T0327127

Two Women

Two Women

～

A Novel

GERTRUDIS GÓMEZ DE AVELLANEDA
TRANSLATED BY BARBARA F. ICHIISHI
INTRODUCTION BY BRÍGIDA M. PASTOR

Lewisburg, Pennsylvania

Library of Congress Cataloging-in-Publication Data

Names: Gómez de Avellaneda, Gertrudis, 1814–1873, author. |
Ichiishi, Barbara F. (Barbara Franklin), 1948– translator. |
Pastor, Brigida M., 1967– writer of introduction.
Title: Two women / Gertrudis Gómez de Avellaneda ;
translated by Barbara F. Ichiishi ; introduction by Brígida Pastor.
Other titles: Dos mujeres. English
Description: Lewisburg, Pennsylvania : Bucknell University Press, [2022] |
First English translation of Spanish novel Dos mujeres. |
Includes bibliographical references and index.
Identifiers: LCCN 2021009984 | ISBN 9781684483150 (cloth ; alk. paper) |
ISBN 9781684483174 (epub) | ISBN 9781684483181 (mobi) | ISBN 9781684483198 (pdf)
Classification: LCC PQ6524 .D6813 2022 | DDC 863/.5—dc23
LC record available at https://lccn.loc.gov/2021009984

A British Cataloging-in-Publication record for this book is available
from the British Library.

♾ The paper used in this publication meets the requirements of the American
National Standard for Information Sciences—Permanence of Paper for Printed
Library Materials, ANSI Z39.48-1992.

www.bucknelluniversitypress.org

Distributed worldwide by Rutgers University Press

Manufactured in the United States of America

Contents

Introduction by Brígida M. Pastor   vii

Translator's Note   xvii

Two Women   1

Afterword   241

Select Bibliography   265

Introduction

Brígida M. Pastor

Gertrudis Gómez de Avellaneda y Arteaga (Camagüey, 1814–Madrid, 1873) is regarded as one of the most important Hispanic writers of the nineteenth century, a pioneer of both Latin American and Spanish women's writing. Her feminist and culturally critical ideas started to develop at an early stage and were consolidated through her own, often tragic, experiences and resulting victimization. Prevented by the oppressive social conventions of the time from openly promulgating her ideas, she was impelled to do so through the conduit of her fiction.

Gómez de Avellaneda was born and educated within the Cuban aristocracy in Puerto Príncipe (now Camagüey) but spent most of her literary career in Spain. In 1836 she left Cuba and moved with her family to La Coruña, her stepfather's home city, and in 1840 she settled in Madrid, discovering a vibrant literary context that helped launch her most creative period. With a prolific career spanning more than thirty years, Gómez de Avellaneda's pre-eminent literary status is borne out by a body of work comprising poetry, six novels, around twenty plays, several short stories (*leyendas*), biographical writings, travelogues, and essays on women titled "La mujer" (Woman) and "Galería de mujeres célebres" (Gallery of famous women).

In her lifetime, she was highly popular and acknowledged as an outstanding woman writer in a male-dominated literary world, but her fame dwindled after her death. Scholarly research over the past three decades, however, has shed considerable light on her public identity and literary output, restoring the critical esteem she deserves within Hispanic literature. The year 2014 marked the bicentenary of Gómez de Avellaneda's birth, commemorated by the publication of several edited critical volumes offering new perspectives on the Cuban writer.[1] The consensus was that Gómez de Avellaneda is not only one of the most important Hispanic writers of the nineteenth century but a major figure in world literature.

Gómez de Avellaneda's body of work reflects the personal conflicts in her unconventional early life and the feelings and concerns she experienced as a woman torn between her individualism and conformity. She first became known as a lyric poet in Madrid in the early 1840s. From the outset, one of her main themes was love, both temporal and spiritual. The pain provoked by her experiences of frustrated love appears in numerous poems: "El cazador" (The hunter), "La Serenata del poeta" (The poet's serenade), and "La venganza" (Vengeance), among others. As a consequence of her disillusionment with love, Gómez de Avellaneda entered a more spiritual phase, which was similarly reflected in her poetry, including "Al mar" (To the sea), "A una acacia" (To an acacia), and "Las contradicciones" (Contradictions). Many of these poems incorporate deep disappointments from her early amorous experiences, but they also show the nostalgia she felt for the idealized Cuban homeland. Poems like "Al partir" (On leaving), which she wrote when she first left Cuba in 1836, and "La vuelta a la patria" (Return to the homeland), written twenty years later when she returned to Cuba, are full of patriotic sentiments for Cuba expressed in exalted metaphors: "Perla del mar" (Pearl of the sea), "Hermosa Cuba" (Beautiful Cuba), and "Edén querido" (Beloved Eden).

Gómez de Avellaneda not only was a reputable poet in the nineteenth century, but, as Gies points out, she "competed successfully with her male counterparts to have her plays staged and published,"[2] despite the difficulties faced by women playwrights of the era. María C. Albin, Megan Corbin, and Raúl Marrero-Fente have written that she was the first woman in the Hispanic literary world whose plays were deemed to be innovative and original, garnering critical praise and enjoying popularity among the theatergoing public.[3] Thus she succeeded in creating a highly respectable space on the Spanish stage, which, according to Alexander Selimov, "at the time was still heavily populated by foreign productions and Golden Age Comedia *refundiciones* (recasts)."[4]

Gómez de Avellaneda wrote seventeen plays, including tragedies on historical themes, such as *Munio Alfonso* (1844) and *Egílona* (1845), or on historical-biblical themes such as *Baltasar* (1858) and *Saúl* (1849), as well as comedies like *La hija de las flores* (The daughter of the flowers) (1852) and *La aventurera* (The adventuress) (1853). Each conveys concern with the three major philosophical currents of the Romantic period: morality, justice, and freedom. In some of her theatrical works, she used the ideas, characters, and subjects of prominent English, French, and Spanish writers, such as Byron, Émile Augier, Shakespeare, Madame de Staël, and Manuel José de Quintana. Her play *La aventurera*, in which she defends the stereotypical femme fatale as a victim of a male-dominated society, is a serious attempt to condemn prevailing social norms. Gómez de Avellaneda clearly identified with her character, as she too suffered discrimination from a censorious society when she rejected the restrictive cultural values placed upon her. According to Gies, "the female protagonists who appeared in her plays were determined women in control of their own lives until they were overwhelmed by forces beyond their power."[5] Gómez de Avellaneda succeeds in creating female characters who free themselves from social death through the act of suicide. For instance, in her first play, *Leoncia*, she creates a female protagonist who defines her own destiny after years of suffering at the hands of a cruel world. Ultimately, Leoncia's self-inflicted death upon failing to achieve her ideal romantic love may be seen as a way of freeing herself from the conflict between her desire to follow her (feminine) instincts and the cultural barriers to expressing her authentic inner self.

While Gómez de Avellaneda's plays and poems are vehicles for her anti-chauvinism on occasion, it is in her novels that her concerns are most consistently and directly expressed. Two novels, in particular, stand out: *Sab* (1841) and *Dos mujeres* (*Two women*) (1842–1843). By subverting traditional norms, both novels turn against the literary paradigms of the time. Her marginal condition as a woman and a writer enabled her to create an abolitionist narrative without precedent—her first novel, *Sab*—which was distinct from other nineteenth-century antislavery works.[6] The analogy of black slavery with the female condition is made even more explicit in the denouement of the novel. The mulatto slave, Sab, compares women's role in marriage with that of his own oppressed race: "Oh las mujeres! ¡Pobres y ciegas víctimas! Como los esclavos, ellas arrastran pacientemente su cadena bajo el yugo de las leyes humanas" (Oh, women! Poor, blind victims! Like slaves, they patiently drag their chains and bow their heads under the yoke of human laws).[7] Through her novel *Sab*, Gómez de Avellaneda demonstrates, according to Selimov, "the technology of domination, which is based on the manipulation of the norms of public and private conduct and their passive acceptance by the subaltern group."[8]

In *Dos mujeres*, Gómez de Avellaneda goes still further and attempts to reveal the institution of marriage as something mutable, with the societal concept of adultery as a sinful and punishable act set in contrast to the reality of simultaneous, virtuous, multiple love. The feminine characterization in this novel exposes the woman writer's dilemma in a tradition from which she has been almost completely excluded and in which she must avoid mirroring traditional masculine models. To some extent the only path available to her was to reproduce well-known characters and stories, recreating the figures of the "femme fatale" and the "angel in the house" that are the traditionally accepted literary constructions of the female. In *Dos mujeres*, the female protagonists are apparently trapped in these categories but escape from this entrapment in their constant search for self-discovery.[9] Gómez de Avellaneda anticipated the censorship of her liberal ideas by prefacing *Dos mujeres* with an apologetic prologue—a recurrent practice in her published work. She appears to undervalue her novel by referring to it as "una obrita" (a little work) and contrasting it with the eminent works of Victor Hugo and Sir Walter Scott. While ostensibly undermining the significance of her work, she simultaneously takes a very feminist stance. Gómez de Avellaneda deliberately uses a rhetorical style that invites the reader to look thoroughly into the real essence of the text. In *Dos mujeres*, beneath the mask of the main protagonist, Catalina, the author protests against the oppressive social position assigned to women and the inevitable condemnation women suffer if they decide to reject it.

Undoubtedly, *Dos mujeres*, like *Sab*, are vessels containing the full complement of the author's personal philosophy and social criticism. Gómez de Avellaneda's voice is overtly heard through her two heroines, Catalina (the femme fatale) and Luisa (the angel in the house), who might be said to depict the complexities of her own feminist identity. Hence, through her work, the Cuban writer demonstrates that she was driven by two contradictory aims—on the one hand, to express her own conception of an unconventional personal life and, on the other hand, to adhere to the dominant social order.

Before entering the exclusively male domain of publication, it was in her private writings that Gómez de Avellaneda began to construct and present herself as a woman. Her *Autobiografía y cartas* (also published under the title *Diario íntimo* [1945]) consists of a vast compilation of personal letters addressed to the object of her unrequited love, Ignacio de Cepeda y Alcalde, between 1839 and 1854.[10] Evidently, Cepeda is the inspiration for Gómez de Avellaneda's epistolary writings, but he also engenders conflict between what the author wishes to express and what she is permitted to express within the dominant masculine discourse available to her.[11] As Susan Kirkpatrick affirms, "as a form of private, very personal writing, Gómez de Avellaneda's autobiography reveals the difficulties that fractured her attempt to construct herself as both a feminine and a Romantic 'I.'"[12]

If her autobiographical and fictional writings demonstrate true feminist intent, it is in her journalism that the author resorts to a militant feminism. These articles, collectively titled "La mujer" [Woman], were published in the literary magazine *Album cubano de lo bueno y lo bello*, which Gómez de Avellaneda founded upon her return to Cuba in 1860, although it was in print for only six months. The more radical arguments in this series of essays claimed that women's intellectual ability was not only equal to but superior to men's.[13] The articles, both claiming and seeking to justify equality of rights, appear to have been motivated by her unsuccessful application for membership in the Spanish Royal Academy, which was rejected solely on the grounds of her gender—as she put it, due to her "lack of whiskers."[14] To some extent this exclusion turned her from a covert into a more overt feminist critic. It is evident that Gómez de Avellaneda took advantage of the key role of the press to place herself at the epicenter of the debate on the "woman question." Hence her journalism became a powerful medium that enabled the author "to exert a decisive influence in shaping public opinion to bring about social change."[15]

In spite of her efforts to promote equal rights for women, Gómez de Avellaneda ultimately felt defeated by the very chauvinistic society in which, against the odds, she had largely succeeded and which she had so often attacked. Her novels *Sab* and *Dos mujeres* not only were banned in Cuba because they were considered a threat to conventional notions of the moral fabric of society but also were excluded by Gómez de Avellaneda herself from the final edition of her *Obras literarias* (Literary works).[16] It would seem that in her later years Gómez de Avellaneda's more fervent feminism mellowed. Eventually she succumbed to the norms imposed by a patriarchal society, just as most of her fellow women did.

Nevertheless, as her posthumously published autobiographical writings conveyed, she felt different from other women: "Ya he dicho mil veces que no pienso como el común de las mujeres y que mi modo de obrar y de sentir me pertenecen exclusivamente" (I have said a thousand times that I do not think like the rest of women, and that my ways of behaving and feeling belong exclusively to me).[17] Her indomitable wish for freedom encouraged her to challenge conventional patriarchal norms by refusing an arranged marriage. She indulged in love affairs and had an illegitimate child. In a similar vein, she did not refrain from expressing her emancipated ideas about marriage, divorce, and chauvinism in her fiction.

Toward the end of her life, she joined with other contemporary women writers who did not dare complain overtly about the obstacles to their careers so they could maintain the respect of, and access to, society and avoid the pain of rejection. Most women writers, when they opted for the "sinful" act of writing, complied with conventional norms and defended the traditional roles assigned to women, almost by way of apologizing for their defiant attitude. Gertrudis Gómez de Avellaneda was an exception. The fact that her novels *Sab* and *Dos mujeres* were banned in Cuba and were eventually excluded from the final edition of her *Obras literarias* (1869–1871) "should not lead us to think her victory was Pyrrhic."[18] For as Beth K. Miller wrote, "she was conscious of being a woman writer and, ever mindful of adverse circumstances, often viewed her life and later her works as exemplary, especially for other women."[19] Miller wrote that Gómez de Avellaneda wanted "not only to survive, but to survive as a feminist," creating an authentic feminine voice through all her writings.[20]

All in all, Gómez de Avellaneda does not hold a place in Cuba or Spain exclusively as a woman writer but as "una de las primeras feministas del mundo en el orden del tiempo" (one of the world's first feminists).[21] Her rhetorical style masks a subversive critique of the forms of self-expression available to her as a writer and as a woman. She fought to cast light on her emancipating views, leading prominent male writers and dramatists like Manuel Bretón de los Herreros and José Zorrilla to describe her in terms such as "es mucho hombre esa mujer" (that woman is quite a man) or "un alma de hombre en aquella envoltura de mujer" (a male soul within a womanly exterior).[22]

Gertrudis Gómez de Avellaneda left written testimony of her feminist ideas, which were considered reprobate at a time when the emancipation of women had not yet been conceived. Thus, Bretón de los Herreros's and Zorrilla's words offer a key to the only way in which nineteenth-century society could understand and accept her. Both her life experiences and her writing proclaim her status as a pioneering champion of gender equality in Hispanic literary history, solidifying her presence within a tradition that could no longer ostracize her.

Notes

1. See Brígida M. Pastor, ed., "Beyond the Canon: A Life and a Literature of Her Own," special issue, *Romance Studies* 32, no. 4 (2014); Brígida M. Pastor, ed., "Gender, Writing, Empowerment," special issue, *Romance Studies* 33, no. 1 (2015); Milena Rodríguez, ed., "Entre Cuba y España: Gertrudis Gómez de Avellaneda en su Bicentenario (1814–2014)," special issue, *Arbor* 190, no. 770 (2014); Cira Romero, ed., *Lecturas sin fronteras (Ensayos sobreGertrudis Gómez de Avellaneda), 1990–2012* (Havana: Ediciones Unión, 2014); Ángeles Ezama Gil, ed., *Gertrudis Gómez de Avellaneda, Autobiografía y otras páginas,* Edición, estudio y notas de Ángeles Ezama Gil (Madrid: Real Academia Española–Espasa-Círculo de Lectores, 2015).

2. David Thatcher Gies, *The Theatre in Nineteenth-Century Spain* (Cambridge: Cambridge University Press, 1994), 30.

3. María C. Albin, Megan Corbin, and Raúl Marrero-Fente, "Gertrudis the Great: First Abolitionist and Feminist in the Americas and Spain," in "Gender and the Politics of Literature: Gertrudis Gómez de Avellaneda," ed. María C. Albin, Megan Corbin, and Raúl Marrero-Fente, *Hispanic Issues On Line* 18 (2017): 13, https://conservancy.umn.edu/handle/11299/192190.

4. Alexander Selimov, "The Making of *Leoncia*: Romanticism, Tragedy, and Feminism," in "Gender and the Politics of Literature: Gertrudis Gómez de Avellaneda," ed. María C. Albin, Megan Corbin, and Raúl Marrero-Fente, *Hispanic Issues On Line* 18 (2017): 250, https://conservancy.umn.edu/handle/11299/192133.

5. Gies, *Theatre in Nineteenth-Century Spain*, 202.

6. Evelyn Picón Garfield, *Poder y sexualidad: El discurso de Gertrudis Gómez de Avellaneda* (Amsterdam: Rodopi, 1993), 54. See also Brígida M. Pastor, *Fashioning Feminism in Cuba and Beyond: The Prose of Gertrudis Gómez de Avellaneda* (New York: Peter Lang, 2003), 70.

7. Gertrudis Gómez de Avellaneda, *Sab*, prologue by Mary Cruz (Havana: Instituto Cubano del Libro, 1973), 316.

8. Selimov, "The Making of *Leoncia:* Romanticism, Tragedy, and Feminism," in "Gender and the Politics of Literature: Gertrudis Gómez de Avellaneda," ed. María C. Albin, Megan Corbin, and Raúl Marrero-Fente, *Hispanic Issues On Line* 18 (2017), 255, https://conservancy.umn.edu/handle/11299/192133.

9. Pastor, *Fashioning Feminism in Cuba and Beyond*, 130.

10. Around 1839 Avellaneda met her great love, Ignacio de Cepeda y Alcalde, a law student who belonged to a rich and important family from Seville. This correspondence ceased when he married another woman, and Avellaneda understood that further pursuit was futile. In spite of many separations and reconciliations, this love continued and was maintained through correspondence until 1854. Upon Cepeda's death, his widow inherited the letters and published them in 1907.

11. According to Sylvia Molloy, "Autobiography is always a re-presentation, that is, a retelling, since the life to which it supposedly refers is already a kind of narrative construct." *At Face Value: Autobiographical Writing in Spanish America* (Cambridge: Cambridge University Press, 1991), 5.

12. Susan Kirkpatrick, *"Las Románticas": Women Writers and Subjectivity, 1835–1860* (Berkeley: University of California Press, 1989), 146.

13. Gertrudis Gómez de Avellaneda, "La mujer," in *Obras literarias* (Madrid: Rivadeneyra, 1871), 5:297.

14. Carmen Bravo-Villasante, *Una vida romántica: La Avellaneda* (Madrid: Cultura Hispánica, 1986), 187–188.

15. Albin, Corbin, Marrero-Fente, "Gertrudis the Great: First Abolition-ist and Feminist in the Americas and Spain," 3.

16. Mary Cruz, ed., "Gertrudis Gómez de Avellaneda y su novela *Sab*," *Unión* 1 (1973): 140. Aurelia Castillo de González wrote that it was at the suggestion of the Jesuits of Belén, Cuba, that Gómez de Avellaneda excluded *Sab* and *Dos mujeres* from the final edition of her *Obras*

literarias; cited in Edith L. Kelly, "Avellaneda's *Sab* and the Political Situation in Cuba," *The Americas* 1 (1945): 305.

17. Gertrudis Gómez de Avellaneda, *Autobiografía y cartas*, with a prologue and eulogy by Lorenzo Cruz de Fuentes, 2nd ed. (Madrid: Imprenta Helénica, 1914), 45.

18. Brígida M. Pastor, "Cuba's Covert Cultural Critic: The Feminist Writings of Gertrudis Gómez de Avellaneda," *Romance Quarterly* 42, no. 3 (1995): 187.

19. Beth Miller, "Gertrude the Great: Avellaneda, Nineteenth-Century Feminist," in *Women in Hispanic Literature: Icons and Fallen Idols*, ed. Beth Miller (Berkeley: University of California Press, 1983), 203.

20. Beth K. Miller, "Avellaneda, Nineteenth-Century Feminist," *Revista/ Review Interamericana* 4, no. 2 (Summer 1974): 181.

21. Max Henríquez Ureña, *Panorama histórico de la literatura cubana* (New York: Las Américas Publishing Co., 1963), 86.

22. Bretón de los Herreros, quoted in Pedro Romero Mendoza, *Siete ensayos sobre el romanticismo español* (Cáceres: Servicios Culturales de la Excma. Diputación de Cáceres, 1969), 1:308; José Zorrilla, "Gertrudis Gómez de Avellaneda," in *Hojas traspapeladas de los Recuerdos del tiempo viejo* (Madrid: Eduardo Mengíbar, 1882), 6:501.

Translator's Note

The life story and work of the nineteenth-century author Gertrudis Gómez de Avellaneda (1814–1873) played out in two hemi-
spheres and cultures: her homeland of Cuba, where she was born
and raised, and the mother country of Spain, where she spent most
of her adult years. While Gómez de Avellaneda's first novel, *Sab*
(1841), is set in contemporary Cuba, her second novel, *Two Women*
(*Dos mujeres*, 1842–1843), transports the reader from the New World
to the Old, painting a picture of upper-class life in early nineteenth-
century Spain. For a translator who has until recently focused on
contemporary literature, the project of recreating a story that ema-
nates from a distant time and social milieu has presented some interesting new challenges. First of these was the existence of multiple
editions of the book, spanning nearly two centuries. The original
work was published in serial form in Madrid from 1842 to 1843;
this is the only edition that the author saw and approved. Since
then there have appeared a number of other editions, both official
and pirated. For many years the novel was banned by the royal
censors in Cuba (along with her antislavery novel *Sab*); the first
Cuban edition of *Two Women* finally came out in Havana in 1914,
as part of the collection of her complete works that marked the
centennial of the author's birth. For my translation I have used
these two editions, both of which I felt were sound in content and
style and true to the author's intent. I have tried to untangle small
mistakes and inconsistencies in spelling, punctuation, and syntax
that are found in these old editions, and on occasion updated certain elements so they conform to modern English usage. In the

case of typographical errors, omissions, and distortions that were hard to decipher, I also consulted modern (twenty-first-century) editions to determine what appeared to be the correct word or phrase in the given context. One persistent problem with both the 1842–1843 Spanish and the 1914 Cuban editions concerned the length of the paragraphs. There was a tendency in both to write very short paragraphs, many of just one sentence; I have consolidated the text into longer paragraphs to provide a greater sense of continuity in the reading experience.

Gómez de Avellaneda is a highly romantic author; her work comes out of the European Romantic tradition. Her writing is emotional and intense; it cuts to the quick of the human experience, unveiling the mysteries of life and death with their endless round of joy, pain, and sorrow. Her narrative explores the intricacies of the human psyche in long flowing sentences that carry the reader along on a wave of sound. The language is beautiful and expressive, the dialogue often high-flown and rhetorical. The writer's style is an integral part of the world she creates and the message she seeks to convey in her work. As a translator, my guiding principle has been to be faithful to the spirit of the author and the work, while striving to have it read naturally in a different linguistic medium. On the whole, I do not agree with the modernizing project undertaken in some twenty-first-century editions of the book. I feel that measures like breaking up the long sentences into two or three shorter sentences, eliminating exclamatory expressions and emotive words and phrases or replacing them with more down-to-earth forms of speech, in order to make the book more accessible and appealing to the modern reader, tend to flatten and distort the nature of an intense Romantic novel, thereby giving a somewhat false and diluted impression of the author and the work. One of the joys of reading fiction is to gain imaginary entry into an unknown world. The aim of the translator, then, is to open the door to that world and seek to bring it alive, so readers can dwell within it.

Sincere thanks are due to those who have offered me help and encouragement along the way. I am truly grateful to two anonymous readers for Bucknell University Press, one of whom went through the text line by line, comparing the English translation with the Spanish original and offering illuminating ideas and comments, and the other of whom gave very helpful suggestions in regard to the afterword and the bibliography. My heartfelt thanks go to Judith Reyna for her careful and thorough reading of the English and Spanish texts and her wise thoughts and suggestions. Warm thanks go to Janet Fishman for her insightful comments on certain parts of the manuscript, and to Al Franklin and Connie Greenspan for their fruitful advice and support. Special gratitude goes to Adriana Méndez Rodenas for awakening my interest in this remarkable author through her lecture on *Sab* at a 2014 Americas Society/Council of the Americas session in New York. I am very grateful to the editors of Bucknell University Press for their enthusiastic response to the work, and for their helpful assistance throughout the publication process. As always, my love and thanks go to my husband, Tatsuro, for his invaluable technical help and his steadfast emotional support over the years of carrying out this project. I hope English-language readers will fall under the spell of this captivating little book.

Barbara F. Ichiishi

Two Women

Prologue

If the warm reception that Madrid's readers have given to the little novel entitled *Sab* obliged its author to offer them another work of greater scholarship and depth, she might not venture to publish her second attempt in such a difficult genre, wary of not adequately fulfilling that obligation. But as she believes it a no less pressing duty to offer such a kind audience a token of her gratitude, and she can manage no other than to present to it her light works, she decided to publish the present novel, without feeling obliged to make a show of false modesty by detracting from whatever merit it may have, or still less to attribute to it any it may lack.

She will just say that the present little work does not belong to the genre of the historical novel immortalized by Walter Scott, or the so-called dramatic novel of Victor Hugo. It does not contain creations like *Hans of Iceland* or *Claude Gueux*, nor has the author tried to fathom the criminal instinct in the human heart. Humbler and less profound, she has confined herself to sketching true-to-life characters and natural passions; and the scenes depicted in the novel, if not always flattering, are never gory.

She leaves it to the critics to elucidate the numerous flaws that these pages must contain as a literary work, and she forestalls any frivolous or harsh interpretation of the work, declaring that she had no moral or social purpose in writing it.

The author does not feel obliged to profess an ideology, nor does she believe herself capable of undertaking a mission of any kind. She writes as a mere pastime, and she would be hurt if some of her opinions, voiced with no agenda, were judged with the severity that might be appropriate for one who presumes to pronounce moral doctrines.

1

"I am telling you for the hundredth time, sister, that it is absolutely essential that my son get to know the world a little, before he undertakes such a serious endeavor as marriage."

"Of course, because casting a poor lad of twenty, fresh out of school, into that Babylon of Madrid, where they can deprave and corrupt him, is the best way to prepare him to be a good husband. Your reasoning does you proud, brother!"

"Leonor, your capricious way of interpreting my words astonishes me. Who intends to cast off Carlos, as you say, to deprave and corrupt him? Can't my son go to the court with a letter of introduction to worthy and prudent individuals who will serve as his guides in your so-called Babylon? Moreover, in Madrid as in Seville there is both good and bad; I don't know why one assumes that everyone who goes there is necessarily corrupted. You're so unfair and stubborn in your concerns!"

"And you with your incredible whims! So it seems that despite my repeated reflections, you are determined to send the boy to Madrid as soon as he arrives in Seville?"

"I'm not saying that it will be right after he arrives in Seville—certainly not. I haven't seen Carlos in eight years, and . . ."

"Thanks to your crazy obsession with making your son into a revolutionary, a heretic, a Frenchman. It was certainly not by my verdict that you sent Carlos to a school in France to obtain what you call a brilliant education: to that new Nineveh, that seat of corruption, of heresy, of . . ."

"For God's sake, sister, suspend your judgment and let me finish what I was saying. I repeat that I haven't seen my son in eight years, and it is natural to wish to have him by my side for a few months before separating from him again. But after that, it's decided, afterward he will have that brief immersion in court life which is so appropriate for a young person of his class and will in no way, I believe, impair his feelings and his good habits. Sister Leonor! No Silva has been a scoundrel or a libertine, and by God I swear that Carlos will not be the first."

"But why does Carlos need that brief immersion in court life, as you say? If he stays peacefully at home beside his father and his wife, tending to his interests, which thankfully are considerable, will he be less of a gentleman, less esteemed by his peers? Is he losing something by not going to Madrid?"

"Yes, señora, because this sojourn, which by the way will not be long, will enable him to revive useful relationships that I have neglected, which will in turn allow him to don the distinguished insignia of Carlos III that I obtained at his age, for my son shall not be less than me; he will get to meet and cultivate the friendship of his cousin who is chaplain to the Queen, a powerful and sickly old man who has no close relatives . . . In any case, even if no benefit derives from the trip, it is my wish and that is reason enough."

"That is your usual argument against all those I present to dissuade you from the foolish plans you concoct every day. In truth, brother, you are crazier at the age of fifty-four than you were at twenty."

"And you more stubborn and domineering at fifty than you were at eighteen, when you married that poor man whom you sent to an early grave with your shamelessness. These pious or devout women are more fearsome than a legion of devils."

"Brother Francisco!"

"Sister Leonor!"

"You go too far."

"You push me to the brink."

At this point when the discussion between the siblings had reached the dangerous line between an argument and an affront, a glass door with green taffeta curtains silently opened, and an angelic blond head, worthy of the brush of Raphael or Correggio, appeared.

"What is this, my dear mother? What's wrong, my beloved uncle? Are you two quarreling? Oh! And it upsets me so much when the two of you have these disputes where you end up getting angry!"

Upon hearing these words, uttered by a musical voice with a light and charming Andalusian accent, don Francisco de Silva's brow cleared, and a smile of maternal pride rose to the pale lips of doña Leonor, which a moment earlier were trembling with anger.

"Come, Luisita," the good woman exclaimed, moving her gaunt and stiff body in a broad damask armchair with silver braid. "Bring me eau de cologne, ether, anything, because I'm not feeling well at all. Oh Lord, what a stitch! These irritations do me in."

"Sister," said don Francisco, looking at her with concern, "I'm really sorry . . . but you insult me so much! Well, forget it . . . if I offended you, forgive me. You know my temper . . . I'm a powder keg . . . but I ask you again to forgive me."

As the gentleman stammered these words, sincerely regretting his sister's ailment, although he must have been accustomed to such scenes which occurred too often, Luisa came out of the study with a flask of ether, and seated on a footstool before her mother, she moved her pretty head close to examine with tender concern the old woman's features, still shaken with anger but revealing satisfaction over the victory that, thanks to her indisposition, she had just gained over her opponent.

Then the lovely girl applied the flask to the sick woman's nose, and turning beautiful blue eyes full of tenderness and mildness to her uncle, seemed to say with them, "Why, for goodness' sake, aren't you gentler with my mother?"

Don Francisco got up from his chair, no longer frowning but with a contrite and shamefaced look, and taking one of his sister's hands he said, "Leonor, say you forgive me. In any case, Carlos will not go to Madrid."

These words were a triumphal hymn to doña Leonor, who nonetheless pretended not to heed them, and making a show of generosity, she exclaimed, "I forgive you, Francisco, and I hope that you as well . . ."

"Say no more, my dear Leonor; forget it. Are you feeling better?"

"I want to go to bed, brother; I need to rest. For three days I've been feeling so bad!"

"And I, brute that I am, with no consideration for your state of health, am constantly giving you more aggravations . . ."

"Come now, uncle, you just said not to say any more about that. Let's carry Mama to her bed and then . . . then I'll give you a hug for how well you made up for your offense."

"Enchantress!"

And the gentleman gazed at the pretty girl, completely besotted, until she nudged him to remind him that they had to take the old lady to her bed.

As the respectable ailing lady is resting on her fluffy feather bed; as don Francisco leaves after receiving the promised embrace; and as Luisa takes advantage of the moments of being left alone to read on the sly behind the curtains of her mother's bed *Paul and Virginia*, which because it was on the list of banned novels was in the latter's view a work that was harmful to youth, we will undertake to give the reader a brief overview of the people we have introduced. There is little to be said about don Francisco de Silva; he was nothing short of the character who appears in the above scene. A good and generous heart, a simple soul, a lively nature, a bit capricious but easy to control after the initial impulse. Prudence was not his strong point, and he often made the most outlandish and risky plans with a nonchalance that the years had not mellowed but had rather brought out. He rarely took anyone's advice but his own; obvious contradiction irritated him; he never yielded to others' arguments; but he could not resist supplication, and a child could make him do his bidding through sweetness. Descendant of an old and powerful Sevillian family, he wed a woman of the same class, whose only offspring was Carlos. His wife died soon after their son's birth, and his only sister, doña Leonor, then took charge of the boy, who knew no other mother. Don Francisco, despite his eternal disputes with his sister, believed he could not have put his son in better hands. Devout, strict, severe, doña Leonor was a woman whose virtue Envy herself would not dare to question. She had all the prudence her brother lacked; she was as thoughtful as he was rash; and if she made decisions less forcefully, she carried them out with more perseverance. While don Francisco constantly criticized his sister's unyielding nature, he was, without being aware of it, dominated by that same nature. Leonor never flinched from the course she had chosen with mature deliberation; and her steadfast, unwavering opposition to everything that went against her principles or thwarted her plans always won the day, often defeating by wearing out her opponent.

Out of six children engendered by doña Leonor, only one remained upon her husband's death, and the loss of so many loved ones had made that last token of their union even more precious to her. Luisa, the lovely Luisa was that dear gift, and her mother had taken the greatest pains with her upbringing. She was not of a mind to adorn her with distinguished talents, and Luisa's upbringing was more religious than brilliant, despite don Francisco's objections to such a rigid approach. She did not have music or dancing lessons, or training in any other kind of skill; but in exchange she knew all the secrets of housekeeping, and excelled in embroidery and needlework; she knew basic arithmetic and geography; she could recite biblical history by heart and was somewhat proficient in the profane; with which, in the opinion of her mother nothing was lacking for her to be called an educated woman. Moreover, although doña Leonor condemned the reading of all novels and love poetry, she generally allowed Luisa to read works she considered both pleasant and edifying, and making the most of this concession, during her leisure hours the girl read and reread *Evenings on the Farm*, *The Lives of the Female Saints*, *The Girls' Store*, *Euphemia or the Well Raised Woman*, and even the works of Fray Luis de León, as long as they were not those in which the poet was moved by some softheartedness. Furthermore, her uncle would sometimes give her on the sly a few novels such as *Robinson Crusoe* and *Paul and Virginia*.

Luisa had no friends her own age; doña Leonor did not want to give her daughter as companions *modern-day youngsters*, as she called them, who were raised with theaters and balls, and who at the age of thirteen went out on their balconies to say sweet nothings to their boyfriends. She was shocked by the freedoms mothers gave their daughters, she declared that in her day things were very different, and ended up devoutly cursing France and the French, for she firmly believed that they had inevitably infected Spain with their evil ways.

Doña Leonor was to a high degree Spanish and royalist. Her veneration for Fernando VII seemed bound up with the veneration she felt for God, and hostility toward the legitimate absolute monarch was in her eyes a sin of heresy, so fused in her mind were the altar and the throne. During the reign of Joseph Bonaparte in Spain she had shut herself away in a small town in the mountains, living in complete seclusion, to avoid hearing talk of that usurper toward whom she maintained all her life a hatred as great as the one she professed for France; the fact that her brother did not concur with her feelings in this regard was in her eyes one of his major faults. Don Francisco, while always a sincere supporter of the King's cause, was by no means an enemy of the Bonapartes, and a number of times he had made his sister's blood boil, assuring her, as a far-sighted man and a politician himself, that the Bonapartes had brought benefits to Spain that would be discernible later on, whether or not that was in line with their intentions. The noble gentleman never forgot to include among these benefits the abolition of the terrible tribunal of the Inquisition, and at that point doña Leonor went through the roof, since the pious woman prayed devoutly every day, after saying her rosary, for the restoration of the Holy Office and the extermination of heretics, as well as for the return of Fernando and the fall of Bonaparte, whom she always persisted in calling Malaparte, although her brother openly mocked her for such a display of childishness.

Doña Leonor returned to Seville around the middle of 1814, to celebrate with religious rites in several convents at her own expense the restoration of the King.

Three years had passed from that day to the start of our story, and although popular enthusiasm for the reinstated monarch had cooled somewhat during that time, this was not the case for doña Leonor, whose emotions on the contrary ran ever higher, as did her religious devotion, the two reaching the point of fanaticism.

One could easily imagine her household and her family being transported back to the seventeenth century with no contradiction. The air they breathed was ancient and monastic; the furnishings, the interior design, everything in doña Leonor's home was pure Spanish, vintage and refined. They dined at one in the afternoon; they had hot chocolate and pastries at five; they supped at nine in the evening; and at ten on the dot, in summer or in winter, everyone was in bed.

Doña Leonor knew few people and was not close to anyone. Her only diversion was to play manille some afternoons with doña Beatriz and doña Serafina, women as old and devout as she was, and her guests of the opposite sex consisted of her brother, her confessor the venerable Capuchin priest, and two beaux who could recall the wedding of Carlos IV to María Luisa, at the celebrations for which Leonor attended the one and only ball she had seen in her life. That worldly entertainment, as well as the theater, were banned in the austere lady's home, and Luisa scarcely knew what the words meant. Of course, it's true that in exchange her mother allowed her to go some afternoons to watch the bullfights, and every year she entrusted her daughter to her friends doña Serafina and doña Beatriz, who took her to the Festival of San Juan on Hercules Avenue to stroll and eat a few fritters.

This was the extent of Luisa's pleasures, but in their absence her life was filled with a thousand small tasks that her mother made her scrupulously fulfill. Every Saturday without fail she confessed and received Communion at the Capuchin Sisters; every Sunday she heard two Masses in the cathedral. Certain days of the year were devoted to visiting hospitals to console and give aid to the sick; others mother and daughter dedicated to sewing clothes by hand for the foundling hospital, which institution was under doña Leonor's special patronage—in short, the multitude of novenas, the various festivals for saints, the visits to convents, in each of which doña Leonor had a relative or friend, all these things combined with domestic chores kept Luisa busy enough to prevent her perhaps from indulging in those ardent raptures that endanger idle youth, from those vague ruminations of the contemplative life that may often lead the purest mind astray.

In any case, nothing about Luisa heralded one of those powerful and active imaginations that consume themselves in the absence of other nourishment. Despite having been born beneath the blazing sky of Andalusia, neither physically nor morally did she possess the characteristic traits of southern women. White and pure as her complexion was her soul, and her temperament as sweet and modest as her looks. Innocence shone on every one of her features, as in every one of her thoughts, and when her serene blue eyes turned upward and a ray of sunlight illuminated her white brow, you could say that it recalled the existence of heaven on earth. That chaste and ideal form seemed to be surrounded by an aura of divine poetry, and one breathed a fragrance of purity in her presence. Upon looking at her, the least chaste imagination conceived vague thoughts of timid pious love; the most jaded heart felt itself revive at the sight of that pure and lovely girl. It seemed that human passions could have no influence on a creature all divine, and that the human voice would hurt those ears accustomed to angelic hymns.

Everything in her corresponded to that divine form; tender, soft, benign, always with a smile on her lips and peace in her heart, she had known neither the pleasures nor the pains of life, and she wore on her brow the stamp of a virgin soul. However, if no one beholding her would dare to imagine that peaceful existence invaded by terrible burning passions, anyone who beheld the wistful sweetness of her brow and the exquisite sensitivity shining through her gaze would understand that that soul was made to love: to love with all the purity of the angel, and all the selflessness of woman. Yet she herself—poor girl!—was unaware of this; had she ever dared to ask her heart why it sometimes throbbed when the lovebirds cooed around their nests, when she heard the sweet trills of the nightingale in the silence of the night, or when wandering alone through the garden by moonlight, she saw the branches tremble, cajoled by the wind, and emit a faint melancholy sound that resembled a sigh?

She was only seven, and her cousin Carlos ten, when the brother and sister arranged their union. Their marriage seemed suitable in every respect: they were both only children, both well-to-do and of similar age; Luisa and Carlos had been raised as siblings, and they loved each other as such. The parents did not envisage any future event that could thwart their project, but don Francisco wished to send his son to be educated in a school in France, and from the moment when he put his plan into effect, doña Leonor constantly predicted that the desired union would not take place.

And in truth, the good woman would have been extremely sorry if her predictions had come true, so whether out of devotion to her family, or the long time she had nurtured the plan for such a union, or because being old and sick she wanted to ensure that her daughter had a protector, doña Leonor passionately wished not only to realize but to hasten as much as possible the marriage of Luisa with her cousin. Given the girl's substantial dowry as well as her worthiness, you would expect there to be many asking for her hand, but the knowledge of the engagement of the cousins and the absolute isolation in which she lived had not allowed anyone else to appear as a suitor, and doña Leonor trembled at the thought that she might die before having placed her daughter.

It was undoubtedly these considerations that made her resist with such tenacity don Francisco's idea of his son's sojourn in Madrid, and her heart did not find complete rest even after hearing him offer to desist from such a plan. She tossed and turned in bed, unable to calm down, and amid the moans caused by her rheumatism and her fits of hysteria, Luisa heard her exclaim in an edgy tone, "No, I will not rest easy until I see them return from the altar."

2

And so we find on a beautiful May morning of 1817, as the gold-finches greet the spring in the lush fields of Andalusia, and Seville, reclining like an Oriental queen in the center of her fertile plain, dons the perfume of orange blossoms and jasmine; when the Moorish courtyards are newly adorned with china flowerpots dotted with geraniums, heliotropes, pinks, and roses; when water jets playfully leap and turn from the marble fountains; when the Guadalquivir River is blanketed with sailboats and light craft, as the orange and pomegranate trees, swollen with pride from having gazed at themselves in its famous streams, raise their florid heads along the shore; as the sun seems to smile lovingly on the reviving vegetation; as the lovely maidens appear with the dawn, as sunny as she, to stroll along the riverbanks; in short, when all of Seville is life, pleasure, and poetry, we find a ship casting anchor on the strand, and two minutes later don Francisco de Silva is embracing his son. Carlos had made the journey by sea from France to Cadiz, where he had just had a stopover of several hours, eagerly awaiting the moment he was now enjoying.

Doña Leonor soon received official word of the safe arrival of her nephew and future son-in-law, and that he would come that day with don Francisco to dine with them. Despite her hysteria and her rheumatism, she immediately sprang into action, and likewise put to work all the domestic staff, to give a worthy welcome to such beloved guests. They say that the venerable old furniture of that ever serene house took fright upon seeing the unusual activity that day, and the old housekeeper, who did not recall ever witnessing such expense and profusion in the thirty years in which she had been working for doña Leonor, crossed herself devoutly and said to the butler in a low voice, "There's no help for it, Tadeo, our mistress is going to die soon, because when people go to such extremes it means that nothing good is in store for them."

None of Luisa's finery seemed good enough to her mother, so although until then she had been staunchly against following the latest fashion, in honor of this great day she allowed her obliging friend to do the rounds of several stores to buy lots of trinkets of feminine adornment. Poor Luisa, who up to that day had heard that it was a mortal sin to waste time at the dressing table, on that memorable morning had to undergo two long hours of toilette. We cannot guarantee that her getup could be called elegant, since it was coordinated by the respectable señora Serafina who, although thirty years earlier had had the reputation of wearing stylishly her satin mantilla, was not very up to date on the fickle ways of fashion. What we do know is that on that day all of Luisa's great-grandmother's diamonds emerged from their steel coffers, and weighed down with them all, that night she complained of a splitting headache. But all in all, by the end of the toilette, doña Serafina declared that she was as beautiful and as decked out as Leonor herself had been on the day she accepted the hand of her deceased husband, and the housekeeper, the butler, the maid, and even the cook were dazzled at the sight of so much beauty and so many diamonds.

The time of the visit was approaching, and doña Leonor, having completed her preparations, had seated herself majestically in her enormous red damask armchair with silver braid, carefully arranging her satin dress the color of dry leaves and adjusting symmetrically on her shoulders her Indian crêpe scarf. Doña Serafina and doña Beatriz, her only friends, filled a couch that went with the armchair, they too dressed in the most select clothes from their wardrobes, and Luisa sat timidly on an antique stool beside her mother, crushed under the weight of her jewels, hearing the prudent advice given in turn by her mother and her mother's friends. Meanwhile the poor girl wondered inwardly, not understanding the reason for all this solemnity. She had been told a thousand times that she was destined to marry her cousin, but the word did not carry the grave meaning it should have for the innocent girl. She recalled a very handsome boy who broke her dolls but on the other hand gave her baby birds and candy, and she did not find anything frightening about the idea of living forever with that childhood companion. Why so much advice, so many warnings? Luisa did not understand it at all, and she was starting to feel a vague uneasiness, which she tried to dispel by telling herself that that so long awaited beau, that so solemnly proclaimed husband, was none other than her friend Carlos, her funny Carlos, whom she still imagined with his little round white face, his long hair, his large black eyes filled with innocence and gaiety, and his loud childish laugh. She almost believed that upon seeing him, despite all the warnings of the venerable triumvirate, she would not be able to stop herself from running up and hugging him. As she had this thought, her mother repeated for the hundredth time, "Girl, you must neither be so serious that it seems as though you are not sharing in the family's joy, nor so bright-eyed and content that one might think you feel entitled to have the greatest share in it. Composure, my Luisa, moderation, and above all, silence. A well-bred girl says only what's necessary, and all the more so on the first visit of her future husband."

At the moment when this harangue ended, probably only to be started up again, they heard the sound of a carriage stopping at the door, and the three women exclaimed at once, arranging their shawls with majestic and almost solemn composure, "They're here."

Luisa's beautiful eyes involuntarily turned toward the door, but doña Leonor slapped her on the shoulder with her fan, saying severely, "Girl, girl! Keep those eyes down."

Luisa obeyed, and remained motionless until she heard her uncle's voice crying out by her side, "Luisita, greet your cousin."

Then she raised her head and fixed her sweet, innocent gaze on the person don Francisco was introducing her to. But in an instant and with no need of a new command from her mother, she again lowered her beautiful eyes to the floor, her face tinged purple.

The cause of such sudden confusion is not hard to guess. Luisa had not found her Carlos. The person standing before her was not the one she had been parted from eight years earlier. The gay, funny Carlos had vanished; the girl had not found his round rosy cheeks, his long chestnut hair, his bright eyes, his laughing little mouth. Perfect black locks framed a large dark forehead, in the middle of which appeared a bluish vein; strong well-etched features composed a face of southern character, ardent and proud; in short, upon seeking the boy's smile, she had found the man's look.

At that moment a feeling without name, a strange blend of surprise, pleasure, sadness and fear, overwhelmed her heart. The formalities among Carlos, don Francisco, and the three women had three times run their course; the new arrivals had already been seated and the conversation had exhausted all the commonplaces, all the trivialities one finds on such occasions, before Luisa again dared to look at her cousin. Finally, taking advantage of a moment when Carlos was telling the women the details of his trip and when Luisa thought he would not notice her, she slowly and timidly raised her lovely eyes, turning them toward him as though on the sly, but . . . as luck would have it, her gaze had barely rested a moment on the young man's face when his suddenly turned to hers, so direct, so brilliant, so ardent, that Luisa went from confusion to alarm. She leaned her burning face on her heaving breast and, not knowing what to do, started breaking the mother-of-pearl ribs of her fan. She felt that she had never been looked at before, had never seen such eyes before . . . in short, she felt that that gaze was oppressing her heart and that she was going to be sick. Doña Leonor, who busy as she was paying her respects to her nephew was still secretly watching her daughter, noticed the girl's distress, as she tore to shreds the precious fan that doña Leonor had been carefully saving for eighteen years (as it was indeed the very one she had used on her wedding day), and could not contain her anger, crying impetuously, "Girl, what are you doing?"

A traveler caught off guard by a thunderbolt would not be more startled than Luisa was by that sudden question, "What are you doing?" Did she herself know by chance? The fatal fan fell from her hands in a movement of alarm that she could not control, and seeing all eyes turned upon her, and then realizing that she had broken her fan and not knowing what to say or do, the poor creature turned to her uncle with eyes full of tears, as though she were imploring someone to defend her from the strange emotion she was feeling. But before don Francisco made a move, Carlos came to pick up the fallen fan, and returning it to Luisa, as though her confusion were contagious, he also blushed and lowered his magnificent black eyes as she lowered her sweet blue ones. Oh, the first moment of a first love! What stroke of the pen can succeed in describing you? When a beam from heaven descends and ignites at once two virgin hearts, the angels smile, languidly flapping their white wings, and they alone can understand the chaste mysteries that the soul encloses and innocence hides beneath her pure veil.

Thanks to the timely intervention of don Francisco, matters moved away from the fan; the conversation started up again, and Luisa could gradually overcome her first emotion. The three women had finally settled into their natural domain, that is, they started talking about migraine headaches, hysteria and rheumatism, and the detailed enumeration of all the proven or unproven remedies that might apply. Don Francisco listened to them, at times breaking in to confirm the infallible nature of some or the ineffectiveness of others, while Carlos and Luisa, sitting across from each other, were silent and gazed at each other in turn; I say in turn because as though by mutual agreement, they avoided having their eyes meet again. When Carlos fixed his impassioned gaze on Luisa, the girl kept hers lowered to the floor, and when Carlos furtively noticed that Luisa was raising her modest eyes toward him, he directed his to two large oil paintings that adorned the walls, one depicting the arrest of Jesus and the other the assumption of Mary. Two or three times the young man tried to say a few words to his cousin, but those words remained frozen on his lips, without being uttered.

Finally the mealtime arrived, which on that extraordinary day was at three, an excess that gave doña Leonor a colic, since her stomach, used to the long habit of being satisfied at one on the dot, could not easily submit to a two-hour delay. The good woman insisted that in commemoration of the last day when her nephew had dined with her at the same table, before his departure to attend school abroad, he take the same chair he had occupied that day, and that Luisa sit beside him as she had then. Having the two young people sit next to each other was not the best way to stimulate their appetites; neither of them could eat, Carlos from looking at Luisa, and Luisa from looking away from Carlos.

At the end of the meal doña Leonor said how thankful they should be to God for having reunited them as a family, in the same way and with the same pleasure that they had experienced eight years earlier. "Yes, my dear nephew," she then said, turning to Carlos, "I give thanks to divine Providence for having returned you to the bosom of your family, and for having allowed me to live to see this blessed day. During the eight years of your absence, not once have I sat at this table without gazing with sadness at the place you occupied, and recalling with emotion your mischief and your charm."

At that point Carlos dared to address his cousin for the first time: "And you, Luisa," he said in a low, rather shaky voice, "have you ever thought of me?"

Hearing her name uttered by Carlos made the girl shiver, and his question put her in a state of inexplicable embarrassment. She tried to answer, and the monosyllable "yes" came out so faintly that Carlos could guess it rather than hear it.

"I too," he added somewhat more boldly, "remembered you, but to be honest, not you as you are now, but as you were when we parted."

"Oh!" the girl innocently exclaimed, "so the same thing happened to you as to me?"

The women and don Francisco were getting up from the table, but the two distracted young people remained seated. "I remembered you as the cute little eight-year-old, Luisa, but now you are so beautiful!"

Luisa again blushed, but she still managed to respond, "You too have changed so much!"

"I would always like to be the same Carlos you used the familiar form with, whom you called your brother. Do you remember,
Luisa?"

"Oh, yes! But . . ."

"But now I am different in your eyes, isn't it true? Now, cousin,
you don't treat me like a brother; you don't love me in the way you
did then."

"I always . . . —love you," Luisa was going to add, but as at that
moment she again found fixed upon her the youth's gaze that
unsettled her so much, the sentence remained unfinished.

Neither did Carlos manage to say anything else, but he stared
at her for a long time, so absorbed that he did not hear doña Leonor
inviting him to go with his father to a sitting room to rest a little,
because even on such a great day the good woman could not do
without her afternoon siesta. She repeated her suggestion three
times before he heard her, and might have done so a fourth time
if Luisa, who could no longer stand the blushing and the emotion
she was feeling beneath the youth's persistent fiery gaze, had not
gotten up and quickly gone to her room.

Then Carlos was led to the sitting room, where upon finding
himself alone with don Francisco, he exclaimed in a burst of enthusiasm, "Oh, Father! How happy I am! How happy we'll be!" At
that moment the young man was certainly thinking that that
divine creature was destined to be his; when he was with her he
had only been aware that she was as beautiful and pure as an angel.

And Luisa, what was she thinking as her mother and her venerable friends were sleeping, while she sat in an armchair reading
Paul and Virginia . . . ? I do not know, but I am confident that
although she was at the most interesting passage of the novel, the
moment when the two lovers are separating, the siesta went by
without the girl's reading about the start to Virginia's boat trip.
We must confess that more than once the book slipped from her
hands, and other times, although her eyes were fixed on it for a
long time, you did not see her turn a single page. It is undeniable
that she was thinking about something that was more interesting
to her than the love of the two Creoles—but who would dare to

express in human language the thoughts of a young girl who has just fallen in love?

The siesta came to an end; the women left their beds, and Luisa and Carlos met again, if with less confusion, with more agitation. But don Francisco, for whom it was as essential to take a walk along the tree-lined avenue every summer afternoon as it was for his sister to take her two-hour siesta, informed his son (we do not know whether to the latter's satisfaction) that it was time to take leave of the two women. Upon which were repeated all the welcomes and invitations exchanged between the hosts and the guests upon their arrival, and doña Leonor concluded by emphatically inviting her nephew to join them in the evenings.

"Although my home is not one of those designed for frequent gatherings," she said, "you can still have a nice time. My two worthy friends here" (upon which doña Beatriz and doña Serafina made a slight curtsy), "the priest don Eustaquio, a most congenial man, and a few other friends usually favor us with their company, and although we do not provide balls or other worldly entertainments, we play a hand of manille, and some nights lotto. In this way, my dear nephew, you will enjoy yourself without offending God or harming your neighbor, and if you find these games boring . . ."

Carlos quickly interrupted his aunt, assuring her that far from being bored he expected to really enjoy himself, because he was a great fan of manille and lotto. But doña Leonor finished her thought, saying, "If some nights you find the games boring, Luisita will talk with you, because she never plays."

"If you had a piano in your home, as you should," said don Francisco, "and if you had not set your mind on not letting the girl study music, we could have had some very good times, because Carlos is a consummate music lover. But you, sister, have deprived Luisa of any agreeable skill, and the upbringing you have given her . . ."

"Brother," doña Leonor exclaimed in some anger, "to hear you, my nephew would think that the girl is ignorant, stupid, and the truth is that just because I didn't want to make her into a music teacher or a dancer, I don't think I can be accused of not giving my daughter a suitable upbringing for her sex. Sometime Luisa will show her cousin the altar cloth she made for the altar of our Lady of Refuge, which is admired by everyone who has seen it, and her two images of the Virgin of Sorrows and of Santa Teresa de Jesús, which she embroidered on white satin with silk and look as though they were painted with a brush. Not to mention her flowers, which are so natural you can almost smell their fragrance—and which she does just as a hobby! It's a pleasure to hear her reading, she writes quite clearly, she does every kind of needlework to perfection, she knows the first four arithmetic rules as well as any shopkeeper, and she can recite by heart some of the books she has read. Come now, I don't think she is as ignorant as you suppose."

"Did I say any such thing? It's impossible to talk to you, sister, because you give an absurd interpretation to the simplest statement."

"It's you, brother . . ."

It looked as though one of the siblings' usual quarrels was about to break out, when fortunately the kindly figure of Father don Eustaquio arrived, cutting off the argument that was getting started. After another half dozen congratulations and welcomes from the family's reverend priest, each one answered meticulously in turn, the father and son took their leave and set out for the avenue, the one saying, "My sister is impossible!" and the other, "My cousin is enchanting!"

3

Carlos de Silva was one of those men whom women judge at first sight, and about whom they say to themselves, "How lucky is the woman he loves!"

Indeed, his eyes revealed an ardent, impassioned soul and a kind heart full of faith that could easily be aroused, as his brow bore the seal of intelligence and noble pride. His features showed all the ardor and enthusiasm of youth, slightly tempered by a touch of pride and melancholy. He was a fine man in every sense of the word, because his was a purely masculine beauty, and observing that young face, one sensed that later it would take on a severe look. But at this time Carlos was only twenty years old.

The first twelve years of his life had been spent in the company of his aunt and the pious, austere atmosphere that surrounded her. His first ideas had been formed in conformity with those of the people he lived with. The strict principles of doña Leonor, her rigid morality, her religious practices and inflexible character had governed his development, exerting a profound influence on his entire life.

During that brilliant period for France, when the great political drama that had begun with the revolution had just ended with the fall of the empire, during that time of new ideas and new principles, Carlos, who was of a bright and thoughtful nature, had absorbed the events of an era that was so fertile in new ways of thinking. His ideas had changed and grown, enlightening him and expanding his intellectual horizons, without corrupting his heart or tainting his character.

Of course, upon returning to his aunt's side he no longer had the same concerns that she had instilled in him, but he kept intact the religious faith and the strict moral code that distinguished this respectable woman. Although of an intense, fiery nature, with strong passions—perhaps more strong than deep—he remained true to his principles, his behavior was stable and consistent, and his impetuous character was tempered by the force of reason. The truth is that up until then his principles and his reason had never undergone the test of a fierce struggle with his passions. Thus Carlos was a strong and beautiful organism that had never been put to the test; a zealous heart that had not yet lived; a high-mindedness that could not yet judge with wisdom and correctness; great ability that was still not self-aware: in short, he was a twenty-year-old man, with the noble instincts of that happy time, with the big ideas and expectations of ardent souls, with all the dangers that go along with inexperience and some of the concerns internalized from his early upbringing.

Ever since his early childhood, he had heard those around him say that Luisa would be his wife; at school in France he had sometimes thought about this. When his heart began to speak, when the blood began to flow hotly through his veins, he thought repeatedly about the fact that his life's companion had already been chosen for him. The image of the Luisa he had left behind no longer satisfied the ambitions of his passionate soul, was not the object of his dreams of love. The youth held in his mind the idea of a beautiful, pure, radiant woman, with a noble brow and a tender look; he created the ideal wife his heart yearned for, and at times he thought, "And I will not be able to look for her! I will have to accept someone else who is not her!"

But by a rare and happy chance, the woman chosen for Carlos by his father was, without his suspecting it, the embodiment of his dreams, the original of the portrait sketched by his ardent imagination. Carlos saw Luisa and he knew her; he recognized his creation, his ideal spouse; this was the pure maiden who smiled at him in his solitary raptures, the enchanting vision he had glimpsed in his dreams. Carlos saw Luisa and loved her; he had loved her for a long time; he now loved her with a double affection. Luisa was the lover he had not yet known; he had found in the girl, in the sister, his ideal companion; and that adored girl and beloved sister was the one chosen for him by his family; the woman they were giving him was the woman for whom he would have searched the world over. Happy Carlos!

One can easily surmise that he did not neglect his aunt's invitation, and showed up punctually every evening at her house. It is true that he did not make a great effort to take part in the games of manille that doña Leonor had described as a pleasant, decent amusement; he preferred his aunt's second proposal: that of talking to Luisa. However, to be honest, I must confess that it was not the liveliest of conversations. While the three women were playing cards, and the reverend priest and don Francisco shifted to the parlor to discuss religious or political matters, or the one denounced the corruption of morals while the other defended them, merely out of a spirit of contradiction, Luisa, seated on a stool before a small mahogany night table, was busy knitting socks or weaving flowers, while Carlos, sitting on another stool near her, watched her work in silence. At times Luisa asked her cousin's opinion about which color to use, or asked him if the socks she was knitting seemed fine enough to him. Occasionally Carlos also commented briefly about how varied nature appeared in her work, and how difficult it would be to imitate with the brush or the needle the freshness and the coloring of those flowers with which she was carpeting the floor, while also admiring the light touch of his cousin's work. If a pair of scissors or a knitting needle fell, Carlos leaned down to pick it up, sometimes daring to fool Luisa by pulling the object away at the moment when she was about to take it. Then the girl smiled in embarrassment; he kept showing it and pulling it away until she got impatient, childishly insisting on taking it from him. If in the course of that kind of game her hand accidentally brushed Carlos's, Luisa immediately withdrew it, her face turning purple, and Carlos, agitated and shaky, stopped the game. This was how the evenings went by in doña Leonor's home, until Carlos got permission from his aunt to teach Luisa how to paint flowers and birds. From then on there was no more knitting socks or weaving flowers. The two seated before an old-fashioned table, Carlos gave his beloved long lessons, which she received with obedience and pleasure. During the daytime, the young man amused himself painting pretty floral bouquets and birds of all kinds, which he brought at night as models for his student.

It was the month of July, which is very hot in Seville, and according to local custom families lived in the rooms on the main floor, the inner courtyards of which were beautifully decorated. The courtyard of doña Leonor's house was not notable for its furnishings, but it stood out for the abundance and variety of flowers that Luisa cultivated in blue and white vases, the fragrance of which filled the air. The tables on which doña Leonor played manille and Luisa painted were in that courtyard. The fragrant ambience of that enclosure seemed like the only kind of atmosphere fit for that angel, and when Carlos, leaning on the arm of his chair bent forward, to follow more closely the movements of the pretty hand that was practicing copying the birds he had painted, gentle breezes blew Luisa's blond hair, which briefly grazed his forehead. If at that moment his heart beat violently and his lips burned, eager to devour that beautiful hair and those snow-white shoulders, when Luisa turned toward him her serene, peaceful eyes, the man bowed his head, confused and respectful of the innocent look of that cherished maiden. Her appearance aroused the soul more than the senses, and the heart's storms grew calm in the presence of that meeting of the sweetest and most powerful qualities that exist on earth: innocence and beauty.

Contemplating her in a silent, devout ecstasy; at times hearing her musical voice utter tender words and express thoughts that were as pure as her heart; breathing by her side that flowery atmosphere beneath the poetic skies of Andalusia; receiving a smile, a gaze; these were such intense pleasures for Carlos, such perfect happiness that he could not recall if there could exist one that would be greater. And Luisa, ah! Luisa . . . The innocent one felt a new life awaken in her heart: a wellspring of strange new sensations rose in her breast, as the colors that sleep at night awaken by the light of day; and without understanding what she felt or what she inspired, she was at once happy and restless. She was frightened of her own good fortune, and when one of Carlos's looks told her with respectful passion, "I love you!" and the girl felt her heart overflow with happiness, she raised her eyes to heaven to ask if it was a sin to be so happy on earth. In that pure and pious soul, every feeling had a mystic character, and often, as her eyes rested sweetly on the adored face, her thoughts rose to heaven to seek beyond earthly life the future of her love. When Carlos was not with her, she took a childish pleasure in touching all the objects he had touched, in sitting in the chair he had occupied, in repeating words he had uttered and mimicking his gestures and the tone of his voice; but when she realized her own craziness she knelt, flushed and repentant, before an image of the Virgin, calling on her protection, and her pure vows and timid hopes rose to heaven on the wings of prayer. The new and powerful emotion that filled her heart, far from weakening her piety, had intensified it; because love in souls that have not yet been corrupted is also a religion: a faith.

And where can you find the man who, upon loving for the first time in his life, before he has seen or felt that love can wear out, that happiness has limits, has not believed that the earth is too small and life too short for the feeling that uplifts him? Where is he who has not then felt the need for a paternal God who offers eternal life for an eternal love? That is why no man is a materialist at the age of twenty. One only stops believing when one stops loving.

But those with virgin hearts and the force of youth, those who love each other without sin, who will soon make their pure and ardent passion into a sacred duty, those who are so chaste and happy, believe in everything: in eternal life, in eternal love. Oh! I will certainly not be the one to mock any faith. I find in all beliefs virtue and happiness. Let those cold jaded hearts mock man's higher instincts, which they call daydreams. Come to me, true or false, come to me, sweet beliefs of early youth! What remains to man when you are lost?

4

Two months had gone by since Carlos had arrived in Seville, and don Francisco had still not said a word about the cousins' engagement. This silence was starting to bother doña Leonor, and even more so because from a few things her brother let slip she strongly suspected that he had not entirely given up on his idea of sending Carlos to Madrid. As we have seen, the good woman was strongly opposed to this plan, fearing that an absence, a long delay in tying the nuptial knot, might lead to some setback that would thwart it, because despite her monastic life she had gained some worldly wisdom over the years, and knew that at her nephew's age one's impressions, while very strong, are not always the deepest, and that it was not prudent to put his fidelity to the test, especially before tying him with an unbreakable bond. Doña Leonor, whose health was more fragile by the day, and as a result ever stronger the desire to get her daughter settled, was carefully observing the rapid progress of the young people's love, and she pointed this out to her brother to rouse him to a definite decision. But don Francisco did not say a word, and doña Leonor was starting to get really irritated. Carlos no longer limited his visits to two or three hours at night; he was spending almost all day in his aunt's home, always with Luisa, gazing at Luisa, bewitched by Luisa. For her part, the girl was half neglecting her household chores, and while she continued to be sweet, humble, and affectionate, she seemed melancholy and restless during the times when she was not with Carlos. Doña Leonor, with her relentless severity and maternal vigilance, found it necessary to curtail many of her religious devotions to constantly monitor the lovers, because despite the respectful conduct of the youth and the perfect modesty of the maid, she felt she would be flouting all the laws of propriety and would be guilty of a sin of omission if she did not keep watch over all their actions, movements, and even looks. When her hysteria or her rheumatism prevented her from scrupulously filling the role of careful and prudent mother, the respectable widow doña Serafina took her place. Doña Beatriz was not assigned such a stately task because, despite being in her fifties, her being single did not make her respectable enough in the eyes of the scrupulous mother. Doña Leonor was getting tired of having to keep a constant eye on her daughter, and she was even reluctant to allow her to spend so much time with her fiancé when she still did not know if the desired union would take place soon. For these reasons, as well as her fear that don Francisco might again bring up the subject of sending Carlos to the court, which might lead to some obstacle to the realization of her desires, she finally decided to resort to a concrete means of forcing her brother out of his inaction. Before putting her plan into effect, she studied her nephew at length, to confirm the opinion she had already formed that he was madly in love.

Indeed, there was no doubt that the young man's affection was increasing day by day. It was a sight to behold how he spent hour after hour sitting with his cousin, intoxicated with gazing at her and as though oblivious to the entire world. Their conversations, which usually took place in the presence of a respectable audience, consisted of mere trifles or words that were meaningless in themselves, but in that small talk there were so many ways for the lovers to communicate! A timid, furtive look, a stifled sigh, the tone of voice, sweeter, slower, more expressive when they addressed each other . . . all the little things that are so great in love came naturally to the aid of our hero and heroine, and without either of them ever uttering the word "love," they both knew that they were loved.

The painting lessons that Carlos continued giving his cousin afforded them some moments when they were less subject to scrutiny, because then they were somewhat more apart from the elders, although never out of sight of the watchful Mama. But it turned out that having more freedom made them shier. Often, finding himself spied on by the inexorable gaze of doña Leonor, finding it impossible to say a single word to his cousin for her ears alone, Carlos desired and promoted the drawing lessons, feeling that he had a thousand passionate things to tell her; but when he found himself in the longed-for state, he tried in vain to express what he so intensely felt. He got confused, he trembled, the words died on his lips, and sometimes when he forced himself to say something, his words were so incoherent that he himself could not figure out what he had wanted to express. If Luisa then turned toward him her demure eyes full of serenity and tenderness, and he heard her sweet, musical voice, the young man gazed at and listened to her in rapture; his agitation calmed down, his confusion vanished, and spellbound, subdued by that pure, peaceful beauty, he felt only the need to love her as one loves God, rendering her a silent devotion. Then he was again bewitched, happy just to behold her, his gaze fixed on her with an expression of tenderness mixed with respect, which sometimes brought smiles to those around them and made the chaste girl blush.

Doña Leonor, who in view of all these symptoms no longer doubted that Carlos truly loved her daughter, resolved to take a prudent step toward realizing her desires, and when she saw her nephew most in love she told him in all earnestness that her own and her daughter's respectability made it imperative that they spend less time together.

"I can't tell you, dear nephew," she added, "how much I regret having to make this request, but it has come to my attention that people are starting to talk about the intimacy I am allowing you with Luisa, because although everyone knows that for many years my brother and I have had the intention of strengthening our family ties through the union of our two children, everyone wonders, and rightly so, why without any apparent reason the marriage is so delayed. Thus for my daughter's honor, you should limit the time you spend together until there is no obstacle to your union."

Carlos, who until then had not felt great impatience for the arrival of their wedding day because the certainty of it removed all anxiety, was unpleasantly surprised to hear his aunt's words, and for the first time thought that he could already be married and was not. He got a bit worked up, and said with feeling, "Stop seeing her every day, every hour! Oh, that would be cruel! An obstacle, you say—what is it? What can impede this union that was agreed upon long ago and on which I am pinning my lifelong happiness?"

"On that point I am as much in the dark as you," the shrewd woman replied. "As far as I'm concerned, you could get married today."

"So who is it . . . ?"

"Your father may have some reason for this delay, which is puzzling all Seville and which leaves room for gossips to spread myriad false rumors to his and my dishonor. But Francisco does not give any of this a second thought, and I suspect that he intends to send you to the court and . . ."

"Send me to the court?" the young man broke in impetuously. "Be separated from Luisa! Oh, no; I won't hear of it!"

It was hard for doña Leonor to hide her glee upon hearing this pronouncement, which dispelled all her fears; but she managed to do so, and told her nephew with feigned strictness that a good son should not oppose his father's will, even when his will was despotic and capricious.

"There is much talk about my brother's resolve," she added, "and it is hard for me, who would like to give you the sweet name of son; but it is not fitting for me to try to hasten that day, as though my daughter were a burden and I would like to relieve myself of her at any cost. Thank the Lord, that is far from my thoughts."

"Who could doubt it?" exclaimed Carlos vehemently. "Luisa is an angel! Want to relieve yourself of her! Oh, who could think such a thing? But you are right; it is not up to you to hasten that day which will make me the happiest of men; if you allow me to, I will talk to my father about it myself this very day, and entreat him on bended knee that he not delay my happiness any longer. Do you agree to this, Aunt?"

Doña Leonor pretended to hesitate, and seeing the youth's resolve, retreated to the point of saying that it might be a good idea to take more time to think it over before taking on the heavy yoke of marriage.

"But then we will continue as we have been, won't we, dear Aunt?" Carlos exclaimed. "I will wait as long as you want; I'll follow your orders; but let me see Luisa every day."

Doña Leonor, who had not expected such resignation, took care not to grant her nephew's wish, and as he, for his part, could not accept seeing Luisa less often, she finally had to agree to his first proposal; but doña Leonor did this so properly, so skillfully, that he was convinced she was doing it almost in spite of herself, and she felt sure that she had not in any way compromised her dignity or lowered her pride an iota.

Carlos talked to his father that very day, expressing his desire to get married as soon as possible. The elderly man explained to him in vain his reasons, good or bad, for not wanting him to get married so young. The impassioned lover triumphantly refuted them all—what eloquence one conjures up to defend the heart's cause! In such cases, the most dull-witted man finds stupendous resources. The father, who while not very prudent was after all a father, who had once been twenty and was now fifty-four, talked a lot about the solemnity of the endeavor his son was undertaking, about the importance of thinking it over wisely and getting to know the world a little before assuming the august state of husband and father, about how horrible it would be to later have regrets . . . but all of this made no impression at all on his son. Regrets! When you are twenty, do you ever think of regrets? When you are in love, do you ever conceive of the possibility of falling out of love?

Youth! Love! If they were allied with prudence and foresight they would not lead to so many mistakes, so many regrets, so many sorrows—but oh! would they then have so much charm?

Don Francisco was reasoning; Carlos was feeling. Carlos had to win, and win he did.

Two weeks later, at seven in the morning in the cathedral, the wedding ceremony was celebrated that united two people unto death. A solemn, moving ceremony in the Catholic faith, which

I have never beheld without feeling a blend of profound tenderness and terror.

Upon leaving the church, Carlos, who was holding his young wife by the arm, was beaming with happiness. Luisa kept her eyes down, her forehead and her cheeks flushed, her entire being emitting a kind of vague anxiety and sweet melancholy; but only upon returning to her home, when she and Carlos were led by their godparents to the armchair where her mother (whose ill health had not allowed her to accompany her daughter to the church that day) was sitting, only then could you see a limpid tear slip slowly down her cheek. Doña Leonor, whose gaunt yellow face made a sharp contrast with the pure lovely face of her daughter, held out her thin arms to the two young ones, who kneeled before her to receive her blessing. The austere, sickly features of the old woman softened and revived at that moment, and placing her shaky hands on the heads of the two young people, she raised to heaven a look that had never before been seen in her eyes: the gaze of a mother who is asking heaven for her daughter's happiness, an eloquent look, indescribable, sublime! Then, in a weak voice but in a deeply solemn tone, she gave the newlyweds a long talk about the duties they had just assumed. As she spoke, her severe, serious tone gradually softened, and upon finishing her speech with these words, which she addressed to her son-in-law, "Keep her as pure and as pious as she is at the moment I give her to you. She has been a good daughter; reward her by making her a happy wife," her features took on a truly poignant look.

Carlos, moved, took one of her thin hands in his, and joining them with Luisa's, pressed them on his heart, exclaiming, "I swear it!"

"And you, my daughter," Leonor continued, "never forget that after God your first love should be your husband; love him, obey him in all things that do not conflict with the salvation of your soul."

Luisa raised to her husband a gaze of indescribable tenderness; Carlos, entranced, took her in his arms, and she, leaning languidly on her husband's chest, whispered in a voice so soft that only he could hear it, "Yes, I will always love you: God and you!"

It was the first expression of love that those pure lips had uttered. Carlos, beside himself, planted a kiss of fire on her virginal brow; it was the first time the youth held in his arms a woman he loved.

"Now," cried doña Leonor in a solemn tone, "I bless you, my children; may God make you virtuous and happy; and may your children be for you what you have been for your parents."

And those present replied in chorus, "Amen."

From his seat in the clouds, the angel of pure loves must have pulsed with pleasure at that moment.

5

If there exists happiness for mankind, if it is attainable on earth, it is only the union of love and virtue that can provide it. Love sanctified by religion, love tempered by security and habit, love that takes the form of duty, duty embellished by love . . . how sublime, what blissful harmony! Why does fickle nature wrest from man this state of divine bliss? Why can we not solidify the concordance between feeling and duty? Oh imperfection and inconsistency of human nature, that eternal love, the soul's desire, cannot be realized by the heart!

But Carlos and Luisa are so happy! Away, cold thoughts, away sad lights of truth, for I want to relish the charming spectacle of a happy and chaste love. But I will not attempt to describe it; pure loving souls will intuit it, while it is beyond the understanding of callous, depraved beings.

For the young newlyweds, the first months were spent in divine rapture; the following months in delightful calm. They had been married for more than a year, and during that time had not known a single hour of boredom or regret; on the contrary, every day they seemed happier and to have gained a better mutual understanding.

Given doña Leonor's rapidly declining health as well as the custom of a secluded life, Luisa almost never went out, and Carlos, content with his home life, had also withdrawn from all society. But what need is there for amusements when one has good fortune? Luisa, who had replaced her mother (now bedridden forevermore) in housekeeping duties, and who looked after the old woman with truly filial tenderness and care, could fulfill these tasks without for a moment neglecting her husband. And she was so lovely, so sublime when she descended from the angelic sphere to handle the smallest details of domestic life! An admirable order reigned in that house. Every moment was occupied, all events were foreseen, all needs anticipated. Don Francisco had moved into his sister's home, and it was now a single family doubly entwined and perfectly united; even the small arguments between brother and sister were now rare, and the peace, the sameness of that innocent and serene life, was so unchanging that it seemed to bear the seal of eternity.

January arrived; Carlos and Luisa had wed fifteen months before, and it seemed to them like yesterday. The long winter nights were for them a delight. That patriarchal family made a picture worthy of being immortalized by the brush of Bartolomé Murillo, if Murillo had been alive at that time. In the center of a spacious bedroom, a large bronze brazier where an ample fire was burning. Seated around the hearth, a lovely girl in simple dress, involved with her womanly chores, and a handsome youth by her side reading aloud a novel by Richardson, from time to time interrupting his reading to caress his pretty neighbor. A little farther out, in comfortable armchairs, a still robust elderly gent between two reverend dames, doña Beatriz and doña Serafina, constant members of doña Leonor's salon, the three listening in silent absorption to what Carlos was reading, annoyed by his interruptions, while often interrupting the reading themselves with outbursts of wonder or pity according to the unfolding fates of the novel's protagonists. How many reflections evoked by the virtue of Pamela and the arrogance of her sister-in-law, the one praised and the other condemned! How much indignation at the wickedness of Lovelace! What sympathy for Clara's misfortune! Luisa often wept during these readings, and as she was never so pretty as when she cried, her husband would often leave his audience in suspense during the most gripping passages to delight in contemplation of his wife. Upon which Luisa was embarrassed that her sensitivity was noticed, the two women got angry at the interruption of the reading, don Francisco took advantage of the pause to criticize the work, although no one paid the least attention, and doña Leonor had to raise a thin transparent hand from the bed and declare in a forceful tone, "Go on!" for the audience to calm down again and the reader resume his task.

Fortune frowned on that serenely happy life, and soon the innocent literary evenings were interrupted. A letter from Madrid brought news of the death of the Queen's chaplain, first cousin of don Francisco, and that he had designated don Francisco and doña Leonor as his sole heirs. The deceased had left behind a considerable fortune in homes and valuables, as well as debts he had with various members of the court. As his affairs were not in good order, the executors of his estate informed the Silvas that one of them would have to go to straighten them out for himself. Don Francisco, who had never completely lost the desire to send his son to Madrid for a brief immersion in court life, declared that it was absolutely necessary that Carlos be charged with this affair. Doña Leonor raised objections, the youth loathed the idea, and Luisa timidly resisted; but at last, after several days of discussion, the matter was decided in don Francisco's favor, and Carlos reluctantly agreed to separate from his wife, in the hope that it would be for a short time, because he planned to devote himself exclusively to finishing the assigned task as quickly as possible. Preparations were made for the journey, and recommendation letters written. There were two women at the court who had ties with the Silva family and to whom Carlos was to be recommended, because Luisa feared that he might fall sick when he was far from her, and in such a case it was essential that there be people of her sex who were favorably disposed to the young man. So the brother and sister wrote two long letters to the female relatives; but an argument arose in this regard that led to one of the two being torn up. One of the ladies was doña Elvira de Sotomayor, the widow of doña Leonor's first cousin, with whom the latter, although she did not know her personally, since the one had never left Madrid and the other had never left Seville, had maintained a long epistolary correspondence, even after the death of her husband. The other was the Countess of S., also the widow of a close relative of the Silvas, but one whose marriage had greatly displeased doña Leonor. The reason for her ill will was none other than the fact that the Countess had been born in France, a nation that, as we have said, doña Leonor despised. In 1811 in Paris, the Earl of S. married Catalina of T., whose Spanish mother had wed the Viscount of T. when he was secretary of the French Embassy in Spain, but the Viscount having returned soon after to his homeland with his wife, Catalina had been born in the country that was so loathed by doña Leonor. When the Earl of S. informed her of his marriage to a Frenchwoman, the respectable lady responded by advising him to take her away from that accursed land as soon as possible, and she never forgave him for the disdain he showed for her advice. When the Countess was widowed, heiress to a large part of the possessions her husband held in Spain, she decided to settle in Madrid, where she was at the time of the Earl's death. Doña Leonor had heard all of this from her brother, who occasionally wrote to the Countess, since for her part, she had never chosen to strike up a correspondence with "that foreigner"; and it must be noted that her designating anyone with that term was a succinct and proper way to show the most complete contempt. Thus, when don Francisco read her the letter he had written to the Countess recommending his son to her, doña Leonor declared that Carlos had no need whatsoever for the friendship of the "foreigner," and that she would be extremely upset if her son-in-law cultivated such a relationship. On that day don Francisco revived his old stance of opposition to his sister, maintaining that no one could be more useful to his son in Madrid than a woman who had connections with the most distinguished houses, who was accustomed to the best society, and who, as he was informed, combined a perfect understanding of society with remarkable talents. But this was not the kind of praise designed to reconcile doña Leonor with her cousin through marriage, and everything her brother said in this regard only served to heighten the instinctive dislike she had felt ever since she first heard the name of Catalina. So don Francisco had to yield this time as on others; the letter for the Countess was torn up, and the only member of the fair sex Carlos was referred to was doña Elvira de Sotomayor, who at least (as doña Leonor said) was Spanish and had been raised properly, and not in lands where altars were defiled, kings were guillotined, and soldiers ruled.

The day of Carlos's departure finally arrived. Luisa had not stopped crying for many days before, and her grief was so strong that the severe mother had to seriously scold her, after making futile reflections on how grave a sin the lack of resignation was in God's eyes, and how it offended His divine majesty that one give to a mortal that immense love that only He deserves and that we owe only to Him. The poor girl listened to her mother with her usual humility and begged forgiveness for her sorrow, but as bad as she felt about it, she could not even try to overcome it. Her frightened imagination gauged the distance between Seville and Madrid as though the immensity of the oceans would separate her from her husband, and it seemed to her that there would be worlds between them. All the tender fears and sad forebodings that generally accompany the first separation from a loved one overwhelmed the timid and passionate spouse, and it seemed to her that life itself was deserting her as the fatal hour of Carlos's departure approached. This was her first sorrow, and while the first sorrow is not always the greatest, it is undoubtedly the most sensitive.

When she was packing her husband's luggage, she kissed his clothes, moistening them with her tears, and she felt a kind of jealousy to think that other hands than hers would fold those handkerchiefs that she had embroidered for Carlos and would administer all those little caring touches that only she should do for him. When she buttoned his jacket and brushed off his cloak, she said in tears, "Carlos, I will not be myself from now on . . ."

And she could not finish, her voice smothered in sobs. Carlos took her in his arms and tried in vain to console her; he too was crying like a child, and was almost on the point of deciding to take Luisa with him when doña Leonor appeared, leaning on her brother's arm, looking so pale and sick that he felt ashamed for even having thought of depriving that old woman who was at death's door of her daughter. The departure of the servants carrying the luggage to the stagecoach, and the striking of the cathedral clock that distinctly chimed the dreaded hour, announced to Carlos that the moment had come for a separation to which he still had not resigned himself. Covering with kisses the blond head of his wife, with a painful effort he uttered the terrible word "Farewell."

Luisa shuddered; she raised her eyes and fixed them avidly on her husband's face, and taking from her neck a black ribbon that held a scapulary of the Virgin, embroidered by her own hand, she put it around her husband's neck, barely able to pronounce the words, "May she protect you."

Then she tried to repeat, but could not, the advice already given a thousand times, that he should protect himself from the thin air of Madrid, that he should not in any way overdo it . . . in short, those precautions that only occur to a woman and that are at once childish and tender.

"Come now, my children," said don Francisco. "Chin up! Soon, very soon you will be reunited."

"May it be so," uttered doña Leonor, coming up to embrace her son-in-law.

But Carlos could not part from Luisa who, clasping him around the neck, repeated amid sobs the fatal word "Farewell."

"Don't inflame heaven, my children," said the old lady. "Don't bring upon yourselves a genuine sorrow as punishment for a grief without cause."

Upon hearing these menacing words, Luisa drew back from her husband with a shiver, exclaiming, "Forgive me, my God, and Thy will be done."

Carlos looked away from her, because he knew that while he looked at her he would not have the strength to leave.

"The stagecoach is about to leave," called the butler from the doorway.

Carlos kissed his father's hand, embraced his aunt, and without looking at Luisa dashed out of the living room.

She wanted to run to the balcony to see him off, to tell him a thousand things that occurred to her at that moment, but the poor girl could not get to the place where she was headed; her strength gave way and she fell, fainting, into her mother's arms.

"Luisa! Luisa!" exclaimed don Francisco, holding back his tears. "Have you no consideration for your poor mother's condition? Do you want to kill her with your grief?"

"Me! Me!" cried the girl trembling. "Oh, no! Mother dearest, may God take my life in place of yours, but may He allow me to see him once again . . . A moment, a single moment . . ."

"He will soon return to your side, my child," said doña Leonor, moved.

"It had better be very soon," the desolate wife exclaimed, "if you want him to find me alive."

6

It was a fine winter's day, one of those winter days that you find only in Madrid, when entering by the Antocha gate Carlos saw for the first time the busy life that circulates on every street of the imperial city, and which takes by surprise those who come from a quiet provincial town. During the journey he had been so engrossed in thoughts of Luisa that he was unaware of his surroundings; even the picturesque grandeur of the Sierra Morena, which always catches the eye even of those who have seen it many times, barely managed to draw him out of his deep sadness for a moment. But upon arriving in Madrid, the noise and hubbub roused him from his gloomy, lethargic state, and accustomed to the silent majesty of Seville, he could not help but be agreeably surprised at the sight of loud and lively townspeople. Along the way he had made the acquaintance of a man from Madrid who was returning home after a two-year absence, and Carlos could not help catching some of his enthusiasm for a moment upon seeing his native city.

"There she is," his companion cried, clapping his hands in excitement; "there's the royal city, the splendid city! with her unexpected brilliance, her many avenues, her forty-two squares, her innumerable fountains, her people always as busy as ants. Madrid is not Spain; Madrid is Madrid, and beyond here is no life. Do you know, Silva," he added, turning to Carlos, "that I have also been in Paris, in the early years of the Empire, and in London, Edinburgh, and Vienna? Well, in those foreign courts I yearned for Madrid. A Spaniard cannot live without Madrid once he has seen it; the Prado and the Puerta del Sol are as essential to him as air and food. Hail a thousand times, oh queen of New Castile!"

The enthusiastic Madrileño asked Carlos if he was planning to stay in a guesthouse or in someone's home, and realizing from his answer that Carlos had not made up his mind about this, he proposed that Carlos join him in renting rooms in one of the best guesthouses in Madrid, where they would be well accommodated for fifty reals a day. Carlos agreed, and as soon as they went through customs they headed for Fuencarral Street, followed by three robust Gallicians who carried their trunks on their shoulders. Despite his travel companion's praise for the place where they were going to live, Carlos found it very shabby, recalling the elegance and orderliness of this kind of establishment in France, even in the smaller cities. The momentary distraction he had felt upon arriving in Madrid vanished as soon as he found himself installed in a small, scantly decorated room, quite dark for one who remembered well the many high windows in Sevillian homes that let the sunlight pour into all the rooms.

Carlos again grew sad, and wishing to conclude as soon as possible the business that had brought him to Madrid against his will, he got dressed immediately and went out with his friend, who offered to accompany him, to go to see the executors of his deceased relative and learn what he had to do. Once he had taken this first step, which aroused the hope that his stay in Madrid would not be long, he went to the home of his cousin by marriage, doña Elvira, to deliver the letter given to him by doña Leonor. Not finding her at home, he left the letter with her servant with the address of his lodgings.

Tired, thoughtful, preoccupied, but less sad thanks to the hope of returning soon to the objects of his affection, he returned to the guesthouse and shut himself in his room, to avoid having his companion divert him from thinking exclusively of Luisa. He was already working out in his mind what to tell her in his first letter, because although he had written her from Cordoba and Ocaña, it seemed like a century to him since he had told her his thoughts, thoughts that were all centered on him and her. He was already counting the days he would have to spend without seeing her, and transporting himself to the day when he would surprise her, throwing himself unexpectedly into her arms, while he tried to guess what she was doing and thinking at that moment, and upon thinking, "Maybe she is crying," neither could he hold back his tears.

He was still absorbed in these thoughts, half reclining on a sofa, when there was a light knock on the door, and a maid came in to say that a woman wished to see him. Carlos thought that it must be doña Elvira, and he came out to receive her, inwardly cursing such an untimely visit. He was not wrong; it was in fact his cousin, and he tried as best he could to hide his annoyance and respond in kind to her gracious warmth. He had heard his father and his aunt speak repeatedly of this lady without paying much attention to their words, and he had somehow imagined doña Elvira to be a respectable matron, close in age to doña Leonor and don Francisco. Thus he was a little surprised to find himself with a woman who was at most thirty, with a graceful figure and elegant bearing, so lively that as soon as she saw him she ran up to embrace him, asking him a thousand questions nonstop.

"My dear cousin! I can't tell you how happy I am to meet such a close relative of my late and eternally mourned Silva! So you are the son of his favorite cousin, his childhood friend, his dear Francisco whom he never stopped talking about? My husband adored your family. And my dear cousin Leonor? How unnecessary her letter was! Did she think she had to refer you to me? All she had to say was, 'My nephew is going to court.' However, I was very glad to receive her lovely letter. Is the good woman in such poor health? Maybe a change of air would do her good—why doesn't she come to Madrid? And you, my cousin, will you be with us for a long time? Leonor told me that some business interests bring you here— it must be the cousin's inheritance, isn't it? I believe that he left his affairs in a muddle. What a character he was! I guess you didn't know him."

This whole stream of words fell on Carlos before he had time to open his mouth, and he took advantage of the first pause to ask her to come into the living room. "I won't hear of it," she replied with the same impetuous vigor that astonished Carlos; "I have come to pick you up. The son of don Francisco de Silva staying in a guesthouse when Elvira de Sotomayor has a home? Impossible. And besides, Madrid guesthouses are vile! My maids have been preparing your room, and we should not delay because it is five o'clock, which is my dinner hour. My footman is downstairs and will take your luggage, so let's go."

And with these words she took him by the arm, and all his attempts to refuse her offer, which he did not want to accept at all, were in vain. Elvira stubbornly insisted, and Carlos had to yield despite himself. So he joined Elvira in her carriage after taking his leave of the landlady and his new friend, whom he offered to visit sometimes, and resigned himself to putting up with the unavoidable company of his talkative relative for the remainder of his stay in Madrid. "All I needed was to live with a scatterbrained, chatty woman," he thought, "to make the torment of being far from my heart's delight complete."

Despite Carlos's ungracious response to her conversation, Elvira did not for a moment lose heart. Her astounding talkativeness left the young man stupefied. In the short space separating Fuencar-ral Street and Príncipe Street, where Elvira's house was located, a space that the carriage traversed at quite a clip, she enumerated all of her husband's relatives, alive or dead; she told about all the letters she had received from doña Leonor; she talked about Madrid, about her house, her children, her visits, her servants, her horses, and even her cats. She constantly jumped from one topic to the next, she said a thousand trifles without stopping to see if Carlos heard them; but amid that flow of empty meaningless words, she expressed herself with a certain grace that would have caused a less distracted audience to listen to her without annoyance, and even with pleasure. Moreover, without being beautiful, she had a very agreeable face, and her light and lively character gave her features an almost childlike grace.

When they arrived at her home, she led Carlos to a pretty sitting room with bedroom that had been arranged for him. "Here you will be better off than in the home of your stout landlady," she told him. "Lord! How lavishly nature has endowed the good woman with flesh! This balcony is on a bottleneck; Príncipe Street is one of the busiest avenues of Madrid. You can see the theater—do you like theater? I really like tragedy; I prefer tragedy to comedy, although Moratín's comedies make me die laughing. The doña Irene character is hilarious in *The Maidens' Consent*! And her baron—what an utter jerk!

"What time do you usually eat? I think people eat early in the provinces. This is my dinner time—is it all right for you? I am going to tell them to serve the soup; in the meantime settle into your new home. You will have complete freedom here; I don't want you to have any inconvenience; you can come and go as you please; you'll have a servant who is entirely at your disposal."

Having concluded her speech she left, and Carlos followed her with his eyes, wondering if he could ever get used to that woman's behavior.

During the meal Elvira talked a lot and said a thousand bits of nonsense, but Carlos began to detect great kindness and sweetness for all her frivolity. Elvira had two daughters, both of whom were being educated away from home, and although Carlos initially viewed such detachment as blameworthy on the part of a mother, her visible emotion upon speaking of them, the pride that lit up her face whenever she said "my daughters," made him judge her less severely.

Elvira left him at seven to go to the theater, after futile attempts to get him to accompany her, and as soon as Carlos was alone he shut himself in his sitting room to write to Luisa, although the mail would not go out for two days. What letters you find between two young lovers upon their first separation! An outsider could not read them without laughing from the opening line! What details, what minutiae! How the same thought is expressed a thousand ways, in a thousand forms! How much ink spilled to finally express one single idea: I love you! What an abundance of sweet lies, which the one who writes believes to be truths! And yet those letters, so trite and childish to an outsider, are life itself to an absent lover; more than life, they are happiness. As they are read, the lover believes, loves, hopes, enjoys; they fill the empty world and the empty heart.

Carlos spent several hours that night immersed in his delightful task, and at eleven he rang the bell and asked if Elvira had returned. The servant smiled. "At eleven!" he said. "No, señor, the señora never comes back so early; after the theater she goes to the salon; but we have orders to serve you supper whenever you like, and you can retire without waiting up for her, since she might not come home until dawn."

Carlos followed the advice; he asked for a cup of tea and went to bed right away, completely exhausted, in the elegant bed they had made up for him, in which he was sweetly transported in sleep to Seville, by the side of his adored Luisa. Sleep is a great enchanter, who has granted us all, to a greater or lesser degree, the sweetest favors. Poets have often called him the friend of the unfortunate, and his name can well be invoked as the flatterer of lovers. How often does he beguile us in their absence! How often does he mock the rigor of ingratitude! How often does he avenge us for abandonment!

So smile, sweet silent Morpheus, on our Carlos in love, and intoxicate him with the fragrance of your innocent lies; while we, so as not to gaze on the fiery ghosts of sleeplessness, your enemy, record faithfully all we know or suppose that Luisa was doing and thinking, from the moment in which she lost sight of the dear object of her one and only love.

7

One of the peculiarities one finds in those who are sad or distressed is the surprise they feel at others' pleasure or mere indifference. When we are suffering, it is hard for us to believe that ours is not a universal sorrow, and we cannot understand that what is for us the cause of profound grief may be insignificant to others. When Luisa no longer saw Carlos, it was not just her heart that was left empty; for her it was also the house he no longer inhabited, the city he left deserted. It seemed to her that, as if her husband's absence were a public disaster, Seville took on a guise of mourning, and the disruption of her happiness was a universal upheaval. The voice of a neighbor singing at the piano a cheerful Andalusian song hurt her ears and her heart, and she thought in dismayed surprise, "People can sing when he is away!"

That night doña Beatriz and doña Serafina showed up punctually as usual, and upon seeing them Luisa burst into bitter tears. "Oh—so Carlos has left?" said one of the women. "It's clear from these little tears. Come on, girl, you should not get so upset; it's nothing. One or two months of separation, after which you will be all the happier to be reunited. Now, now . . ." she added, wiping Luisa's eyes with her handkerchief, "calm down; since we don't have our reader here tonight, his beloved wife should replace him; otherwise we will have a very dull evening. Don't you agree, Leonor?"

"I told her the same thing myself, my dear Serafina, but this girl is getting too spoiled; it's her father-in-law's and her husband's fault, who have gotten her used to always having her own way and never having to face any setback. Before getting married my little Luisa was not like this at all, nor would she ever have become like this if I had lived alone with her. But all this pampering, flattery, extreme indulgence . . ."

Luisa's crying increased, and don Francisco rushed in to defend her, calling his sister cruel, unjust, and cold. "Isn't it natural," he asked, kissing the tearful girl on the forehead and hair, "that she takes very hard the first separation from her husband? What is wrong with that? Leonor, do you really have to find every possible excuse to torment your daughter and slander your brother? Cheer up, my dear, don't cry anymore; do it for me, and don't pay attention to what your mother says; it's her own trouble that makes her speak that way. Don't be upset, Luisa." And the old gentleman took Luisa far from the invalid so the latter would not notice how little success his advice had had.

"Come now, let's not talk about this anymore," doña Beatriz now said, "and speaking of absences, do you know, doña Leonor, that our good friend Father don Eustaquio has also gone off to Madrid?"

"Is it possible?"

"Yes, señora, I will tell you the story, because the reason for his departure makes quite a story."

"Tell us, tell us," the two women exclaimed, and doña Beatriz began her tale, after taking out her gold snuffbox with the portrait of Lord Wellington and offering snuff to her listeners.

Luisa, sitting in a corner of the room, tried to calm down, and don Francisco, after whispering in her ear some consoling words with the assurance of the speedy return of Carlos, also went up to the narrator to hear the story of the departure of Father don Eustaquio. The conversation on this topic lasted more than an hour; then they talked about the cold weather they were having and the illnesses it was causing in Seville, according to doña Leonor's doctor; about the Mother Abbess of the Capuchins who suffered terribly every winter; about a visit that doña Serafina and doña Beatriz had made to her and of what they were planning to talk about on the next visit to the Reverend Mother; in short, the evening passed in a very similar way to others, and poor Luisa saw with surprise and dismay that what had the power to destroy her happiness was in and of itself a very insignificant event. In the meantime, she soothed her sorrow by contemplating all the objects that most vividly reminded her of her husband: the chair he usually occupied, the books he had read and those that were still spread out on the table . . . Luisa noticed that in one of them a small ribbon was inserted in the last page Carlos had read, and she secretly took the ribbon, which from then on remained forever hidden in her breast. Upon leaving, the two women repeated their usual words of consolation, and afterward doña Leonor seriously urged her to curb a sensitivity that was extreme to the point of dangerous, if not blameworthy, succeeding by her lecture, if not in calming her, in making it seem excessive and unjust in her own eyes. She went to bed telling herself that it was in fact crazy to get this upset over a short separation, but despite her precise reasoning, a mournful feeling continued to weigh on her tender heart, as though an inner voice were crying nonstop that that separation would forever destroy her life's happiness.

And why should we condemn premonitions as crazy? The heart has its own intuitive foresight, and what often seems to us a fanciful anxiety may be an advance warning of a huge misfortune.

From the day following Carlos's departure, all of her days were the same, with no interest, no object, no thought other than that of receiving letters from her beloved; it seemed like centuries between the mail days from Madrid. The only activity she willingly devoted herself to was to write long journal entries to her husband; she could not bear anything that did not relate to him. The caregiving required by her mother's condition, chores that were so sweet when she shared them with Carlos, became tiresome to her. She was no less diligent and painstaking in caring for her invalid mother, but her actions no longer held for her the same ease and the same charm. When she was with her mother she tried to hide her sadness, and this pretense made her continual attendance on the sick woman painful. Often, after an entire day at the patient's bedside, trying to distract her with trivial conversation, she withdrew to her room at night with her heart swollen with tears, and she made up for the day's oppressiveness by devoting the whole night to writing and crying. Her natural shyness seemed to increase with her sadness, and hiding her sorrow like a fault, she hardly dared to raise her beautiful eyes, red from crying. Her complexion withered and she got visibly thin, to a degree that within a month of Carlos's departure her beauty had undergone a striking change for the worse.

Nonetheless, her husband's letters were long and frequent, they all breathed the same passion, the same sadness at not seeing his Luisa, they all assured her of a speedy return, so amid her sorrows, the poor girl at least did not know the terrible, devouring pain of jealousy. Not once did the thought cross her mind that her husband could love another; she never considered the possibility that absence could weaken the strong affection he had sworn to her, and the slightest suspicion to that effect would have seemed to her a crime.

8

Carlos realized that he had been mistaken in his concern that he would feel put upon in the home of his cousin Elvira. Many days went by without his even seeing Elvira except at dinnertime, busy as she was with her numerous visits and amusements, and when he was invited to chat with her for a while in the morning, he did not find her flighty talkativeness as unbearable as he had thought at first. Elvira was such a sweet and obliging person, so frank and easy to get along with that one did not feel put upon by her at all, and when one got to know her well enough to appreciate her kind heart, one could easily forgive the frivolity and shallowness of her character. Carlos actually came to enjoy her glib small talk and no longer avoided the rare moments when he could see her at home, because although she repeatedly urged him to accompany her to the theaters and salons she frequented, he always refused, citing his many occupations and his lack of relish for diversions where he would not encounter friends or relatives. Elvira made fun of his misanthropy and gaily went her way, without taking offense at his unsociability. Carlos wondered at that dissolute way of life, so different from that which prevailed in the home of his mother-in-law, and although he was becoming fonder of Elvira by the day, on the whole he judged harshly women like her who made of life an endless round of pleasure. The unchanging order, the sensible home economics that he had observed in the household of doña Leonor seemed to him worthier of praise than the indulgence that reigned in Elvira's, who Carlos moreover knew was not rich enough to be able to sustain her extravagant lifestyle for long. The flippancy with which a mother gaily ruined her children's future seemed to him as unthinkable as it was criminal. Carlos was more than a little surprised when he later learned that this in his view thoughtless, spendthrift woman had salvaged her daughters' inheritance through great sacrifice and hardship, that within several years she had paid off the considerable debts that remained upon her husband's death, and that she was so quick and adept at making her assets profitable that her expenditures were always less than her income. It is true that the person who gave Carlos this information also suggested, in a vague and confused way, that no one believed that doña Elvira could have renewed her depleted fortune in such a short time by herself, and that some powerful friend had probably come to her aid. But this did not diminish the good impression the preceding story made on Carlos, and from then on he sincerely respected his cousin.

Thus he now sought out occasional conversations with Elvira with the same eagerness with which he had previously avoided them, and that distraction was all the more necessary to him since he rarely went out except to take care of the business that had brought him to Madrid. In the morning he usually met his friend at the Puerta del Sol and strolled with him for a while, and at night he occasionally went to visit the wife of don Eugenio de Castro, executor of the estate of his deceased relative whose heirs were his father and his aunt. He saw no one else, he had no dealings with anyone, and the occupation of writing to Luisa, as long as the letters might be, left him much free time that he did not know how to fill.

On the day that marked one month since his departure from Seville, he was feeling sadder than usual and was planning to ask Elvira if he could spend the day with her, but as he was about to go to her bedroom for that purpose, he received a polite note from the señora de Castro inviting him to go to her home at five for dinner, because that day being her birthday, she had invited a few friends over. Carlos, who longed for any change of routine that would dispel his deep sadness, accepted the invitation and arrived punctually at don Eugenio's home at the appointed hour. However, he soon found that being in society, instead of distracting him, heightened his annoyance, and during the meal he tried in vain to mimic the joviality and studied high spirits of the guests.

They were serving dessert and Carlos was yearning for the moment when he could slip away without attracting attention, when the mistress of the house asked him a question that obliged him to hide his impatience: "Are you going tonight to the concert that the Countess of S. is giving in her home?"

"I don't have the honor of knowing her," Carlos answered.

"What? You don't know the Countess, when she's the close friend of your cousin doña Elvira?"

"And the most beautiful and distinguished lady of the court!" one of the gentlemen at the gathering added brightly.

His words caused a stir among the ladies present, who looked at one another and whispered in each other's ears with signs of strong impatience, and some with a disdainful smile. The señora de Castro spoke up and asked the gentleman who had committed that offense against gallantry, in an ironic tone, how he had meant the word "distinguished" in regard to the Countess. "As concerns her questionable beauty," she added with a smile, "I will not be the one to analyze it."

"I call her distinguished," the gentleman responded in some embarrassment, "in view of her brilliant talents, her excellent upbringing, her exquisite elegance and lovely qualities, which although her envious rivals might wish to denigrate . . ."

The speaker was interrupted by the low murmur of many female voices, quivering with indignation, that repeated with feigned scorn, "Envious? Envious of the Countess?"

"Ladies," resumed the gentleman in ever more confusion, "I did not mean to offend anyone, and I just meant to say that I called the Countess distinguished because of her . . ."

"Astounding flirtatiousness?" said sharply an unmarried woman in her fifties, who in her younger years had undoubtedly been a good judge of the subject.

This witty remark (for it was taken as such) was received with roars of laughter, which showed the perfect solidarity of the female audience.

"I don't deny," resumed the gentleman, "that the Countess is rather flirtatious . . ."

"Rather, rather!" the women repeated in chorus. "And he doesn't deny it! Oh, what a praiseworthy concession not to deny that the Countess is rather flirtatious!"

And the laughter and gibes rose to a point that the poor gentleman finally had to leave the field to his female opponents, saying humbly that his opinion was not infallible, and that as a friend of the Countess he could not be an impartial judge.

"Friend of the Countess!" said the woman to the right of Carlos, close to his ear. "Do you know the origin of that friendship? It's none other than that this gentleman is seeking employment, and the Countess has influence, so to speak, with the Minister . . . And you, Count?" she added, turning to a blond young man who was probably her lover. "Are you also a champion of the distinguished merit of the Countess of S.?"

"As for me," the man in question answered smugly, "I detest these mannish women who discuss everything, who know everything, who need no one . . ."

"Oh! As for not needing anyone," one of the señoritas stuck in maliciously, "you are wrong, and you don't do Catalina justice. Do you think that goddess could survive without the worship of her numerous admirers? It is clear that she zealously seeks them out."

"And she finds them," said a married woman, whose ninth lover had abandoned her for the Countess, but who nonetheless, thanks to her great prudence and severe moral principles, which she displayed on important occasions, passed for a woman of extraordinary virtue. "No matter what people say," she went on with refined malice, "the Countess is an exceptional woman. No one else in Madrid sings with her skill and relish; I am told that she does fine painting and drawing; and it is said that she is so well educated that she discusses with the most knowledgeable men matters of ethics, religion, and politics. Gifted in all the arts, she is no less so in her independent nature, and I doubt that there exists in Spain a woman of freer ideas. I confess that I cannot abide taking a harsh view of what might seem questionable in her; in cases like this

I always give the person the benefit of the doubt, to the point that I overlook my own convictions to take her part."

"That is not surprising," said a septuagenarian who was aspiring to console the woman for the desertion of her ninth lover, with respectful mature gallantry. "That charming leniency in you is not surprising, so appropriate to the refined virtue and Christian charity that distinguish you."

"Certainly not," replied the woman with such enchanting humility that it elicited general praise. "I do not believe that my virtue is so rare in my own sex that it sets me apart. I am in no way a notable woman; I cede that honor without regret to the brilliant Countess of S., and I am content with my obscure mediocrity. My mediocrity does not allow me to set myself up as judge of the conduct or opinions of others, and I will only raise my voice to preach indulgence. As regards the friendship that the gentleman who initiated this conversation claims to have with the Countess, I say that it is very natural and understandable. I am not surprised that the Countess has many friends, although I admit that I would not choose her as a friend for my daughters."

"I feel the same way as you," said a young woman with a sentimental air. "The Countess is so natural, pleasant, and easy to get along with that men must really enjoy her company. The only thing I bitterly censure is that she does not use some caution, some discretion . . . In my opinion, only scandal is unforgivable. Oh! I really respect public opinion."

Upon hearing these words, it seems that some of the listeners looked at each other with knowing smiles, as though they recalled some event that could belie that assertion. Nonetheless, one of the gentlemen present hastened to approve what the beautiful young lady had said. He was an *afrancesado*, a staunch supporter of Bonaparte in 1809, and an ardent legitimist and absolutist since 1814. He raised his head with affectation, which until then he had held in a position suitable for chewing, and with a witty imitation of the faulty accent of a foreigner speaking Spanish, he said decisively:

"Oh! This woman is certainly right, and I am of her opinion in everything. Decorum in woman and integrity in man; these are the qualities I most esteem. The Countess of S. does not think or speak as she should, which is a striking flaw, and the truth is that on that account she is an exception to the rule in the country where she was born, because the French are models of discretion and know very well how to conform to social conventions. I, who know France better than if I had been born on its soil, declare that the Countess would be as severely judged there as in Spain."

"You are speaking too harshly of the Countess," the master of the house at this point observed, "and I believe that señor de Silva is related to that woman."

All of the women looked at Carlos, who had been listening to the conversation in silence, and they awaited his response in some embarrassment, like people of good taste who fear having violated the social proprieties.

But Carlos had heard too well what had been said about the Countess to admit his family tie with her, and with flushed cheeks he answered with a brief, emphatic "no."

"So now that I am not afraid of offending anyone," continued señor de Castro, "allow me to ask you, ladies, what great offense, what scandalous affair there has been in the Countess's life that has lowered her so much in your eyes?"

The women hesitated for a while, and looked at one another as though to consult about what answer to give to this unexpected question. Finally the most assertive one spoke up:

"Great offense!" she repeated. "Do coquettes commit great offenses? Their hearts are too cold and their character too shallow and fickle to commit great offenses."

"The Countess is a very astute woman," added another. "She knows how to do things with great finesse."

"I thought you condemned the Countess for being indiscreet," señor de Castro observed, "and I find an obvious contradiction in . . ."

"Enough!" his wife interposed, throwing a fearful look at her tactless spouse. "It is not necessary to examine the basis of any opinion. It is always right when it is the prevailing view."

Carlos could take no more; he was ashamed that the woman they were discussing had ties with his family. It seemed to him that if she showed up at that moment he would turn his back on her with supreme disdain, and yet he was starting to feel indignant with her detractors and more than once had trouble refraining from insulting them.

He pretended not to be feeling well as an excuse to leave.

When he returned to his room, the valet informed him that doña Elvira was waiting for him in her dressing room and that she wished to speak with him. Carlos showed up in a bad mood, finding his relative before a mirror, decked out in magnificent attire, and giving a final touch to her headdress.

"Welcome, esteemed cousin," she said without stopping her preparations; "I was waiting for you with impatience."

"What can I do for you, dear cousin?"

"Oh, that we will see to afterward—what I want to know now is your opinion of my dress: do I look nice?"

"I know little of such things, dear cousin, but nonetheless I think you look very beautiful."

"This is the first time I have heard you use gallant words to your dear cousin—but speaking of relatives, it appears you do not know that there is another person in Madrid with whom both you and I have family ties. Catalina, the widow of the Earl of S., was surprised to learn that a son of don Francisco de Silva is in the court and that she has not yet had the pleasure of meeting him."

This allusion could not have come at a worse time. Carlos made the most frivolous and trivial excuses.

"Although a scrupulous person in matters of etiquette would not accept such excuses," said doña Elvira with a smile, "I who know Catalina declare that she would find them sufficient, and in her name I am inviting you to the concert she is holding tonight in her home."

"Cousin," Carlos replied emphatically, "I cannot accept that honor. I am grateful to you and to the Countess for these so little deserved attentions, but you are aware that I am only in Madrid to take care of the business matter that brought me here, and moreover I am not inclined to social gatherings."

"The Countess's will be the most select; once a week she holds concerts in her home, attended by the most brilliant social circle of Madrid."

"That is a reason more for me not to attend," said the youth coldly; "since my stay in Madrid is to be brief, I am not trying to meet people or be introduced into that so brilliant circle, which moreover should not be very interested in a poor lad from the provinces, who longs to return there."

"You certainly are different," said doña Elvira laughing, "and since you display with so little embarrassment your desire to leave me, I am going to take my revenge by obliging you to confess that Madrid is not as unbearable a place as you now think. I must attend our relative's gathering tonight, and I am ordering you to accompany me."

"Cousin . . ."

"No excuses! If you refuse to accompany me, you will oblige me not to go."

"You will go, cousin, and I will accompany you, although it will surely be a sacrifice."

"I can see that there is no way to make you into a gallant gentleman, but despite your curt frankness I am sure that Catalina will like you very much; just from hearing me relate some of your singular traits, she is really curious to meet you."

"So according to what you say, you want to take me to this gathering as a curiosity piece, designed to amuse the brilliant Countess of S.?"

"Cousin, sometimes you are impossible—where did you get that idea?"

"Don't get angry," said Carlos smiling; "I am willing to go with you wherever you want to take me, and it will be a pleasure to give you this proof of my obedience, even at the price of being the object of ridicule of twenty coquettes."

"You are hard on my friend, Carlos, and without having met her I don't understand on what grounds you believe her to be a coquette."

"I did not go that far, señora; I was speaking in general."

"But look, admit that you have heard something that has induced you not to form the most favorable view of Catalina."

"Cousin, today is the first time I heard talk of the Countess, and the people engaged in that conversation all granted her the merit of brilliant talent and a fine upbringing."

"That's an understatement."

"It is generally believed, I think, that she excels in all the arts."

"They must have also told you that she is beautiful."

"Some said so."

"And that her manner is enchanting."

"Yes."

"And in the course of that long conversation of which it seems Catalina was the object, they did not fail to attribute to her faults strong enough to spoil all the merit they could not deny her."

"I see, dear cousin, that you know perfectly well the society in which you live."

"No, not as well as Catalina, but in any case, let's see if I can guess. Didn't they say that the Countess is shallow, fickle, frivolous, and mocking?"

"They said more."

"More! What, for example?"

"I would hope that the woman whom one of my father's relatives made his wife would not be considered the coldest and shrewdest of coquettes."

"Ah! Is that all?" said Elvira with a laugh. "If so, all the better for her husband. Everyone knows that the Earl was never jealous."

"Was not jealous!"

"No; the woman who needs the homage of all does not give preference to any one."

"And the Earl coldly watched his wife seek out and accept these tributes?"

"The Earl, my dear Carlos, was a man of the world."

"I confess that I do not understand that kind of man. As for the Countess, she may unite all the talents and all the charms of her sex, but I could never like or respect such a woman."

"You are too severe," said Elvira, "and I don't want to aggravate the bad mood that seems to have taken hold of you tonight. I am going to the theater; I will leave you to your own devices. In three hours I will come to get you and take you to the Countess's home, where I hope to reconcile you with her."

Carlos took her to her carriage and returned to his room, very annoyed about his commitment to accompany Elvira. While awaiting the appointed time, he wrote a long letter to his wife, the most notable paragraph of which was the following: "Tonight for the first time I will attend a social gathering in Madrid, having been unable to find an excuse not to accompany Elvira. The soirée is at the home of the widowed Countess of S., a woman who arouses in our dear mother an instinctive dislike, which I believe I will find justified, since according to everything I have heard about her character, my Luisa, she in no way resembles my angelic partner, nor our respectable mother."

He closed the letter with the usual vows of eternal love, indestructible happiness, and so on; he gave it to the courier and in a bad mood got dressed and waited for Elvira. She soon arrived; she called for Carlos without getting out of the carriage, and he had hardly gotten in when she began singing the Countess's praises, although we must confess that these praises were not of a kind that would recommend her to Carlos. Elvira enumerated with her witty joviality all of her friend's admirers; she spoke highly of her influence with several figures at the court, an influence that was all the more admirable considering that the Countess held opinions contrary to those of the current regime. She praised to the skies the talent, kindness, and discretion of Catalina, and she recounted, as outlandish flashes of wit, some tricks she had played on her admirers.

"She is a strange woman," she said; "she has aroused violent passions, without ever returning them; she only loves her friends, she worships friendship; her heart is impervious to love, and thus she plays with her lovers like chess pieces. No one knows like her how to disconcert a rash suitor, to humiliate a proud one, how to make a wise man lose his head and make an idiot look good. She laughs at everyone without falling out with anyone. Furthermore, no one has such a gift for taking revenge against a jealous rival, while obliging her to return to the lover she has stolen from her, the man now covered with disdain and ridicule. Oh! It is highly amusing to follow her in the sea of her flirtations, and see with what calm and serenity she observes from the port the storms she excites."

"Which is to say," said Carlos with an ironic smile, "that she is a cold executioner who delights in the convulsions of her victims."

"No, certainly not. Catalina has a beautiful heart, but she says, and rightly so, that it is a useful and permissible skill to know how to turn back upon our enemies the weapons with which they wish to harm us. But she is not cruel at all; on the contrary, she is a good and generous person. Her money and her friendship are at the disposal of all, and she is so open, so easy to get along with . . . ! She has so little pride that she rarely takes offense. She is so tolerant of others, always inclined to forgive them, that many people believe her to be very humble. But Carlos, don't you think that that kind of broad tolerance of human faults arises out of excessive pride? Catalina has such an innate conviction of her own superiority, joined perhaps with an exaggerated idea of human imperfection, that her goodness to all at times seems to me more like scorn than generosity."

"I cannot now judge the Countess," said Carlos with disdain, "and I do not think that I will ever get close enough to her to know her true nature."

Amid such conversation, Elvira and Carlos arrived at the Countess's home, and despite Carlos's irritation about attending the party, he could not help but have a pleasant impression upon entering the drawing room gleaming with lights and beauty.

Everything in the Countess's home had the mark of good taste and the most refined elegance; all that you saw, and even the air you breathed in that enclosure, was as though filled with perfume. The Countess assembled in her home the most select and brilliant society of Madrid, and she had introduced there the kind of open familiarity and simple elegance that made the Paris salons so pleasant and enjoyable.

Carlos had to admit, finding himself among this brilliant circle, that in the absence of real happiness, the imagination and even the heart must need that heady perfume of wealth and harmony, those fleeting impressions that leave no place for boredom by evading reflection. Elvira introduced Carlos to the Countess, who had come up a few steps to receive them, and despite the grounds for complaint that Catalina must have found in Carlos's neglect of her, her welcome was so warm and gracious that her indulgence made him feel ashamed and guilty. He found himself embarrassed and almost confused, and the momentary crimson of his cheeks lit up his proud eyes. All the women who were nearby seemed to wonder at his expressive and virile beauty, and although one noted some timidity in his manners, his looks were so noble and majestic that that defect seemed to make him look kinder. The Countess gazed at him for a moment, but upon meeting his eyes she looked away, and for the first time Carlos could examine that renowned foreigner. She was of slightly less than average height, and her figure more notable for its delicacy than for its perfection. The Egyptians would not have considered her a beauty, nor would she appeal to those men who love a robust figure bursting with health, so to speak. She was slim, and although her neck and shoulders were very shapely, and her figure really lovely, one could see at first glance that she lacked the voluptuous majesty of full-bodied women. Nor did she have pronounced features; her mercurial feelings were sketched on her face, whose expression was so fleeting, so variable, that from moment to moment she seemed to have different features. Her large brown eyes, sparkling with wit, had a quick, almost dazzling look, but when that gaze alighted, it was hard to defend yourself from the impression produced by her expression, which was both proud and passionate. Beyond this, there was nothing striking about her looks; she did not have classic features, and it was only when she lit up in conversation that you could see the admirable effect of the whole. It was noteworthy that despite the rare mobility of her face and the charming awkwardness of her entire person, the shape of her face and the natural position of her lips gave her, when she was idle, an admirably aristocratic air, and that without the least affectation there was an unlooked-for dignity in her bearing, combined with the most amiable abandonment. The gown she was wearing set off that kind of beauty, for it consisted of a dress of lace on satin in a pale pink color that went well with her pale white, almost transparent complexion, and in her abundant black hair were entwined with studied carelessness thick strands of pearls. Her feet, in white satin shoes, could compete with the trimmest feet of girls from Cadiz, and her hands, in light perfumed gloves, were small and fine. Carlos thought, upon examining her, that while she was not as beautiful as Luisa, no woman could be more seductive, but he did not commit the sacrilege, which it would have been in his view, of comparing the charming and elegant figure at whom he was gazing with the celestial image that was engraved on his heart. Perhaps at the very moment when he was admiring the graces of the Countess, the dear memory of his beloved came to disturb his fleeting distraction, because Elvira, who was watching him, saw him go to the far end of the drawing room and sit in the least visible spot with a pensive, melancholy air.

"Look at our Sevillian," she said smiling to the Countess; "look how he seeks out solitude in the middle of a ball. You could not imagine a more aloof, reserved character—and it's really a shame, for I'm sure you will agree with me that he is very handsome."

"Yes," she answered with a kind of amused disdain, "he's not bad-looking."

"Not bad-looking! You are very frugal in your praise, cousin," said Elvira, fixing her gaze on Carlos, "and I believe you are the first woman who does not think him worthy of more flattering words. Have you ever seen, hard-to-please one, more beautiful eyes, a more graceful figure, more perfect features?"

"I hadn't noticed, in truth," answered the Countess, throwing a quick glance over the object of the conversation, and immediately added, "but what unbearable insolence, my dear! To withdraw as though he's bored when he has not been ten minutes in our company!"

"Didn't I warn you that he's different, a mixture of pride, timidity, and eccentricity?"

"Oh! Your protégé just seems to me a rustic from the provinces, dear Elvira."

"You're wrong; he is not the least bit foolish. If you got to know him you would see that he has talent, imagination, and above all, modesty, although he has enough merit that he could be pardoned for the lack of it. But I see that the law of likes and dislikes holds, because you, who are so tolerant with everyone, at first sight judge unfavorably a young man who I thought would captivate you, and he, without even knowing you, has taken an insurmountable disliking to you."

"What?" said the Countess, turning intently to her interlocutor. "To me? An insurmountable disliking?"

"What I mean is that what he heard about your character put him so much on his guard against you that he would not pardon your bold gesture, even taking into account your talents and charms, and I had quite a time getting him to accompany me to your home."

"Is it possible?" said the Countess, turning again to look at Carlos, who still maintained his thoughtful stance, and then slowly turning away to look at Elvira with an expression of interest. "What? Does he find me so dangerous?"

"Dangerous? Not at all. Didn't I tell you that he's different? Do you know what he said about you tonight?"

"What did he say?" the Countess asked intently.

"That he could never love or respect such a woman."

The Countess blushed slightly, and her features clearly reflected a poorly repressed spite.

"You mean they spoke so badly of me? What did they tell him?"

"Rubbish. But he seems to be a confirmed enemy of coquetry. Oh! He is a man with his head full of dreams of delight, and he speaks incessantly of love, of joy, of virtue."

"Ah!" said the Countess, smiling sadly. "He believes in love, in virtue, in happiness . . . How fortunate he is!"

"He believes in everything, except that there is something noble and good in the soul of a coquette. He is severe, very harsh in his judgments, although he has a basically kind nature that I find enchanting."

"He has delights!" the Countess repeated absently. "He believes in love and happiness! Then he is right to scorn cold or jaded hearts; he is right."

And she turned to gaze fixedly at him again, while Elvira glibly went on, "Moreover, it's sad. He is always thoughtful, although never in a bad mood, and I assure you that he has a beautiful heart. Apart from you, I have never heard him speak ill of anyone. The smallest thing moves him. And despite that apparent timidity and aloofness, he is the sweetest, most obliging person in private. So . . ."

Catalina did not let her finish the sentence. "Elvira, if I recall correctly, the day after tomorrow is your birthday, and I would like to come to eat with you. I would like you not to have guests so we can be alone. However, he can be there—he lives with you so it's unavoidable—but no one else. Will you give me that pleasure?"

"I'd be delighted, cousin, but I fear that the two of you, that is, you and Carlos, will have a hard time, if you do not manage to overcome the mutual antipathy that seems to divide you."

At that moment the concert began, and the Countess, not heeding her friend's last words, seemed to focus entirely on the music. However, Carlos kept the same posture and seemed completely estranged from everything that surrounded him. Oh! At those moments his imagination was in Seville. Several ladies and gentlemen of the gathering sang in turn, and Carlos scarcely gave the signs of approval required by courtesy, continuing with his earlier train of thought. Finally they asked the Countess to sing, and she was led to the piano without once taking her eyes off the corner where Carlos was sitting, then standing at the piano in such a way that she could continue to gaze at him. She chose an aria by Rossini, and her voice, so whole and melodious, was a little weak and insecure upon starting the song. But she soon overcame such an inexplicable emotion, and her wondrous talent and great gifts shone forth in their full splendor. At the delightful strains of the song, Carlos raised his eyes toward her and could no longer withdraw them. The Countess's face was divine as she sang; never did such expressive features accompany beautiful music. As Catalina sang, Carlos could not breathe, totally captivated by the power of the melody. The music was not at all touching, and could more rightly be called bright than passionate, but even in the gaiety expressed by the song there was an indefinable feeling of melancholy. That fleeting joy, like all joys on earth, leaves in the soul a feeling of sadness, as though one wishes to hold in the air the pleasing sounds, which like the illusions of hope, vanish the very moment we think we enjoy them.

When Catalina stopped singing, she was surrounded by her numerous admirers, whose loud applause seemed to Carlos a petty and vulgar show of the enthusiasm that should be felt upon hearing her. By an involuntary movement he drew a few steps closer, although without a conscious desire to speak to the Countess. The latter, who while busy responding to her admirers' gallantries did not miss a single one of Carlos's movements, turned toward him as though to encourage him with her look, but that look had the opposite effect of the one intended. Carlos, who saw he had been noticed, immediately returned to his place, and Catalina could not suppress a gesture of spite.

The women wanted to waltz, and Catalina, who wished to show off her great ability before Carlos, gladly accepted. She chose as her partner the young Marquis of —, who, it was said, was at that time her favored admirer, and the two attracted attention by their superiority in dancing. Catalina paused upon passing by the spot where she had seen Carlos at the start of the waltz, but upon seeking him out she found the seat he had occupied empty. Carlos had left the salon, and an observer could have easily detected that from that moment on the Countess danced with less spirit. When the waltz was over, she too left the drawing room and found Carlos in a corridor leaning on a window ledge, seemingly completely detached from what was going on a few feet away from him. Catalina slowly came up, and upon reaching him she said in a voice so sweet that it renewed the impression produced by her song:

"It seems señor de Silva is not fond of dancing—would you perhaps give us the pleasure of serving as a third in a game of ombre?"

Carlos turned, and for the first time the Countess heard his voice.

"I am so ignorant of every kind of game, señora," he told her, "that I cannot accept that honor."

The Countess placed a chair next to the window, and sitting down she invited Carlos to sit in another that was by its side.

"I believe that you have been in Madrid for a few weeks, and yet I don't recall having seen you on the promenades or in the theaters. Has dear Elvira been neglectful in offering you entertainment? In that case I would be glad to rectify her shortcoming. I have a box at the Príncipe Theater, and it would give me great pleasure if you would accept a seat there."

Carlos thanked her rather dryly, and explained that he was too busy with the matter that had brought him to the court to be able to think of distractions. The Countess asked him about his family, to whom she said she was pleased to belong, and Carlos realized, nonetheless, that she knew very little about them. He answered her questions tersely—and as though he were embarrassed by Catalina's conversation, although it was of the simplest, easiest kind, he made it clear that he wished to return to Elvira to see if she was ready to leave.

At that point Catalina left him and returned to the salon at the same time that Carlos and Elvira were leaving.

"I am leaving, my friend," said the latter, "because my companion is becoming very bored at your brilliant gathering, but to make up for the annoyance of leaving you so soon, as you know, I am expecting you to come for dinner the day after tomorrow."

The Countess affectionately saw Elvira off, but her farewell to Carlos was colder and drier than was to be expected, given her warmth toward him in their recent conversation. As the Marquis of — was present, Carlos attributed her reserve to fear of irritating the Marquis, but when he said this to Elvira, she roared with laughter.

"Catalina show consideration to her lover? That's crazy, dear Carlos! She is a despotic queen, who does not have to justify her actions to anyone, and whose whims are law for the humble flock of her admirers. Besides, the Marquis is a pleasant rake, whose only ambition is to embellish himself in salons with the title of the lover of the Countess of S. Do you think he loves her? Nonsense!"

Carlos thought he was dreaming: a woman who allowed a man she did not respect to be called her lover; a man who prided himself on the capricious preference of a coquette he did not love; another woman who spoke of such improbable relationships as a matter of course . . . All of this seemed to him so strange and scandalous that on the way home he remained stubbornly silent, as though he feared being drawn into the petty secrets of that brilliant life at court.

However, it was not these thoughts that kept him awake that night. He thought of his wife, of his father, of his peaceful and innocent home life, and he resolved to leave Madrid and its corrupting pleasures behind as soon as possible.

9

On Elvira's birthday Carlos was informed that the Countess would
eat with them, and although he was anything but pleased, he
showed up at the appointed time. He found the two women alone in
Elvira's sitting room, and in the daylight, in a simple and elegant
dress of dark *alepín*, a fine wool, and with no other adornment on
her head than her lush, curly black hair, Catalina looked more beautiful to him than she had in full evening dress. Carlos, although
rather constrained at first, soon came under the influence of her pleasant, open manner which, without her making a conscious effort,
naturally inspired trust. During the meal and after, Catalina's conversation was both diverse and entertaining, and Carlos was surprised
to find neither the pedantic self-importance of an educated woman
nor the lightweight chatter of Elvira. There was an indescribable
magic in the natural elegance with which she expressed herself, and
the most trivial topics were treated in a fresh new way with spontaneous fitting remarks. When Elvira was with her the former talked
less than usual, because she took such pleasure in listening to her
friend, and Carlos himself began to understand the power of attraction that was attributed to the Countess. The hours passed quickly by
her side, and although he was usually quiet with people he did not
know well, that day he enjoyed talking with Catalina, thereby allowing her to get to know his own vitality and penetrating gifts, as well
as his keen judgment. Catalina also enjoyed drawing him out, and to
get him to talk she sometimes pretended to contradict him, but always
with such finesse, such natural grace, that Carlos found in her opposition only new cause for admiration.

Elvira was astonished to see how well two people got along who she had supposed did not like each other; she was so delighted to see this that, wishing to cement their good relations, she invited Carlos to accompany them to the theater. He did not refuse, and Catalina could not hide her satisfaction at what she considered to be her triumph. That happiness caused by satisfied vanity was not lost on the young man, and he was about to withdraw his acceptance. As the two women got ready to go to the theater, he walked restlessly around his room, trying to understand the reason for the imprudent delight the Countess had shown upon hearing his acceptance of Elvira's invitation. Carlos was not vain, and we could even say that he was too simple and modest to interpret the Countess's gesture in his own favor, so instead of suspecting that she was flattered to go to the theater with him, it occurred to him that he might just be an object of ridicule for the artful Countess. "Maybe she has in mind," he thought, "to take advantage of my character, which Elvira has described as strange and extreme, as an amusement when she is bored; maybe the pleasure of ridiculing a man who has not paid her homage would be a triumph for her petty feminine vanity."

And Carlos was on the point of sending his apologies to Elvira when she showed up at the door of his room, saying, "We are at your orders, dear cousin, pleased and proud to have you as our chaperone for the evening." At the same time the Countess appeared, and Carlos could no longer back out. He took them silently by the arm and left, determined to thwart any plan the Countess might have formed by behaving with extreme coldness and reserve toward her in the theater. And he carried out his plan to the letter. Seated in a box next to Elvira and face to face with the Countess, he carefully avoided having their eyes meet, and although the women often tried to draw him into the conversation, he made a special effort never to address the Countess.

Once during an intermission in the comedy, Elvira said, laughing, "I have noticed, Catalina dear, that it might be better for you not to bring our cousin to the theater with you, because he is stealing from you many looks that when we are by ourselves are directed to you alone. I notice many opera glasses from other boxes trained on ours, and fixed, if I am not mistaken, on the new and handsome figure that today adorns it; and even your admirers are anxiously examining a person whom they perhaps take for a new rival."

"In that case," the Countess replied, absentmindedly playing with her fan, "their notion is as wrong as their curiosity is impertinent."

"One person who is not paying any attention to us," Elvira added, "is the Marquis of —; I believe he has not even seen us. Tonight he is paying court in the Duchess of R.'s box. Have you noticed?"

"No, of course not," Catalina answered indifferently, and turning suddenly to Carlos, she asked with a little pout, "Do you find that Englishwoman very beautiful whom you've been staring at for the past hour?"

"She is, in fact, beautiful," he answered without looking away from the lady who inspired the question, "but what attracted my attention, señora, was less her beauty than the resemblance I noticed between her face and that of another absent person who is very dear to me."

The Countess was a little disconcerted, and took a while to reply. Then, regaining her enchanting but rather scornful smile, she said to Carlos, "So you like blondes? There is certainly poetry in those sky-blue eyes, and in those locks surrounding a mother-of-pearl brow like a crown of gold. In Spain, and especially in Andalusia, such types are rare and as such have all the merit of novelty. Elvira told me that you were educated in France. Could it be that under the less burning French sky you met the person whose memory is so dear to you?"

"No, señora," Carlos answered coldly. "She was born on Andalusian soil, as pure and fragrant as its flowers."

"Now I understand," said Catalina, quickly and mechanically pulling the petals off the bunch of flowers she was holding according to local custom, "now I understand why you are so sad and withdrawn from society. You are in love, and you are separated from the object of your love."

"From my first and only love!" he exclaimed with zeal. "Yes, señora, I have been away from her for a month, from my Luisa."

"Your Luisa!" Catalina repeated, turning pale and dropping her tattered bouquet. "What? So you really love her?"

"Didn't you know about it?" he rejoined in a tone of frank surprise.

"It's true," said Elvira, laughing. "Now I recall that I didn't say anything about it to Catalina. The truth is that I myself keep forgetting, but later I will tell her what I know about your story."

As Elvira was speaking, Carlos was astonished to see the sudden change in the Countess's appearance. Why had Catalina's expression changed? What did she care if Carlos was in love or not? Was it possible that that headstrong and so flattered woman could have taken a serious liking to an obscure young provincial, whom she had met twice? These thoughts were crowding into Carlos's mind, and his eyes, fixed on Catalina's face, were seeking an answer to his conjectures, when the door opened and the Marquis of — came in, filling the box with the scent of his musk cambric handkerchief, and with a rose in his buttonhole. The Countess made a gesture of annoyance, and her lover had barely come up to speak to her when she said in a rather loud voice, so Carlos could hear her:

"Why have you come, sir? How did you resolve to leave the Duchess for an instant? Perhaps she warned you that I had noticed how she responded to your pleas by graciously awarding you that rose that a moment ago adorned her breast, and that now shines on yours? Did she tell you to come out of compassion, to pay some attention to a woman who, as a witness to your inconstancy and the triumph of a rival, was not clever enough to hide the spite and surprise that despite herself must have been painted on her face?"

The Marquis, astonished at hearing these terrible charges leveled at him, tried in vain to refute them, swearing on his honor that that rose had never belonged to the Duchess and that he had brought it to the theater with the express purpose of giving it to Catalina, but she would not listen to him and seemed so furious that Elvira, who had never seen her take so seriously the Marquis's infidelities, thought she was dreaming. As for Carlos, Catalina's words made him realize the stupidity of his original conjectures, and convinced that the wily coquette was observing her lover as she pretended to pay attention to him, turned back to the stage and focused entirely on the second act of the comedy, which had just begun.

In the meantime, Catalina and the Marquis kept up a very lively conversation in low voices, confined on the one side to accusations and complaints and on the other to humble excuses. Elvira, who did not miss a word, whispered in Carlos's ear, "I'll bet anything that the proud Catalina is really starting to fall in love with that playboy. I've never heard her say the kind of things she's saying tonight . . . And if she is going to get married some-day, all in all it's better that it be to the Marquis, who may be a reckless fool but is rich and has a distinguished title. Don't you agree, Carlos?"

"I don't care, señora," Carlos answered, "whether the Count-ess loves or does not love the Marquis, or whether she will or will not be his wife . . . but I think that a woman capable of making such jealous scenes in public for a man she does not love and whom she does not plan to marry, is undoubtedly crazy."

"Talk more softly, for God's sake! Why are you shouting? If I'm not mistaken, I think Catalina heard you. There's no doubt about it; see how she's looking at you; she is completely distracted from what the Marquis is telling her, and is staring at you with such a look . . . !"

"Let her, then," said Carlos, smiling and turning back to the stage with a look of disdain worthy of Catalina herself.

"Will you do me the honor of receiving me after the theater?" the Marquis asked.

"This is intolerable," said the Countess distractedly. "This is a mark of clear contempt."

"What, señora? Is it possible that you take like that a natural wish on my part? The desire to justify myself in your eyes . . ."

"Marquis," Catalina interrupted him, suddenly brightening up, "I had not planned to go to señora B's salon tonight, but I have changed my mind. I will wait for you to pick me up at my home after the comedy."

The Marquis, although he was certainly familiar with many of the Countess's whims, did not know what to make of everything he had heard her say that night. It was a puzzle to him, and his vanity could only deduce that he had finally subdued that fickle heart. So he left the box swollen with pride, and with a scornful look at Carlos, whose handsome figure had drawn his attention, but whose nonexistence in the Countess's eyes he had just witnessed in the show of preference she had given him in his presence.

How many men as savvy as he have founded their apparent triumphs on even more mistaken evidence! How many would be disabused of their vain dreams if they could guess the secret motives that were often behind the signs of interest given them by a woman! But it is not our purpose here to reveal all the small and invisible means of feminine cleverness and talent, so it will suffice to pay her the just tribute of our admiration.

The Marquis left the Countess's box as the second act was ending, and Carlos, who no longer had a pretext to have his eyes glued to the stage, turned to Elvira, ignoring her companion. "I will leave you for a moment, dear cousin, to greet señora de Castro, who is in the front box."

"Go then, but I think," Elvira added in a low voice, "that it would be good to first say some conciliatory words to Catalina. I am sure she heard what you were saying, and she is really angry."

"She would be wrong to get angry over a remark that anyone else in my place would have made," Carlos returned, "and as I don't know what I could say to dispel her anger, which I moreover could not care less about, I ask you to excuse me from attempting it."

After saying these words he left, with a slight bow to the Countess, who followed him with her eyes until the door of the box closed behind him. "Now," she said to Elvira in an irritable tone that she had not used with her until then, "why did you have to bring to my box that coarse, unbearable Andalusian?"

"I'm sorry," said Elvira, taken aback. "It's just that you yourself invited him, and you were so insistent . . ."

"Insistent! You are raving, Elvira. So who is this divine creature he is so in love with? Are you in the confidence of this peerless, so lovesick lover? I thought you said that you would tell me his love story. Come on, it must be curious, poetic."

"It is just very ordinary and prosaic," Elvira replied, looking again at Carlos who was in the front box talking to the señora de Castro. "I think it's a shame that they bound such a young and inexperienced man with such formal ties, because I think . . ."

"What?" the Countess interrupted her impatiently. "Are his ties so serious? What do they consist of? What are they?"

At that moment several gentlemen came in to greet the two friends, so Elvira could not satisfy the Countess's curiosity. As the curtain went up and the new visitors left, Carlos returned, and since his seat next to Elvira was taken by another, he remained standing near Catalina. The latter could not hide the anxiety that had taken hold of her, and after trying in vain to focus on the performance, she turned to Carlos and said, "Señor de Silva, I am not feeling well, and I don't want to distract Elvira from the entertainment. Would you mind taking me outside? I need a breath of fresh air."

Carlos ungraciously offered her his arm, and after saying something in a low voice to her friend the Countess left with him, without either one saying a word. As they went down the stairs, Carlos asked her dryly where she wanted him to take her. "To my home," she said rashly, "to my home . . . The carriage has not come yet. It doesn't matter; I will walk."

"As you like," said Carlos, and they walked on in silence. When they were almost at the Countess's house, she said to her moody companion, "Sir, I beg you to forgive me for the hard time I have given you, taking you away from the theater where you could enjoy gazing at the beautiful blonde who revived such sweet memories."

"Señora," he answered, still with his curt dry tone, "those memories are inseparable companions of my heart and my life."

"So you love your Luisa so much?" Catalina said, trying to smile.

And Carlos suddenly lighting up, and his face and voice taking on an expression of enthusiasm and of an indescribable, sublime tenderness, answered: "Do I love her? Yes indeed, señora! And I pity all hearts that find ridiculous or extreme my pure undying passion! I love her as one loves life, as one loves happiness . . . even more! I love her as a mystic can love God, with a blind, immense, absolute love. I love her as my first and final love, as the source of all my pleasures and virtues, as the consolation for all my sorrows, as my tender lifelong companion. You ask if I love her? Ah, señora, ask yourself that question after seeing the emotion that has involuntarily taken hold of me, upon hearing you utter the adored name of Luisa."

And Carlos turned away to hide a tear that rose to his eyelids, ashamed of a tenderness that he thought must seem ridiculous to the Countess.

She said nothing in response, but her arm that was leaning on Carlos's trembled a moment, and upon arriving at the door of her house she stopped, as though tired, putting her hand on her heart. "Señor de Silva," she said in a shaky voice that revealed her emotion, "a love like yours is rare, very rare in life, and is never felt by a vulgar heart. But love, however grand it may be, at your age is not eternal. Sometimes the heart deceives us . . . Be that as it may, the woman who could inspire such a love is fortunate, very fortunate, and if she is worthy of it . . ."

"Worthy of it!" Carlos exclaimed, giving her his hand to help her up the stairs; "Señora, my wife is an angel."

"Your wife!" she repeated, drawing back her hand as though it had been stung by a viper. "What? Are you married? Tell me, are you married?"

"What new trick is this?" Carlos wondered, astonished at Catalina's gesture and shaky tone of voice. "What is this woman up to? What is she trying to appear?"

"Answer," she repeated with the same anxiety, stopping in the middle of the staircase as though she were nailed to it. "Are you married?"

"Yes, señora," he answered calmly, although ever more surprised at the tone of his interlocutor. "For more than a year I have been bound by the most sacred and indissoluble ties to the best and most beloved woman."

"That's enough," said the Countess coldly, giving her hand again to Carlos; and she continued quickly up the stairs, although visibly trembling. When she arrived at the door, she bade him farewell with a silent bow.

On the way back to the theater, Carlos mechanically crossed the streets without being able to digest what he had just witnessed. He found the Countess's behavior so extreme, so puzzling, so incomprehensible that the more he tried to understand it the more he got lost in a labyrinth of conjectures.

He arrived at the theater without having made any headway from his long examination, and on his way up the stairs he bumped into Elvira. "The comedy is over," she told him, "and I don't want to stay for the dance or the farce. When I'm not with Catalina, I find it all boring. But where is she? Isn't she coming back? What's the matter with her? She told me she was going out to get some fresh air."

"I left her at her home," Carlos said, "and I think her slight indisposition is nothing. In fact, she must be getting ready for the Marquis, who is supposed to take her to a gathering."

"As for me, I am not going to go with her tonight, so I'd appreciate your taking me back home."

Carlos, destined to be a women's escort that night, gave her his arm and the whole way home answered in monosyllables the countless questions from Elvira, who could not stop talking about her friend's behavior toward the Marquis and asking Carlos his opinion.

10

A week had passed since the one that occupied the entire last chapter for our obliging readers, during which Carlos had only seen the Countess upon casual encounters at the theater where he occasionally went, for Catalina had not returned to Elvira's home, nor had Carlos returned to the Countess's despite Elvira's repeated insistence that he accompany her there, while the Countess continued with her brilliant and dissipated life, augmenting day by day the number of her admirers.

But when both women were again immersed in the sea of their diversions, Elvira suddenly fell dangerously ill, showing alarming symptoms from the start. In this situation, Carlos felt it his duty to devote himself entirely to caring for his cousin, and he did so with both diligence and tenderness. The Countess, for her part, had scarcely learned of her friend's sickness when she flew to her side, redoubling her efforts as the disease seemed to worsen. She and Carlos thus met often at Elvira's bedside, but as though they had both forgotten what had transpired during their last conversation, they treated each other with cold politeness.

On the third day of the illness, Elvira's condition got so serious that the doctors declared her in imminent danger, and they feared that the night would bring on a crisis. The Countess declared that she would sit up all night at her friend's bedside, and by her order Elvira's servants were sent off to rest, worn out by their nursing duties of the previous nights. Carlos thought he should not leave the sole care of the patient to the Countess, and he asked for permission to stay up with her when he saw that it was futile to try to persuade her to entrust Elvira's care to him alone. In this way they found themselves for an entire night at the bedside of a sick woman, united in a sense in the same endeavor and the same concern. He felt rather embarrassed in such a situation. He could hardly believe that he was seeing the most brilliant woman in Madrid, now, like him, turned into a nurse, and he thought that despite all the warm feelings that Catalina claimed to have for Elvira, she would be awkward and out of her element.

Toward midnight the patient got more agitated, and the Countess, who until then had only watched her slightest movements with silent, passive attention, now went into action. Carlos was amazed to see the ease and care with which she attended the patient, being in a dozen places at once to do whatever would be of help to her friend. She changed her position, fluffed up her pillows, prepared and gave her her medicine, guessed her desires, avoiding any annoyance with tireless care. Carlos's attempts to help always came too late. Catalina anticipated and filled all her needs with calm vigor and unaffected vigilance.

Seeing her in her simple calico robe and knitted cap, down on her knees to warm the patient's feet, or herself stirring up the fire to heat the drinks, in short, going through all the trouble involved with ministering to a patient, Carlos did not recognize the beautiful Countess of S., whose friendship he had up to then studiously avoided, and he began to suspect that she had not been judged fairly, and that he himself was guilty for having treated her so harshly. It moved him to see the tenderness with which she treated her friend, and during the long hours of that difficult night he gazed at her more than once with an expression of kindness that he had not shown up to then.

The sick woman's agitation grew from moment to moment, and she began to rave. Catalina redoubled her attentions, and Carlos, who was not needed, confined himself to supporting Elvira's head with his arms, since she seemed to feel better that way. In her delirium she was as talkative as ever. She talked about balls, about clothing, about her girlfriends, and then, without any transition or logic, about her daughters, her illness, her predicted death.

Carlos tried in vain to calm her down.

"Leave me alone, señor," she said, her feverish eyes fixed on Carlos's face, "leave me alone. Who are you to come and give orders in my home? Can't I even speak about my daughters—my daughters who will be orphans! Because I am dying . . . there's no help for it, I am dying! Get Catalina; bring her at once. She must be at home or at the theater or out for a walk . . . it doesn't matter; I know she'll come. I want to entrust her with my daughters' care. Don't you know, señor, that she is their mother more than I am? Yes, señor, because they and I were ruined . . . the creditors were raining down on us and there was no recourse—we were ruined!"

"For heaven's sake, Elvira," said the Countess, interrupting her and clasping one of the sick woman's hands in hers, "be quiet; calm down."

"So bring Catalina. Didn't I tell you, señor?" the young woman went on. "Wasn't she the one who saved my daughters from ruin? Wasn't it she who paid off many of my debts, who forgave those my husband had with hers, who managed my assets until they were returned to me free of debt and increased? Hasn't she been my constant benefactress, my comfort, my support?"

"Elvira, Elvira!" the Countess exclaimed. "Here I am, by your side, but if you do not stop going on like this I will leave here pierced through with grief."

"Let her speak," said Carlos with emotion; "let her speak. What she has just revealed in her delirium is the triumphant response to all the vile attacks of your enemies and hers. Señora! I too needed to hear it in order to learn to appreciate you and repent of my shallow judgments."

Elvira's agitation was followed by a great weakness and a huge sweat, which led to a happy outcome. By the next morning she was in a deep sleep, and the Countess, worn out, sat on a stool at the foot of the bed.

"The danger has passed, I believe," said Carlos, who had just taken the patient's pulse. "You too should rest; you have had a terrible night."

"Of course," Catalina answered. "It is terrible to see a person one loves suffer without being able to share in her sorrow."

"Ah!" said Carlos. "You have a kind heart."

"Speak more softly, for goodness' sake," she said anxiously. "She is asleep, and she has suffered so much."

Carlos fell silent, but he positioned himself so he could see the face of the Countess, who had rested her head on the edge of her friend's bed. The dim light of dawn penetrated the joints of the balconies and weakened upon passing through the curtains on the glass doors of the room. The light of an oil lamp still burning on a table was also covered with a thick veil of green crêpe so as not to hurt Elvira's eyes; and in the feeble light of the room the pale white face of Catalina stood out against the crimson bedspread as, succumbing to fatigue, she fell asleep.

Carlos saw the uncomfortable position she was in, and after hesitating a moment finally decided to take advantage of her sleep to make her more comfortable. He arranged some cushions around the Countess, and seeing that her arms and back were bare, he carefully covered her with his cloak. At this gesture she awoke, rather startled.

"Ah! Is that you, señor de Silva?"

"Catalina," he answered (and it was the first time he called her by her given name), "you are very uncomfortable; please let me bring an armchair in which you can have a better rest."

She agreed, and Carlos helped her get settled in an armchair that he adorned with silk cushions, covering her again with his cloak, and he sat on a stool next to her, also leaning his head on the back of the chair. She soon fell asleep again. Carlos felt her slightly tired breathing on his forehead, and he stared at her superb eyes, sweetly closed.

"She is more beautiful like this," he thought, "than when she appears splendid and radiant among her circle of admirers."

A little later he added, "Luisa is not more beautiful. Why didn't I realize that until now?"

He continued gazing at her and almost inhaling her breath, and he started to feel agitated. This time his mouth pronounced clearly and involuntarily the thought that was on his mind: "No free heart," he said, "can know her with impunity." And he moved away from Catalina feeling dissatisfied with himself, although without an awareness of what he felt by her side.

He went out to the parlor and walked for a while in a strange haste, running his fingers through his abundant curly black hair. He thought about what Elvira had said in her delirium, and he was glad to have a reason to respect the Countess, whose kind heart he could no longer doubt. After making twenty rounds around the parlor he returned to the sick woman's room, where he found Catalina still asleep. He contemplated her for a moment, and involuntarily repeated, "It is impossible that she not be good, being so beautiful." At that moment Catalina again woke up.

"Did Elvira speak?" she asked anxiously.

"No, don't worry; it was I."

"You!"

"Yes, but I will not interrupt your rest again."

"No, it's already day, and I am leaving, señor de Silva . . ."

"Why don't you call me Carlos, like Elvira? Aren't we also relatives, Catalina?"

"All right, Carlos; I hope that you will retire now to rest. I will have Elvira's servants come right away. She is better now, and if there is any new development they will let me know immediately. Please rest so that tonight we can do our duty by our dear cousin."

"So you're already leaving . . ."

"Until this evening."

"Goodbye, Catalina."

She extended her hand to him; this time Carlos raised it to his lips. She did not take offense, but upon leaving she stopped a moment at the door, and putting the hand on her heart, she appeared to want to bury there the emotion that despite herself her face revealed. Carlos watched her depart, and sat down thoughtfully in the spot she had occupied. Soon after Elvira's servants came in, and he went to his room, leaving the one in which he had spent the night with far different thoughts from those he had had upon entering it.

11

Elvira was out of danger, but her condition was so fragile in the doctors' view that she was in need of constant care. Therefore that night, like the preceding one, Catalina wished to keep vigil at her bedside, and as expected, Carlos offered to keep her company. The hours spent together in that room the night before had established a kind of intimacy between the two of them that years of friendship amid the hustle-bustle of the outer world might not have produced. They met again that second night with the pleasure of two comrades in arms who had not seen each other for years, and they settled in near the sick woman with the ease of knowing that they got along well.

As Elvira was resting peacefully, Catalina moved away from her, sitting in a chair at the far end of the room, and said to Carlos with gentle familiarity, "Since we are staying up with Elvira, and at the moment she doesn't need anything, while she is asleep we can talk in low voices. Come, Carlos, I would like you to tell me your story. I would have expressed my curiosity a few days ago, if your stubborn coldness had not restrained me."

"My story!" said Carlos, sitting on a footstool at her feet. "Do you by chance think it will be long and entertaining?"

"At least it will be beautiful and pure, like your soul, like your life. I believe that you are happy, and happiness is so rare in this world that my heart will take pleasure in inhaling the divine perfume given off by a joyful, innocent life."

"You are certainly not wrong in believing that I am happy," said Carlos, "but my story and my happiness can be summed up in two words: I love and I am loved."

"And yet," said Catalina, "Elvira told me that your marriage was arranged between your families, and as in such cases happiness is extremely rare . . ."

"Your observation might be correct," Carlos answered, "but I had the singular good fortune that the wife who was destined to be mine since childhood was the very one I would have chosen out of all the women in the world. As children we loved each other as tender brother and sister; then we parted, Catalina, and when we came together again, now as young adults at the age to fall in love, we loved each other as lovers, as husband and wife! I recognized in her the other half of my soul; she gave me all of hers. Never have a pair of siblings loved each other so tenderly, nor two spouses understood each other better and made each other so mutually happy. Close in age and in feelings, her character has the sweetness and gentleness that mine lacks, while my soul perhaps offers the strength and vigor needed to support her fragile, delicate existence. We each need the other to complete one soul, one life, one happiness. Heaven has joined us, and as tight and holy as are the religious ties that bind us, they are without doubt surpassed by the ties by which our hearts are forever united. That is my story; that is all, Catalina. Are you satisfied? Maybe you find my conjugal enthusiasm ridiculous?"

"You are indeed lucky," said the Countess, who had heard these words with great emotion. "Why doesn't heaven grant the happiness that you have attained to all those souls who are capable of appreciating it? And if heaven were to concede it only to those who are privileged in His love, why did He not at least endow the others to whom He has denied this joy with sterile hearts that would keep them from needing it? Oh, Carlos! Happy are those who are granted the destiny of loving and being loved—and happy as well are those who do not feel the futile voracious need for a good fortune that they have been denied!"

As the Countess was speaking, Carlos had gone up to her, and seeing the profound sadness painted on her face, he felt moved and involuntarily took one of her hands in his. "What?" he said to her with interest; "have you by chance not known that happiness?

I cannot believe it, Catalina; no matter what your enemies may say or shallow souls who judge without understanding, I cannot believe that you have a cold heart, only inclined to vain, ephemeral pleasures. No, Catalina, you yourself cannot undo the opinion that these hours spent by your side have made me form of the excellence of your soul and the exquisite sensitivity of your heart."

"I appreciate that opinion," she replied, "although I think it is only just; but justice is so rare that we should take it as a favor. Yes, I am much obliged to you for the favorable judgment you express, because while I usually do not give weight to other people's opinion of me, I am very sensitive to the approval or disapproval of my friends. And I would like, Carlos," she added in some confusion, "to count you among them."

"Yes," he said eagerly, "from now on I too would like to have a place among the people you honor with your friendship. And perhaps, Catalina, perhaps I will not be the last in knowing how to appreciate it, despite having been the last to obtain it."

"I believe so," she replied, "because you may also know me better than many of those I have known for years. I think that you can easily understand me."

"And for that reason, because I now understand your heart, I understand less than ever how you can live content with that stirring life of frivolous pleasures that you seem so keen on. Excuse my frankness, señora, but I must confess that the more you make me respect you, the more severely I will judge your conduct, and that which I might pardon in the cold and vain coquette, I find blameworthy, very blameworthy in my eyes, in the woman of talent and heart."

"And why is that?" she asked with a smile that combined irony with bitterness. "Is the person blameworthy who, weighed down with a sterile burden, throws it off for a few moments to be able to breathe? Talent! Heart! Do those who have been endowed with these fatal gifts incur certain obligations vis-à-vis the world? If so, those obligations would surely not include spreading to others the sorrow and bitterness that these very gifts attract; they would not include cursing the world because it cannot give them all they ask for; they would not include disturbing others' happiness with the spectacle of their own deep unhappiness. What more can they do than smother their groans, harden their hearts, and accept life as it has been given to them, forgetting how they had conceived it?"

Carlos turned away from her, unable to contain a gesture of contempt. "What is this, señora?" he exclaimed, fixing on her a severe look. "Do you think that divine goodness endowed man with the precious gifts that bring him closest to His supreme intellect only to torment him? Should the ability to feel and to think just be considered an inexhaustible source of suffering, and should we believe that the greatest moral perfection of man only serves to make him more unhappy?"

"That is a question that I can never resolve," said Catalina, "not because I doubt that inherent in the greater ability to feel is the greater ability to suffer, but rather because I believe in the eternal law of exchange, and he who is capable of great pain is also capable of great pleasure. As for me, I can only say that I would rather not have been endowed at birth with a voracious imagination, and a heart that eats away at itself, unable to find nourishment for its insatiable need. I do not know if all men with common hearts are happy; at least their happiness would not suffice for me. But when you say that you are happy, when I see that for others that longed-for adventure of loving and being loved with enthusiasm and purity is possible, then I feel angry with destiny, and I ask, 'For what crime have I been deprived of that supreme joy?'"

Upon uttering these words, the Countess's voice revealed the strongest emotion, and Carlos returned to her side, his expression, which had darkened for a moment, once again serene.

"You are a remarkable woman," he told her, "and the more I try to reconcile the contradictions that I find in you, the less I succeed. If you are satisfied with the happiness of a pure, intense love, why do you scorn it? If your heart thirsts for fulfillment, why do you get high on the vapor of those fictitious pleasures, empty of meaning and emotional worth? This is my eternal appeal, because it is my constant doubt. You are not content with that brilliant, tumultuous life that you seem to love—so why have you chosen it? Why have you sacrificed to it the happiness that your heart desires?"

"It was not a sacrifice," the Countess replied. "I have sacrificed nothing. This way of life was not a choice, but a necessity. When a person is in extreme pain, he often takes opium, not to lessen its intensity but to dull his ability to feel it. There is also opium for the heart and for the soul, and that opium is a life of dissipation. Those who are happy would be wrong to take this course, but shouldn't it be granted to the wretched?"

"And are you wretched, Catalina?"

"I am."

"Why? Why are you wretched?" Carlos asked, taking her hand with visible emotion.

"Because I am not happy," she responded. "Don't be surprised at my answer. I believe there are people who, although they are not happy, do not consider themselves to be wretched, people who do not complain if they do not have real concrete misfortunes. I am not one of those, and I can only explain my misfortune by saying that I feel it in my soul."

"But what are you lacking in order to be happy?"

"I lack everything, because I am not."

"But do you think you could be happy with a destiny like mine, like Luisa's?"

"Oh! Yes, I could," she exclaimed without thinking. "I would be completely happy—I'm sure of it now—with the destiny of Luisa . . . and with yours, Carlos," she added, blushing at the words she had just uttered.

"Weren't you loved by your husband? Didn't you love him, Catalina?"

"No."

"Have you never been in love?"

"I don't know. At the moment I think no: I have never loved in the way that you love your Luisa, in the way I imagine that she loves you. I have never known the kind of love that yields lifelong happiness."

"And yet, you have a passionate heart. It is not an inability on your part that has prevented you from enjoying that happiness. Perhaps you have not found in any man the kind of love you needed."

"If I am honest and can open my heart to you, even at the risk of your finding it ungrateful and capricious, I will confess that I have known men who were violently in love with me, and who did not shun any kind of sacrifice to convince me of it. If it is a crime of the heart not to obey the dictates of the will, I am guilty of this, for unfortunately my heart did not love when my reason advised it to. There was a period of my life when I valued only the qualities of a man's heart and thought that they alone would suffice to captivate me forever; but I soon learned that I was wrong, and that the most perfect goodness and tenderness, in the absence of outstanding intelligence and character, are not enough to assure one of the love of a woman who needs to admire, respect, and even fear the man she loves. Emerging from one error, I fell into another, that of attributing to the superior intellect of a man more weight than it actually has in the happiness of the woman who loves him. In fact, superiority in this domain, if it does not go along with a superior heart, is more to be feared than loved. There is something monstrous in the union of a huge intellect with a mean or hard heart. The influence that a man acquires over the heart of a sensitive woman by dint of his talent alone, turns tyrannical and soon makes him hateful to her. Only love grants the right to enslave her. And if love not supported by talent does not always succeed, great talent that is not aided by love never achieves its goal. Your sex, Carlos, is afraid to find superior intelligence in the woman he loves, but in ours the opposite occurs. Woman, who in her weakness seeks out and requires support, needs in the chosen object a superiority that inspires confidence. No matter how great a woman's talent, no matter how lofty and even proud her character, she wishes to find in her lover a talent superior to hers; and if a superior woman really comes to love a less distinguished man, you can be sure that that man has a wonderful character that replaces and makes up for the lack of talent, endowing him in another sense with the superiority he lacks. But as difficult as it seems to me that an uncommon woman could fall in love with a man who is in every way morally inferior to her, it seems to me even less likely that she could long be deluded by a man who only possesses an elevated intellect and character. For woman, the essential thing is the heart: she wants to admire without being dazzled; she wants to be dominated without tyranny; she wants and needs to be loved; and she appreciates man's superiority only insofar as it lifts her up, it ennobles her. But when this superiority does not lift us up, it humiliates us; and it will always humiliate us if the love we inspire is not strong enough so the man lays it aside when he is with us.

"But Catalina," remarked Carlos, "you who have such outstanding spiritual qualities, could you feel humiliated by those possessed by your lover? Would you need to have him lay them aside with you?"

"I don't know," she answered; "to tell you the truth, if I have found in any man real moral superiority to me, I can assure you that it was because I wished to find it. And yet, when I have seen that the great talent or character of a man often gives him means of domination apart from love, I have developed a horror of those same qualities; and based on my own experience, I think that women will forgive the lack of intelligence more readily than the lack of love."

"So," Carlos said, "you have never fallen in love because you have not been able to find that rare blend of intelligence and goodness, of strength and gentleness, of honor and love. It is indeed difficult, maybe impossible, to find that kind of perfection, and only a very bold man would dare attempt to satisfy the desire of your heart."

"Did you say perfection?" she replied. "You did not understand me, or I did not explain myself well. I strongly doubt that a perfect man would inspire passion in me. There are faults that I might easily forgive, or rather, that I would adore him for. However, there are others that would estrange me from a lover forever. Coldness or hardheartedness and a mean character are defects that I abhor. The greatest talent and the noblest temperament inspire respect but not love if they are without goodness and tenderness; cruelty horrifies me, and what men call "bravura" seems to me savage. I could never love a fierce man, even if he were considered a hero, nor a man swollen up with ambition and devoid of feelings, even if he were considered a genius. But neither would I love a coward or an idiot, no matter how kind and tender his heart. Apart from that, I think it would be very possible for me to love a man who had many flaws: I can easily pardon a great temperament for some arrogance and even apparent curtness; for a brilliant talent I can disregard his flightiness, and even enjoy his inconsistencies. In short, Carlos, if I could find a man who possessed, along with a fine character and clear intellect, an impassioned heart . . . I would ask for nothing more. He could have faults, and even virtues, that frighten me, but I would fear him without loving him the less for it, and even if I occasionally suffered I would be happy. You might be criticized for being too stubborn in your ideas, and the impetuous nature that often makes you disregard social conventions and that men of the court would call lack of refinement might annoy many women, who would only let you off on account of your handsome looks. I myself could in all fairness scold you for the harshness with which you judged me at first, and I might find you too proud in your way of making up with me. But I am sure that neither the severity and obstinacy of your beliefs, nor your curt frankness, nor that pride and rigidity at times barely contained by the goodness of your heart are obstacles to the happiness of your wife."

"Ah!" he replied, sighing at such a sweet memory. "My wife, Catalina, is a unique person. I am sure that she has never asked her heart why she loves me, nor if my faults should or should not influence her happiness. She, the adored angel, only thinks of *my* happiness; her own consists in that which she gives me, and therefore must be perfect. Moreover, the flaws you find in me, how could they affect her? I am not tolerant enough? She doesn't need my tolerance. My beliefs are stubborn and severe? She respects and shares them. I lack polite manners? In the auspicious isolation in which we live we have no critics, and my impetuous nature is always tamed by the divine serenity of her gaze. Oh, Catalina! You do not know my Luisa! I am sure that you would love her; you would find her much more appealing than I do."

The Countess abruptly got up and moved a few steps away from Carlos, unaware of what she was doing. The young man looked at her in surprise, and quickly controlling herself she sat down again, saying with apparent calm, "I thought Elvira called, but I was wrong; she is asleep."

It did not occur to Carlos to doubt that explanation, and he went on, again grasping the Countess's hands in his: "Catalina, I also think she is capable of understanding you, and of loving you, because I am convinced that you have an excellent heart and character. Indeed you might confide in her more completely than in me, and if you unveiled your entire soul to her, I am sure that she would hold you in high regard."

"My soul!" repeated the Countess. "Perhaps it is worthy, as you say, and my heart is too good for my own happiness. But you who speak of confiding fully in another, would you like me to do this? Would I find in your heart the understanding that I need? Because unfortunately I am not like that Luisa whose shining good fortune has never been obscured. I have been unhappy, and I must seem to you blameworthy."

"Blameworthy! No, Catalina, you could never be that to such a degree that my heart would not absolve you. Isn't the humiliation of confessing a fault a form of atonement?"

The Countess raised her head with pride.

"I don't know what you would call faults," she said, "but I will never feel ashamed nor will it be painful to me to confess mistakes of the imagination that have led to my unhappiness. The most careful scrutiny could not uncover anything low or vulgar in my soul or in my life, and if you could say you respect me while having this in doubt, either you were lying or you are not the person I believed you to be."

"No, I have not seen a trace of anything unworthy of a noble heart since I met you, Catalina—but can't noble hearts also go astray? You who call me severe, will you compel me to defend errors that I may condemn without looking down on the one who has fallen prey to them?"

"Condemn errors!" Catalina repeated. "You are severe even in your tolerance. If errors are to be condemned, who is the mortal free of faults? If he exists, I could not respect him; the person who is never wrong must be evil from his birth. As for me, I confess that I have been mistaken many times, and I even believe that I have made great errors. Do you want to judge for yourself if they are inexcusable? If so, hear my story."

Carlos was in fact listening to her with keen interest, and she went on, with a serenity that she was losing as she spoke.

"When I was sixteen, my mother took me out of the school where I was being educated to marry me to the Earl of S. She explained to me that marriage was a contract in which a woman gave herself to a man in exchange for a social position that she received from him, and the position that was being offered to me was brilliant. My father had died in the fateful days of the revolution, a martyr to the King's cause, and his widow was left penniless. The Earl had great wealth in Spain, and he was living with dazzling ostentation in Paris. His personal enmity toward the favorite of Carlos IV made his stay in the Spanish court unpleasant, and as he had been educated in France and had always had a great affection for that country, he decided to live in Paris as long as the political situation in his homeland did not change. He could not have picked a better time to carry out his plan. The French emperor had just signed the Treaties of Tisilt, which appeared to consolidate forever the new dynasty, the new principles, and the glory and prosperity of France. When the Earl arrived in Paris, the entire capital was celebrating with one voice the glory of the French army and the genius of the great man who was guiding their destiny, and the constant festivities made it into the most joyous capital city of the most powerful nation on earth.

"The Earl, who was not involved with politics, was happy in Paris, and forgetting Spain, he seemed to want to settle permanently in his new country, taking a wife there. In early 1811 he met me, and a few days later he solemnly asked for my hand, which was granted.

"Although I was so young and ignorant of the passions, I could see that the contract that he alone was to approve had nothing to do with love, but I was told that only those of humble birth had the right to just consult their hearts upon choosing a new master for life, while I, as a member of the nobility, was not free to choose. Pride and vanity should be the determining factors, and they were. You must know that your relative, the Earl of S., was no longer young when he proposed to me, but despite his forty years, he was still handsome, although a bit faded, and his elegant manners made him rather attractive. I think that he could have been loved in return if he had loved, but the Earl, although of exceptional gifts, always had a heart of ice. Moreover, he had been dissolute in his youth, and not moved by ardent passions or subject to a fiery temperament, his profligacy had been merely the result of a life of ease, great wealth, and the contagion of a corrupt society. Thus he had never invested his heart in a relationship, and his withered existence was all the more unpleasant in that it did not bear the mark that a fiery soul leaves on the face of its victims. When we witness a spent heart, we think how much he must have loved and suffered; we are so forgiving to the one who has been unhappy, and we glimpse so much sorrow in an existence consumed by terrible passions! But the enervation and languor of a cold man is the image of vice in its brazen nakedness. My husband, who had never loved, said that he was tired of love. So I found in him a genteel and attentive friend, and a nice and obliging companion, but I would have sought in vain the ardor of a lover or the jealous tenderness of a husband. He had been a libertine by design and he had married by design, when he realized he could no longer play the role of the brilliant roué. Carlos, don't you think it was a sad lot for a girl who at the age of love and dreams finds her pure blooming life tied to the arid existence of that coldhearted, wasted man?"

"But you, Catalina," he answered dryly, "you who had sold yourself for a social position, you who at the age of sixteen speculated with the sweetest and most sacred bond, could you expect or deserve a different fate?"

"That is a cruel remark," said the Countess, "and you forget that at the age of sixteen a woman has no will; you forget that I did not know love, and that upon leaving school that fearful destiny was presented to me as an enviable lot. In fact, it even seemed enviable to me at first. My husband's wealth offered me all the pleasures that would delight a heart as young and ignorant as mine. Carriages, footmen, balls, rides, theaters, social gatherings, everything that satisfies one's vanity was lavished on me. One of the most elegant Parisian circles met at my home. The events I hosted were considered the most brilliant; my dresses served as a model; and I myself was regarded as one of the most amiable women. In fact, my husband enjoyed adorning me with the talents and skills he possessed, and this study along with pleasures filled two years of my life, during which time I was always so busy that I did not have time to ask my heart if it was happy."

"And you were satisfied with that brilliant, tumultuous life," Carlos said in some anger. "Oh, Catalina! I fear that you are also deluding yourself when you call it insufficient."

"Would to heaven that your fear were well founded!" the Countess replied. "But no, Carlos, that way of life was not enough for me, despite being so full of things that do not constitute love or happiness. My ardent imagination soon tired of such impressions, and my satiated vanity let my heart speak. Then I realized that there must exist a joy superior to that offered by social standing and wealth. Always extreme in my reactions, in a short time I moved from the wildest life of pleasure to the most austere seclusion. My joys and sorrows have always stemmed from such a keen and delicate sensibility that receives no weak impressions, and from an imagination that magnifies and diminishes everything to the extreme.

"The situation that had intoxicated me, that for two years my imagination had portrayed as the supreme good, all at once became odious to me. The magic brush that had embellished it now tinged it in darker colors. Intense people rarely go halfway, and they are not content with compensations. As for me, I can say that few situations seem to me just pleasant or unpleasant: I am in bliss or anguish; I am joyful or in complete despair.

"Thus when my existence, void of affection and full of unsatisfying pleasures, stopped intoxicating me, it was only to inspire in me the deepest scorn and the most extreme boredom. In vain did my husband and my friends try to keep me engaged; I would have died of ennui amid all the pleasures and gaiety. So I persuaded the Earl to let us spend the summer in a small city in southern France, and I spent several months there in complete seclusion. The Parisians made strange remarks about my absence and my melancholy. Some thought my husband was ruined, some that I was immersed in a passionate affair, and some even found in my conduct a piece of refined coquetry with the object of giving my gay, brilliant return to the elegant circle I had abandoned all the appeal of novelty. No one suspected the truth; it did not occur to anyone that I had finally come to feel the emptiness in my heart. However, solitude, the idle contemplative life that I adopted did me more harm than the dissipation I had fled. Beneath the beautiful sky of Provence, amid the fields I had chosen as my home, life was revealed to me, the life of love that I was condemned never to know. To prevent my feeling bored, which my husband thought was the inevitable result of solitude, he gave me what he called entertaining books. What novels! Jean-Jacques Rousseau's *Julie*! Goethe's *Werther*! Fiery pages from his cold hands that my eyes devoured during hours of devouring sleeplessness! Many times throwing the book down in despair, I went out into the fields like a madwoman, and I got drunk on the gentle night breezes that were like a promise of love, and I prostrated myself before the moon that seemed like a divine beacon from the celestial spheres designed to illuminate the mysterious joys of lovers; and I listened trembling to the silence of the fields—that silence whose voice is the whisper of a leaf or the breathing of a bird—and I seemed to detect in it a silent call to the love that offered the repose denied to my heart; when my hair soaked in dew let the moisture enter my head, I felt that the tears of heaven had come to console me in my abandonment, and I too cried, and eagerly prayed for love and happiness. That feverish state was usually followed by hours of deep depression. And little by little that way of life was destroying my health, and perhaps even unbalancing my mind. The solitude that is so praised in theory by tender souls and vivid imaginations, and that when of short duration can spread before them such profound and melancholy impressions, is dangerous and fearful if it goes on for too long. Solitude is only borne well by resigned souls or sterile imaginations, never by young hearts in the throes of thoughts and sensations. In that case, Carlos, I know from experience, solitude is voracious and terrible. Self-analysis can do one great harm. If the spectacle of society can strip one of many illusions and stifle many noble impulses, the solitary life necessarily gives rise to erroneous opinions and dangerous desires, and in a vibrant imagination perhaps also to sinful excesses.

"We returned to Paris in the winter of 1814, to witness the fall of the imperial colossus. Everyone was dismayed by this upheaval that would change the destiny of Europe; and this global situation as well as the poor health of my husband justified my complete withdrawal from society, so that during the four months when we remained in Paris I hardly left his bedroom. Believing that the climate of his homeland would help him regain his health, the Earl resolved to return to Spain, so in the month of May I trod for the first time the soil of the birthplace of my mother and my husband, a place for which I had always had a special affection. But the air of his homeland did not have the favorable effect on my husband's health that he had hoped for; I had the sorrow of losing him several months after our arrival in Madrid. Yes, Carlos, I did feel real sorrow, but after the first few months of widowhood I began to think with secret joy that now I was free, and could embark on that joyful future that I had dreamed of for so long. I spent two years filled with hopes, dreams, mistakes, and disappointments, two years in which my heart, eager for emotions, burning with the desire for happiness, latched onto every object that attracted it for a moment. I divided those two years between Paris and Spain; I showed up everywhere with that naive credulity of youth, that reckless confidence of a kind and noble heart. Nothing seemed easier than to find all around me tender and sincere friends, passionate and attractive lovers. Young, beautiful, rich, enthusiastic, and generous, I set out with sublimely innocent boldness and abandonment in search of an idol at whose feet to lay the virgin treasures that were stored in my soul.

"Oh! How dangerous for a woman of a vivid imagination is this period of her life when she needs, seeks, and waits for a protective, loving being to whom to offer her soul, her future, her very existence! How she deludes herself! And how is she to avoid that inescapable misfortune? If I were to relate to you how carried away I was by my romantic flights of fantasy, you would laugh at my naivete and be touched by my enthusiasm. A man I saw for the first time was sometimes the object of my thoughts for many weeks. It was enough to make such a strong impression that he have a noble appearance and a distant melancholy air, which I interpreted as proof of great and profound thoughts, just as a pale complexion or prematurely gray hair were for me the sure sign of some beautiful and poetic misfortune. Everywhere I sought and believed I found men of lofty character, ardent passions, noble adversity; my inexhaustible imagination idealized every object, and I could not judge a single one correctly until the rose-colored prism through which I viewed him cleared. But thanks to a rare blend of enthusiasm and judgment, no one gets more impassioned of those who please her, while no one is so quick to discover their flaws. The instinctive analytical spirit to which my judgment involuntarily subjects even my most tender affections, has breathed a cold wind on all of my desires. However, I have come to have friends and have sincerely liked some of them, despite knowing their faults; but as for love, which lives only on enthusiasm and dreams, I have not found a single man who did not lose upon knowing him what he had gained on being imagined. Because friendship is, if I may say so, a luxury for the soul's happiness, but love is a necessity. It is enough to be able to respect a friend, but we must both love and respect a lover. We never ask for joy from friendship—it is enough that it console us for its absence; but we demand happiness from love, and it is worthless if it does not provide it.

"However, for me friendship itself has only developed as the sequel to a failed passion. Going into the relationship with high hopes, I only suffered disappointments. Now that I know life and men, I have come to appreciate that sweet sentiment and take it for what it is, for just what it can be; but at that time, when I knew life only through the senses and could judge things only by instinct, love and friendship were equally impossible for me to find. In everything I was seeking the fulfillment of a dream, a phantasm . . . I was seeking happiness, which I later doubted that love itself could give.

"In such a frame of mind, you can imagine how many false beliefs, how many absurd infatuations life offered me, and how many cold disillusionments quickly followed my brilliant mistakes. The girlfriend in whose affection I basked most freely, the one I esteemed most highly, played with my feelings for a while, tapped its treasures, and then scoffed at my blind faith, abused my simple candor, and all the better for me if she didn't make hay out of my impulsive, passionate nature to slander my conduct and my heart! The lover in whom I thought I had spied my ideal mate abruptly turned into a vulgar, hateful, and petty being. Sometimes I found the stale, corrupt playboy in what I thought was the noble unfortunate soul; stupidity and hardheartedness beneath an exterior that I read as denoting kindness and virtue; frivolousness and idiocy in the elegant gracious form that had heralded the union of all that was lovable and appealing; an unbearable ridiculous vanity in certain natures that had seemed great and original; weakness and timidity in others I had believed to be sweet and tender; hardness and ferocity in many who by some isolated traits I had considered dynamic and nobly powerful. Carlos, I repeat, for the person who knows men, there are many in whom one can find some beautiful, praiseworthy qualities, but for the blind ardor of youth, when one still seems to recall heaven and asks for as much on earth, reality is always a letdown. The imagined always surpasses the real, and it is experience alone that makes us indulgent.

"During those two years I went through a costly and sad apprenticeship. My affections were disappointments; my hopes madness; my very virtues disastrous to me. My experiences day by day, hour by hour showed me that whatever good, great, and beautiful there was in my soul was an obstacle to my happiness: that my enthusiasm led me astray, my credulity made me the plaything of so-called clever people, my lofty indiscretion attracted the censure of those who took pride in their good sense and composure, that my inability to lie was called tactlessness, my yearning for affection insatiable coquetry . . . in short, Carlos, my very intelligence, that priceless gift that brings us close to the divine, was for common minds a dangerous quality that would sooner or later be my undoing.

"Brokenhearted, I again withdrew from the society that I was starting to understand, but that I still could not discount. The poorer and more unjust I found the world, the more I felt the need for a noble, sensitive being who would understand and love me, and protect my fragile, lonely existence. But oh! I still searched for him in vain. When loving would have been a crime for me, I thought there was nothing easier than to love; when my heart was free, it seemed powerless to give the very thing it overflowed with.

"I never found what I was avidly seeking, and I began to blame myself. In the absence of passion and enthusiasm, which no man inspired once I got to know him, I thought I could find happiness in one of those gentle and serene emotions that fill the lives of many women. But mild feelings are not in my nature. Lord Byron notes that in certain climates one does not experience the soft coolness of twilight, the melancholy haze of half-tones. The sun does not slowly descend toward the horizon, weary in its course, but rather abruptly disappears, full of light and force, as though its powerful movement could not go through a gradual decline. Isn't it the same for fiery, powerful souls? Their passionate nature never allows for lukewarm emotions; they love or they hate, they admire or despise, they go far or they remain far behind.

"Soon I lost heart; that powerful imagination tired of deluding me, and I could only feel the extent of my unhappiness as an icy cloak of doubt shrouded all the lofty beliefs of my youth. Wishing to shake off at any cost the germ of death that was sprouting in my soul, I sought in the intellect what I had sought in vain in feeling; I had seen man in society, and now I wanted to study him in books. I convinced myself that enlightened by the experience and talents of the great moralists, perhaps my ideas would change for the better, and that freed of the elation that impedes correct judgment, I could find safeguards against discouragement in the illuminating lessons of philosophy. I was hoping to find, if not the joy of dreams, the calm of convictions and the torch of truth to guide me through the dark ocean of the human passions.

"I have spent many nights reading the works of the great ancient and modern moralists and philosophers: I have breathed, pulsated with the poetry of Plato, I have followed him in his ideal and wildly sublime Republic; in my sleepless nights I have reflected on the dreams of Rousseau, I have plunged heart and soul with him into the world of ideas, and like him have fallen from the heights of the intellect into the abyss of human failure. Thus, after poring over the great questions and getting drunk on their exalted theories, I have become even more haunted by the vague specters of doubt, and in trying to understand all I became a stranger to myself. The just and the unjust, right and wrong all blurred in my mind, and in my loneliness of heart I soon found growing the icy colossus of egoism, because when I analyzed the virtues, I always found them to be grounded in self-interest. Frightened of myself, I returned to the world, no longer to seek there love, happiness, justice, truth, but rather an opiate of pleasures and riches that would lull me to sleep. I returned there to cloud in its steamy marshes the fatal spark of my intellect, to smash on its bronze facade the piercing dart of my sensibility.

"From that time on, the world that stabs me in the back has strewn roses at my feet; since then I am no longer a victim because I can be a tyrant; since then no one pities me because some envy me. No one looks down on me, because many hate me. I have no disappointments, because I believe in nothing. I have enemies who slander me, but my indifference kills their joy in mortifying me.

I have friends who love me, because I am tolerant of their faults and I give them the pleasure of censuring my own. Do you know what society is for me? What a courtesan is to you men. You seek her out; you lavish on her false and fleeting allurements; you pay her well for hers, as false and ephemeral as yours; and you discard her with scorn.

"Society is for me a necessary evil. I who cannot accept its code do not rebel against it, because I am both strong and weak, one who can neither conform to the straitjacket of social hypocrisy nor is of such a great heart as to deprive herself of its dazzling pleasures. And what else can I desire or hope for? When one arrives at a state where the dreams of love and happiness have vanished, Carlos, man finds before him the path of ambition. But for woman, what recourse is left to her when she has given up on love, her only good, her unique destiny? She must fight hand to hand, weak and helpless, against the frozen phantoms of boredom and starvation. Oh! When we still find ourselves fertile in thought, thirsty in soul, and our heart does not give us what we need, ambition is very beautiful. Then one should be a warrior or a politician, one should create for oneself a campaign, a triumph, a ruin. The thrill of glory, the turmoil of danger, the zeal for and fear of success, all those vital emotions of pride, valor, hope and fear . . . all of that belongs to a way of life that I do not understand. Yes, there are moments in my life when I imagine the pleasure of battle, the intoxication of the smell of gunpowder, the sound of cannons; moments when I penetrate the winding path of the politician, and I discover the flowers of fame and power amid the thorns that make his position more appealing . . . But poor woman, with only one destiny in the world! What can she do, what can she be when she cannot be the one thing that is allowed to her?

"She will do what I do, and like me she will be unhappy, without her unhappiness being able to be confided to others or understood. Oh! If anyone understood, they would feel for me . . . And my pride repels compassion. I need to appear happy because I am not."

The Countess fell silent, and Carlos remained still, unable to turn his gaze away from that expressive face with its look of haughty sadness. It was rare and terrible to witness that blend of passion and reason, activity and weariness, flippancy and depth, indifference and pride. Catalina inspired in him a feeling of painful admiration, the kind of impression made by a high tower as it collapses or a huge fire consuming great buildings. He no longer saw in her the cold and frivolous coquette, or the attractive slandered woman he thought he had seen moments before. That woman had been transformed in his eyes into a person of terrible misfortune, a living drama that excites at once pity and terror as a mysterious symbol of life in its two phases: one of gold and the other of lead. However, he ventured to make a comment to the Countess.

"It is no doubt true," he said, "that in the brilliant world of great cities, you find vices and evils that are unknown in those places where individual lives are more exposed, and where civilization has introduced fewer elements of corruption. But I cannot believe, señora, that anywhere in the world the majority of men have lost all virtuous principles and all kind feelings. I cannot do mankind the injustice of believing it to be so bad that it is a misfortune and an exception to have high, noble feelings. In short, I will never understand how the imperfections in society can justify the scorn of society as a whole, nor that we should live without respecting or loving anyone for fear of being deceived."

The Countess smiled.

"I believe you, Carlos," she said in a sweet and melancholy voice. "For you, with your young and pure heart of twenty-one years, who have not yet suffered, who have not yet caused another to suffer, the sad voice of a wounded existence must seem like an angry blasphemy and not a cry of pain. Lord keep me from blaming you for your noble trust, for your generous faith! But you are wrong if you think that I judge man by his behavior in society. You are also wrong in assuming that I scorn man or detest him. No, on the contrary, I do not believe that a single one exists who is completely bad. I think that deep within the most corrupt and sinful existence we can still find fine, noble qualities, and that there is no crime or vulgar act that, taking into account the cause and the circumstances, is without a valid defense. It is events, more than instincts, that make a man evil. Both the seed of good and the seed of bad exist in all souls, and I cannot easily accept the fearful hypothesis that there is an innate goodness or an innate evil within us. That would be an offense against God's justice. Because I know man I do not hate him, and because I know him I am tolerant of his faults. I repeat, only youth that has not yet lived or judged is severe on this point. The man who knows himself and knows others forgives many things. Do you think that I do not find lovely qualities in men who are full of flaws, or that for me their flaws outweigh their virtues? No, Carlos; as I said before, there are flaws that can make a man lovable; and I will add that not one exists who is so hateful and ugly that I consider him to be wholly contemptible. But if I am indulgent, it is because I am no longer enthusiastic; if I do not scorn, it is because I no longer admire; if I do not ask for sublime virtue in humanity, it is because I know that humanity does not possess it, and that only in the first blush of youth can the human heart emit that perfume of poetry that is soon swept away in life's downpours.

"The world, as Shakespeare says in *Hamlet*, is an arid field gone to seed that yields only coarse bitter fruit. Every man in isolation may offer some more or less rare virtues, and proportionate flaws; and I still do not doubt that there are well-balanced individuals living in favorable circumstances in whom we find a genuine kindness that is incapable of wrongdoing.

"At home we may find a father who loves his wife and children, and who is good because he is loved. But if we seek that same man in the collective mass known as society, it is possible that we will find him plotting to destroy a rival who is an obstacle to his promotion. We may see a youth in whom we find many honorable feelings, who would blush if we suspected him to be capable of a vile deed, and in society we watch him show off his vices, deceive an innocent heart, stain with foul words a mother's name. The woman who at heart has the sweetest, most lovable nature, and at times even more beautiful qualities, will tear apart a rival whom she might secretly respect, and stoop to lies and hypocrisy to deceive a husband, and use vile schemes to avenge herself on an enemy, and tricks to rid herself of a critic.

"No one enters society to display his virtues. Kind feelings are reserved for private life, for intimacy, for familiarity. One goes into society armed with the distrust that provides self-defense, and the malice that allows for revenge. Society, especially in the civilized, corrupt cities, is the sewer into which is poured all the filth of the human heart; the hollow rock that echoes all lies; the furnace in which are forged all daggers to wound the unwary heart. I prefer crime to baseness. The solitary man may perhaps commit a crime; you do not find crime in society because crimes are grand and need space, but you find there petty passions, conflicting interests, silent revenge, base machinations, vile schemes. By following its code you keep up appearances, and if you are clever enough to give a polished veneer to your ugliest acts, you will not be held accountable."

"But señora," Carlos replied, "if you know what society is like, how can you live in its ranks? And if you believe there are men who are not unworthy of esteem, why don't you enjoy the more pleasant and less dangerous company of a small group of select friends?"

The Countess smiled.

"Wherever three people come together," she said, "they can be divided by conflicting interests; they will be a fragment of society at large and contaminated by its vices. But I admit that I could gather a small group of friends, and we could isolate ourselves from the larger group and disengage ourselves from anything beyond our own narrow circle; and I even think it possible that nothing would come between us and the interest of one would be the interest of all. Would such a monotonous life borne of egoism bring us happiness? Carlos, only love can fill one's life, and in its absence we need the whole world to daze us with its roar, to provoke us with its baseness, to move us with its unhappiness, to whisper to and flatter us, to caress and mistreat us, so as to arouse in us some emotion.

"I had resigned myself to this fate for quite a while, but you have done me harm—great harm. You have come to proclaim to me that happiness, love, virtue *do* exist. Carlos, since I met you I find my life wretched indeed, and believe me . . . when I arrive at the days of old age and loneliness, I will have only one warm memory of my days of pleasure: the memory of these moments spent with you."

Upon uttering these last words the Countess's voice trembled, and she fixed her gaze on Carlos with a melancholy look. A tear seemed to cool the impassioned fire in her large eyes, and Carlos was so deeply moved that taking her hand, he tenderly raised it to his lips.

At that moment Elvira sat up in bed. Catalina ran to her side, and Carlos remained lost in thought until the Countess came back to bid him farewell.

"I am leaving, Carlos," she told him; "it is already dawn and Elvira's condition is stable. I think this has been the last night when we need to sit up with her. I will still see you here on some days, but Elvira is getting better and then . . ."

"Then," he said emphatically, "I hope that I may be allowed to spend some moments with you in your home."

"I was desiring that," she said, "but I did not dare to ask for it. And yet, Carlos, why should you deny me that pleasure? You take no risk in granting it to me, and I," she added, blushing, "I believe that I will always respect your happiness."

She departed, and Carlos withdrew to his room, where he nonetheless did not seek the rest he needed after two sleepless nights. He paced up and down the room in long strides, recalling all he had heard from the Countess. He examined the life and soul of that singular woman in light of what she had revealed to him; he was moved by her simplicity and candor, enchanted by her gifts and the magic of her conversation, and frightened by her insatiable soul of fire no less than by her bleakly cold and implacable reason.

"Everything she is saying must be true," he thought. "She will never be able to love; she will never find a man who can subdue both her passionate heart and her brilliant and powerful imagination. But if she did come to love . . . what pride, what satisfaction could compare with making that brilliantly unfortunate woman happy!

"And yet, could anyone make a lasting impression on a woman with this kind of temperament? Can this feverish exaltation," he continued, "paroxysm of the soul, ever know the tranquil joy of a strong reciprocal love? No, without doubt Catalina will never make a husband happy, but I can easily conceive that she could send a lover into ecstasy. It is better that she keep up her frivolous and contemptible role of coquette . . . it is better that way. Catalina, as I have seen her tonight, is a terrible woman, a woman who, if she cannot give or receive happiness, can open the way for herself and the one she loves to a nightmare of suffering and crime . . . crime!" he repeated fearfully, "—but why? She will certainly not love a man who is not free, and no one who is would be criminal in loving her. He may be unhappy, but . . . wouldn't there be a kind of joy in being made unhappy by and with her?"

At that moment his servant half opened the door, and seeing him still up said, "I wanted to remind you, señor, that today is the mail day for Andalusia, and if you are going to bed it would be good to give me now the letters I am to send."

Carlos shuddered. It was the first time that his letters to Luisa were not written the evening before their dispatch, and this time he had even forgotten that it was the mail day.

He dismissed the servant and started to write. We do not know if his letter was as long as the previous ones, but we can assure the reader that it was still tender and sincere.

12

"So how are you getting along now with Catalina?" Elvira asked her cousin one morning. "It seems that during my illness you have become friends."

Carlos, who was sitting rather far from the sofa where the convalescent was resting, got up and came over to her side. "The Countess," he said, "must have as many friends as people who have the good fortune to know her."

"Which means," said Elvira smiling, "that your opinion of her has changed a lot. Twenty days ago, a month at most, you assured me that you could never like or respect such a woman."

It annoyed Carlos that Elvira was reminding him of his bias against the Countess, and he answered rather dryly, "That just shows that if I was then too hasty in my judgment, I am at least sincere enough not to have to pretend to be consistent at the expense of doing justice."

"I had already told you," Elvira added, "that Catalina was an irresistible woman, and I am very glad to find that the two people I am closest to in Madrid are finally on good terms."

At that moment the Countess arrived. Elvira had been sick for a week, and her friend had visited her every day with the precision of a doctor and with the painstaking and natural affection of a sister. From noon until four in the afternoon she did not leave the convalescent's room for a moment, entertaining her with her varied conversation or with pleasant light readings. She read admirably; verses in particular turned into real music, intoned by her lilting, melodious voice. As she had a complete command of French and Spanish, and translated and spoke quite good English, Italian, and German, no author of worth was foreign to her. She had a good understanding of Corneille, Schiller, Shakespeare, and Dante, and translated them with peerless talent and ease. Her pleasant voice expressed with the same sweetness and grace the ideas of André Chénier as of Garcilaso de la Vega, and Jean Racine as well as Calderón de la Barca would have been pleased to hear their beautiful dialogues in that enchanting mouth, which gave them a new luster.

Carlos, who was always there during the two friends' readings and conversation, admired ever more the Countess's great gifts, and her vast and yet modest learning. Since he too knew several languages, he could appreciate more than Elvira the quality of the beautiful improvised translations she did of foreign poets, without giving the least importance to this difficult and arduous work. He was no less delighted to hear her recite the most beautiful lines of the great French and Spanish poets with exquisite sensitivity and understanding, and when he discussed with her the quality of various poets, he was always surprised at the speed of her analysis and the accuracy of her judgments. The Countess combined the ardent poetic imagination of a Spaniard with the wisdom and refinement of a Parisian. She analyzed like a philosopher and painted verbally like a poet, her ideas had the vigor and independence of a man's, and she expressed them with all the charming fantasy, and even some of the pleasant versatility, of a woman.

She was, in short, a unique blend, an amalgam that was difficult to analyze; but whatever the essential nature composed of those contrasting qualities, there was undoubtedly a striking originality and an ever renewed appeal in her external behavior, or in her features, as it were, because temperaments also have features, which are sometimes more deceptive than facial features.

Catalina, the Countess of S., was known to the world as a person of lively, amiable character, but he who observed the volatility beneath her apparent gaiety, who noticed that that woman was at once too cold and too hot, that her heart and her head seemed to be constantly at odds, could not help but study her with curiosity and perhaps with fear. There is in some stormy, contradictory natures a kind of sinister influence. Some psychic makeups are so difficult and complex that we cannot analyze them for fear of tearing them apart.

Carlos, however, was day by day more captivated by the pleasantness of the Countess's company, and the more he felt he got to know her the higher was his opinion of her heart. He rarely left Elvira's house; he got up early and awaited with great impatience the hour of Catalina's usual arrival. When the clock chimed that hour, his heart beat faster with the sound of every passing carriage, and when the Countess finally showed up, Carlos was surprised at the happiness he felt at the mere sight of her; in a sense he felt drunk in her presence. When he was with her, he could only admire her, applaud her, avidly relish the moments of joy that her talents and her sweetness afforded him, and congratulate himself on having the friendship of such a distinguished and amiable woman. But the moment Catalina left, he felt restless and discontent. He could not think of her without feeling a kind of painful distrust, he was afraid to examine the very happiness he enjoyed when he was with her, and although impatient to see her again, he felt a kind of anxiety, which increased as the time of her arrival neared.

Nonetheless, not the slightest suspicion of being in love had crossed the mind of Luisa's husband. Carlos did not believe that the feeling the Countess inspired in him could be love. Even if he were free, he would not have chosen as his wife that brilliant notable of the court; even if he were free, he would not have believed it possible to be loved by a woman who was the object of such adoration. Catalina only inspired in him feelings of admiration, and at times shyness, and although his respect for her increased the more he was with her, his distrust also increased. He believed her to be good, generous, sincere, and intense, but he could not persuade himself at times that she also possessed the gentle qualities and modest virtues that promise happiness and are worthy of trust. Thus he was an enthusiastic admirer of the Countess, he even went so far as to declare himself her most ardent friend, but he could not understand how one could wish to be her husband, and he pitied, although he did not condemn, her apparent lovers. So Carlos refused to admit to himself that there was danger for him in that intimacy.

As for Catalina, who for a week had only had Elvira and Carlos on her mind, who had had no distraction other than being with them, and who saw with chagrin that she would soon have to return to her life of pleasure, she savored greedily those hours of sweet intimacy that she knew so well how to embellish, and did not take care to avoid frequent contact with a young man to whom she was well aware that she was not indifferent. Catalina was under no illusions. She knew that if her initial desire to win over Carlos had been motivated by wounded pride, for many days now he had made a strange impression on her heart. When she was with him, she often found to her surprise that she was drinking in the sight of his large black eyes with their proud, ardent look, and his head as noble and pure as that of Milton's Adam. When he spoke she held her breath, and heard with an interest she could not conceal his gifts and his shyness, his pride, his ignorance of life and of the world, his perfect understanding of his duties, the natural goodness of his heart, and the severity of his principles. In short, the inexhaustible delight she took in studying that active soul and southern head, still young and powerful yet always dominated by a strong will; the novelty it was for her to have to win through genuine and substantial qualities of the heart an homage that had always been paid her for her gifts and her beauty alone, all of this drew her more and more to Carlos. Every day she was more preoccupied; every moment spent with him increased the strong and deep impression he made on her heart.

But far from avoiding him, she rushed to be with him, to study him, to understand him and to quench her thirst, as it were, in the poison of his looks, looks that had an unspeakable power over that singular woman. And do not think that Catalina behaved this way from a lack of prudence, or that she set out to capture Carlos's heart at any price. Her actions actually arose out of a contrary desire and a wise calculation. She knew that her dreams never survived analysis; she knew that no man once known by her was the man she had imagined; she confided in her fickleness, in her delicate sensibility that could so easily be hurt, in her remarkable perception of faults . . . In short, Catalina behaved in regard to love the way one should behave regarding the feeling of panic. She knew that fear is not dispelled by fleeing from the object that inspires it, because the imagination will magnify and exaggerate it the less we actually experience it, so the best remedy is to approach, to touch, to take apart, if need be, the unknown object that has frightened us. The said object, once examined, often inspires contempt, and we laugh about our past fear.

So this, no more nor less, was what the Countess hoped for. She knew herself well enough to know that fleeing from her enemy would only make him stronger, and as a woman who understood the passions and relied on her gifts, she wished to engage in hand-to-hand combat, convinced that she might find a shadow in what her imagination portrayed as a formidable giant.

This was her conjecture, and yet she was amazed to find that after a week of almost continual contact and severe scrutiny, her fervor had not weakened at all.

When Elvira was completely recovered and declared that she was going to return to her former way of life, Carlos and Catalina shuddered. They looked at each other at the same time with the same expression, and each of them realized that the thought of not seeing each other every day was now unbearable for the other.

"Maybe he loves me!" thought Catalina, with a rash, involuntary joy.

"Maybe she loves me!" Carlos dared to think for the first time. And he shivered with fear and perhaps also with pride. Each one judged the feelings of the other, and did not examine his own. Why? Catalina, because she was starting to fear them; Carlos, because he was not yet aware of them.

13

It was two in the afternoon on a lovely mild April day when Carlos for the second time in his life entered the home of Catalina of S. It had been three days since he had seen her. Elvira, back to her former lifestyle, was almost never at home, and Carlos, who had not made up his mind to visit the Countess, had spent those three days in almost complete solitude, although while involved with his affairs he could not stop thinking all too often of Catalina.

"She has undoubtedly returned with pleasure," he thought, "to that stirring atmosphere in which she lives, and in the crowd of pleasures that surrounds her the memory will quickly fade of the two weeks of friendship and openness we shared. Perhaps at this moment when I still seem to inhale the fragrance of her hair in these rooms, among her circle of elegant admirers she has forgotten the very existence of the modest, obscure youth with whom she shared hours of solitude and sorrow at the bedside of a sick woman. Her memories of me must be associated with the tedious circumstances that motivated our acquaintance, and how do I know that if I were bold enough to plunge into the world of her triumphs, to claim the friendship she offered me in the solitude of night by a sickbed, I would not be treated by her as a lunatic or a fool?

"But I cannot complain," he added, mechanically pressing to his chest the reliquary of the Virgin that his wife had given him upon his departure. "I should be glad that the impression that those days may have made on her heart is as fleeting as it seemed strong and true. No doubt she was not lying; her pleasure when we were together was not a fiction, her sadness upon parting, her sad tender look when she said, 'Carlos, these sweet hours of intimacy and openness are now over for us.' No, none of that was a fiction, because you cannot pretend like that, because she is too sincere and good to shamefully mock the credulity of a pure heart. But those feelings cannot last. They are fleeting sensations borne of an ardent, intense imagination, which will pass without leaving a trace. That is for the best. What would I gain by being loved by her? Loved by her . . . what madness! Thank the Lord it is impossible. Loved by her! Heaven forbid! And I would not fear it so much if only my happiness were at stake . . . but Luisa! My Luisa!" And the young man kissed the reliquary of the Virgin, and recalling his wife's words upon placing it on his chest, he repeated them with a kind of superstitious fervor: "May she protect you."

But after three days spent in a state of continual melancholy and poorly contained agitation, he decided to visit the Countess, feeling that he could not neglect paying her this courtesy without seeming ungrateful and rude. So he went there, but upon arriving at the Countess's home he felt so stirred up that he was about to leave without entering. Yet just as he was about to do this, he saw Elvira who was leaving the Countess's home, and who upon seeing him said emphatically, "Thank heaven that finally, once in your life, you are attentive and courteous to your friends. Poor Catalina is not well, and it would have been cruel and ungrateful not to come to personally find out about her health."

"She is not well!" Carlos exclaimed, but Elvira was already far off, so it was the doorman who answered, "Yes, señor, the Countess is rather unwell, but she is up. According to what her maidservant told me this morning, her indisposition is more sadness than anything else."

Carlos heard no more. He ran up the stairs and hardly gave them time to announce his arrival, so great was his impatience to reach the sitting room where they had said the Countess was. All of his confusion and reserve vanished upon learning that Catalina was not well. He had expected to find her content, splendid, triumphant, and the words "she is not well," "she is sad," turned his thoughts and his feelings upside down.

Catalina was lying languidly on an elegant sofa, whose elastic cushion gently gave way beneath the light weight of her delicate frame. She was wearing a white dressing gown, which competed that day with her extremely pale face, and her hair, loosely tied back in a bun, left entirely clear her beautiful forehead and her large bright eyes.

Upon hearing Silva's name she sat up with a movement of surprise and doubt, but upon seeing him her gloomy face lit up, and her eyes shone with the strongest joy.

"Carlos! Carlos!" she cried in a tone that could drive him mad. "At last I'm seeing you again!"

"Catalina," he said, taking the hand she held out to him with a shiver of pleasure, "I did not know that you were ill."

"Which is to say," she replied with a wistful and enchanting smile, "that it is only due to my indisposition . . ."

"No," he interrupted her, sitting by her side, "but I feared . . . Excuse me, Catalina, but I was afraid to find you in the circle of your admirers, in the world of pleasure that surrounds you in that brilliant society that is foreign to me. I thought you might find my presence annoying . . . that it would irritate me to see you surrounded by your numerous friends, and that perhaps my . . . egoism—if you want to call it that—would make me feel ridiculous."

"You wretch!" she said, then struggling to maintain a serene and friendly tone. "You are unfair to take me for so frivolous and fickle that for the sake of pleasure I would forget a friendship that I had accepted with such pride and returned with such tenderness. No, you could never think that it would annoy me, and if you did, you should not have told me so, because in so doing you shattered my hope that you had understood my heart. But in any case, now I am seeing you after three dreadful days in which I have cruelly suffered."

After uttering these last words, which naturally slipped out, she realized that she had said too much, and added with little hope of being believed, "I have been ill."

"So what is wrong? What do you have?" Carlos asked anxiously.

Catalina seemed to consider what answer to give, and to seek in the catalog of stock illnesses one that would seem appropriate, but as her lively imagination immediately came up with a list of usable ills, she did not pause to choose and answered after a brief moment of thought, "Migraine, nerves, a bad cold, dizzy spells . . . surely some bile."

The truth was that her indisposition was simply due to the spite and pain caused by having spent three days awaiting a visit that did not take place, and that her pale face, the dark circles under her eyes, her sadness had as their source the lack of sleep and appetite and the constant sorrow from finding herself rejected by a man whose love she had felt flattered to have attained three days earlier, and with whom she was, despite herself, madly in love.

Carlos said he was sorry to hear about all the ills that had afflicted his friend over the past three days, and then expressed surprise at not finding any of her numerous lovers and friends with the beautiful patient. The Countess said, "That is because yesterday and today I refused to see anyone. I was incapable of concealing my trouble, and besides, I wanted to see if by focusing entirely on one thought, I could reduce its effect."

"And what is that thought?" Carlos asked, fixing on hers his superb Arabian eyes, which seemed to want to penetrate the depths of her soul.

"What is it?" and she too fixed on him her bewitching look. "Do you want to know?"

"Yes! . . . Yes!" And upon saying this "yes," he almost guessed what he was asking; it was told him by his heart and by Catalina's impassioned look. But he was not in his right mind, and swept along by a crazy desire to hear what he already knew, he repeated, pressing the Countess's hand, "Yes, I want to know."

"Well then, Carlos," she said, "I was thinking that I am very unhappy . . . that it would have been better for me not to have met you."

Carlos could not find words to respond to that reckless admission, but he was no longer in control of himself and he fell at the

Countess's feet. That action, and his facial expression full of passion and sorrow, aroused the Countess from her dangerous self-abandonment. "Carlos," she said, trying to feign a serenity she did not feel, "please believe me because I am assuring you of it: it would have been better for me not to have met you. Because your happiness makes me constantly aware of the happiness I lack. But if you can, if you would be my friend . . . my brother . . . do you agree? Then I can still find my destiny sweet."

"Your friend? Your brother?" he cried, with a mixture of fear and hope. "And what other title can I hope for? What other tie can exist between the two of us? Your brother! . . . Yes, I would like that, Catalina. You must make me your brother, because I cannot and should not be anything else for you, because if you tried to inspire in me other feelings, a day would come when you would repent of it, a day when you would desire and would be unable to return to me the happiness you had robbed me of, and when you would be weighed down by a terrible remorse: that of turning an honorable man into a criminal and of making an innocent girl unhappy; because what might for you be a whim, a pastime, would for me be a passion, a delirium, a misfortune, a crime!"

"Oh, Carlos! Stop, stop," the Countess cried, covering her face with her hands. Carlos perceived a muffled sob, and more than ever moved and disturbed by the unexpected position in which he found himself, he took Catalina's hands away from her face, and seeing it bathed in tears and embellished by a kind of terror that was etched on her features, he pressed her hands to his heart and called her by the sweetest names, begging her to calm down.

At that moment a servant announced the arrival of Elvira, and Carlos barely had time to get up from Catalina's feet when his cousin entered. Catalina complained of a strong headache, which explained the change in her face and her moist eyes. Elvira put her in bed, declaring that she would spend the whole day by her side, and Carlos left, so worked up, so beside himself, that he walked all over Madrid before finding his way home.

The scene he had just played a part in shed a baneful light on his feelings. For the first time he realized that he was in love with the Countess, and that when he was with her he could not answer for his own behavior. He also believed himself to be loved with more passion, with more zeal than he had been up until then . . . And yet his affection for his wife, far from diminishing seemed to have gained force from his remorse, and upon realizing his guilt Luisa became much more attractive to his heart.

"The poor angel!" he said, rushing around his room. "If she knew that her husband, at the feet of another, had felt a delirium such that it was all he could do not to offer that other a heart that should belong to her alone! . . . If she knew! . . . Oh! She would forgive me, I am sure, because her divine soul was only made to love and to forgive, and her divine voice to utter blessings and prayers. But that innocent, peaceful creature could never understand a crazy, frenzied passion . . . She would not have loved me if, like Catalina, loving me had entailed a crime!"

And he, the still virtuous but already ungrateful and unjust husband, almost wanted to find in his wife's virtue a rationalization for his criminal passion for another, and upon thinking, "She would not have been capable of being guilty on my account," the natural deduction he made was, "so she does not love me as much as Catalina." And therefore this conclusion: "My infidelity is excusable."

Such is the logic of the passions, and so will it be always, despite the fact that upon considering it objectively, we understand and denounce its sophisms.

Carlos spent an agitated evening and a worse night. Elvira, who had come home from the Countess's house at eleven at night, told him that Catalina was running some fever, and his imagination exaggerated her suffering and the danger. The poor fellow did not sleep a wink that night, yet during all those long hours feverish, ravenous dreams impeded a moment of reflection. What mortal who has loved and suffered does not know those terrible night visions, during which in vain are one's eyes open and one's body erect? Despite this, the mind is not awake nor the heart free of nightmares. The imagination roams without giving reason the time to challenge its excesses, and the heart, its victim, yields trembling to the deadly blind power that enslaves it.

It will always be easier for a man to answer for his actions than for his thoughts, and there is surely no greater folly than to ask him to justify the latter.

14

The following day Carlos learned from Elvira that the Countess was feeling much better, and that night, that she had gotten up. He decided to visit her the next morning, rationalizing this second dangerous visit by resolving to show the Countess such a noble, pure, and tender friendship that under such a sacred name their relationship would not dare take the form of a guilty passion. He still counted on the willpower he had garnered to support him in his virtuous resolve, and he also counted on Catalina herself, who would no doubt manage to combat a hapless inclination.

But throughout the day he did not for a moment feel he was in the serene and composed frame of mind needed to go and see Catalina, and it was already well into the night when he set off for her home. Two days earlier he had arrived at her door upset by the thought of finding her happy, radiant, forgetful of him and entirely devoted to her pleasures and triumphs; this time he felt a fear of a different kind. Maybe he would find her paler and weaker than on his last visit; maybe he would find himself alone with her in a risky solitude . . . In short, he was afraid that if he were put to such tests, his victory was far from certain.

Shivering, he climbed the stairs. He did not notice that the house was all lit up, and it was just when he got to the entrance hall that he heard the sound of voices. In his extreme agitation a horrid thought came to him at that moment, and hitting himself on the head he said, "She's very ill! Oh, God! She's very ill!" And he rushed into the living room.

He made a really theatrical entrance, and to make the scene even more comic, no sooner had he arrived pale, flustered, shaken amid the splendid society that the Countess had assembled in her home that night than he stood stock-still, frozen, as flushed as a moment before he had been pale, and with an almost foolish air.

A low murmur went through the room.

"Who is that?" some people asked.

"Is Elvira de Sotomayor's cousin crazy?" said others.

"It's a surprise," said some nasty women; "one of the Countess's tricks to amuse herself at that poor fool's expense."

"How handsome he is!" remarked the youngest.

"But he's a fool—what is he doing standing there like the stone guest at Don Juan's banquet?"

Indeed, Carlos's surprise, confusion, embarrassment, and indignation had left him standing stock-still for some moments, and when he realized the ridiculous part he was playing in that dazzling salon, he dashed out of the room as impetuously as he had entered, without greeting anyone or even knowing what he was doing.

In any other set of circumstances this strange episode at the party would have been met with general laughter and gibes, but the extreme pallor that spread across the Countess's face, her anxious looks toward Carlos, and the visible emotion that obliged her to sit down although she seemed to want to go after him, all of which were not lost on the discerning people around her, gave a very different complexion to the scene. Everyone suspected a love affair, a novelistic scene, featuring either a laughable chance event or the awkwardness of a novice suitor, and no one dared to make fun of it. On the contrary, a thousand different remarks were made in low voices; the men were jealous of the emotion that the mere sight of Carlos stirred up in the Countess, and the women, who saw in it a romantic indiscretion on the part of a highly intriguing youth, secretly envied the woman who could complain of it.

Meanwhile Carlos ran down the stairs like a lunatic, and finding himself out in the street started walking aimlessly around the city. He had enough pride to feel embarrassed and almost furious at having made himself into a laughingstock before the Countess, and thinking she should have foreseen it and that it was her fault, he was indignant and almost hated her. He recalled seeing her all dressed up and beautiful among her admirers at the moment when he showed up like a lunatic believing her to perhaps be at death's door . . . He doubted her love; he doubted her goodness. It even occurred to the fool that she might be laughing along with her lovers over the rare spectacle he had just offered them, and in his outburst of rage, spite, and grief, he was on the point of returning to the Countess's home to crush her with insults before her entire gathering. At that moment, in his mind she returned to being the shrewd, cold, implacable coquette. At that moment he did not think of Luisa, nor of anyone except that woman whom he despised, and whom he was resolved nonetheless to scorn.

He found himself on the Prado without having intended to go there. The crisp freshness of an April night, the solitude and silence of that place at that hour, and above all some moments of reflection there, calmed his seething blood and his angry heart. Upon examining carefully what had happened, he had to admit that the Countess was not to blame for what was merely the result of his own imprudence, and when he returned home at midnight, while deeply thoughtful, he was in a calmer state of mind.

He shut himself in his room and tried to sleep. It was not easy, but he finally did, and in his dream he saw his wife flying amid an angelic choir that came to watch over him and intervened between him and the Countess, who appeared in the dream in the same ballroom, as dressed up and beautiful and treacherous as she had appeared to him that night.

He awoke very late the next day; his servant came in at noon to serve him breakfast and to say that Elvira would like him to go to her room before leaving. He did in fact comply. She was still in bed, complaining of not feeling well, and she asked him to take a chair near her bed. "I wanted to talk to you so you could explain to me your conduct last night," she then said, smiling.

"What? Were you there?"

"Of course."

"So why didn't you tell me anything about that party? Why was it kept a mystery?"

"I don't know what kind of a mystery it was," Elvira answered. "As for not telling you that there was a gathering last night at the Countess's, it was your own fault for not leaving your room the whole day, even refusing to eat with me. Besides, since I knew you would not go, having only visited Catalina once, while she before yesterday did not seem to want to hear about you . . . frankly, Carlos, I thought the two of you had fallen out again."

"I will never be either the Countess's friend or her enemy," said Carlos strongly. "I'm not up to being either one or the other."

Elvira looked at him more astutely than usual. "Well then," she said, "what I'd like is for you to explain your behavior last night." Carlos told her the truth, without going into detail, and attributed his confusion to his surprise upon finding himself at a party when he thought the Countess was sick.

Elvira was starting to gently scold him for his lack of social graces, his inability to dissemble—in short, that he should have known how to control himself and make a virtue of necessity, pretending that he knew about the gathering—when the door of the room abruptly opened and the Countess came in in a black dress and mantilla, with a really sickly countenance. Upon seeing Carlos she got so upset that she could hardly greet him, and he for his part was confused, not knowing whether to stay or to leave. The Countess sat down on Elvira's bed, saying she would only stay a moment, and Carlos decided to stay, trying to look as calm and indifferent as possible.

"What lovely jewelry you wore last night!" said Elvira. "How beautiful you looked! Do you know that the Marquis of — really fell in love with you last night? And the Colonel of A—do you know that you won his heart?"

Catalina paid no attention to these words and said to Carlos in a slightly shaky voice, "Why didn't you stay, once you had come?"

"Señora," he answered dryly, "I was not in the mood for a party."

"But," she went on, "why didn't you at least wait a moment? Then . . . I would have gone out, would have thanked you . . ."

"For what, señora?" he quickly asked.

"For the interest you took in my health."

"Then you knew that I thought you were sick, that I entered the room extremely anxious, with a thousand fears!"

"I guessed it, Carlos; your action made it clear."

"I must have seemed to you a lunatic, an oddball . . ." said Carlos with a forced smile.

"To me!" she exclaimed, with an inimitable expression.

"Certainly, señora, but I am delighted," he went on with an affected jolly air, "I am delighted that at the cost of a little vanity on my part, I could give you solid proof of my friendship, of the interest you inspire."

The Countess leaned forward a little and said in a very low voice, "Is it true, Carlos? Can I believe it? Will you always be my friend?"

"Who can doubt it?" he answered, in the most impertinently ironic, but unfortunately rather comic, tone. Then his face, which could at times take on a stern, domineering look, suddenly changed, and getting up and absentmindedly clearing his handsome brow, whose bluish vein stood out strongly at that moment, he added, looking with cold pride at the flustered Catalina, "My friendship, señora, must be of small value to a person who has as many friends as men who have seen her. Moreover, my friendship could not even be understood by someone with your brilliant gifts. I appreciate your kindly expressing your desire for it, but convinced that there cannot be any kind of fellow feeling between you and me, I am relinquishing an honor that it would be very hard for me to retain."

Upon concluding this statement he began leafing through a book he picked up from the table, and the Countess, who had listened to him without batting an eyelash, silently got up and left the room.

"Where is Catalina going?" said Elvira, standing up. "Run, Carlos, don't let her go . . . I have to speak to her . . . run."

Carlos went out rather slowly, despite Elvira's appeal, and without stopping leafing through the book he was holding in his hands, as though he were extremely interested in counting the pages. He found Catalina standing before a table on which she was leaning with both hands. He approached her slowly and said, "Señora, your cousin wants to talk to you."

She raised her head, and he saw that her eyes and her cheeks were full of tears. A heart of twenty-one years cannot watch coldly the tears of a beautiful woman, even of one he is not in love with. Carlos suddenly felt disarmed, and his face and language changed.

"Catalina!" he said, taking her hand, "Why are you crying? Is it out of sympathy or anger? Are they tears of repentance or spite?"

"They are tears of sadness," she answered, "of sadness, Carlos. And not because I believe that I am as alien to you as you have tried to pretend, not because I do not know that it is resentment rather than the heart that dictates the cruel words you just pronounced, but because that resentment shows me that I am not understood, that I am harshly judged."

"Catalina," he said, "I am not accusing you nor do I have the right to complain, but allow me to flee from a woman who appears sensitive and tender to the point of driving me mad and shattering my peace, only to return to being the happy, unfeeling coquette whenever she pleases, to add to my remorse the shame of having been contemptibly mocked."

"When you found me sensitive and tender," she answered, "I had not stopped to think that your happiness and that of another were in danger. I only thought that mine was at risk. What's more, I will confess all! Yes, I did hope that the feelings I had recklessly given in to would not have much effect on either your fate or mine. But from the day, from the moment when I found you at my feet, when you reminded me of what a huge responsibility had fallen upon me . . . Carlos! Since I realized to my great sorrow the extent of my love, and from your words the enormity of my fault . . . since then I knew that I should not, and could not nourish a senseless hope. Since then I vowed to respect your happiness, and that of a woman who is so dear to you, and no matter how difficult it might be, to try to combat my fatal passion and return to you, even at the cost of your friendship and esteem, the mistaken idea about me you had conceived at the outset. But such heroism was beyond my power, Carlos. I now realize that your unhappiness, hers, mine, that of all living beings, is less bitter to me than the mere idea of being scorned by you."

Her tears gave Catalina's face an irresistible expression, and the vehemence of her words drained her to a degree that her supple frame doubled over like a reed, tumbling into a chair.

Carlos, who was as shaky as she was, held her in his arms. "Then it's true that you love me!" he cried, with a kind of mournful pleasure. She did not respond, but leaned her head on Carlos's chest, and a soft moan revealed more than her action the force and vehemence of the feeling that overwhelmed her.

Carlos was beside himself. He pressed her wildly to his breast, and as though in a dizzy spell muttered incoherent words.

Elvira's voice roused them both from such dangerous ravings. Her bedroom bell was ringing and she was calling for her servants. Carlos fled from the Countess and wildly shut himself in his room.

Catalina tried to get up and fell into her chair again. Elvira's lady's maid, upon seeing her, ran to her aid. "Mariana," the Countess told her, "please give my excuses to your mistress for not going in to say goodbye to her; I am suddenly ill . . . Please help me go and find my carriage."

The maid took her almost in her arms, and when she went in to see her mistress she told her what the Countess had said to her and the state she was in. Elvira jumped up from the bed with a gesture of anger and sorrow. "Oh, my Lord! My Lord!" she cried, without trying to explain herself to Mariana. "If that were the cause, I would never forgive that man. What a boor! What an idiot!" she added, stamping her delicate bare feet on the floor. "Can't he understand his good fortune?"

The servant helped Elvira get dressed, and she went to eat with her friend without trying to see Carlos or leaving him a note, as she usually did.

"Señor don Carlos," said the familiar voice of his servant, knocking softly on the door of the room where our hero had shut himself in.

In a notably altered and irritable voice, Carlos replied, "What do you want, Baldomero?"

"The mailman just left the letters that have come for you from Seville."

The door opened, and Carlos held out a shaky hand to receive the letters. Seeing Luisa's handwriting, which he recognized at first glance on the envelope of one of them, stunned him as much as if he had suddenly seen Luisa herself standing before him, asking him to account for his thoughts. The letter slipped from his hand, and it took him two minutes to work up the courage to pick it up and open it. As soon as he unfolded it, something heavier than paper fell at his feet, and his nerves were such that he was afraid to look for it, as though he sensed that he would find there new cause for sorrow and regrets.

"My beloved Carlos," the poor girl wrote, "I feel sorry for the deep sadness I found in your last letter, and I know that this cruel absence is as painful for you as it is for me."

He slapped his forehead, repeating, "Ah yes, cruel! Very cruel, because it can make me most unhappy!" and he went on reading.

"I think that if this separation goes on longer it will do us both great harm; it will make us very unhappy."

"Very unhappy! Yes," he cried again, "You too, poor angel! No, no! I will not allow it." And with shaking hands and vision dimmed by tears, he continued reading.

"If you could see how changed I am! I am no longer pretty, my husband, because I have lost weight from tearful sorrows, and what you used to call roses of innocence and youth have vanished from my cheeks. But you will return them to me soon, won't you? Along with happiness, you will restore to me beauty and health, because I know that you are as impatient as I to leave that wretched court where you are so bored. Mama tries to convince me that you are not as bored as I think, but I know that there are no pleasures or distractions for you far from your Luisa."

"Pure and sublime faith!" he exclaimed. "May misfortune and shame fall upon the man vile enough to deceive her!" And after two turns around the room, he again picked up the letter.

"The dress you sent me is very pretty, but I will only wear it on the day of your return. However, to show you how grateful I am for your gift, I am reciprocating with another, which you must have seen before you read these lines. Isn't it true that it is more precious than your dress? Give it many kisses, my dear, and keep it on your chest until your wife herself can remove it."

Carlos hastily picked up from the floor the object that had fallen upon opening the letter. It was an ivory with a miniature portrait—the portrait of Luisa! Carlos gazed at it with a hesitant and ardent look. She was so young, so serene, so lovely! She, with her blue eyes beseeching tenderness, inspiring virtue! She with her rosebud mouth, which seemed to be formed expressly to pray and to bless, with her modest bosom covered with three-layered gauze, and her golden hair never defiled by the hand or curling iron of a hairdresser. It was her, his friend, his sister, his wife, the woman of his heart's desire, of his mind's design . . . And yet, he saw it with a kind of chagrin; he held it in his hands without pressing it to his chest or his lips. The awareness of his fault inhibited him at that moment in a way that could be mistaken for coldness. It seemed to him that that silent mouth was scolding him, that fixed look penetrated the depths of his soul, and he threw off the unlucky image with an involuntary movement of terror. He covered his face with his hands and wept like a child.

Then he got up, picked up the portrait, asked it to forgive him with a sad and humble look, kissed it respectfully and kept it more serenely, because he had made a decision: a firm, irrevocable decision, the only one that could reconcile him with himself, and that he must carry out very soon.

This decision will soon be made known to the reader, but for the moment, we would like to return to Catalina's side and reveal what was occurring in that woman's heart, flattering ourselves to have awakened some interest, or at least curiosity, in this. The Countess of S. received her friend in her dressing room, that mysterious sanctuary of coquetry where everything you saw revealed the luxury and pampering of a sultan's wife. At that moment the brilliant foreigner was lying on a sofa in complete disarray, her face revealing profound reflection.

"Catalina," Elvira said softly.

The Countess raised her head and could not suppress a gesture of annoyance upon seeing her friend. "Is it you, Elvira?" she asked, with a forced smile.

Elvira sat down next to her without waiting to be invited, and she said in a sad and serious tone, which did not seem to go with her cheerful, almost childlike features, "Catalina, you seem like a different person over the past few days."

"Do you think so?" the Countess answered, in a would-be comic tone.

"Yes, I think so," Elvira went on, "and what upsets me most is that I can guess the cause."

Catalina did not bat an eye, and threw her friend the regal look that she knew how to assume when she wanted to disconcert an insolent person. But Elvira was not intimidated.

"Yes, Catalina, I now realize that you, the most favored woman in Madrid, who can boast of the most triumphs, the most glorious conquests, the most submissive homages; you, the cold indomitable beauty who mocks the passions you inspire, have succumbed to the whim of overcoming the primitive virtue of a poor lad from the provinces, with no social standing, no refinement, no attraction other than a beauty of which he himself is unaware."

The Countess smiled ironically as Elvira was speaking, like a person who finds herself judged by an incompetent judge, but she inwardly had this thought: "My passion must be visible and striking indeed, if such a shallow and thoughtless woman has noticed it."

Elvira, who had paused for a moment to organize her thoughts, which despite herself were never very sensible or consistent, went on: "And it greatly hurts your pride to see all your attacks founder on the hard crust of that rustic marital fidelity."

The Countess sat up sharply, and assumed a cold, ironic tone. "What? Do you think I am trying to assail that fidelity, that I am the bad angel who has come to tempt virtue? What's more, do you think that my criminal attempts are unfruitful, that I have only gained the humiliation of defeat?"

"No, I just think that you would like to punish a foolish young man who has not paid you homage, compelling him to love you, no doubt later to reject him. That is all that I wished to say. But you know that that young man is not free, that he has a wife, that his love for you would be an insult, not an homage."

"Do you think me capable of finding amusement in causing a rift in a marriage? Do you think I would assail the happiness of two people to satisfy a cheap vain impulse, even in the case that I found such a conquest flattering?"

"But," Elvira observed, beginning to feel confused, "as your conduct with him could be interpreted . . ."

"So what?" said the Countess impetuously.

"So I thought it my duty as your friend to tell you that you are doing wrong to behave that way."

"Is that all?" said Catalina smiling, but without her artificial joviality enabling her to hide the spite that was disturbing her. "As a prudent, conscientious friend, you want to warn me that I am doing wrong in attacking the virtue of your cousin and that that virtue is impregnable?"

"I know that he dearly loves his wife, and that he is not worldly enough to understand your behavior toward him, and that he can interpret it in a way that is offensive to you."

"Has he said anything to you about it?" the Countess asked intently.

"No, but for days I have noticed him feeling discontent, in a bad mood, and just today he spoke of you disparagingly."

"In that case," said the Countess with an irrepressible gesture of anger, "you are very foolish, Elvira, to reproach me for my conduct toward him. If he does not respect me, he must look down on me, and I . . . listen," she added, with a fierce angry look, "I never forgive the scorn of those to whom I cannot return it."

Elvira was almost afraid of her. She had never seen that look or heard that tone from Catalina. Then for the first time in her life, she instinctively realized that violent passions slept in that woman's soul, which she, gay, frivolous, inoffensive creature that she was, could not understand.

The Countess struggled to calm down, and asked her, "When did you talk to Carlos about me today?"

"Before you came to my house."

"Ah!" said Catalina. And that "Ah!" which Elvira did not understand, contained the full triumph of pride, the full satisfaction of the heart. It was when Carlos was offended, jealous, that he had spoken harshly of her. It was before the scene that had made him sure of being loved.

"And since then . . . ?" she asked.

"Since then I have not seen him. I think I am starting to hate that man," Elvira answered simply.

"And do you think that I love him?" Catalina asked, looking at her with a kind of anxious curiosity.

"No; I just think that you would like him to love you."

"And in your view that is impossible."

"I don't know, but in my view that would be a very mean triumph for you and a great misfortune for him."

"A great misfortune for him!" Catalina repeated, and remained thoughtful a moment. Then she raised her head, and her beautiful face looked as clear and pale as usual.

"I appreciate what you have told me, my friend," she said, getting up and taking Elvira by the arm. "You chose your words badly, but I can see your good intention. I assure you that he will not be unhappy on my account . . . I swear it! Come, I want to get dressed to go out for a walk with you. Tonight we are invited to a ball at the home of my rival the Duchess of R., the Marquis's new conquest. You know that I must outshine her."

Elvira embraced the Countess, crying with joy. She had just regained her friend. She saw her once again bright, flirtatious, happy, and she thought with pride, "This is my doing." She skipped along behind her, like a child whose mother has promised him a nice toy, and Catalina looked at her with the tender indulgence of a mother, who makes herself childlike so as to be better understood.

15

Carlos returned home when it was almost dark. He was serious and calm. He had just booked a seat on the stagecoach (at that time recently established in Spain) that was to leave for Seville at dawn. He walked around the room. Then he called for his servant and asked, "Baldomero, is my cousin available?"

"She is not at home, señor. She ate with the Countess, and came just now and left again with her maid and one of her best dresses, because I think she is going to get dressed at the Countess's home and then go with her to a ball."

"That means she won't come back until tomorrow; all the better. Baldomero, something unexpected has come up, and I must leave at dawn for Seville. Since my cousin will be affected by the news, it is better that she not hear about it until she returns from the ball. I would like to ask you to pack my suitcase while I write two farewell letters. One you will give to your mistress tomorrow; the other you will take afterward to the Countess's home."

He sat down and quickly penned some lines in which, on the pretext that a letter from his father had urgently summoned him to return to Seville, he apologized to his cousin for being unable to await her return to say goodbye to her in person, and ended with the usual courtesies in such circumstances.

Then he took another sheet of paper and meditated a long while before starting to write. His serene brow darkened, and his hand was unsteady as he traced the first lines. Several times he left his task and walked nervously around the room; several times he went up to a window as though he needed to inhale the fresh night air.

Finally, as the clock struck midnight he concluded the following letter, which will reveal better than all our observations his state of mind during those hours:

"I am going away, Catalina, I am leaving Madrid, without saying goodbye to you, without expressing all the gratitude you have inspired by your kindness. If I saw you again, I would not have the strength to realize a sacrifice that honor and duty urgently demand. Catalina! When sacred ties that I respect have joined me forever with a pure, innocent girl, worthy of adoration, I would have to be a villain to remain longer near you, the most seductive, irresistible, superior woman who exists. I do not know if it was compassion, a whim, or an unfortunate fellow feeling that impelled you to utter words that have driven me wild, words that would have brought me pride and glory . . . words that would have lifted me to the heights of human happiness if I were free and worthy of you, but that have made me profoundly guilty and unhappy upon recalling my condition, my duties, the iron wall that separates us. Catalina! Until this morning I was unaware of the nature of the feeling you inspire in me. How foolish I was! I did not think it possible to love more than once in life. I thought that a heart bestowed on an object that was worthy in God's eyes would be protected by that same God who had authorized their vows . . . Catalina, I was a fool who did not know myself. No, I did not suspect that my heart could be ungrateful, false, fickle . . . And is it so? Ah, no! Don't believe it, señora; don't scorn me like a cad. I love and worship the angelic woman who for more than a year has made me the happiest man on earth. I have sworn to make her happy, and I would sooner die than betray that sacred trust. But I must flee from you . . . and I flee because your presence has become essential to my life. Because if you did not see in me more than a friend, the least distinguished of the many who surround you, I would suffer cruelly without having the right to complain, and if you loved me . . . you love me! Catalina, what fool would shun such happiness? Forgive me, I don't know what I am saying. If you were in love with me, I would flee from you with greater cause. If that love were for you a passing whim, I would only be unhappy; if it were a passion like mine, we would both be as criminal as we were unfortunate. In any case, we must part, and would to God we had never met! If this decision causes you some pain, please forgive me, Catalina—but no, that will not be the case. At this moment, as I am taking my leave of you forever with an anguished heart, you are dancing, you are collecting tributes from your admirers, you are beautiful and charming to all . . . and all are worth much more than a poor youth like me, with no treasure other than a heart that is no longer his own to give, that cannot be offered to anyone, Catalina! All must be fleeting for one who lives in that tumultuous world of pleasure. Soon, very soon the weak memory of your unhappy friend will be erased from your mind. But as for me, heaven grant that I find in the satisfaction of having filled a sacred duty compensation for having sacrificed an immense happiness. Happiness? I am raving. What is it; where is that happiness? Can it exist in crime? Crime linked with you, Catalina! Crime through your love! Oh, this is impossible. But the hours fly by . . . I am still speaking to you, in the hope that you think of me for a moment. Within a few hours all will be over. Feel for your friend, Catalina, but be happy . . . yes, be happy, and allow me for the first and the last time to say that I love you, that I wish that I were free . . . that I am very unhappy!"

After finishing this letter and giving both to Baldomero, Carlos made the final preparations for his departure and awaited the hour in sad anxiety.

Shortly after two he heard a carriage stop at the front door, and soon after he heard Elvira go up. He listened carefully, fearing his valet might mention something about his departure, but he calmed down upon hearing his cousin say, "Mariana, you weren't expecting me back so soon, were you? Catalina, who was dancing like a madwoman, did not feel well and left, and when she is not at an event I no longer have fun. But come with me to my bedroom; I want to go to bed right away because I am extremely sleepy. It is understandable, because I did not sleep last night and I got up very early—at noon!"

Elvira went on to her room talking to her maid, and soon after the profound silence that reigned in the house informed Carlos that everyone was asleep.

"She danced like a madwoman!" he repeated several times, as leaning on the balcony, his eyes followed the course of some small clouds snatched up by the wind, which at intervals blocked the pale light of the moon. "Everything passes," he added; "everything moves rapidly through that insatiable heart, so rich in emotions, so poor in attachments. So much the better! Oh, Luisa! You will never be able to utter such fine words about feelings, but you understand them better. You cannot dazzle a man with the image of an impossible happiness, but you can make the man you love enjoy it. Oh! I was really unworthy for a few moments, to think that she was more capable than you of an ecstatic, profound love. I will atone for that error through love, veneration, worship."

He left the window and sat fully dressed on the bed, where he could only sit for a few minutes; he could not stay still. He got up again, walked around the room, sat down, picked up a book, put it down and returned to the balcony, and remained in this constant state of agitation until it began to get light and Baldomero came to tell him that it was almost dawn. He had him take his suitcase, gave a long sad look at his cousin's room that held so many memories for him, and left without a sound, with the emotion we always feel upon leaving a place to which we never expect to return.

When he arrived, the stagecoach was ready to depart. His seat was in the berlin, and the coachman said that he had been waiting only for him. He got on right away, wrapped himself in his cloak because the early morning air was very raw, as was usual in Madrid in the month of April, and sank into his seat without saying a word to his only neighbor, who by the scant light of dawn he could tell was a lady.

The stagecoach departed, and Carlos breathed deeply, as though relieved of a heavy burden. The fatigue from several nights of sleeplessness and agitation, the motion of the carriage, the monotonous sound of the bells, the sleepy moisture of the early morning soon made him drowsy, and he fell asleep. Something similar must have happened to his neighbor, because wrapped in a large merino shawl and her head covered with a velvet cap, which she had donned in place of her hat for greater comfort, she leaned forward, resting her elbows on her knees and her head on her hands, and was soon dozing like Carlos.

The sun was already high when the latter awoke. His neighbor had changed position and was almost falling on his shoulder. Carlos did not deny her his support. He moved closer so the traveler's head would rest more easily on his shoulder, and since this was no more than a natural protective gesture that any young man would extend to the weaker sex, he at once leaned his head the other way and abandoned himself to his own ruminations. The stagecoach stopped to change horses without his neighbor's waking up, and not wanting to disturb her he did not get off, as did all the other passengers.

They were already very close to Ocaña, where they were supposed to eat, and the position Carlos was in was starting to make him uncomfortable so he was thinking how to free himself from the weight of his neighbor's head, when she stirred a little as though she was starting to wake up, and she muttered some words among which Carlos thought he made out his name.

The woman in fact woke up. She sat up, and her eyes naturally turned toward the man from whose shoulder she had raised her head. A scream rose at once from both of their chests:

"Carlos!"

"Catalina!"

16

The stagecoach was entering Ocaña, and the two travelers, who were devouring each other with their eyes, had still not managed to sort out what stroke of chance had brought them together. Their first words to each other said nothing, clarified nothing.

"You, here, Catalina?"

"Carlos, is it you? Is it really you I am seeing, or is my imagination, my eyes, my heart playing tricks on me?"

"Oh, Catalina! So we are still seeing each other, talking to each other!"

And they fell silent, pressing each other's hands with warmth. There are feelings in life that one cannot understand or explain at the moment of experiencing them. You relish them in silence, without trying to examine them; you do not seek their origin or foresee their consequences. It seems that the least effort, or the slightest touch, so to speak, will spoil their charm, so we abandon ourselves without trying to explain them. The Countess and Carlos asked each other nothing, said nothing. They were together; they were happy at that moment; they did not care to know how or why.

But the stagecoach stopped at a roadside inn, and the travelers hurried off to move their stiff limbs. Carlos got off, took the Countess's arm, and requesting one room went in with her, not caring what his travel companions would think of that act. He strongly needed to be alone with her, to see her, to hear her, to savor a joy that half an hour earlier he thought he would be deprived of forever.

When he was alone with her, he threw himself at her feet. "Catalina, Catalina! Is it chance, heaven, or hell that has reunited us? Catalina!" he repeated in fits of pleasure and pain, "Did you decide to follow me? Is it your will, your heart that has thrown you into my arms when I was fleeing, when I was sacrificing myself to a despotic duty? Catalina! Speak, speak, for God's sake!"

"You were fleeing from me!" she cried with a gesture of surprise. "What? Weren't you in the stagecoach to thwart my cruel plan? Didn't you discover the news of my voyage and its reasons? Carlos, explain it to me; I don't understand it at all."

"Ah, Catalina! I do, yes! I'm starting to understand . . . And if that is the case, see the power of an inexorable destiny. Oh, my Lord! This will make me fall into a blind fatalism. Catalina! I left Madrid to flee from you, because I love you! I love you madly! And I don't have the right to offer you my heart! I fled from you because it was my duty, and a letter that was to be delivered to you several hours after my departure would have revealed to you the fulfillment and the magnitude of my sacrifice."

"You are right," she said after a moment of silence; "there is a destiny. There is a fatality more powerful than human will. Carlos, I too left a letter for you in Madrid, but I kept the draft . . . in my purse. Read it."

Carlos took the paper that she handed him, and going up to a window anxiously perused it, as the Countess, resting in an armchair, looked drained with weariness or emotion. The letter read as follows:

"Farewell forever, Carlos! I do not have the cruel strength to destroy your happiness, or to conquer mine. Today Elvira uttered words that sealed my fate. Upon learning that I was loved, I forgot everything—everything! even the insuperable obstacle that divides us. The voice of friendship came to arouse me from such a dangerous dream, crying out to me: 'He is happy and virtuous—do you want to be at once the assassin of his joy and of his virtue?' Oh no, never! Carlos, I want to earn your respect, since I am not allowed to earn your love.

"I own some property in a town in La Mancha, and I am going to stay there the whole time you remain in Madrid. I long for solitude, and I hope it will afford my spirit the rest I seek in vain in big-city life. I have tried to daze my heart with the parties and pleasures I have devoted myself to for the past four years. I have come to realize that the remedies I have used to cure my ill only make it worse.

"I have not told anyone my decision, which I made this morning. It is now three in the morning, and I am still in my ball gown. I heard people around me say, 'How happy she is!' when I was dancing with a smile on my lips and death in my heart! Because for me death is not seeing you. It is renouncing forever . . . Carlos, adios! Be happy, and if some day you hear that I am too, don't deny it, but know that it is impossible."

After reading the letter he went up to her, and grasping her hands in a kind of despair he said, "Now you see that we have both tried to sacrifice ourselves on the altar of virtue, but virtue has not accepted our sacrifice. We tried to flee, and we are reunited in spite of ourselves. Catalina! I love you and we are still together. Happiness or misfortune, virtue or crime! Tell me what you wish. My fate is in your hands."

"We will separate!" she cried, struggling with herself. "We will not be overcome by a whim of fate. We will separate, Carlos, and not without the joy of a final tender farewell. We still have before us sweet hours of closeness and affection. We will travel together like two friends, like brother and sister. In La Mancha we will part, and the memory of these final moments of joy borne of chance will long fill my solitude." And leaning toward him, she shed in his hands many tears.

Carlos gazed at her with the ardor of a repressed love. His look held a strange blend of the lover's frenzy and the child's timidity. He looked handsome in that inner struggle which gave his face a particular expression, and in which any woman would have read that life still held many new and unknown sensations for that heart.

If the conquest of a wild or worldly heart is flattering to a woman, it is also pleasing to possess a young impassioned soul, who recklessly throws her all the treasures of his tenderness and dreams. Carlos's love held these two attractions, and was satisfying for both reasons. It was a triumph to overcome at once his pride and his virtue, and there was still in his passion that inexplicable charm, that divine fragrance of respect, submission, and purity that women who are loved by "men of the world" sorely miss.

Catalina was inhaling with delight the fragrance of such a pure, although guilty, love. Carlos was by her side, holding her in his arms, and did not even touch with his lips the locks of hair that brushed his face. At that moment she felt so happy that it did not seem possible to her to be guilty.

"Carlos," she said, closely fixing on him her bewitching eyes, "the virtue that condemns such a pure joy is a cruel virtue."

"Well then," he answered, with the rash impassioned resolution of a young heart, "if virtue condemns us, let her punish us! Aren't these moments worth a lifetime of atonement?"

"And why slander our hearts, believing them to be incapable of noble, pure feelings?" said Catalina. "What is love? Isn't it the most involuntary and the most beautiful of the human emotions? They say adultery is a crime, but there is no adultery for the heart. Man can be held responsible for his acts, but not for his feelings. Why is it a crime for you to love me? Can you only feel for me an adulterous, criminal love? Couldn't you love me, not as one loves a wife, not as one loves a sweetheart, but rather with an intense chaste love, purified by sacrifice, with the love that must be felt by souls in heaven? Couldn't you do this, Carlos?"

"Oh, yes!" he answered excitedly. "I would spend my life at your feet getting drunk on a look, a word, a smile. I would watch over your sleep as you slept in my arms, and you would awaken as pure as the light of dawn. Yes, Catalina, give me the joy of living by your side without crime, and I will ask for nothing more; I will be happy. Happy with all possible earthly happiness!"

"And I would too, Carlos! Ah no, my heart would never ask you to abandon your duties. The happiness you gave your wife would heighten mine, and the more just, noble, virtuous your conduct, the more I would consider my affection justified. Would your virtues make you less lovable in my eyes?

"Oh, Carlos! The most fortunate one, the one with the most honorable virtues may be your wife, but she is not the proudest. Your friend, who does not have the right to adorn herself with those virtues, would adore them in her heart of hearts, and she would be content to reward them with a look that only you could understand and relish."

"Quiet, quiet, for God's sake," he cried, pressing her hands on his pounding heart. "Be quiet, because you're driving me mad. Catalina, beloved woman! Yes, the love you feel, the love you inspire, is not subject to general laws. Your sublime soul uplifts it and purifies it. So do not talk of our separating. Be my friend, my sister, but never leave me."

A rough voice shouted at the door. "On board, señores! All on board!"

"Catalina!"

"Carlos!"

"Do you agree?"

"I love you."

"I promise that you will never regret it."

"Señores, on board! On board!" the coachman repeated.

Carlos opened the door. "Coachman, the two travelers who were in the berlin carriage are leaving it free and at your disposal. Please take down our luggage."

"Carlos . . . what now?"

"Now to Madrid, because now that I am happy I am no longer sad; I have no more remorse or concerns or jealousy . . . Now I will share in your pleasures, follow your triumphal carriage, join the chorus of your admirers. Shine, enjoy, be adored, but keep for your friend that look, that smile which must be his one happiness on earth."

"But," she said, "couldn't we both stay in La Mancha . . . ?"

Carlos looked at her with an expression that made her understand what he did not dare to say.

"It is true," she said, taking his hand; "we are better off in Madrid. But wherever we are, my friend, even in the depths of solitude, I will vouch for your heart and mine."

"I can always vouch for my heart, Catalina," he replied, grasping her in his arms, "but not for my reason. I have sworn to be worthy of your sublime, chaste love; leave me the means to fulfill it."

"Do what you will," she said; "my life is yours."

17

"Three months! It's three months today since I last saw him!" said the sad Luisa, leaning her blond head on her hands, sitting before a small night table on which were spread some letters from Carlos. "And he does not talk of returning!" she went on, sitting up and looking for the last letter she had received. "Nothing! He says nothing that can give me hope!"

And she picked up the letter, commenting on it as she read:

"Dear Luisa: What you say about the condition of our esteemed mother causes me the greatest sadness, and I regret being unable to share in the attentions you lavish on the dear patient."

"He regrets it! So why doesn't he come? My God! Is all the wealth in the world worth the sadness of being separated for three months from those one loves?"

"I have still not completed the business that is keeping me in Madrid, because the accounts of the deceased are in such a muddle that all of my efforts and those of the executors have not been enough to disentangle them."

"And yet a month ago he said that it would all be done soon!"

"Some days ago I decided to return home, and I told this to my uncle's executors, proposing that upon my arrival I would tell my father to name a representative who was more suited than I am for this task. But after two days of reflection, I realized that it did not make sense to hand it over to mercenaries after having come, and that my father might not approve . . . so I finally returned to the executors to tell them that I had changed my mind."

"Oh, how easy it was for him to change his mind! . . . but the fear of displeasing our father! . . . And yet, he is so good! Yes, he would have forgiven him. I am going to talk to him today about this; I will throw myself at his feet and beg him to let my husband return to our side. I'll do it; I am resolved. For goodness' sake! Will I never have the courage to tell him that I am unhappy?"

And the poor girl cried, sobbing bitterly for quite a while.

Whether by chance or by design, the sobbing increased to such a degree that upon leaving his sister's room and crossing a hallway adjacent to the room where Luisa was, don Francisco heard her, and the good gentleman rushed in, calling out to her in alarm, "Luisa! Luisita! Where are you?"

"Here," she muttered. "Here I am . . ."

"My child, what's wrong? What's bothering you?" her uncle exclaimed, coming up with paternal affection and lifting her head to see her pretty face bathed in tears.

"What's wrong?" she stammered, with a childish gesture as if to say, "You know perfectly well!"

"What did Carlos write you, my child? Did he give you some cause for complaint? Tell me, Luisita; it's your father who is asking you." And the old man, sitting beside her, took her on his knees.

"Complaint! No, he's not the one I should complain of . . ."

"Then who is it, my dear? Who has offended you? Who could offend you!"

"No one . . . but he cannot return without your orders . . . and you don't give that order . . . and it has been three months since I saw him—three months! And it will go on like this . . . poor me!"

And the tears and sobs started up again, and the good man could do nothing to stop them, for all his cuddling and caressing.

"You don't love me!" Luisa responded periodically, going on like this.

Finally don Francisco took the letter she had read for the twentieth time a moment before, and upon arriving at the paragraph in which his son spoke of not leaving the court out of fear of displeasing him, his paternal pride made him forget Luisa's tears for a moment.

"So," he cried, "he has done well! This shows that my efforts have not been in vain. Carlos is a respectful, obedient son, which is hard to come by these days. I should take pride in this. For all that my sister goes on that if he is good it is due to his own nature, not to the upbringing I have given him, I will always maintain that no soil, no matter how good, yields the best fruit without being carefully cultivated."

"But if he is a good son, you should not be a cruel father," said Luisa with a boldness that was so out of keeping with her usual behavior that it took don Francisco aback.

"Me, a cruel father!" he exclaimed, after a moment of silence. "What do you mean, Luisita?" And the distressed girl threw herself at his feet, asking for pardon, with a humility that touched him.

"I don't know what I'm saying," she said; "I know that everything you do must be fair and good, but I am suffering so much! I haven't seen him for so long! I will die very soon if things go on like this."

And resting her head on her uncle's knees, she abandoned herself to her grief.

We have already seen that don Francisco was a man who could not long resist pleas and tears. He raised Luisa up, kissed her on her pretty eyelids swollen with tears, asked for pen and paper, and on the same night table that held his son's letters wrote these lines: "Carlos: You can come home whenever you like, because I will appoint someone who is better equipped than you to deal with such entanglements. Your wife impatiently awaits you, and your father is pleased with you and wants to give you a hug."

He handed the paper to Luisa, who upon reading it cried with joy as much as she had earlier cried with sadness. Her Papa hugged her and left, advising her to calm down.

Luisa was overjoyed, but she did not jump for joy or show her happiness through those childish extremes appropriate to her seventeen years, but rather, ever shy and religious, the girl kneeled to give thanks to the Virgin for the favor she no doubt owed her. Then she wrote a long and enchanting letter to her husband, and upon returning to her mother's side she was more tender, more humble, more angelic than ever, because in that kind, innocent soul, happiness was like a divine fragrance that was felt by all those around her.

18

No one in Madrid except Elvira knew about the departure of the Countess and of Carlos, or about their return. Elvira herself was not informed of the details of that sudden voyage and sudden return; but she was no longer the only one who knew of Catalina's love. Upon her return to Madrid, Catalina appeared with Carlos at theaters and promenades, without making any mystery of her attachment. That woman, so extreme in everything and proud to the point of believing herself capable of prevailing over or scorning public opinion, had never learned or wished to practice the art of pretense; and Carlos was still too bewildered by his own defeat to think about social conventions. For him the big step was already taken. He had offered and accepted a guilty love; he had forfeited in his heart his severe moral principles; he had betrayed his wife and perjured himself before God. To not feel regrets he had to avoid thinking about anything, and he himself urged the Countess on and led her from one party to the next, trying to intoxicate himself to the point of losing the power to think.

Catalina, rash and exultant in her triumph, while fearful of losing it, deceived herself with her showy sophisms to convince herself that she was not betraying her virtue as long as she did not forfeit her honor; and the more she strove to deserve Carlos's respect and affection, the more she felt justified, as though stealing the heart of Luisa's husband were not the most terrible and irreparable wrong she could do to the unfortunate young woman. And yet, she was naturally kind and understanding. Her great flaw, as she herself had told Carlos, consisted in that her keen imagination magnified or diminished everything to the extreme; and the most outlandish theories seemed possible to that woman who was capable of the most sublime endeavors, and of the most deplorable aberrations, but for whom there was no happy medium.

She knew well that Carlos's eagerness to revel in every worldly distraction arose from the fear of being alone with himself. She understood the power held by duty over that noble and upright heart, duties that he was abandoning for her sake, and always wary of a remorse that would have wounded both her pride and her heart, she skillfully supported his efforts to forget his crime.

She had never looked so beautiful, so magnificent and splendid. She constantly gave parties where she put on display for Carlos's benefit her good taste, her elegance and wealth. She often intoxicated him with her magical talents; her admirable voice sounded sweeter and more expressive when she sang with him or in his presence. When she danced, she was a sylph who seemed to leave earth to wander through the air. When she rode on horseback and Carlos went out riding with her, he noticed that everyone's eyes were bent on the elegant Amazon, who made a proud Andalusian horse champ at the bit, seemingly impatient at being mastered by the delicate hand of a woman. If Carlos talked about painting, Catalina painted ingenious allegories and handsome heads that all resembled him. If he praised the beauties of nature, she organized a country outing, and they went with a small select group to spend sweet relaxed days in the most picturesque spots.

In short, if she found him for a moment restrained and distrustful of her affection, she proved to him its strength through a thousand passionate indiscretions. If, on the other hand, she suspected that he was starting to take his happiness for granted, she aroused his unease through clever, fine flirtations. She was sweet, tender, and obedient when appropriate, and haughty, ardent, and domineering when necessary. All in all, she was the antithesis of the woman who had made Carlos happy for eighteen months, and the only one who could enthrall him to the point of making him forget her.

Thus it had been two months since the day when Carlos returned to Madrid with the Countess, and in all that time the thought of leaving her had not once entered his mind. Despite himself, he found himself chained by Catalina's side. He could no longer conceive of living without her: without her talents, which beguiled him, without her pleasures, which dazzled him, without her reckless passion, which drove him wild, and even without her flirtations, which infuriated him. He needed all these new and varied emotions so as not to feel the void caused by the innocent happiness he had lost, and if he was still not criminal enough to deny his fault, he was by now too weak to wish to examine it.

More than a month had gone by since he had received permission from his father to return to Seville; he did not even dare to speak of this to the Countess. He gave various excuses to postpone his departure from Madrid, and when a tender, plaintive letter from Luisa reminded him that it was now by his will alone that they were still separated, it almost seemed to him cruel of the poor innocent girl to ask of him a sacrifice that would cost him so much.

His letters were now shorter and less natural; they all came down to justifying with childish reasons his ongoing stay in Madrid, and assuring her of his loyalty, his constancy, and the tender love he professed for his wife.

And he did in fact love her; yes, he still loved her, as the most tender brother can love his sister. But oh! it was no longer she who held the key to his heart. It was no longer she who had the power to make him rave with passion, or rage with jealousy. In short, she was no longer the woman with whom he was in love.

19

Malice and envy, which often dog lofty, brilliant people, in the same way, as a poet observed, that lightning always seeks out towers, could applaud the Countess's indiscretion, especially as Catalina, in some sense confirming the unfavorable opinions of her, seemed to give up any means of self-defense and yield like a resigned victim. However, as she had never been more generous with her wealth, more gay and open than now, the same people who cruelly shattered her reputation eagerly sought out her pleasures, and while the number of her enemies increased day by day, so did the number of her flatterers. Slander is like a cowardly dog, who barks from afar at those who approach him disdainfully and pounces and vents his rage on those who run from him in fear.

Elvira, who was hearing every day the gossip that was circulating to her friend's discredit, was not a woman of strong enough mettle to rein in the talk; the timid but sincere friend was content to wound her critics behind their backs, without daring to tell them off face-to-face. However, she did not neglect to inform Carlos of all that was being said, and even timidly scolded Catalina from time to time for her lack of concern for her reputation; but there was something about that woman that intimidated Elvira, and she had such a strong influence on a weak, frivolous nature that even the Countess's excesses seemed somehow respectable in her friend's eyes. She seemed so above public opinion that Elvira was afraid of looking ridiculous if she seemed to fear it, and the friend finally decided that she should not go to the trouble of defending the Countess against what the latter deemed an incompetent judge.

This was not the case for Carlos; he suffered terribly upon learning that the Countess's love for him gave society new arms against her, and his violent indignation could barely be contained by the fear of doing her greater harm by taking it upon himself to avenge her. The wild intoxication with which for two months he had indulged in worldly pleasures and seen his beloved shine was quickly fading. When he accompanied her to a gathering, he could not take part in the joy and self-assurance with which she presented herself. He spied out the looks of everyone around her, he listened with alarm to every nearby conversation, always wary of the aim of insulting Catalina, and always interpreting the least evidence at its worst. Without suspecting her in the least, he felt day by day more wary of anything that could relate to the Countess, and his love and his pride were equally up in arms at the thought that the woman who was now mistress of his life would not be respected by all.

Day by day Catalina watched Carlos's declining happiness. In vain did she provide parties to distract him; and in vain did she exhaust her magical eloquence to instill in him scorn for the society she flaunted. Carlos did not share her opinions on this point, and the more he loved her, the more sensitive he was to the world's view of her. But if Catalina could not inspire in him her indifference to public opinion, he could not help but convey to her his sadness.

"Carlos," she said one night when both of them were about to leave for a ball, and at a moment when his irritation was painted on his face, "I think we had better not go to the ball."

"But you wanted to so much!" he answered with a sad smile.

"I thought you would enjoy it, but I see now that I was wrong." And taking from her hair her lovely crown of pearls, she threw it far off and fell onto a sofa in tears.

Carlos looked at her a moment in silence. Then he said, "Catalina, I am a poor wretch who has only appeared in your flowery path to sow thorns. Your life of triumphs was no doubt very beautiful, but despite myself I cannot follow in your path."

"Carlos!" she exclaimed, fixing on him an anxious look, "Are you by chance jealous? Ah, if so, for heaven's sake tell me, and you will lift a terrible weight from my heart."

"Jealous? Yes I am, and surely will be jealous! Jealous of your talent, of your beauty, of the happiness you do not owe to me. Yes, I am jealous, even of the wind that blows your hair, of the inanimate object your eyes happen to rest on. But that is not what is tormenting me, what makes me hate men and want to tear you away from a society that I curse."

"Tell me, tell me then!" she cried, reaching out to him with pleading hands.

Carlos grasped both hands, and with a look full of passion said, "How beautiful you are! How could you not excite envy? Oh! If I could take you in my arms, press you to my heart, and introduce you with the words, 'Here she is, my wife, the woman of my heart's desire,' then I would defy the world, I would be happy, because I would have the right to adorn myself with your love, to take pride in my good fortune. But wretch that I am! My sterile love can do nothing for you, and I am condemned to give you in return for your affection only the world's persecution, perhaps discredit and shame. Oh, my heart's beloved! Can you ask me to be happy?"

Upon finishing these words he sat down beside her, hiding his face in his hands so she would not see two tears that, in spite of himself, were running down his cheeks. But it was too late; she had already devoured them with her gaze. It was the first time she saw Carlos cry. And what woman ignores the power of a man's tears, when he is loved? They say a woman's tears are all-powerful, but how much more omnipotent are a man's tears! Weeping borne of weakness can move us, but such weeping is natural, easy, frequent. But when a tear dampens a masculine face, when force and pride momentarily give way to sensitivity and tenderness, the emotion one feels is profound, unfathomable. It contains a mixture of sadness and pleasure, of fear and assurance. The emotion that makes a man cry is a feeling whose nobility intimidates the woman who beholds it, but she takes pride in her power to produce it.

The Countess, overcome by this emotion, was about to throw herself at her lover's feet. He took her in his arms and pressed her to his chest. "Catalina," he said, "we must both make a terrible sacrifice. My appearing with you everywhere only fuels the malice that is raging against you. I am starting to understand that pretense is the most necessary art for those who live in society, and only appearances constitute virtue or crime. So we must be slaves to this."

"And what do I care?" she cried vehemently. "What do I care about the respect or scorn of a society that mainly consists of fools and rogues? Good grief! Is it necessary to don the mask of a hypocrite, to degrade one's character, debase one's feelings to earn a glance from a world we scorn?"

"Oh!" he answered with a bitter smile, "we should not scorn it as long as we need it."

"So let's renounce it forever."

"Catalina!"

"Yes, we must. As of today I want to free myself from the world; I want to lead a quiet, obscure life. The only homage I aspire to is yours; my only pleasure consists in gazing at you, my sole joy in being loved by you. Carlos, as long as that happiness brightens my days, the entire world cannot give me a moment of sorrow, and if I lose it . . ."

"Oh, be quiet! I cannot give you happiness—no! And it is that thought that torments me even during the sweetest moments of my life. But my love is yours, yours as long as I exist, yours if you accept it, yours if you reject it—yours forever, my friend!" And the foolish man swore false oaths, and what's more, the impassioned Catalina, even more foolish, erected her future happiness on those rotten foundations.

From that day on there were no more gatherings at the Countess's home. Her social life was reduced to a small number of friends, and she and her lover were alone most of the day. They loved their new situation at first. What long and intimate conversations! How many hours of delightful solitude! Each lived entirely for the other. Their thoughts were in perfect harmony. They achieved that closeness that is the strongest bond of love, when it does not destroy it. That habit of seeing each other, of telling each other everything, which sometimes survives love, and which when it is lost leaves a void in the heart greater than love itself.

For Carlos this was a new situation. With the sweet and simple Luisa, private life had more softness than charm. The Countess had the rare talent of giving color to a uniform life. The more her conversation was open and spontaneous, the more it was pleasant and seductive. She knew how to evade boredom by constantly bringing into play her talents or her heart, and it almost exasperated Carlos that she had so many charms with which to captivate him, while he believed his only resource was his love.

And yet, his modesty deceived him on this point. The Countess's passion grew day by day, and the intensity of her love frightened her. Carlos was unlike any other man who had loved her. She certainly could not ask for the ardent and wholehearted passion of that young soul from those courtiers with stale hearts and petty ideas; nor was there any resemblance between the insipid gallantry of those salon beaux and the continuous, although sometimes silent, homage of a repressed love. Carlos was certainly not one of those conceited men who crop up everywhere, always vain and self-confident, eager for courtly triumphs as the only fame they can aspire to, nor was he in the ranks of those unhappy lovers who are more concerned about being lovers than lovable, and who are too irritating from the start to be tolerated until one gets to know them.

Always worthy and sincere, now yielding to the feeling that mastered him, now fighting against it with all the strength of his reason, Carlos was by nature the kind of person designed to captivate the Countess. He was irresistible in his ravings and respectable in his resistance. He showed the whole power of his passion, while at the same time inspiring such a high idea of his virtue that it prevented her from ever having complete confidence in the former.

Catalina loved him madly; she loved him because he was worthy of her love, and perhaps also because she was not supposed to love him. She considered herself unfortunate that her capricious destiny had brought her the only man she had ever really loved when he was already bound to another by the closest ties. The impossibility of being happy by rightfully belonging to him constantly poisoned her heart, and she lamented her fate. But she deceived herself in attributing her unhappiness to blind fate. If each of us could judge himself impartially, he would often avoid the trouble of looking outside himself for the causes of his misfortune.

Catalina's nature was such that she could not greatly enjoy an easily won happiness, and could only grow attached to those goods that she could not be sure, or perhaps even have the hope, of attaining. An insatiable need for emotion constantly devoured her fiery soul. During her early years it had been fueled by feverish dreams of a love she did not yet know; then with the disappointments of a world and a life that gave her nothing she had asked of them, but offered in exchange the sharp sensations of frustrated hopes and vanished illusions. Later, proud triumphs, flirtatious projects concocted by design and necessity, the pride of knowing how to deceive a world of which she had been the victim, persuading it that she was happy in spite of them all; the benefits she spread around like a fragrance that only she could exude; all of this still stirred up emotions that day by day, it is true, were growing fainter and less capable of satisfying her, but that kept her from the calm of inaction that meant death to this extremely volatile and stormy personality.

Passion, and a hapless passion, finally came to bring her a new life, and this passion that made her deeply unhappy nonetheless placed that woman in her natural element, and led her to fulfill her destiny. That passion which is always the same in essence had all the varied facets needed by a sensibility that was hyperactive and prone to tedium. The great passions, like everything truly great, are immutable in essence and variable in their aspects. Like the sky, now blue and splendid, now covered with clouds, like the sea, sometimes looking like a dreary plain, sometimes like a steep mountain, passion holds within itself its own opposite, and if it lasts long, it is surely due to its continual variety.

20

If the Countess's love grew more ardent day by day, it was also day by day more unhappy. That woman who keenly relished a moment's happiness, whose philosophy consisted in impulsiveness and indiscretion, was suddenly assailed by a new form of torment, and during her sweetest moments with Carlos, the thought that that joy could not last aroused her passion while shattering her soul. "He is not free! He has a homeland, a family, a wife!" Catalina thought every minute of the day. "He must return to them—he must! And I . . . my Lord! What will become of me when I no longer see him?"

And she resolved many times to follow him to Seville, to live in the city where he lived, to give up everything for him. But then she recalled that in that city, which was foreign to her, where she would follow him only by trampling on her reputation and renouncing her free, brilliant life, she would find a rival adorned with a spotless name, a rival young, lovely, and pure, to whom would belong the man for whom she would sacrifice herself, who would have the honored title of his wife, and whom he would make it his duty to protect and love, while his unhappy lover would only have as the reward for immense sacrifices and humiliating sorrows a tender word uttered in solitude, which he would condemn himself for as a crime. Oh! How different theory is from practice! When Catalina had described to Carlos the supreme happiness she would enjoy just from loving and being loved by him in their heart of hearts; when she assured her lover that his domestic virtues and the happiness he gave his spouse would make him more lovable in her eyes and would also exalt her; when she declared herself generous enough to leave all the honor to her rival, contenting herself with a secret glance or smile from her lover, was she shamelessly lying or was she deceiving herself? Yes, of course she was deceiving herself—and doesn't everyone fool himself who in the grip of an ill-fated passion tries to live out the brilliant theories inspired by his raving dreams? That is why you rarely find in passionate temperaments the worthy quality known as consistency.

The Countess was now far from the heroism she believed herself capable of at the start of her relationship with Carlos. She constantly trembled over the expected announcement of his departure, because whether she followed him or remained behind, she was convinced that that moment would seal her life's unhappiness. She could neither conceive of the idea of living without Carlos, nor still less that of seeing him live with another. The terrible emotion of jealousy was germinating in her heart, and there were moments when death looked appealing to her. She was no longer the brilliant Countess of S., nor even the gifted woman who invented means to keep her lover. Her pale complexion; her expression, now at a fever pitch, now listless and demoralized; her uneven moods; her nervous movements; her absentmindedness when Carlos was not at her side—all revealed the agonizing secret that was oppressing her more each day.

But if she was suffering, in truth Carlos was no happier than his beloved. His passion was consuming him; he was a man after all and in vain did he try to forget it. If remorse for his fault at times faded from his heart, it was because the suffering from a thwarted passion made him so unhappy that it seemed to him to be atonement enough. Drawn by his heart to the Countess's side, they spent days and days together in the closest, most dangerous intimacy, and each time he withdrew from her feeling more in love and more unhappy. When everyone believed him to be in tranquil possession of Catalina, he was going through the torture of a passion that was constantly inflamed and never satisfied. His own resistance had flagged more than once with Catalina, but it seemed that the man's weakness had strengthened the woman's pride.

There was something unfathomable to Carlos himself in the long resistance of that rash and impassioned creature. He could not understand why she sacrificed her good fortune and her reputation for the sake of love, only to subject that same love to an eternal struggle. Most women are restrained by the fear of public disapproval; but in Catalina's case, what did she respect when she threw at the feet of the idol of her guilty love everything her sex most prizes?

In reasoning this way, Carlos was ignoring the power of pride, the great pride that is a law unto itself. Yes, the Countess's only champions were pride and love. She knew that her resistance ennobled her, and she enjoyed buying that apparent heroism at the cost of both of their happiness. She would have succumbed if she had loved him less and if Carlos's esteem were not so vital to her. But when she loved him enough to sacrifice for him her triumphs, her pleasures, her reputation and her peace of mind, when for the sake of love she was making herself his slave, she needed to be admired, respected, and loved. She enjoyed offering him every sacrifice except the one that might appear to give her happiness, and preferring to see her lover suffer than to see his passion fade, she found the secret of her virtue in a feeling of egoism, which was nonetheless the best kind of egoism possible, and which could be given much rarer and more exalted names.

Her hope was not disappointed; Carlos was unhappy—although he might have been more so if she had been less virtuous—but he did not complain or dare to blame her. In his eyes Catalina was an exceptional being whom he idolized more and more, and he was almost glad to find her so great and so superior that it was impossible to stop loving her.

One always finds weakness in the sacrifices made by a woman who is overcome by love, so it is natural that she inspires pity more than admiration. But if a woman who subordinates everything to her passion at the same time masters that passion strengthened by her sacrifices, through sheer willpower, we admire her as much as we feel for her. In that case we do not see her as the weak blind victim of a crazy love; we see woman in all her dignity and all her self-denial.

Was Catalina unaware of this? We do not know. And if the reader wants to see her resistance as pure virtue, he is free to feel assured of this. But if those who think that all human virtue is rooted in egoism (in other words, self-interest) insist that it is due to egoism and pride that our heroine does not wish to acquire the label of a common woman, neither would we feel obliged to contradict them.

21

It was the sixth of July. The morning had been hot, and the afternoon no less so. As a result, the elegant set from Madrid rushed to the Prado, saying they went to get some fresh air. There was a long line of carriages, and the salon was filled with perfumed hair covered with transparent veils, slender waistlines, and polished footwear, because the year was 1819 and we had still not adopted the exotic fashion of dresses with trains. Close to nightfall, there appeared in a light carriage, a vehicle that was uncommon in Spain at that time, the Countess of S. and her friend Elvira de Sotomayor. It had been more than two months since they were seen in any public place together.

"Who are those women?" asked a Marquise to another great lady who was accompanying her in her carriage.

"If I am not mistaken, the Countess of S. and her inseparable."

"Oh! Has the Frenchwoman come out again into the light of day? Has she left her last Adonis?"

"He might be on horseback . . . but no, I don't see him."

"But my dear, I think you are wrong; that is not Catalina of S."

"It is certainly her, but she is as thin as a rail. What has become of her so lauded beauty?"

"Her last love must have worn her out." And the women smiled.

Several such dialogues arose upon seeing the Countess, but she did not seem to care much about the stir caused by her presence, and her face radiated a strange and sad brightness, like that caused by a fever. She was talking to Elvira without looking around her.

"Yes, my dear, that is the reason for my coming to the Prado, and tomorrow I will give a ball, and the next day and the next forever . . . I want to return to life!"

"You want to return to life," Elvira commented sadly, "and you are letting yourself die? If you could see how pale, how washed-out you look! Catalina, I feel sorry for you!"

"Sorry! . . ."

And her mouth took on her old disdainful and ironic smile; but then her eyes filled with tears, and she added with deep bitterness, "I surely deserve it! Telling me that he absolutely had to leave . . ."

"So the boor told you that?"

"Yes, that his mother, that is, the mother of . . . that woman they married him to, is very ill; that his father strongly orders him to leave Madrid . . . In short, that he is leaving and that I . . . I should not go with him!"

"Well, what did you expect?"

"I wanted to go with him, as his sister, as his friend, as his lady or as his slave . . . Yes, I wanted to."

"My God!" Elvira exclaimed, staring in terror at the Countess, who went on, "You don't know how much I love him! You cannot conceive of a passion like mine."

"But tell me, have you seen him today?"

"I haven't seen him since yesterday . . . maybe he has already left . . . what difference does it make? Didn't I tell him yesterday that I hated him, that our ties were broken, that I was going to forget him?"

"You told him that, Catalina?"

"So what? Do you disapprove? Do you know that I had kneeled before him, bathed in tears, begging him not to desert me? Do you know that I fainted twice at his feet? And the wretch, oh! the wretch repeated, 'I cannot!'"

"And then . . ."

"Then I hated him! I told him that I abhorred him and that I should abhor him. Have you seen him today?"

"No. Since he moved out of my house, I don't see him often."

"Maybe he has already gone . . . Elvira! I must know . . . to . . . to die! Because this is impossible!"

"My God! What's wrong, Catalina!. . . . Driver, go quickly to my house."

The Countess was in terrible distress. Elvira held her hands, and the carriage sped to her house. But before arriving there, it had to pass in front of the house where Carlos was living, and despite her turmoil Elvira noticed this and said, "And that stupid driver had to come this way!"

The Countess heard this, and her face lit up with a strange expression. She pulled on the cord while haughtily ordering the carriage to stop, and as soon as it did she dashed out before Elvira had the time or the nerve to stop her. Given the situation, all she could do was to follow her.

She entered the house where Carlos lived and ran up the stairs, but upon arriving at the door to his room she stopped, breathless and pale, and she would have fallen had Elvira not held her in her arms. Two or three minutes passed without Catalina having the will or desire to pull the bell cord, and she might have finally given in to her friend's pleas to return to the carriage without going in, when the door abruptly opened and Carlos's servant appeared on the threshold. Upon recognizing the Countess, he cried, "I was just going to your home."

The Countess asked with extreme anxiety, "Why? Why were you going to my home?"

"Señora, please don't take it badly; I was alone and the master is so ill that he doesn't recognize me and keeps talking nonsense, so . . ."

Elvira tried in vain to restrain the Countess, who rushed into the room calling out to her lover. By the time she could catch up with her, she found her kneeling by Carlos's bed. He was in the grip of a raging fever, with delirium painted on his contorted features and in his burning eyes. The Countess kissed his hands and called him by the most tender names. The patient's agitation seemed to subside upon hearing her voice, and he sought out Catalina, who held him in her arms.

"I'm here; I am Catalina, your lover. I am here to live or die with you, Carlos, my Carlos!" And she kissed his hair and his burning forehead.

Carlos recognized her, but his words were so incoherent that the Countess, grief-stricken, was close to fainting.

Elvira, who on this occasion showed a presence of mind that she did not seem capable of, succeeded in making her friend understand that what the patient needed was care, not tears, and when she found her more willing to act sensibly, immediately sent the Countess's carriage to find her doctor, and managed to get information from the servant about Carlos's illness. The servant said that two days earlier his master had received a letter from Seville that disturbed him; that since then he had been worried and preoccupied, and last night he had run out like a madman without even his hat; that the servant had run to take it to him and had reached him when he was close to the Countess's house. That his master returned very late, and that from the moment he saw him he knew he was unwell. He heard him up all night, pacing the room in extreme agitation and sometimes talking to himself, until around daybreak he called him complaining of feeling cold, and he looked so pale that the servant urged him to go to bed, which he immediately did.

"From that point on," he added, "the fever kept rising and he seemed to be quickly getting worse, so I decided to inform the señora Countess, whom my master kept talking about in his ravings."

Kneeling by Carlos's bedside, the Countess heard these words with an expression of painful pleasure. "He loves me!" she repeated, wildly kissing his hair and his hands burning with fever. "He loves me alone! Only me! He is suffering, dying for my sake! . . . Then we will be united in the grave with bonds more eternal than those tyrannically imposed on us by men! Carlos, Carlos!" she added with ecstatic love. "Death alone can make you mine, freeing you from the yoke that enslaves you in the world. So by all means let it come! We should both greet it as a liberating angel."

Elvira managed to calm her down again, and the arrival of the doctor obliged her to contain as best she could her extreme emotion.

From that moment Carlos started to revive, as though his lover's presence had a physical effect on him, and after a large bloodletting, on the doctor's orders, his mind grew completely clear and his feverish pulse slowed to a normal pace.

Carlos thanked Elvira for her care, and taking the Countess's hand, said in a low voice, "Why are you saving a life that I cannot devote to you?" Her only response was to give him one of those looks that disarm reason and unman resistance.

Throughout the night the two friends did not leave Carlos's bedside for a minute. He said nothing. Periodically he dozed off, and during those times you could hear him mutter in turn the names of Luisa and Catalina, but when he was awake he maintained a sad silence and seemed preoccupied with some sorrowful thought.

The following day at dawn, upon being alone with the Countess for a moment, he said, taking her hand, "Upon returning me to life, you return me to the sense of my duties. I thought I was dying, and at that moment I was at peace with my conscience and with the world. But you have plunged me again into this horrid struggle, which will leave my heart shattered. Take this letter; read it, my dear, and tell me if I can forget it without being contemptible in your eyes."

The Countess took the letter and read it, trembling. It said the following:

"Carlos: my sister is at death's door. When you receive this, your wife will be an orphan. The unhappy girl, overcome by the sorrows that she absorbs in silence since the moment when you could return to her side but willfully stay away, and the trials and pains she has gone through in caring for her mother, is in almost as grave danger as the latter. For days she has been cruelly suffering, and there are times when I fear for her sanity. Grief has entered this house, once so serene and happy, and in the name of your wife's tears and my authority as your father, I am ordering you to leave Madrid the moment you receive this sad letter. Your duty and my will are recalling you to Seville, and if you are deaf to one and the other . . . But no, it is not possible! Come, my son, come if you do not want to compel me to curse the right I have to call you by that name."

The Countess returned the letter to Carlos without saying a word.

"Well," he exclaimed, "what do you advise me to do, Catalina?"

"You can't go now," she answered; "you cannot obey your father's orders in the state you are in. Later, when you are well . . . then . . . then you will leave, if you can and will . . . if it is necessary."

Then she called for Elvira, who with Carlos's approval wrote the following lines to don Francisco de Silva:

"My cousin: Upon Carlos's orders I am informing you that he cannot immediately obey your order due to illness, but he will return to Seville as soon as he is in a condition to do so without danger. We share in your great sadness over the grave condition of our dear Leonor. I ask heaven to grant you the Christian resignation that in this situation can be your only source of comfort, and I respectfully send you my kind regards, etcetera, etcetera."

This letter was mailed out, and Carlos quickly improved, although you could see that with his return to health his sadness seemed to increase.

The Countess did not leave his side, but oh! how much more was she suffering than the one for whom she was concerned! The two most terrible passions consumed her fiery soul: love and jealousy. There at the head of the bed where she constantly watched over him, lavishing tenderness, there above the head of the man she loved, the man for whose love she would gladly give her life, there like a severe judge, like a jealous master, like an eternal witness, hung the portrait of the other. Catalina would have guessed who the model was even if she had seen that portrait elsewhere. Her heart told her that only such a heavenly image could withstand for so long the power of her passion. She gazed constantly at the portrait, which aroused in her an unspeakable emotion, and Luisa's beauty, enhanced by her imagination, seemed to her so irresistible that all her pride, all her passion, all her confidence in her own worth faltered and gave way to the restless and anxious feeling of jealousy.

"What!" she thought. "Am I to return him to her arms? . . . Will I agree to restore him to that lucky rival, after having sacrificed my entire future to a crazy love?"

And upon fixing her eyes again on the angelic image, the innocent smile on its lips seemed to her a sneer. "She is laughing!" she thought, with her ivory teeth biting her lower lip, which got bloody. "She is happy, virtuous, pure! Hers is the honor and good fortune; mine the desperation and shame! Oh no," she added, getting up with the force of rage. "No! She can keep the glory of virtue, I will accept disgrace, but I want happiness at any price."

Carlos, who was sleeping, had just woken up with a start, and a name slipped from his lips: "Luisa!"

The Countess turned pale, and then red as a beet. She went up to the bed, and sitting by Carlos looked at him with an unusual expression. The terrible feeling she had at that moment gave her features a particular kind of beauty.

Carlos gazed at her a moment and shuddered, as though he read in her face the desperate resolution she had made in silence. But she was so beautiful! . . . He took her in his arms and said, "No, I will never have the strength to leave you if you do not give it to me yourself, Catalina. If you don't hide from me that turmoil, that forceful grief I see on your face. So please have mercy on my heart . . . Oh! you do not know how it has suffered! This separation that breaks it was necessary, unavoidable. The passion that consumes me makes it as imperative as the duty that calls me elsewhere. At least, my friend, I leave worthy of you. I leave without having cursed the cruel tyranny of a virtue that has made you superior to a mad passion. But this struggle could not go on. Destiny is parting me from you at the moment when my exhausted strength was breathing its last. Oh, my beloved! Our love, which men may call guilty, has been as pure and chaste as that of the angels . . .

but I am only a man, and my heart would have asked more of yours."

The Countess fixed her gaze on him with a passion that made Carlos's heart leap in his chest.

"So!" she said, "Are you afraid to bind yourself to me with closer ties? . . . Is the happiness that I have given you not enough for your heart?"

Carlos embraced her wildly.

"Oh yes!" he cried. "A moment of supreme joy, and in exchange, a lifetime of atonement! I would have accepted this, Catalina: to call you mine for a moment, and then, Hell! What do I care? No," he went on, "you do not know how much I have suffered, because you do not know how madly I love you; you do not know that at this very moment your look is scorching me, your breath drives me wild, and the touch of your hand devours me . . . Catalina! Why are we separating without having known happiness?"

And she, without dodging or giving in to his raptures, riveting him with her burning look, exclaimed, "Do you want me to be yours forever? Do you want me to devote my entire life to you? Do you want us both, in the arms of happiness, to forget about heaven, the world and its laws? Do you . . . ?"

He overwhelmed her with ardent caresses. "Yes, I am yours, I want you to be mine, I long for joy or death," he repeated.

"Then joy for us both," she said; "joy! Tomorrow we will leave this country forever and find refuge in some corner of the New World. I am rich, and happy lovers have few needs. Let's flee this society that makes a crime of feelings it does not endorse, that it cannot gauge with its icy compass. Beneath the skies of the young America we will be free, we will be virtuous . . . we will live obscure and unknown, but alive! Oh, Carlos! Isn't life an eternal struggle between nature and human law? The only crime of the heart is found in falseness and treachery; hypocrisy cannot be virtue. Let's tear off its cowardly mask, and since we have not been able to be angels, let us at least be human. Loving each other is a misfortune, but deception would be infamy. I love you enough to follow you wherever you go, to where I can live as your wife."

Carlos sat stock-still, listening to her. His elation had given way to surprise, and the fear provoked by such an unexpected proposal.

His reaction was not lost on the Countess's keen discernment, and the indignation and jealousy she felt in her heart exalted her eloquence. "What? Do you hesitate?" she cried with a strong show of grief. "You hesitate? Perhaps you are afraid," she added with bitter irony, "to compromise my reputation, which is already lost? Are you afraid to look egoistic accepting as your lifelong companion the woman who is publicly called your lover? Or is it perhaps that a name and position whose sacrifice she asks for are worth more to you than that woman and your own happiness—a woman who did not wait until you asked to make an equal sacrifice with pleasure, with pride!"

"Enough, by God!" yelled Carlos, who had been deeply moved by these last words. "Oh! Don't ask me for what I could only do by turning myself into a monster. No, no, I cannot break a solemn oath taken before God and men. I cannot sacrifice the angel who has been entrusted to my care . . . I am guilty enough for not loving her as she deserves to be loved! I cannot plunge into the tortures of Hell that innocent soul that was formed for heavenly blessing . . ."

"Stop, you brute!" the Countess cried in despair. "You have just annihilated me. You have trampled on the unhappy woman whom love for you has covered with shame." And she fell, choking with anger and grief.

Carlos jumped out of bed and lifted her in his arms. "Catalina!" he told her. "I love you, I worship you . . . but what do you want from me? Would you be content being disgraced forever in the eyes of the world? Would this hapless love that has led us astray always be enough for your heart?"

She removed herself from his arms. "For me," she said, "this is the only alternative: your love or death! I ask you for one or the other. But your love, for me alone, mine, all mine! Do you want to witness my final humiliation? Do you want me to reveal to you all my heart's weakness? Then know the truth: I am jealous! My jealousy is killing me, is driving me crazy! Carlos, Carlos! What a state you have reduced me to!" And she fell at his feet, pale, her hair undone, bathed in tears.

"This is too much," he cried, clasping her in his arms. "Catalina, I am yours! Do what you will with me! I will follow you wherever you want to go; I will commit a thousand crimes if your all-powerful voice in my heart so commands. Come! I'll forget all: God, the world, honor . . . Come! Intoxicate me with love and pleasure, and may we be as happy as we are guilty."

22

With the agitation of that memorable day, Carlos's fever returned in full force. The Countess cared for him, and when he was better she withdrew with him to a house she owned a few miles from Madrid. Her business agent took care of the sale of various country houses she thought it wise to dispose of, and Carlos, sad, upset, but resolved to follow her anywhere, surrendered completely to her and her love, with the kind of dejection with which we succumb to a fate we have tried to struggle against in vain.

As he surrendered, weak and blind, to his crazy passion, the Countess, from her retreat, made all the arrangements for their departure, to take place as soon as Carlos was fully recovered; while Elvira, who without knowing her friend's plans was starting to vaguely fear some reckless act on her part, wrote her long letters to which the only reply she received was, "I am happy; don't tell me anything."

"Poor Catalina!" said Elvira in tears, while looking in a mirror to see if some strands of pearls she had just bought were becoming. "I am very worried about her, and I will hardly be able to enjoy myself at tonight's ball, which I'll attend with my eyes red from crying." And bothered by this thought, she stopped crying and quickly wet a fine towel to refresh her pretty eyes.

23

The affairs of the Countess were in good order and everything
was prepared for her long journey, which was nonetheless a secret
to all. Carlos, still weak and sad, in chains at the feet of his impassioned lover, watched the day of his exile approach with a kind of
indifference. He no longer had the energy to feel either pain or
pleasure. He felt it necessary, however, to go to Madrid to entrust
his father's affairs to friends of the latter, and to write him at length,
as well as to Luisa, confessing his guilt, begging their forgiveness,
and relinquishing in his wife's favor all the assets he held from his
mother and those he would have inherited from his father.

The Countess, who was detained by some affairs at her country home, let him leave, saying she would meet him late in the
week (it was Monday). Carlos, upon finding himself alone, no
longer seeing the eyes that entranced him or hearing the voice
that went straight to his soul, felt at the same time how impossible it would be to live without her, and remorse for the enormity
of an act that he only grasped when he was no longer with his
beloved.

He did not waver, however, and upon his arrival in Madrid he
immediately visited the people to whom he had resolved to entrust
the family affairs, and then he began to write, first to his wife. This
letter was not written in a tranquil frame of mind, as the reader
can well imagine. He had loved the poor girl so much! He still
felt for her such tender affection! Often as his hand traced the
lines that would deal a death blow to her heart, overcome by the

enormity of his crime he felt the impulse to kill himself, thereby putting an end to the dreadful struggle that was ravaging his soul.

However, he finished the letter. Broken, he fell on the bed, and a flood of burning, bitter tears poured from his eyes, relieving somewhat his heart. He had spent the whole night writing. It was already dawn, and succumbing to fatigue, he dozed off for a moment. In his dreams he saw Luisa, pale, thin, dressed in mourning, weeping at once for her dead mother and for her unfaithful, fugitive husband, and with the anxiety caused by the nightmare he awoke with a start. But the vision had not fled with his dream. There she was, as conjured up by his imagination, pale, thin, and in mourning! It was Luisa, standing at the foot of his bed, gazing at him with her sweet, merciful look, holding out to him her white, innocent hands, as if begging for compassion.

Carlos screamed, and in his feverish state he got down on his knees, exclaiming, "Forgive me, forsaken angel! Ah! Alive or dead, forgive me!"

"Carlos, my husband," responded a musical voice that Carlos had not heard for seven months, "we just arrived; I wanted to surprise you. Our father is waiting for you at the inn where we are staying. We were afraid that we would find you very sick. Thank the Lord, we learned from Elvira that you are well again. Here I am . . . how I have suffered! I have come to find my husband . . . I no longer have a mother!"

And the innocent girl lifted him up, embracing him and shedding many tears on his chest. Carlos did not know if he was still asleep or if he was awake. He seemed completely dumb.

"Come," repeated Luisa; "a coach is waiting for us at the door." And she took him with her without his offering any resistance.

However, upon crossing the living room where there were some preparations for his voyage, he suddenly stopped, and looking at his wife in a kind of fright, exclaimed, "Tell me right now: Are you really Luisa? Are you in Madrid? Why have you come?"

"You wretch!" she answered tenderly. "I knew you were not well, and you ask me why I came? Does it bother you, Carlos," she added, looking at him with vague unease, "does my coming perhaps bother you?"

Carlos slapped himself on the forehead. Now he understood all; he knew the truth.

"No," he said, taking Luisa's hand and avoiding her eyes. "No, my friend; you are welcome!" And he followed her in silence.

24

When two powerful emotions are at war in the human heart, the victory gained by one invigorates rather than blots out the other. One sees this kind of phenomenon above all in the case of love. If we find ourselves caught between a despotic passion and a sacred duty, passion typically wins, but all the sacrifices it entails, all the laurels with which it is crowned, seem to weaken the feeling for which they were conceded. The duty that has been sacrificed, like all innocent victims, will excite pity along with remorse, whereas its proud conqueror, oppressing the heart that has renounced all for its sake, may end up wearing it out. But if at the moment when we almost repent of the idea of going through with a huge sacrifice for the sake of conquering love, an obstacle outside our will abruptly appears to stop it, the result is that instead of rejoicing over the unexpected aid, it provokes and irritates us. Duty, which as a victim had gained strength, now appears as a hangman, and love, which triumphant wears us out, gains through adversity a new force that is conveyed to the will.

Pride and pettiness of the heart! You will always find it so; in every climate, in every social order, with only little difference, the human heart is the same. You find it constantly longing to surrender all to the passion that consumes it, and repenting in proportion as it gives. You find the heart unruly to whatever denies its passion, to later become the tyrant of its own idol. All its force comes from setbacks; give it the strength to sacrifice all, and that very strength will soon wear it out.

If Carlos had gone through with his flight to America with the Countess, perhaps the value of all he had sacrificed would have risen in his imagination, and his remorse and grief would have adequately avenged the abandoned Luisa. But the sudden turn of events caused by that woman who had appeared without being summoned to return him to the path of duty that he was on the point of deserting, silenced the inner voice that still spoke in favor of that very duty; and that which if carried out would have seemed to him a painful sacrifice, upon being undone became a thwarted happiness.

There he was in the arms of his father and his wife, trying in vain to respond to their caresses. One thought, one single object was on his mind: Catalina! At that moment she was the real victim in his eyes. Upon seeing himself returned, despite himself, to a forsaken wife, he was less moved by the naive ignorance of the victim than by the grief of the perpetrator. His imagination painted in vivid colors the suffering of his passionate, jealous lover upon learning of this unexpected development, and the ungrateful man did not consider how the innocent Luisa would also suffer if at that moment she fathomed the guilty heart of her husband!

Luckily that did not occur. Love is so blind; innocence so rich in illusions; faith so credulous! Carlos's disarray only seemed to Luisa the natural effect of pleasure and surprise. She was so happy at that moment that there was no room for sad suspicions in her soul. Sitting on her uncle's lap and holding her silent and confused husband's hands in hers, she related with simple eloquence how she had suffered, how she had wept. She revealed to him, blushing, the secrets of her pure heart, secrets fit for angels' ears. No suspicion, no distrust showed through the most hidden sorrows of that tender soul; no reprimand slipped from those so sweet lips.

Carlos was suffering. He often lowered his eyes fixed on Luisa, full of tears, but his heart, his guilty heart quickly stifled the impulse of a momentary repentance. And yet upon seeing her, hearing her, recalling how he had loved her and feeling how he was still loved, in those moments he felt as though he had been the victim of some painful dream and that everything that had occurred in the past six months was only a figment of his imagination.

Lost in confusion, Carlos remained by Luisa, not knowing what decision to make in this existential crisis, when a coach stopped at the front door and soon after Elvira appeared. Her family ties with the visitors, and their visit to her upon their arrival, obliged her to return the courtesy, but it was clear at first glance that she was obeying the strict rules of social convention with some repugnance.

Upon seeing her, Carlos felt as upset as if he had seen Catalina herself, and Elvira threw him a look that was as jealous as if it had been the former's. Then, as she distractedly kept up a terse and trivial conversation with don Francisco, in which there was no sign of her usual cheerful talkativeness, she gazed often at Luisa, and admiring and moved by her perfect beauty, she turned back to Carlos with an angry expression as if to say, "You are equally unworthy of your wife and of my friend."

Carlos could not bear for long the awkward position in which he found himself. On a flimsy excuse he took his leave, ignoring the timid protest in his wife's look. He rushed out of the house, the atmosphere of which was stifling him. He looked like a madman, and no one who saw him could be unaware of the terrible conflict that was raging in his soul.

As soon as he returned to his lodgings, he sent a letter to the Countess that contained only these incoherent words: "My wife has come; my father too. Lightning has struck my head. I am out of my mind. Don't worry, Catalina; I love you more than ever . . . oh, wretched one that I am, more than ever! I don't know what to do; the alternative is dreadful. But didn't I swear, upon accepting your sacrifices, to make all those you would demand of me in return? I had made an earlier vow, as you well know—will eternal perjury be my fate? And yet, my unhappiness exceeds my guilt. I await your orders. I can obey by dying, and this would be a good thing for me, for you, and for her."

After sending this letter, he felt even more stirred up. What would be the Countess's resolve? Would she again demand that he desert his wife, his innocent wife who had come orphaned and sad to rest her head on his heart? This idea made him tremble; and yet, when he considered the possibility that Catalina might desist from her plan and perhaps renounce their love, he felt such violent thrusts of anger and despair that they almost made him detest the innocent cause of his unhappiness.

The day passed without his working up the courage to return to his wife's side. Such a long absence began to surprise don Francisco, and to worry and afflict Luisa. "What is your husband doing?" the old gentleman said with disgust. Luisa gave no answer, but her own heart was asking her, like her uncle, "What is your husband doing?"

It was near sunset, and Carlos still had not appeared. Don Francisco could not take any more and went out to look for him; when Luisa was alone she shed a flood of tears. However, she still did not suspect the truth. Her heavy heart, full of vague and indefinite fears, did not emit a single impulse of distrust, and she imagined every misfortune except the one she was really the victim of.

When don Francisco arrived at his son's house, the latter had just left and was running wildly to see Luisa. He had received the mail two minutes before with these lines penned by the Countess: "I understand you; the sacrifice you offered me would for you be death. I will not accept it. I can give you up; I can never toy with you. I give you up! All is over for me. Be happy."

Carlos's despair knew no limits. He would have thrown himself off the balcony if a momentary thought had not stopped him. His voluntary death might ruin the Countess in the eyes of the world; on her would fall public censure and the accusations of his family.

In his extreme delirium, Carlos had the idea of confessing to Luisa all his secrets, of imploring on bended knee not just her forgiveness, but rather her consent to be guiltier still. The brute did not flinch at the idea of tearing from that tender soul the voluntary sacrifice of all her happiness. Thus he flew to Luisa's house, and with a decided air rushed up the stairs that led to her room.

He found her sad and alone, lying languidly on a sofa. She had grown tired of waiting for him, and grief and dismay were painted on her beautiful face. But upon Carlos's arrival she got up brightly, her eyes shining with a ray of happiness, and held out her arms to him.

"Carlos!"

That was all she could utter, but the sound of her voice, its tone, her look in an instant troubled the heart of the guilty one and shook his resolutions. The violent, determined expression on his face was covered by a sudden cloud of sadness, and pale and trembling he fell at his wife's feet, as she grasped him in alarm.

"Carlos, my husband, what's wrong?" she said in an anguished tone. And drawing him to her breast she felt his flowing tears.

"Oh, my God," she exclaimed, trembling, "you are suffering! You are hiding from me some terrible secret! Carlos, for pity's sake!"

He withdrew from her arms with a convulsive motion, and started walking mechanically around the room in extreme agitation. Luisa followed him all atremble, joining her white hands in a gesture of supplication. Carlos suddenly stopped, and grasping her by the arm in a kind of rage, "Don't ask me anything," he told her. "Nothing! I beg you by God and by your mother's ashes. I am very unhappy—that is all!"

"You are unhappy!" she exclaimed in terror, and fell at his feet thunderstruck. Carlos carried her in his arms to the bed, deeply moved, and revived by his caresses Luisa fixed her eyes on him with ineffably sad tenderness.

"Did you say that you are unhappy, Carlos?" she said. "Didn't I hear you wrong? Is it true that you're unhappy? Today! The day of our reunion!"

And quickly reviewing her recollection of her husband's voluntary stay at the court, and the words that had slipped from his lips in the first moment of surprise upon seeing her, she added in deep terror, "Carlos! Do you no longer love me?"

"Always!" he told her. "You will always be the sister and the friend of my heart. I will always love you with all the tenderness of my soul. But can I make you happy? Can I be happy myself . . . ? That is now as impossible as it is to return to you your lost freedom. Society has chained us together with eternal bonds, and you, poor angel, like I, will be the victim of its tyrannical, absurd institutions."

Such ideas could never have occurred to Luisa, but these foolish words shone a baneful light on her blind innocence. She had no words, no gesture to express what she was feeling at that moment, what she was guessing. She buckled beneath the icy hand of her first disillusionment, like a humble shrub beneath the wings of the North Wind.

Don Francisco returned to the inn at nine that night, tired of searching for his son in vain, and found him at Luisa's bedside. The poor girl was in the throes of a violent fever, but don Francisco did not suspect that Carlos was to blame. He cared for her so tenderly, showed such real and strong concern, that the old gentleman forgave him for his strange conduct during the day, and ascribing Luisa's indisposition to fatigue from the trip, he retired to his bedroom, fully convinced that the couple loved each other with the same passion he had witnessed on the day they took their vows in the cathedral of Seville.

25

Three days had gone by since the Countess had received and responded to the letter from her lover, without hearing back from him. This was more than enough to arouse that naturally intense soul. Despair took hold of her, and horrid resolutions took shape one after the other without being carried out.

Her grief was not the profound and resigned suffering of Luisa; it was grief in all its force, its fury, its delirium. Twice she set out on foot, alone and frantic in the midday heat, with the intention of somehow reaching her happy rival and her spineless lover and offering them a cruel spectacle, stabbing herself in the heart in the presence of both. Two other times her servants followed her in the middle of the night, watching her wander crazily around the surroundings of her country home, and stand for hours at a time at the edge of a deep pond, as though she read in its murky waters some dreadful counsel. They saw her shift in an instant from the most convulsive activity to a state of complete inaction; and there were moments when her facial expression and the incoherence of her words seemed evidence of a real state of insanity.

On the third day her despair took on a more silent, constant cast, which might have led to the outcome of this story had Elvira not arrived in time to prevent it. The Countess's good but cowardly friend ran to her side, guessing the state she was in, yet she was frightened by the somber nature of her grief, and conceived fears she had not had before. Eager to temper Catalina's bitterness at any cost, she informed her of Luisa's illness, which in some sense justified Carlos's conduct, at the same time giving assurances that she herself did not feel of his firm resolve to devote himself entirely to his lover, as soon as he could without scandal wash his hands of his unhappy wife. Elvira went further; she exaggerated the gravity of Luisa's illness, emphatically declaring that she was at death's door.

It was not possible for Elvira to fully understand the soul of her friend; she was not on her emotional level. That presumable death, announced as good news, affected adversely the magnanimous heart of her friend and visibly disturbed her thoughts. That passionate, violent woman was perhaps capable of murdering her rival in a fit of jealous rage, but she was not capable of tallying up the advantages she might gain from her death, or of erecting on her grave the edifice of her hopes. We must be fair: there was no soul more noble or generous than the one that animated that guilty woman.

At the thought of Luisa dying, the innocent, betrayed wife expiring by the side of a criminal husband, she could feel the pain and remorse of the latter. She would have deeply scorned him if she believed him free of these emotions. Until that moment the happiness of her rival had exacerbated her grief. Now her grief devolved upon the sufferings of her victim.

She judged herself harshly and found herself guilty. The erring ways of noble souls have no need of judges or executioners; they judge and punish themselves, sometimes too cruelly.

She spent the day in deep, silent sadness. Elvira tried in vain to get her to talk or weep. She spent hours completely motionless, her eyes glued to the floor, her pale face clouded as if it reflected a mournful thought. At times she raised her eyes to heaven, and her lips murmured confused words. Those words that no one heard were sublime. They expressed a vow of which God alone could understand the grandeur and heroism: the vow to never lay her guilty head on the chaste bed of the dying wife, to never succeed her in the nuptial bed of Carlos, the nuptial bed that she had left so pure and that he had profaned.

Oh! Say what they will the ignorant detractors of the weaker sex who claim to know its nature, there is in woman's heart a sublime instinct for self-denial. In the woman who has been most corrupted by the world, the one most led astray by her passions or twisted by her upbringing, there still exist beautiful feelings, generous instincts that are rarely found in men.

Ask men at the right moment about their brilliant deeds inspired by ambition, glory, honor. Ask them about their daring courage, their open freedom, their proud strength. In many, although not in all, you will find some of this. But ask woman alone for that obscure, and therefore all the more sublime, sacrifice; that silent heroism that brings no glory whatsoever in its wake; that boundless generosity and inexhaustible tenderness that make her entire life into a long, silent sacrifice. Ask only of her the exquisite sensitivity that can be deeply wounded by things that do not leave a trace on the lives of men. A sensitivity that gives rise to their flaws, which they exaggerate and stupidly divulge, and to their virtues, which they are unaware of and distort.

That is why woman is always the victim in her associations with man. She is the victim not only because of her weakness, but also because of her kindness. Seek her out as lover, wife, or mother, and you will always find her sacrificed, whether by force or by her own will; you will always find her generous and unhappy—oh yes, very unhappy!

But don't tell this to those kings perforce, who claim to give them such lauded protection; don't tell them, "The sex that you call weak, and that for being weak you have bound with chains, could say to you, 'You are cowards,' if courage were only measured by suffering." Don't tell men this, because after disqualifying her for the high positions that they have appropriated for themselves, after barring all the paths to a noble ambition, after railing against any laurel she may have laboriously and gloriously snatched from their proud hold, they would still be bold enough to dispute with her the sad privilege of unhappiness; they would still like to strip the victim of her crown of thorns and convince her that she is happy.

On the fourth day, a letter from Carlos arrived at the Countess's country home. Luisa was out of danger. Catalina took a deep breath, as though a big weight had been lifted from her shoulders.

Carlos's letter was full of compassion for his wife, but also full of love for his beloved. He beseeched her not to worry, and swearing to die if he withdrew his love from her, he placed the destiny of the two in her hands. Yet while offering all to his lover, he made clear his certainty that his wife would not survive his desertion, and he suggested that neither would he be able to bear for long an existence poisoned by the horrid remorse he would feel for having been Luisa's murderer.

The Countess read that letter through three times and afterward appeared deeply thoughtful. Elvira, respecting her long inner reflection, did not dare to ask her resolve, but the expression on her friend's face made her hopeful. The storm clouds that had disturbed and darkened that beautiful face seemed to clear, and an expression of proud calm replaced the deep despair that only hours before was painted on each of her features.

"She will triumph," Elvira thought. "She will triumph over an insane passion; I will regain my friend." And going up to her and taking one of her hands in hers, she said, "Catalina, only your pride can now save your virtue, and I am pleased to see that that strong champion has not deserted you."

"Yes," she answered with a smile that made Elvira shiver. "Destiny's rage would not be fulfilled without that invincible pride. Yes, it was essential at this moment to make the contest more dreadful and the triumph more difficult."

And quickly writing a few lines, she held them out to Elvira, who read them trembling. They were as follows: "Is a victim necessary? So be it. I will be the victim, but one alone is enough. Please hide from the innocent one your crime and mine. May she live happily in her ignorance, and if you can, be happy in your treason. Make every effort that she not find on your lips the mark of my kisses. I accept the destiny you are offering me."

"And what is that shameful destiny?" Elvira exclaimed, beside herself. "Catalina! Have you considered what you are going to do? Do you understand the position you mean to put yourself in?"

"The most humiliating position," the Countess responded, "the one that will draw tears of blood from my guilty heart. But this alone can serve as atonement for my crime. I who saw fit to arouse in a man's soul a guilty passion am surely not the one who has the right to punish him for it. May he be happy, and may his happiness bring tears to me alone."

Elvira, indignant, at that moment forgot the respect she instinctively paid to her friend, and said bitterly, "Fine! You're right to conceal the shameful cause of your fall! But can you be overcome to this degree by a senseless love? Can it make you lose, along with your reason, all sense of decency, all feelings of pride? Can the result of your long reflection be the decision to accept, close to the respected and beloved wife, the infamous title of the husband's mistress? If so, of what use is your talent? Of what use your much vaunted superiority?"

"Of what use indeed?" answered the Countess with a bitter smile. "The use it always has! To attract unhappiness and repel compassion; to showcase our faults and make incomprehensible our virtues."

26

Luisa had gotten over her illness. Don Francisco, delighted to renew old friendships and full of ambitious plans for his son, had decided to remain in the court, and the gentleman, his son, and his daughter-in-law were now lodged in a lovely suite of rooms on Alcalá Street.

We have already seen that señor de Silva was not without a certain vanity, which was no doubt excusable, and it will not surprise the reader to learn that upon finding himself again associated with the court and in touch with aristocratic and political circles, the thought entered his mind to give some standing to his only son and heir. With the same persistence with which in former days he insisted on sending Carlos to Madrid, he now decided to obtain for him at any cost some honorary appointment that would highlight the benefits of his distinguished birth, his excellent education and substantial wealth, advantages that could only be brought to light through some position in the political sphere. His favorite had always been a career in diplomacy, and he now strove tirelessly to obtain for his son the title of embassy secretary in one of the major foreign courts.

However, Carlos did not care about such aspirations at first. His heart was too concerned with his position vis-à-vis the two women whose fates were entwined with his.

The Countess remained in her country home, where every day Carlos spent many hours in her company. More impassioned, more affectionate than ever, he was determined to make Catalina forget the bitterness of her position, and it was always a painful struggle for him to leave her.

She knew that she had never been loved to the degree she was now. She knew that she held sway over him, reinforced by the generosity with which she was sacrificing her pride and the jealous exclusiveness of her passion for the sake of her lover and even of her rival, but she was nonetheless very unhappy.

Could she obliterate the pride that she had boldly trampled on? Could she forget the brilliant life she had renounced, her reputation lost forever, her freedom enchained by guilty bonds? Would the passion of that stormy, delicate soul have the perseverance to weather times of weariness, when we look back to the past and are amazed to see how far we have come, and we think with profound discouragement, "There is no more turning back!" Still consumed by her passion, the Countess was already analyzing the sorrows it had brought upon her, and her sweetest moments were those when the rack of jealousy tortured her enough to deprive her of the ability to gauge her own misfortune.

It was surely an awful thing for that so passionate and delicate woman to have to divide possession of her lover with another: to touch his warm hand, still infused with Luisa's warmth; to inhale his breath, still imbued with Luisa's breath. Men do not understand the nature of this torture for women. They think they have the sole right to be delicate on this point, which is why we find them so demanding, so jealous of their wives' purity, while they have no qualms about offering the most immaculate virgin the impure remains of a dissolute youth. But while tormented by jealousy, the Countess was always generous, and the life of the rival with whom she divided her lover's attentions consoled her for her own unhappiness.

She had never seen her. Luisa's rare beauty had not aroused her fears, and she always recalled that she had been at death's door, perhaps from finding her husband's heart without the warmth to shelter her fragile existence. She felt compassion for this tender young woman who no longer had a mother, who was entering the world timid and inexperienced, without arms to defend herself against treachery, with no antidote for her suffering. The happiness Carlos gave Luisa inevitably caused the Countess envy and sadness, and yet she needed that sadness; she needed Luisa's happiness.

Carlos gave her a thousand assurances of it. He told her often that his wife's innocence and credulity prevented her from having the least suspicion, that after the first unpleasant scenes that took place between the two, the kind and overly indulgent Luisa had been easily consoled, fully believing the false explanations he had given her. Carlos claimed he was certain that Luisa was incapable of jealousy, and that as long as he was attentive and affectionate, she asked for and needed nothing more. In his judgment, Luisa was a highly worthy and placid creature—all in all, necessarily a happy woman, since she never complained.

But how he deluded himself! The quiet and seemingly tranquil wife was indescribably unhappy. She was no longer blinded by innocence, or sustained by trust. The light of a terrible truth had shone before her eyes. What did her ignorance of her husband's infidelity matter? The certainty of not being loved was enough to make her profoundly unhappy.

Could Carlos's words, those words that had thrown her to the brink of the grave, ever be erased from her memory or her heart? She heard them always, endlessly; when she was with Carlos, far from Carlos, waking, sleeping . . . Those words rang constantly in her ears and etched on her soul the bitter certainty that the eternal bond that united them was now for him a heavy chain.

It is true that she did not complain. She had listened with care and kindness to the explanations and excuses of her husband, and despite her inexperience, she understood that he regretted his sincere outburst and was trying to make up for it. He was still kind and compassionate enough to wish to deceive her, and she pretended to go along.

It was the first time that she had to pretend; this is also the first thing taught by the world that Luisa was entering. She was being introduced, despite herself, to its secret treachery and deceptions. So she remained silent and watched her husband. Soon after the sorrow of feeling herself unloved would come the painful suspicion of being betrayed.

Carlos was with her less every day. He left on horseback every afternoon after the midday meal and did not return until late at night, always giving trivial excuses for his long absences. Don Francisco was so involved with his ambitions and plans, and so besieged by old friends, that he did not notice Carlos's behavior. He left every afternoon before or soon after Carlos, and did not return until bedtime, which for him was at eleven on the dot. Before going to bed he went to Luisa's room for a moment, where he sometimes found Carlos, and since he did not notice any change in their tender relations, he withdrew feeling very confident of the couple's happiness. It is true that he more often found Luisa alone, but when the good gentleman showed up he was always greeted with a sweet smile which dispelled the clouds of sadness darkening the face of the poor abandoned one, who excused her husband's absence, leaving the old man satisfied.

"Are you content?" he would ask her upon leaving.

"Yes, Father," she answered. So don Francisco left feeling very pleased, and a flood of tears atoned for the unhappy girl's generous lie.

She could not confide her sorrow to anyone; she could ask no one for advice or compassion. She was extremely careful to avoid don Francisco's having the least suspicion, because she was afraid of destroying the harmony that reigned between father and son, of subjecting the latter to the violent rage of the former, and perhaps poisoning the final days of the old man, who felt happy with his children's good fortune. Her fears were so great in this regard that when Carlos came back too late, she waited up for him and sneaked him in, to avoid having don Francisco, knowing the unusual hour of his return, demand explanations that Carlos might not be able to give or that might have painful results.

But amid such incredible kindness, her discontent was growing by the minute. She now suspected the full extent of her misfortune, and jealousy was secretly gnawing at her soul. Often in the middle of the night she left her bed to spy, so to speak, on her husband's sleep, hoping to hear some words from his lips that would dispel or confirm her fears. Upon awakening in the morning, Carlos found her still at his bedside.

"You have gotten up so early, my dear?"

"As you see," she replied, "since your occupations deprive me of your company for many hours a day, I like to get an early start on those when I can see and hear you."

If Carlos then gave her a tender look, an affectionate word, she withdrew to hide her extreme emotion, thinking gaily, "Maybe he will again love me; maybe his heart has not completely changed. Doesn't he still have that look that made me happy, that tone that always touches my soul?"

When we have once been truly loved and have had faith in the feeling we inspire, we never foresee the possibility that it may cease to exist. But the moment comes, sudden, unexpected. The entranced heart has not recognized the preliminary symptoms of its arrival, and often we still doubt, even after hitting upon the terrible truth. The heart seems to cling more stubbornly to the dream that is slipping away. Thus Luisa, in the presence of the one who had made her and could still make her so happy, thought it impossible that her unhappiness could last.

But when he was not there, when alone in her room she counted off the interminable hours of anxiety, when she looked around without finding a friendly bosom on which to rest her aching head, then her resistance failed and shedding her usual meekness she dared to complain to heaven.

"My God, my God!" she cried. "It is not fair that a poor woman be oppressed with such unhappiness."

Meanwhile days and days went by without giving rise to any change in Luisa's favor; on the contrary, her situation grew ever worse. One day at the usual dinnertime, Carlos, who was walking around the living room, suddenly went into the study where she was sitting absorbed in sad rumination.

"What's going on?" he said with thinly veiled impatience. "Aren't we eating today?"

Luisa answered, "Our father hasn't come out of his room yet."

"What's he doing? What's keeping him?" Carlos angrily asked. "How is it that at five in the afternoon we haven't polished it off?"

"I don't know," she said sweetly.

Carlos's impatience was as understandable as don Francisco's delay. The one wished to fly to his lover, while the other, who that morning had seen his hopes dashed of obtaining a brilliant appointment for his son, was in a dreadful mood that even made him forget the need to eat.

Carlos kept pacing, but as the minutes passed without his father leaving the room where he was hiding his spite, the young man's anger grew more and more apparent. "It seems we won't eat today," he said again to his wife.

"I don't know," she again answered, holding back a tear.

"This is impossible!" Carlos exclaimed. "I absolutely have to leave, and my father will get angry if I go without eating with him. Isn't that so, Luisa?"

"I don't know," she said again.

And Carlos, angry at her terse replies, abruptly turned his back on her. His watch, which he kept looking at, already said six and he could take no more. He thought of the impatience, the anxiety his delay would cause the Countess, and turning again to his wife with an expression that showed his desire to leave her, he said, "Luisa, could you please go into my father's room and let him know the time."

Luisa obeyed and returned to tell her husband that the two of them should eat alone, because don Francisco was not feeling so well and did not want to join them.

Carlos ran in to see his father, but upon realizing that his condition was insignificant he quickly came out again and told his wife, who was waiting for him to sit down to eat, "You eat alone today, dear, because as I was saying, I really have to leave right away." Luisa looked down, and as much as she tried to hide her grief, she burst into tears. Carlos, who was about to leave, stopped, hearing her smothered sobs.

"Luisa, what's wrong?" he asked her.

"Nothing," the girl answered, her voice buried in tears.

Carlos went up to her, clearly disturbed.

"What does this mean, Luisa?"

A sudden wave of indignation gave her strength; she answered with profound bitterness, "That I am very unhappy!"

Carlos stopped short, surprised and moved, without finding words to ask his wife for a clearer explanation. Luisa kept on crying, and he was tempted to stay with her, to console her, to lie if necessary to calm her down; but the timing was bad, the Countess was waiting and time was flying. He took his wife's hand, asking her awkwardly to calm down, and he rushed out promising to return soon.

Luisa was drowning in sorrow. Her husband's conduct seemed to her crude and humiliating. Not only did he no longer love her, but he no longer even tried to deceive her. Carlos washed his hands of her; he scorned her grief; he trampled on all kinds of considerations and neglected all his duties. These thoughts drove her crazy, because she was feeling strange new impulses that were foreign to her nature—impulses of hatred and revenge, which in similar cases have destroyed many women, who would never have been blameworthy if they had been oblivious to outrage. Her tender heart was convulsed in agony, and she cried in sadness and anger, "Who is it, I want to know, who is the woman who has stolen from me his affection, who sees him, listens to him, while I, poor abandoned one, in solitude dress myself with the empty title of his wife? Traitor! Why did he swear to love me forever? Why does he deceive me like this? . . . and God! Yes, the unfaithful one has also betrayed God! Oh Mother, Mother! How bitter your final moments would have been if you had foreseen the fate that awaited your daughter!"

She cried bitterly, and gave in for a while to the exhaustion her ongoing sorrow produced in her delicate frame, since the situation was not new; every day was filled with the same misery, and by letting her husband know that she was suffering, she had only succeeded in making him feel more blameworthy in her eyes.

In fact, Carlos was no longer deluded; he knew that his wife was unhappy, and this discovery was all the harder for him because he knew he could not restore to her the happiness his new passion had robbed her of. His position was more difficult vis-à-vis Luisa, and as a result, his behavior less natural. When he thought she was unaware of his fault, he still took pleasure in her company, but once he could only feel in her presence like a criminal before his judge, or like an executioner before his victim, he avoided being alone with her as much as possible.

Aware that he could no longer satisfy his wife's heart, who no longer tried to hide her discontent, he observed all the outward amenities with greater care, taking pains not to give her any apparent cause for complaint. When he could not avoid being alone with her, he was confused, embarrassed, and as a result, cold; but in public he redoubled his attentions and care; you can be sure that no unfaithful husband ever honored so much the wife he was betraying.

But what did all these superficial amenities mean to a creature who had no vanity and an extreme love for her husband? More tender than proud, Luisa would have traded for one tender look all that external show that seemed designed to hide her misfortune.

The situation worsened over time. Day by day the poor girl was losing the hope of a change for the better. And she was drained not only by the sorrow of feeling unloved, but also by the idea that her husband was guilty in the eyes of God, which was deeply sad for someone of her religious nature. Now convinced that a new passion was the cause of his indifference to her, she trembled upon considering the enormity of that sin, and in those moments said with pious fervor, "My God! What I ask for is not my happiness but his salvation. If necessary, may his heart never again be mine, but may it be Yours alone. I will cover my face with ashes and drag myself through the dust to atone for his sin. Forgive him, Señor! And return this lost sheep to the fold!"

But God appeared deaf to her angelic plea. The sheep did not return to the fold, and Luisa often lost her divine resignation. "It isn't a whim!" she said. "It isn't a passing affair! I have lost him forever! He has forgotten God, in whose presence he swore to love me his entire life! How is this extreme wickedness possible? How is it possible, my God?" the innocent one repeated with deep sadness. "How can he break an oath sanctioned by You!"

In early youth, and even after, tender hearts have complete faith in the solemnity of an oath, and cannot conceive of breaking it without losing the loved one's respect. Thus a woman demands of her lover the promise of an eternal love, and a lover asks his beloved for the same, as though the duration of one's feeling depended on it, and as though one should respect it.

This is about as sound as an oath affirming that we will be as healthy tomorrow as we are today, or that we will be as youthful at the age of forty as we were at twenty. But such is love's blindness that the person who would declare absurd a vow never to have wrinkles or gray hair, or to endure stomachaches, migraines, or fits of nerves, trusts in the oath uttered by beloved lips, obliging the heart never to undergo the irresistible influences of time and circumstance.

It is an everyday occurrence to hear from the lips of the one who is no longer loved the terrible question "What has become of your vows?" Why not first ask Nature, "What has become of the leaves and flowers that bedecked the trees when the winter wind blows them away? Finally, what happens to the life of man when it no longer animates the body?"

She, Nature, would respond, "All changes; all passes! This is my law, the unchanging, eternal law!"

27

Luisa's life was bitter; she almost never went out, nor found any kind of consolation in solitude. On one of her saddest days Elvira went to visit her, and was astonished to find the deterioration of her beauty. She tried to be discreet and not seem to notice the suffering revealed in the despondent face of the young wife, but the signs of grief were so obvious in her conversation that Elvira was moved. The poor girl could not keep up the slightest conversation; she asked odd questions without listening to the answers, and answered Elvira's so incoherently that the latter could not understand her. Sometimes she stopped in the middle of a sentence and, unable to finish it, started another, which she also left unfinished.

Elvira looked at her with surprise and pity. She asked for Carlos, and the poor girl shuddered at the mere mention of his name.

"Does he go to your house?" she asked anxiously. "Does he visit you often? I thought he was spending all his afternoons with you."

"No, of course not," said Elvira, lowering her eyes, because she was well aware with whom Luisa's husband was spending his afternoons. Then, wanting to turn the conversation in another direction, she asked her cousin why she was so withdrawn from society, and invited her to join her in some entertainment.

"I am so alone!" Luisa said in deep sadness. "I am always alone! I have no friend in this court."

Elvira answered, "I thought you would honor me with that title."

"It is true," said Luisa distractedly, "it is true that you must like me a little . . . feel for me! You are my only relative in Madrid."

Then, suddenly and for the first time remembering that she had another female relative in Madrid, she added simply, "The widow of the Count of S. is also my relative, but I do not know her; she has not visited me."

Elvira's confusion upon hearing these words was so obvious that it could not help but catch Luisa's attention. She pretended to be involved with the backing of her fan, but as Luisa was looking at her in some surprise, she tried to say something and said in an indifferent tone, "If the Countess has not visited you, it is certainly not out of neglect or a belittling of the tie between you, but because she has been away from Madrid, in her country home, for the past five months."

"I did not mean to complain about the Countess," Luisa answered.

These simple, innocent words alarmed Elvira, who more kindly than wisely hastened to add, "Indeed you have no reason to complain. The Countess has enemies who slander her, and you should not believe anything they say."

"I don't know any of her enemies," Luisa responded as simply as before. "No one has spoken to me of the Countess, and I did not expect, although I would have appreciated, her visit." And then, influenced by her mother's warnings despite her angelic kindness, she added, "And I think that I should not be surprised by her absence, since there have never existed friendly relations between 'that foreigner' and my family."

Elvira found in every one of Luisa's words a strong indication that she was aware of Carlos's love for the Countess, and with that thoughtlessness that so often made her commit the worst indiscretions with the best of intentions, she set out to justify her friend as best she could. "I see," she said, "that you have been greatly influenced by the slanderers who are determined to harm Catalina of S., and as I am honored with her friendship, I feel bound to refute slander that disturbs your happiness and wrongs my friend."

Luisa stared at her. Those indiscreet words awakened suspicions that until then had not remotely crossed her mind, since she had not even recalled the existence of the Countess until that moment. Her fixed stare disconcerted Elvira, who kept muttering incoherent words: "Envy, malice—Carlos knows how the Countess has always been maligned. His friendship for her is so disinterested and pure! You should not believe rumors and gossip."

After this truncated speech Elvira fell silent, clearly embarrassed by her position, and Luisa was silent too. The visit was not long. Elvira left without mentioning the Countess again, and Luisa remained lost in thought until her husband's return.

Carlos appeared sadder than ever that day. In contrast, Luisa met him with a more cheerful demeanor than she had had for a long time. As the dinner hour approached, she started talking to her husband, although this custom had been broken in the past months, and among other things she said that Elvira was a devoted friend to him. Carlos praised that woman to the skies, as well as a few others that Luisa named in turn, after which she said, "The one you have never told me about is the Countess of S.; according to what I hear, she also claims to be a great friend of yours."

Carlos shot her an eagle-eyed look that seemed to want to penetrate her soul, and as Luisa managed to keep her simple demeanor, he got up and said boldly, "That great friendship is an unwarranted concession made to me by the public. The Countess of S. is not as great a friend of mine as they suppose. But who has talked to you about her, dear Luisa?"

"Only Elvira," she answered.

Carlos, who felt bolder upon hearing this, added, "I am much closer to her than to the Countess. So what did Elvira say about her friend?"

"That she is very beautiful," said Luisa, daring to fix her gaze on her husband.

"Very beautiful! . . . No, not so much. She's pretty average," he answered, feigning indifference.

"And even before coming to Madrid," Luisa added, "I remember hearing her praised as a woman of great gifts."

"Yes . . . people do say that," Carlos stammered, not knowing what stance to take, "but they exaggerate. Aren't we going to eat today, dear? It's five o'clock."

Luisa got up, and with the excuse of going to give instructions for dinner went to her room to cry. Now she knew all! Her rival was the Countess of S.! And she was beautiful! and highly talented!

This conversation that shed so much light on the suspicions Elvira had awakened in Luisa, was in contrast somewhat reassuring to Carlos. Many times recently he had believed his wife to be perfectly informed of everything related to his fault; and as he could not suspect the simple girl of cunning, as he did not know how quickly the world and misfortune teach women this art which at times serves as a shield and far more often as a dagger, he deduced from the unhappy girl's words that she was in complete ignorance of his accomplice in crime, and he again thought it possible to calm her down, inventing excuses to rationalize his obviously strange behavior.

Unfortunately, his mistake was short-lived. That very day he was destined to discover the full extent of his fault and of his wife's unhappiness. Luisa, succumbing to the heartbreak of that morning, by nightfall was in the throes of a violent fever. When Carlos returned from the Countess's country home, he found her delirious. Luckily don Francisco, who did not know about his daughter-in-law's illness, was not with her, because if he had been he would have learned everything that night.

Luisa, in her delirium, named the Countess and Carlos, spoke of treachery and unfaithfulness, and sometimes invoked death crying, "Maybe he wants it for me! It's the only way for him to regain his lost freedom!"

Carlos, grief-stricken, begged her in vain on his knees to calm down. Luisa looked at him without knowing who he was at first, and when she finally recognized him, cried, "Come! Don't abandon me without mercy! I will learn how to please you and guess your desires, even the most fanciful! Do you need talents in the woman you love? I will acquire them for your sake. I want to possess all the charms, as she does; I want everyone who sees me to say, 'She is the first lady of the world, because she is Carlos's wife.'"

The fever lent her an eloquence that she could never attain in her normal state. She was beautiful, poignant, sublime in her delirium. Carlos, holding her in his arms, thought he would die of grief, and there were moments during that terrible night that three months earlier would have been enough to decide the fate of the two women he was caught between. Moments when the voice of love, which spoke in favor of Catalina, would not have been heeded, nor would the memory of her sacrifices have freed her from being immolated on the sacred altar of duty, by the sad bedside of the chaste wife.

But it was no longer possible; Catalina was no longer only the seductive lover, the sublime friend. Nature, dressing her with majesty, with an indisputable right, now tied her to Carlos with the sweetest and most sacred of bonds. This bond was stronger than all those created by men, and the new duty and new emotion that filled his heart were more powerful than all the tender, pious impulses aroused by Luisa's situation. He was suffering terribly, but he could not make any decision that would release him from this agonizing state. He could not make any promise that would console Luisa in her heartbreak.

Caught between the two women whom he was making equally unhappy, one of whom held the sacred title of his wife, and the other a no less respectable right, impelled by the strongest tenderness for the one and the most violent passion for the other, and the most profound compassion for them both, he despaired of being able to reconcile the happiness of the two, and did not have the strength to sacrifice either. His position was deplorable, and of the three characters in this story, Carlos was at that time surely not the least unfortunate.

That night was really terrible for him, but it passed like any other. Luisa, after getting over the fever brought on by the agitation of that day when she discovered the identity of her rival, returned to her usual state of silent sadness. And Carlos, who saw her resigned although unhappy, and who thought his presence must be painful to the woman who was so offended and so silent, tried to think of a decent way to remove her from that difficult situation, which was also unbearable for him. Luisa already knew all, he could no longer try to deceive her, and since neither could he really satisfy her, the only remaining alternative was to give her heart a rest, removing from her sight the wretch who had betrayed her. That's what Carlos thought—that only his absence could console her, after knowing the full scope of her loss. That absence, which was now necessary, would perhaps lead to tranquility and oblivion. It was cruel to abuse her discretion, always placing her offender before her eyes. It was also unbearable for Carlos to be all day long awkward and tremulous in the presence of that silent victim, who asked for nothing, who complained of nothing, yet whose silence accused him and whose resignation humiliated him.

Then he remembered his father's aspirations, and he began to consider them a plausible means for getting out of the situation they must free themselves from at any cost. By obtaining the appointment of embassy secretary in some foreign country, he could separate from his wife without calling it to anyone's attention, and with a satisfactory excuse that she herself would approve.

Luisa seemed to be in poor health. Some doctors were of the opinion that she would be better off returning to Andalusia, and in any case Carlos decided to say that a long voyage would be harmful to her, and a colder climate not advisable at all. He was counting on Luisa's docility and on what he thought must be her own desire to facilitate that necessary separation, and he was also counting on the Countess's influence to obtain the desired appointment.

In fact, Catalina, who was free and could follow him anywhere, should rejoice over her lover's decision. The doctors could prescribe for her some baths that would explain her departure from Madrid, if she wished to conceal the truth, and in the condition she was in, nothing could be more suitable than an obscure life in a foreign country, near the man she loved and whom she would finally have all to herself.

The happiness she had so longed for some months before, and for which she was willing to sacrifice her position, her name, her future, that happiness that had been her dream of love was now at hand, and obtaining it had not involved a scandal, nor her lover's sacrificing his career, nor mortally wounding a father and a wife. Catalina should have considered herself as happy as it was possible to be in the situation she had gotten herself into—but that was not the case!

The powerful new feeling that energized Carlos's heart, had broken the heart of his friend. For that intense soul, to have such a feeling in such a position was something dreadful. A great and devastating upheaval had taken hold of that woman; only then did she understand the full extent of her offense and the horror of her fate.

What happiness could exist for her? Love? No! Love was no longer the ruling passion in her burning heart. Oh! It was to love that she owed the boundless misery of finding in the sweetest of feelings the most humiliating of sorrows!

Catalina would have been strong in confronting her own misfortune, but she was now concerned with a destiny other than hers; a life a hundred times more precious than her own was in the grip of misery and shame. That same judgment of a world she scorned when its verdict could only fall on her, took on a terrible authority when she envisioned it falling on an adored victim. Far be it from us to exploit that soul in order to paint in detail her secret sorrows; it is enough to sketch them. You women who are mothers! We leave it in your care to complete the picture. Your hearts will tell you more than anything our imagination can reveal.

28

These were the gleaming final days of autumn. The trees were starting to shed their bright foliage, pale leaves carpeted the earth, and the migratory birds, taking flight, went to find on the African coast the heat that the winter would soon steal from the handsome sun of Castile. Sharp winds descended from the snowcapped peaks of the Guadarrama, and you could already feel their biting breath in Madrid, where life was taking on the activity that nature was laying aside. Salons were being formed, solitary theaters regained their splendor, and the life and gaiety that were leaving the fields shifted to the townspeople.

Nonetheless, there was still in nature's aspect that melancholy beauty that is more pleasing to wounded or weary hearts than the cheerful pomp of spring. The last days of good weather are lovely, lovely and sad like the final affections of a once forceful heart. I for one am glad to contemplate a pale, as though weary, sun. Then it does not seem to be an impassive witness to human misery; then it is a friend who, subject to sorrow as we are, bids a faint farewell to his beloved nature. I like to gaze at that same nature some days earlier, bursting with life, youth, and flowers, like a maid of fifteen years; and then, withered and faded, preparing her mourning clothes, like the forlorn widow who laments the loss of her earthly loves. I like the first sounds of the wind that follow the sweet murmurs of the spring breezes: the one is like the tender sighs of a first attachment, sighs of desire and hope; the other like the moans from a mysterious sorrow, when desires are exhausted and hopes fade away. I savor, yes, I savor these melancholy emblems of life in decline more than the rosy images of youth and joy.

Swift and mild October sun! Your light never tired eyes weary from shedding tears, and you have often known how to illuminate the dark depths of a ravaged soul and make sprout there, like those pale, imperceptibly fragrant flowers you give to the earth, sweet and sad memories of a past happiness.

The Countess too loved those days, cloudy like her heart, that nature withered like her youth. She too had passed through the ardent summer of passion, and many dry flowers had fallen from her tree of hope.

She had lost the flirtatiousness that made her so amiable. Her black hair often fell in disarray down her thin back, and her extremely pale complexion was set off by the dark color of her dress. You could hardly tell she had been beautiful. Beauty, like gaiety, passes without leaving a trace; only sorrow can engrave on the human face those deep furrows that not even death can erase.

On the coldest nights you could see her wandering through the fields silent and alone, like a ghost conjured up by despair. Her footsteps hardly raised a moan from the dead leaves covering the ground. But amid the silence, she often stopped to listen intently, as though trying to fathom mysterious words. It was her heart alone that was speaking to her, and who would be bold enough to translate into the conventional language of men the intimate voices of a suffering heart? Who can give a worthy reading of the oracles of grief?

Poor Catalina! Poor, ever deluded soul! Poor soul who ten months earlier lamented feeling empty, and is now exhausted from being too full!

Why are people who have such an inflated thirst for happiness powerless to enjoy it? Why does calm kill those who shipwreck in every storm? What incomprehensible contradiction is there in certain psychic makeups, who in inaction grow restless, eager for movement, and in movement wear out and break down?

What element is found in those souls, at once weak and powerful? What is their fate? Did they just come to earth to bear witness to another existence that they recall, that they yearn for, and that they reveal to common souls by their very impotence to understand or enjoy the present? If this were the case, who would dare ask them to account for their misguided ways?

Nothing entertained the Countess: music, painting, all the arts that she cultivated during those days of splendor and indifference meant nothing to her in her life of love and hardship. If she tried to sing, her voice was out of tune, and deep discordant sobs rose from her breast. Her brush wandered over the canvas without managing to give form to any idea.

In her bitterest days of tedium and melancholy, she had found distraction in books, but now not a one could please her. Even the saddest poetry did not resonate with her soul, because poeticized grief, expressed in lyric verse and adorned with imagery, can only move hearts that have not yet felt it in its naked, harsh reality. It is a sorrow that speaks to melancholy hearts, but not to wounded hearts.

She found novels even more tiresome. Those stories that shared some similarity with her lot afflicted her without arousing her interest. It is painful to see a pallid sketch of the sorrows we are feeling, and if the picture were correct, it would horrify us more than move us. The unfortunate person whose face bears the pitiful scars of a cruel disease would not seek to find his wasted features reproduced in a mirror.

One of the worst aspects of genuine, deep sorrow is that it blinds us to all others. The saddest spectacle is incapable of moving us. Our own misfortune, when it is immense, makes us oblivious to the plight of others. He who has suffered feels compassion; he who suffers needs for himself all the treasures of his soul.

For that reason, there is a terrible kind of egoism in sorrow. The noblest souls give in to cruel impulses in the moments when they feel tormented. A great sorrow needs to overflow, to spread to everything around it, to see all of nature suffer. A unique, solitary sorrow is the most unbearable of all.

Poor Catalina! In earlier times she doled out benefits to those around her, and the pains eased by her hand gave off a fragrance that sweetened hers. Now she does good without taking part in it; the misery she alleviates is much less bitter than her vain wealth. She envies the beggar who struggles to her door, and throws him, without pity, the gold that can do so much for him and can do nothing for her.

She often gets letters from Elvira, cruel letters despite being dictated by a kind heart. They always hint at the public censure that a strong will can scorn when it is unjust, but that always hurts us if our conscience is not clear. In vain does pride rear its head like an avenging angel to proclaim its strength and chase off the dark shadow of regret; in vain will it be trampled on without admitting defeat. Pride can cover with a fake mask humiliations of the heart, but it cannot fool the heart itself.

Poor Catalina, who in her misfortune cannot find the comfort offered by a divine religion, long proudly disdained and now implored in vain from a shaky faith. The hand that wounds her still does not deem her humble enough to be worthy of being consoled. And yet that rational skepticism grows superstitious, and overcome with terror seems to find in a thousand natural events, in a thousand accidental trifles, the threat of a God who judges and condemns her. A cloud that covers the moon at the moment she gazes at it; a black bird that hovers over her head in flight; a portrait of her as a pure child, by chance stained and almost blotted out; a nightmare in which she dreams of falling from one chasm to the next, without ever reaching the bottom; a mystical book opened by chance to a passage that describes the despair of the damned, a despair that lasts an eternity without ever growing weary or old—the most horrific thought the human mind can conceive! Everything seems prophetic; everything frightens her. Such was the lot of that woman whom the world condemned, and whom Luisa in her sadness often called her triumphant enemy, her happy rival!

We have compassion for the murderer, for the outlaw whom they lead to the gallows. But there is none for those guilty of crimes of the heart, the secret atonement for which is so long and painful!

We are all ready to cast the first stone at the unlucky mortal who has fallen; we all want to punish those sins for which no punishment is assigned in our legal code, because God alone should impose it, judging them in His court of justice. But we usurp from Him the right that, in general, we have granted Him; we individually set ourselves up as judges and turn ourselves into executioners, and we call ourselves just and virtuous when we are closed to pity and mute to forgiveness.

29

Carlos was appointed secretary to the Spanish ambassador to England, and he had to leave to assume his position without delay. Don Francisco had intended to accompany him with Luisa, but Carlos got him to change his plan, while being careful not to offer overt resistance. He persuaded him that the British climate would be very harmful to his wife in her delicate state of health, and that his father's absence would be highly detrimental to his affairs; the only thing that made the kind old man waver and not give in entirely to his son's wishes was the fear of dealing a death blow to his daughter-in-law with this second long separation from her husband.

Nevertheless, Carlos prepared for his departure without the slightest indication of his wife's accompanying him, and she, who had remained silent up until then, finally decided to learn her fate. One morning she went into don Francisco's room, where Carlos was too, and trying to remain calm she asked categorically if she should not go with her husband. Don Francisco, embarrassed at the question, stammered, "That is for the two of you to decide. I will not separate you again, nor do I think it is good for either of you."

"In that case," said Luisa firmly, "there is nothing to prevent me from accompanying my husband. That is my duty and my wish."

Carlos, a bit taken aback, hastened to reply, "Your health is delicate, my dear, and for the time being you should not think of exposing yourself to the hardships of the voyage and the rigor of a northern climate. You will go to spend the winter with my father in Seville, and you can plan to join me later on."

"My health will be much better when I breathe a different atmosphere from this," Luisa replied. "I will be better off in any country in the world with you than I can be in Seville without you."

"She is right," said don Francisco. "I think the greatest harm to her will come from your absence."

Carlos lowered his eyes and, visibly annoyed and upset, said that it would be crazy to allow a fragile woman to undertake a trip to a cold country at the start of winter.

"I grant you that," the old man replied, "but it would be worse if she stayed, because this poor girl cannot live without you. I will not take responsibility for her suffering. If she is really determined to go with you, she should go."

"If she is really determined," said Carlos with vehemence and anger, "of course she can go, but neither do I take responsibility for anything bad that comes in its wake."

Luisa stared at him intently, and realizing that her husband wanted to get away from her, she lowered her eyes bathed in tears, and said with sad resignation, "I won't go, Carlos; I won't go!"

Carlos took her hand and squeezed it tenderly. That demonstration of gratitude provoked her. He dared to thank her for consenting to her own unhappiness, to her own abandonment!

She got up and quickly left the room. Shut in her own room she gave in to a bitter lament. And yet, she was far from believing her husband to be as guilty as he really was. She did not even remotely suspect that the Countess was accompanying him to England, and she still found some solace in the thought that if she had to undergo a long separation from Carlos, there remained the hope that by leaving Madrid he might be cured of his guilty passion.

"He cannot bear being with me," the unhappy woman said to herself, "because his heart is weighed down by the separation from his lover. But time will ease that sorrow and extinguish the flame of a sinful love, and when heaven reunites us, my husband will be more worthy of this boundless tenderness that he cannot now value or return."

So she swallowed her sadness fortified by that hope, and arrived at the eve of Carlos's departure without losing heart. During those days Carlos had been so tender and affectionate to her that Luisa, who had not found him like that for many months, inwardly rejoiced thinking, "He still loves me! That adored heart will once more be mine alone! Perhaps he desired this departure as the only way to break off a guilty relationship. Perhaps he is denying me the pleasure of his company because he wants to atone for his misconduct far from me, and return to my arms freed of a shameful passion." And the innocent girl got down on her knees and gave thanks to God, because He had finally heard her prayers and snatched her husband from the jaws of sin.

This was how she was spending the last solemn day she was to have with Carlos, when don Francisco came in, saying, "I just fulfilled a social courtesy that out of laziness and forgetfulness I had neglected. I went to call on the Countess of S. at her country home. I should have done this upon my arrival, but now it was indispensable, because I have learned that it was through her influence that Carlos obtained his appointment, and I would have gone from being inattentive to being ungrateful if I had not gone to thank her."

"Her!" Luisa exclaimed in surprise. "She was the one who wanted to get him away from Madrid!"

"Get him away from Madrid!" the old man said with a smile. "She was certainly not thinking of that, but the only thought on your mind is that your husband is leaving. The Countess learned of my aspirations, and despite our inattentiveness to her, she used her influence to help us, without giving a thought as to whether my pretty Luisa would have to separate from her Carlos."

"And you were in her villa! You saw her!" said Luisa with eager curiosity. "Is she beautiful? What did she say to you? Does she know that my husband is leaving me?"

"I will answer all of your questions in turn," said don Francisco with a calm that exasperated the girl. "She is beautiful, or rather, she is attractive, with a very delicate figure, very fine, quite distinguished. You can see that she was pretty, but she is ill and sad; that is why the doctors have recommended for her a change of climate."

"A change of climate!" Luisa exclaimed in an anxious, worried tone that caught the old man's attention. "So will she do it? Tell me, will she do it?"

"Of course, my dear. I told her how glad we would have been to have Carlos accompany her, because the Countess has also decided to go to London, but she has to stay a few weeks longer in Madrid, and Carlos cannot delay his departure. 'We will see each other there,' she told me, 'and your son will have a true friend in that foreign land.'"

"She is going away with him! She is following him!" cried Luisa, beside herself. "Ah, now I understand it all! For this I am abandoned! For this . . . !"

Crazed and unaware of what she was saying, pale, shaking and possessed by a kind of fury, she got up and grasping her uncle's hands, "And you agree to it!" she continued. "You went to thank her for making me unhappy, for stealing my husband, for dragging him into crime! This is too much; no, no, I will not put up with it."

Don Francisco looked at her in astonishment: "Luisa! What are you saying?" he exclaimed. "You are raving, my child!"

"No, I am not raving," she replied, more and more worked up. "It is the truth—the shameful truth that my discretion has concealed until now! But no more; I can't take it anymore. You will know all: that woman is my husband's lover, the one who has stolen his heart from me, the one who tears him away from his homeland and his family in order to have him all to herself . . . because she considers me too fortunate to be living with him even when scorned!"

"Luisa, watch what you're saying! Do you know that if this were true . . . ? Good Lord, Luisa! Who planted in you this mean suspicion?"

"All of Madrid!" she answered in despair. "Everyone knows it! Only you haven't seen my tears; only you have been unaware of my abandonment, nor observed the pitying looks I've received wherever I went. You who saw me at death's door and did not understand the blow that had killed me!"

Don Francisco was shaking from head to foot, and anger darkened his brow and blanched his lips. "Could it be?" he yelled in a voice like thunder. "Have I been the plaything of a loathsome adulterer and his vile accomplice? Carlos! Could my son Carlos be both a criminal and a hypocrite? Did he let me go to congratulate a despicable woman for his triumph so that she in turn could laugh at me? Me! Luisa! What are you saying? Do you know what you're saying?"

"Yes, the truth, Father," she said, throwing herself at his feet. "But it's not him; she is no doubt the criminal—the most to blame! Father, give me back my husband, or this very instant take this life that he may already be cursing. Death or my Carlos, Father!"

"Yes, I'll return him to you. By God, I'll return him to you!" the old man screamed, more and more enraged and completely carried away by his vehement nature. "I'll restore your honor, or with my own hands tear out the vile heart that has taken it from you. Don't worry, Luisa! I will come before them like the avenging God they have offended, and I'll trample with my feet on that brazen courtesan, and I'll drag to yours that sinful husband. Yes, yes, I'll tear off their masks: dishonor and shame to them both!"

And that rash, violent man who could never control his first impulses ran out in a frenzy, leaving Luisa terrified.

Then she understood what she had done; then the fit of jealous rage gave way to softer feelings in her timid, sensitive heart, and she trembled for the culprits. She imagined her husband battered with harsh reprimands, exasperated by their rigor, perhaps showing a lack of respect to his father and furious with the indiscreet wife who had caused the scandal; and her rival dishonored by the recklessness of don Francisco and even of Carlos himself, humiliated, completely ruined, and more precious to her lover on account of her very misfortune, because when is self-interest not mixed with the nobler instincts?

Poor Luisa, whose imagination exaggerated all the possible consequences of her indiscretion, now felt as overwhelmed by fear as she had earlier been by jealousy. Like a madwoman she ran out of that fatal room where she saw only images of terror, and upon learning that don Francisco had left she cried in despair, "He went there! There! He'll kill them both! My God! He'll kill them without knowing what he's doing!" And stirred by impulses that were foreign to her timid, peaceful nature, she called for a carriage, quickly got in and told the driver to take her to Elvira's house.

Upon arriving, she found Elvira who was going out, and summoning her into her carriage, she said in a tone and with a look that made the woman think she was not in her right mind, "Come with me, señora! Come with me to prevent sensational scandals, terrible misfortunes."

Elvira gazed at her in astonishment, and Luisa exclaimed in profound sorrow, "I am not mad, no! But I was a few minutes ago, and I told all! The painful discretion of so many months lapsed for a moment, and my mistake may be irreparable. Do you understand me, señora? They, as you know, are lulled in the warmth of their happiness, because they are going off together, because they love each other! And meanwhile an enraged father is flying to them to do . . . who knows what? Neither you nor I can tell, but my uncle is in a blind fit of rage, and he told me, 'I will trample on that woman.' Carlos will not allow it . . . he'll rebel against his father! Oh, my God! Do you understand, señora?"

And she wrung her hands in despair.

Elvira had in fact understood, and as frightened as Luisa, she said, "What should we do? You give the orders."

"Go there, go there," cried Luisa. "We must go where they are—to save them! She is your friend, and he is my husband!"

Elvira had heard enough. She ordered the coachman to drive at full speed to the Countess's country home. "Ride the horses into the ground," she said; "I'll pay for them." And the coach set off, racing down the street.

30

When don Francisco had gone to visit the Countess that day, he left Madrid rather early, but not so early that Carlos, informed the night before of his resolve, could not warn her about it. Therefore she received the old man with relative serenity, a few minutes after Carlos had left her, since the latter got there before his father. It was a short visit, and Catalina, who did not expect her lover to return until nightfall, had shut herself in her room in her usual state of sadness.

It was around four in the afternoon when she heard the sound of a carriage, and she thought that Carlos had come a few hours early, which would be natural considering that his departure was set for the following day so he would have to leave her earlier than usual.

She called for one of the servants and said, "Let him come in," without going out to greet him as usual. Her low spirits had affected her body. That had been one of her hardest days. Don Francisco's visit, the hypocrisy it had entailed on her part, Carlos's imminent departure, her decision to follow him, all combined to make her more anxious than ever. That formerly so lively creature had been lying motionless for an hour, her head leaning on the marble mantelpiece, which was less white than her face, and she did not move even upon hearing footsteps she believed to be her lover's.

Elvira rushed in. Luisa, trembling and overcome by conflicting emotions, remained motionless at the door.

Catalina looked up languidly, and upon seeing Elvira a melancholy smile accompanied her "Oh, it's you!" her only greeting.

"Yes, it's me!" her friend exclaimed with her usual indiscretion, heightened by her inner turmoil at that moment. "Catalina! We have come to save you, if there is still time." And she threw herself crying into her arms.

The Countess repeated her friend's last words, fixing her eyes with surprise on the unknown person who was a silent witness to the scene. Luisa lowered hers, and the strong crimson color that her embarrassing position brought to her cheeks contrasted with the deep pallor of her rival.

The Countess trembled. We do not know if she recalled the beautiful facial features she had seen as a painted image, or if it was by an instinct of the heart, but her sudden agitation made clear that she already knew the identity of the woman who was in her presence.

If it were not for the words uttered by Elvira, this visit could have been explained by that of don Francisco, but what her friend had just told Catalina made her vaguely intuit some of the truth. She tried to get up but was stopped by the shaking in her knees, so inviting Luisa with a gesture to sit down, she said weakly, "I believe I have the honor to receive . . ."

"Señora de Silva," said Elvira hastily, "Carlos's wife, Catalina. She knows everything! Everything! And she has come . . ."

"For what?" the Countess broke in vehemently, her face seeming to light up with indignation. "For what?" she repeated, fixing on the disturbed girl a penetrating, almost terrible look.

Luisa, although overcome by the extraordinary position in which she found herself, managed to regain the dignity of a noble, innocent soul, and moving forward timidly but firmly, she said in a fairly audible voice, "Not to scold you, señora, nor to complain of my unhappiness; not at all, I swear it!"

These words aroused all of Catalina's pride, and her eyes flashed with anger, as convulsively grasping Elvira's hands she tried in vain to respond.

Luisa, moved by her agitation and not comprehending all that was going on at that moment in that proud soul, said in a soft tone,

"No, no, I have not come to insult the fallen one; may God forgive you, señora, as I forgive you!"

Catalina could take no more. "Take back that pardon," she said in a muffled voice; "I do not accept it. I am fallen—it's true! I am guilty in the eyes of the world, and you are pure; you are virtuous! What more do you want, señora? As a proof of love you have accepted the honor of being called Carlos's wife, of being respected as such. As a proof of mine, I have accepted affronts, the world's condemnation. And you are the one who pardons, flaunting your generosity! And you are the one who pursues me to the depths of my retreat, to tell me that you do not reproach me for the crime of having sacrificed myself for an emotion that brought you so much honor, so many advantages!"

In response to this bitter sarcasm, Luisa, hurt and indignant, could not utter a single word, and Elvira exclaimed, "Catalina, that is not the way you should talk to her! She feels for you and has come to save you."

"To save me!" said Catalina sarcastically. "I am grateful. But no, señora, I have no recourse. I have wholly sacrificed myself, and I am forever lost. I am his lover and you are his wife. The world will feel for you and call you the victim. If you relate what you have just done, you will not be denied compensation for the generosity you have shown me. But as for me, I expect nothing. You know what my fate should be; fulfill your glorious destiny with as much resolve as I accept mine."

"No," Luisa exclaimed, with an energy borne of the triumph of her goodness over her jealousy and indignation. "No! You will not fulfill that shameful destiny. It is never too late for repentance, señora, and if men do not have mercy, God's is infinite. He never leaves the sinner without recourse; he never closes the door to atonement. I have come, señora, I have come . . ."

"To insult me!" screamed the Countess, enraged. "That's enough, señora!" she went on in a lordly tone. "Leave!" she said, choking with anger, jealousy, and shame. Luisa was about to reply, but she did not let her. "Leave!" she said again, and in standing up made her condition more apparent.

Luisa looked at her and let out a scream, covering her face with her hands. The Countess understood that scream and that gesture, and she fell down, almost overcome. It was a moment of supreme humiliation for that proud soul.

But oh! what was going through Luisa's soul was surely no less painful. Jealousy, the cruelest pangs of jealousy were ravaging her upon understanding her rival's rights over the heart of her husband. And yet, those sacred rights were respectable in her eyes and seemed to invest Catalina with a majestic character. "It's her!" she thought; "she is really his wife! Nature has endowed her with a right that to me was denied!"

The profound emotion caused by this thought prevailed over all others and allowed to rise only the noblest, the worthiest feeling: compassion!

Luisa was no longer a woman; she was an angel beyond all human weaknesses, and when she removed her hands, revealing the divine expression illuminating her face, Catalina herself bowed her proud head, overcome by a feeling of respect.

"Señora," said Luisa in a poignant tone, "only my death can set Carlos free, and at this moment I implore it from the mercy of heaven. If I could without sin end my unhappy life, I would in that way bear witness to the feelings of my heart. I hope that God will soon allow me to leave this vale of tears in which mine have been so bitter. The blow that has pierced my soul offers me that hope."

The Countess no doubt understood all the sublimity of that peerless self-denial, because she then burst into violent tears.

Luisa went on, "In the meantime, go live in the foreign country you have chosen. I will appease an angry father by deceiving him, as I rashly revealed to him the truth. There is still time. I will look for him and calm his anger, and as long as I live I will not leave the abandoned old man . . . and I will not die, señora, before attaining for you and for *him* pardon and grace."

Luisa was leaving. The Countess got up and stopped her. She hesitated a moment . . . then she threw herself at her feet.

Luisa opened her arms, and each at the other's breast they both cried for a long time. Elvira was also crying, the only witness to that moving scene. Two souls, two noble souls bound together at that moment by every generous feeling, opened their hearts to each other. And they were nonetheless two women's hearts!

Luisa advised the Countess on how to effect her departure more discreetly. Catalina listened to her with reverence, and seemed disposed to blindly obey her. Luisa was divine in those moments. A sublime resignation was painted on each of her features, and on seeing her so beautiful, so young, so saintly, the Countess found very guilty and very foolish the man who was deserting her.

At nightfall they parted. It was decided that the Countess would go to join her lover a week after his departure, and that to dispel if possible the gossip against Catalina and avoid people's knowing the real aim of her departure, Luisa would visit her publicly in Madrid, where the Countess had to return before her departure, and they would publicize the friendship to which they now swore.

Luisa and Elvira returned to Madrid, and the Countess, upon finding herself alone, exclaimed with a kind of gaiety unusual in her even on her happy days, "It's done! This agonizing drama is drawing to a close! I give you thanks, destiny!"

Don Francisco was at home when Luisa arrived. When he had gone out full of that violent rage that aroused the young woman to such a daring resolve, by a lucky chance he bumped into an old friend who in earlier times had enjoyed his full confidence. With his usual rashness, heightened at that moment by his blind anger, he told him everything that had occurred and his violent plans, and the friend, who was clearly both kind and clever, got him to desist from his plans without openly contradicting them. The friend placated don Francisco by convincing him that his change of course was purely based on his own reflections, and he returned home resolved not to take a step further without having clearer proof of his son's crime. His wise and prudent friend had made him suspicious of Luisa's testimony, and the good gentleman said to himself in a low voice, "Good Lord! I was crazy to believe in the fantastic notions of a jealous girl!"

When he returned home and found that Luisa had gone out, he went to look for her in vain in every place he thought he might find her, in all the churches and all of her acquaintances' homes. Fortunately he did not give in to the desire to tell everyone he met of his concern upon not finding his daughter-in-law because of the jealousy she had revealed to him that day, and he returned home tired and alarmed, but resolved to act with caution. A few minutes after his arrival, he saw Luisa come in with a calm, serene expression. This change bode well, and Luisa confirmed his hopes by confessing that she felt she had misjudged her husband, that upon hearing his words of praise for the Countess she had become jealous, a jealousy that seemed justified upon learning that they were going to meet in England, but that having later confirmed the degree of friendship that existed between the Countess and Carlos, she was ashamed of having been too hasty in her judgments.

Don Francisco did not have the slightest suspicion of her generous lie, and after holding forth at length about women's shallowness and indiscretion, their jealousy and spite and so on, he ended up praising himself to the skies: his reasonableness and good sense in not having given full credence to Luisa's accusations against her husband.

Luisa listened to him patiently, and when she could finally go back to her room, she got down on her knees and exclaimed, "My God! I have made myself an accomplice to an adulterous love, which is sinful in your eyes. The generous feelings that I have embraced are culpable weaknesses before your severe justice. Oh, my Lord, my Lord! I humbly submit to the punishment you wish to impose on me, but let my crime not be in vain! May *he* be happy, my God!"

31

It was just a few minutes after Luisa and Elvira left the Countess when Carlos arrived at her villa. He had passed the coach on the road, but he was far from suspecting that it carried his wife, and she for her part was too lost in her own thoughts to notice a man on horseback who passed the carriage heading in the opposite direction.

Catalina received Carlos in a calm, almost cheerful mood. It had been a long time since Carlos had seen her like that, and he was delighted at the thought that he could finally offer his unfortunate friend all the solace he could muster in the sad situation he was placing her in.

It had not been a peaceful day for Carlos. Upon separating from Luisa he was not only suffering for the pain he was causing her. His own heart was providing ample bitterness, because he still tenderly loved the poor girl, and in those moments his tenderness was heightened by the sacrifice of her he was making. Moreover, he was alarmed at the thought that his wife's virtue might not always withstand the dangers to which his abandonment was exposing it, and he was tormented in turn by the image of a heartbroken, desolate Luisa succumbing to despair, and by the cruel thought that she might get over it, forget him, despise him, and perhaps place in another the affection he had so poorly rewarded.

He was sad and pensive all day, and upon reuniting with the Countess he needed her to show him all her love and intoxicate him with all her delights, to relieve for some moments the gloomy sadness that was engulfing him.

He sat down beside her and gazed at her with pleasure.

"You look lovely, my friend," he said; "you look cheerful. Tell me, yes, tell me that you hope to be happy; I need to hear it. I am going to be apart from you for a few days, and I want to hold in my ears the melodious sound of your voice. Talk to me, Catalina; tell me that you love me; take me out of myself and plunge me, bedazzled, into that obscure future that is opening before us."

"Yes," she answered. "Come and sit close beside me . . . even closer. There, good. I will talk to you. I too need to talk about the future that I will owe to your love. You are doing so much for me; you are sacrificing so much! No, don't pretend. Don't hide from me what I am costing you. I know that in these moments your heart understands the value of what you are sacrificing on my account, and that very fact heightens the gratitude of mine.

"Fate had given you as a companion a woman worthy of your adoration, a woman who should cross the world's quagmires without soiling the fringe of her mantle of innocence. Unlucky me! A very different fate has fallen to my lot. I have been your ruin; I have drawn you with me to the ghastly abyss that a criminal passion opened before me. She was given the mission of making you happy and virtuous, and I that of destroying you. Why has my evil destiny conquered hers? On this supreme day when the die is cast forever, I do not know if I should take as a consolation or as a final dose of bitterness the profound belief that my poor reason could not avoid it. And yet, I was not born with evil instincts. On the contrary, I believe my heart was naturally good, and that no noble feeling was foreign to it. I will not excuse my errant ways by attributing them to an unfortunate psychic makeup that would inevitably follow the impulse of innate tendencies. So what has been the hidden force, the mysterious power that has ruined me? Am I to believe that virtues in and of themselves can lead to evil, and that crimes are usually only the result of great qualities carried to the extreme and led astray by events and circumstances? I do not know if I can make such a generalization, but in my case I think it is correct. I loved in you the virtue that was to make me forget my own. Incapable of giving in to petty impulses, I have immersed myself in vice without self-contamination, and my love of virtue has often led me astray.

"I had conceived mistaken ideas about the human heart. In my early youth I asked for too much, and upon finding my hopes frustrated I gradually came to expect too little. Both extremes were wrong, and yet both had a noble source. My high demands were borne of enthusiasm, and when I no longer hoped or asked for anything, I could still be generous and use the goodness that no longer deceived me as a source of boundless indulgence. This indulgence was more than a quality; it was a virtue, because I confess that it did not come naturally to me. Tolerance did not come easily to one with such a fervent heart and such a severely virtuous soul. It took a great effort to descend from enthusiasm without falling into a total dejection that would lead to scorn, or into a profound bitterness that would lead to hatred. It was a triumph of my will over my nature, and just as a thousand times my enthusiasm for good led me to ill, now I could only avoid this by loosening the strong fibers of a too severe virtue.

"The world that had not understood my enthusiasm, now did not understand my indulgence. Society did not know what it had cost me to forgive it for so many beautiful beliefs it had snatched away; it did not appreciate the virtue in my tolerance. It demanded more; it found me indulgent and it wanted me respectful, but I could not bow before the false idols that its institutions had erected as gods. I could not offer to conventional virtues the homage I had wished to bestow on the true virtues I had sought in vain.

"Always misunderstood, always meanly slandered, I still took pleasure in that generosity of spirit that pardoned injustice. How many times, Carlos, have I needed injustice to call forth some of the generous feelings that reason had buried in the depths of my soul! It is so sweet to pardon!

"I had survived my enthusiasm without falling into despair, but oh! can I also survive my pride? Now that I am at the world's feet, in need of that forgiveness that I had so often granted it, now that I find in myself a more severe judge than that same world that condemns me, now that I am dragging the man I love with me into my deep fall . . . now, Carlos, I know that nothing can save the victims claimed by destiny, and that akin to those dogs whose remarkable sense of smell detects the scent of death in a still living body, so the world senses and predicts the fate of those unfortunates who are destined to offer them the spectacle of a pitiful downfall.

"But Carlos, never blame yourself for my unhappiness. Perhaps it was inevitable. If passion has led me to crime, the eternal void of an empty heart would have done me greater harm. I was convinced that I was already condemned to that horrid fate, and interpreting inaction as death I was unjust to my own heart. My heart has proved me wrong, showing that enthusiasm never dies in souls capable of feeling it, and that, like the poetic bird that is reborn from its own ashes, the power to love never dies in fervent hearts. Whether they are weary or wounded, enervated or withdrawn, there always exist those mysterious ashes that a divine spark can abruptly reignite.

"The love that has ruined me has been my sole good on earth. I confess my guilt without repenting of it. I deplore my destiny, but I accept it. Carlos! Only the wrong I am doing to you gives me regrets; that which I have done to myself gives me no pain. I prefer this unhappiness to that of a life with no object, and now that I am guilty I am worth somewhat more in my own eyes than when I had resigned myself to being nothing. Pride suffers, the heart endures . . . but I have lived! I have loved! May the world condemn me and heaven punish me—I am resigned to this."

"Catalina!" Carlos exclaimed. "These are not the words my heart was seeking. What does that world or that heaven matter to us now, my love? Speak to me of our love, of the joy you are going to bring me . . . I can never fully repay it; it is worth a whole eternity of atonement. Isn't it true, dear friend, that I can still make us both happy?"

"Yes," she said, "I believe so. We will be happy living each for the other, but only by breaking all the ties that still bind us to the world and neglecting all of our duties. There may be moments when remorse strikes us amid our pleasure, moments when you recall an old father and an innocent wife whom you have abandoned, moments when I sense your remorse and hate myself for being its cause . . . but what of it, Carlos? Those moments will pass and we will again be happy. It is true that our joy will have to be buried in mystery like a crime; that our children will not be able to call us by the sweet names of 'father' and 'mother'; that someday they may curse the lives they owe to us; and that when we reach old age and hold out our arms in search of a homeland, a family . . . we find nothing! But we are still young, Carlos, and our love should suffice."

Carlos shuddered and said with profound bitterness, "It's true!"

"Your wife," Catalina went on, "is more deserving of compassion. So young, so in love, so worthy of being loved, and forsaken for another! For another who is not worthy of kissing the soles of her feet! Her misfortune would be our cruelest remorse if we did not nourish, as we should, the hope that time will heal her heart's wound. Yes, time, because you will undoubtedly never return to her side. Upon following you I will be a complete outcast to the world, and you will not want me to return to be its laughingstock, much less try to abandon me. The ties that bind us will soon be tighter and more sacred, and our destiny is perforce an eternal exile. Luisa will finally find consolation; perhaps a new and happier love . . ."

"Stop!" Carlos broke in in a kind of rage. "Stop in the name of heaven, Catalina! What unheard-of pleasure do you find in breaking my heart? Who the devil is inspiring words that fall like molten lead in my ears?"

"I want to paint for you a picture of our future with all its possible consequences," she answered calmly. "But why are you trembling, my love? Amid all the unhappiness, all the humiliations, how happy we will be to know that we will always be together, and that the curses of our family, the world's censure, the threats of heaven are so many more ties that bind us, cutting us off from whatever could serve as an obstacle to our love!

"Carlos! If you are sometimes weak enough to miss all you have sacrificed for me and you are cruel enough to let me know it, you will kill me! Of that there is no doubt. But I am hoping that you will never ever remember your homeland, your father, your wife. There will never come the day when you need to be something in the world, never the time when you need public respect, your family's affection, your friends' regard. I will always be enough for your heart, my love—isn't it true? I will console you if your father curses you on his deathbed; I will help you withstand the pain of having caused the unhappiness and the possible infidelities of your wife. If that angel succumbs to the harsh trial to which you are submitting her innocence, I will ease your remorse; I will compensate with my love for all those goods that the world esteems. Oh yes, we will be happy in spite of everything!"

Carlos could take no more.

"Catalina," he said, standing up abruptly, "this is too much! You should not be the one to punish me for the offenses I have incurred from the love you inspired in me. You should not be the instrument of divine punishment. Why are you speaking to me in this way? What more do you want from me, Catalina?"

"All I want from you is happiness. Can you give me that? Answer, Carlos: Do you hope to make me happy? Do you think happiness is possible for us?"

Carlos was silent.

She went on: "Many will tell you that there is no happiness without virtue; that there is no love with dishonor; that if love often succumbs to the weight of an eternal bond, it never survives for long in an atmosphere of shame. They will say that the day will come when we will stop loving each other, and this, to our misfortune, before we have stopped living! But I will not utter such blasphemies. I, Carlos, hope that our love will be as lasting, as powerful as our resistance was weak. It is true that you loved Luisa, and you have stopped loving her; it is true that I myself have felt I was in love other times and no longer love the same objects; it is true that everything passes, everything ends! But our love, Carlos, will defy that eternal law of nature, because what would become of us if we stopped loving each other? When passion between a married couple fades away, there still remain sweet ties that bind them; there are still compensations: they can still feel mutual respect, still be friends . . . But if we stopped loving each other, condemned by the world, sacrificed for the feeling that has abandoned us, each guilty in the other's eyes . . . we might curse each other!"

Carlos sat down again in a state of deep dejection, and lowering his head he stayed for a long time in gloomy silence.

Catalina showed no mercy and went on: "Whatever might be the effect on your heart of what I am going to reveal to you, I want to obey a generous impulse of my own. Before you sacrifice for my love the unfortunate girl whose happiness you swore to dedicate yourself to, I want you to know how great a good you are forsaking and to understand the extent of the gratitude I owe you.

"Luisa, the wife you are offending, the rival I have abhorred, knows and approves of our decision. I can repeat from my own lips words from hers: 'Only my death,' she said, 'can set Carlos free, and I implore it from the mercy of heaven . . . I will devote my remaining days on earth to the abandoned old man, and I will not die before obtaining grace and pardon for Carlos and his beloved.'"

"You saw her?" Carlos screamed. "Catalina, for pity's sake answer me. You saw her? What do your words mean? What are you suggesting?"

"I saw her!" the Countess answered, and she then related her entire conversation with Luisa, describing with moving eloquence the sublime abnegation of the saintly girl.

Carlos relieved his agitated heart with an outpouring of tears. The Countess received them on her breast, and her harsh language vanished upon seeing her lover's grief.

"Don't distress yourself so much," she said in a sweet tone; "perhaps you are not as guilty as you now judge yourself, nor is the unhappiness that oppresses you as irreparable as you think. Men had joined you and Luisa with permanent bonds, which are perhaps too heavy a weight for a fleeting life; but souls are destined for eternal life, souls will meet in heaven; if the weakness of the flesh divides them on earth, there, where all loves are compatible, there, where there is no crime in love, where love never fades, there they will be reunited with ties that cannot be broken by faithlessness or death.

"Don't you hope for this, my Carlos? Don't you believe at this moment, as I do, in the immortality of thought and feeling? Don't you need a God and an everlasting life, and an all-encompassing love? Yes, there is a God whose mercy is borne of His justice, a God who knows that the human heart is too weak to be judged with severity. Mercy, that divine feeling that He placed in the depths of our souls, springs from His.

"We are guilty, but don't you feel, as I do, the sweetest hope descend to your soul upon speaking of mercy? Don't you feel that that moonbeam that shines through the window and bathes your handsome brow has come down from heaven to bring us pardon? Carlos! Let's not worry about tomorrow, let's not concern ourselves with an uncertain future, and as if this were the last night of our lives, let's talk about God and about our love."

Carlos was listening to her, but he no longer understood her. He was completely distracted, and was growing more and more stirred up by the minute. Oh! That night that Catalina told him to consider the last night of the two of their lives was not—but it *was* the last that he would spend with his Luisa, the angel who now appeared to him more beautiful, pure, and darling than ever.

Divine words were flowing from the Countess's lips, but he could no longer hear them. It was nine o'clock at night, and although she asked him to stay a moment longer, he refused and rose to leave.

At that moment Catalina's serenity faltered somewhat. Her hands shook as she held them out to Carlos in a gesture of farewell.

"In a few days we will meet again," he told her, "never to part, and horrid as is the future you have described to me, I accept it with you. But grant me the last hours of this sad night, which should be devoted to solitude and bitterness. Let me mourn in silence the destiny of the one whom I will sacrifice on the altar of my love, and before leaving her forever let me hear from her pure lips a word of pardon."

"Pardon!" repeated the Countess. "What a beautiful, sublime word! What mortal over the course of his life has not felt a need for it? I am asking for yours, my friend, because at this moment I am greatly suffering. Come, revive in my soul a flagging faith.

"The hope for a life beyond the grave is a paternal smile from heaven. I feel a need for it at this moment of our separation. How sad and solemn is the word 'Farewell'! The look we receive from the loved one from whom we are going to separate may be the last! The events of tomorrow are as obscure as those of twenty centuries from now. What angel spreads his wings to shelter the adored head from the sudden blast of death? Who can assure us, my beloved, that this is not the final hour of life for one of the two of us?"

Some tears moistened the Countess's cheeks, and Carlos, moved, said, "No, my friend, don't torment yourself with gloomy thoughts; if our faults do not find mercy before God, His punishment should fall on me alone, on me who has poisoned the life of two angels! Yes, you will live to brighten my days on earth, and when I die blessing you, I will offer myself resigned for an eternal atonement."

"How you love me!" she said. "Oh! Never blame yourself for the wrong you have done me. Upon feeling myself so loved, I enjoy a happiness that could not be bought with a thousand sufferings. Carlos! I owe you supreme moments of joy. If I died now, I would still carry with me to the grave a fragrance of love, which might later have disappeared. Why would death be a misfortune for me? Why? I still love and am loved, and perhaps this divine flame would go out before our existence. It must be a terrible thing to outlive one's own heart! To be a corpse, and not be able to rest in the tomb!

"Carlos! If death took me by surprise now, my final moments would not be hard. Death would reconcile me with myself and with heaven, and the love that is shattering my fragile frame would gain strength from my soul at the moment when it triumphantly broke free of coarse matter.

"My death at this time would spare you many years of regret, and as my body rested in the grave, my soul would keep watch over yours. If the effects of my guilt did not survive, if the tears of our innocent victim did not come to disturb the peace of my ashes, how beautifully the sun would shine tomorrow on my tombstone! And that is as it should be, my friend. If I died, my voice would rise from the grave to ask you for peace. 'Earn,' it would say, 'earn with your virtue my ashes' repose, my soul's pardon! Atone on earth for our common faults, and make yourself worthy of eternal life and eternal love, which God grants to the repentant as well as to the innocent.'

"Woe to you if, ignoring my pleas, you close to my soul the gates of mercy! If your life on earth were longer than mine, if heaven chose you to make amends for our faults, I would be waiting for you at the door of that eternal abode that your repentance and atonement should open for me.

"Oh, Carlos! What fate will this path of crime lead us to? What will become of us when the love that now ruins us but justifies our existence stops illuminating our guilty future? What depravity will my soul fall into when it is no more than the tomb of all my virtues and all my dreams?

"The legacy of happiness that God's justice should bestow on all mortals was not granted to me in this world. So I must seek it in the beyond; your love was designed to make me understand this. The happy moments that I have enjoyed with you have been a divine voice that has told my soul, 'Don't despair, poor exile! The eternal source of that beneficent love whose glimmers have illuminated you, exists for you in another life, in a better world.'

"Love and sorrow have wrung from my heart healthy tears that have watered my soul, which was lying in arid indifference and rest. Fatigue arising from inertia is a terrible thing. Sorrow reveals God to us; boredom makes us conceive of nothingness. God summons all men on a single road; even the path of crime can lead to

Him. Repentance is very beautiful. Carlos! Much should be forgiven to the one who has suffered much."

The Countess's ideas flowed from her lips, disordered and incoherent, but her face had an expression of hope and faith that Carlos had never seen before.

"Yes, dear friend," he said, "much should be forgiven to a soul like yours. I too need a great, immense faith in divine mercy. But right now I only ask for your love, Catalina, and a final look and a last farewell."

"Must it be so soon!" she exclaimed, shuddering, but she instantly overcame that weakness, and taking Carlos's hands in hers, she said, "Farewell; don't forget the conversation we have just had. Before leaving, obtain for you and for me the pardon of that angelic woman whom we have so greatly wronged. Yes, get on your knees at her feet, and may her mercy encompass us both." Carlos embraced her in tears.

"And if heaven should call me before you," Catalina went on in a shaky voice, "swear to me this moment that, accepting the atonement that is your destiny, you will devote your life to the sacred fulfillment of your neglected duties, and that I will be allowed the hope that an unhappy wife will not curse my ashes."

Carlos swore it.

"Now," said Catalina, "look at me once again with your loving gaze. And give your blessing to me and to your unfortunate child. I give you mine," she went on, placing her hands on Carlos's head, who had thrown himself at her feet. "May God guide your path, and may the angel who was given to you on earth accompany you through the quagmires of the world without soiling the fringe of her white mantle!"

Carlos did not heed these words. Overly moved, he withdrew from the Countess's arms and returned three times to embrace her.

Catalina was very pale, and her voice and hands were trembling greatly, but her courage did not fail and she saw Carlos off without a word of weakness slipping from her lips. Standing at the window, she listened intently to the gallop of his receding horse, until the gradually diminishing sound completely stopped. Then she wiped a few drops of cold sweat from her forehead, and she left the windowsill with a sad but serene expression.

It was nasty weather. Black clouds, like a cloak of mourning, shrouded the pale face of the waning moon, and the wind battering the old windowpanes made moaning sounds, the only voice interrupting the grave silence of the night.

The Countess slowly wrote a letter. Her hand did not tremble, nor did her brow darken. She looked beautiful and tranquil, as on any of her most brilliant days. However, when she finished the letter, some tears moistened the paper that she carefully folded.

Then she called for her servants. She told one of them to take the letter early the next morning to Elvira's house, and as the night was getting progressively colder, she had them light two large braziers and ordered her servants to go to bed.

32

Upon leaving the Countess, Carlos's emotions grew as he was approaching Luisa. He felt feverish and sick at heart. His head and his heart were burning, and he could not absorb all the tumultuous feelings and sorrows that assailed him.

He arrived home in a delirious state, and Luisa, who was awaiting him with sad impatience, was alarmed upon seeing the change in his face. The poor girl had spent the hours of that night in fervent prayer, but although she had called to her aid all her strength and all her resignation, although she had implored God, crying over her guilt and pleading for courage, she felt completely shattered upon seeing her husband.

She held out her arms, and he threw himself into them. It was still her Carlos, her husband who was sobbing on her breast; he was still hers, and within a few hours she would lose him forever. At such a bitter thought a sea of tears sprang from her eyes, and she murmured those famous words: "'Lord, if Thou art willing, take this cup from me . . .'"

"Luisa," said Carlos, "are these your tears that are falling on my burning brow? What good they do me! Cry, my friend, cry on the head of this odious criminal. Maybe your pure tears will wash away my sins.

"Tell me," he went on, ever more delirious, "tell me if it's true that you know everything, that you forgive everything? Is it possible, Luisa, that you can forgive me? Will I not bear on my head the weight of your curse?"

"No," she answered; "no, my Carlos. I forgive you for everything except that you could doubt the heart of your Luisa. I was not enough for your happiness; I had vowed to give it to you but I could not. My desire would be to be able to return to you this instant the freedom that you sacrificed for me, in exchange for which I could give your heart nothing—nothing!—since it could not dwell as mine! But Carlos! Tell me that you do not abhor me; the idea of being an object of your hatred would make me die of bitterness."

"Abhor you! Oh, Luisa! No woman has ever been so tenderly loved; nor has any woman been so worthy! And if my heart is not breaking at this moment, it is because it feels more unhappy than guilty. Luisa, my sister! There is no peace or virtue for my heart; may it at least find in yours mercy and compassion!"

"They are yours," she answered, sobbing; "yours are all the tenderest feelings of this heart. Oh! it has been very badly treated, it is true, but it still holds for you many treasures of kindness. Carlos! If, when we grow old and love deserts you, this sad childhood friend still exists, return to her and you will always find her waiting. Return, yes; her heart will never be closed to you."

"No, mine is not worthy of it," Carlos exclaimed. "I do not deserve this indulgent tenderness that aggravates my crime. Luisa! Why do I not die at your feet this instant? Why go on living?"

"To make happy the one who has sacrificed so much for you; for her, who has deserved your love!" said Luisa in a muffled voice.

"No, she cannot be happy!" Carlos exclaimed. "I have been the murderer of you both! My heart is bursting with remorse, and at this moment I feel that I adore you both equally, and yet that I would like to obliterate one of you."

"Me! Yes, me!" cried Luisa in extreme sorrow. "I am the one who is of no use on earth."

"No, not you!" Carlos exclaimed, ever more feverish and incoherent. "Not you! Because you are the angel who should save me . . . because I need you, your mercy, your religion, your virtue!"

His raving increased, and Luisa put him in bed and knelt at his bedside.

"Is it true," said Carlos, "is it true that this is the last night we will spend together? All the rest of my guilty life will be hers; let these last moments of love be yours. Because I love you, Luisa! I love you!"

Although these words were uttered in delirium, they still made Luisa's heart throb with pleasure. The angel was a woman, and a woman in love.

"Do you love me?" she exclaimed in a trance. "Is it true that you love me? Is it true that you cannot be happy without your wife?"

"No, I cannot—no! Come, Luisa, come and blow a gentle breeze of purity on my burning head! Come! I am pursued by visions of crime, phantoms of regret. The passion that has led me astray is a hell that envelops me in stinging, devouring flames. Come! I need freshness, calm, innocence! Come and speak to me of those tranquil days of our pure love. Remind me of those pleasures without crime, and of that happiness that cost no one tears. Do you remember, Luisa? Bring me the locket of the Virgin that you took from your neck to place on mine—a precious talisman that was to save me! Where is it? Why have they taken it from me? Bring it, Luisa, and put it on my heart to quiet its violent beating. There! Thank you; I feel better. Now speak to me. Your voice is heavenly music to my ears. Remind me of my life of innocence; summon to this bed in flames the pure breath of our love. What has become of those days? Are they gone forever, Luisa?"

"Do you long for them, Carlos?" she said, cooling his burning head with her delicate hand.

"Yes, return them to me; just one! at least one! I have had so many cruel ones!"

"Very well. God will return to us that happiness that we both need equally, and I will lull you to sleep with those sweet words that we said to each other during the peaceful time of our love. 'Luisa,' you said to me one day, 'if there exists a happiness greater than mine, I don't want to know about it. I do not want any pleasure that does not come from you; nor do I fear any misfortune, if you help me bear it. We will live together, and die together, and our souls will fly as one to the bosom of God, of that God who created you so beautiful for my happiness, and of whose goodness will always be worthy a heart where you reign.'"

"Go on," said Carlos, "your voice does me so much good."

"And we were in fact virtuous and happy," Luisa went on. "We were the pride of our parents, a model couple, and we hoped to be an example for our children. I imagined that we would grow old together, and that upon leaving the earth we could bless our children, as our parents had blessed us."

"Yes," said Carlos, "and they too would have blessed us, because those children would not owe us a life of shame; they could not reproach us for having thrown them into a world that would close its doors on them. Speak to me, Luisa; tell me of the happiness of those parents who can stand before their children without blushing."

Luisa continued talking, but Carlos was succumbing to the fever, and he was soon sunk in the lethargic sleep that usually follows a great agitation. Luisa kept watch on her knees by his bedside, and she cried and prayed, and now asked for something more than resignation; happiness again seemed possible to her.

The day dawned, and as Carlos was not supposed to leave until close to noon, Luisa asked don Francisco to let him rest, and as the old man prepared for the journey, she returned to her husband's side; his fever was subsiding, allowing him to sleep more peacefully.

As the clock was striking ten and don Francisco was ordering that Carlos be awakened, Luisa received word that Elvira de Sotomayor wished to speak with her.

She received her in the chapel, where she had just entered to fortify herself through prayer, and Elvira came in so pale and contorted that Luisa's words of greeting died on her lips.

"Has Carlos left?" Elvira quickly asked.

"He is supposed to leave in an hour," Luisa answered.

"Not alone," Elvira added, "not alone. You must go with him."

"Ah, yes! So you know that he is ill? And you think that he should not leave alone in that condition?"

"That is the excuse you will give him," said Elvira. "You will tell him that you only wish to accompany him for the first day. At the end of that day you can reveal the truth to him and accompany him to his new appointment. Don Francisco must know everything right away; I will inform him. Luisa, you must get ready to leave, and prepare your heart to console the unhappy man for whom you must be the sheltering angel. Your husband has been restored to you. The Countess of S. is no more."

"She is no more!" repeated Luisa in terror.

"By taking her own life," Elvira said, "she wished to return to you the husband she had usurped from you. Only her death could break forever the criminal ties she had imposed on Carlos, and she chose to die. May God take pity on such a generous and guilty soul!"

"Suicide!" Luisa screamed.

"Yes," replied Elvira with a deep moan. "She asphyxiated herself!"

"Suicide!" repeated Luisa, and falling on her knees before a crucifix, "Oh, my God! my God!" she exclaimed. "Do not judge the act, but the feeling. Look away from the means, Lord, and just consider the end!"

"Her sufferings on earth," said Elvira, "make that comforting hope possible. Even her suicide has been atoned for by her long and terrible throes! Enclosed in a small room, suffocating from the poisonous air, that horrid death must have seemed unbearable to her, and she apparently tried to flee when it was too late! The position in which we found her proves that in her last moments she tried to find air, but in the darkness, in the dazed state she must have been in, she could not open the door which she had double-locked, and she died suffocated beside it. What a long and horrid agony she must have suffered! Her corpse showed signs of terrible suffering. I found her still warm . . . but oh, I could not be there for her final breath! All I could do for that unhappy woman who was my only friend is to religiously carry out her last wish. Here it is. Please respect it, and pray to God for her soul."

With these words Elvira left, leaving in Luisa's hands the Countess's letter, written to her friend several hours before her death. Luisa read it, sobbing. It read as follows:

"The moment you receive this paper, run to see Luisa. Tell her that she should leave with her husband, and only after they are far from Madrid should she tell him what she will know before him.

"He has loved me, and his suffering will be great. God and she will soften it. The guilty woman who has caused the unhappiness of two spouses will entreat heaven for the pardon she does not hope for or desire from men. But *hers* will ring sweetly in my tomb; *hers* will give peace to my bones and sweetness to my torment. I implore her pardon on bended knee, and I believe I will receive it. Her divine soul cannot deny mercy for repentance.

"May Carlos not know, if possible, that I die by my own hand; he would feel remorse. May the angel to whom I entrust that beloved existence lavish on his wounded heart the immense treasures of her tenderness and kindness, and may he someday be able to return to her the happiness she bestows on him.

"My final prayer is for them, as is my final wish.

"As for you, my dear Elvira, you know that yours alone has been my most tender friendship. Do not cry for me; no. Do not mourn for my life cut off still in flower! For me, death is not a gloomy prospect; I see it as the liberating angel that God sends to the unfortunate. He is not armed with the bloody scythe; rather he bears a divine torch, more brilliant than the sun that my eyes will see no more. No, my soul will not pass unguided into the night of the tomb; hope awaits me on its threshold; and the faith that flew over my cradle awakens from its long sleep at the call of death and comes to open to me the doors to another world.

"Proud reason dies out with life, but when its insufficient light fails me, the light of hope is reborn from its ashes. To enrich my heart, God in His kindness granted me love; but to punish me for my pride, that beneficent love had to be a crime. The divine will has been done! Love has saved my soul, and my death atones for my love."

Luisa held the letter to her heart, and for several minutes she prayed in silent fervor. Compassion shone on every one of her features, and her eyes, raised to heaven, seemed to long to penetrate its eternal vaults to find mercy. Never did such ardent pleas of innocence beseech pardon for repentance; never did such a pure soul intercede for a guilty soul!

Her prayers lasted the length of time that Elvira used to inform don Francisco of the woeful catastrophe of that day and of its sad history. When the two came to find Luisa, Elvira was tearful, don Francisco, terrified; only on Luisa's face shone a ray of hope. She had just offered God her earthly life and the happiness that had been restored to her in atonement for the faults of her deceased rival, and she was convinced that her plea had been heard.

Carlos awoke in his wife's arms. "What a long sleep I have had!" he said. "It has been so long since I slept so deeply or enjoyed such a sweet awakening! How beautiful is the daylight after a dark night!"

Then suddenly remembering that this was to be the day of his departure: "Luisa!" he exclaimed in a kind of terror. "Is it really day? Is this already the hour of our separation?"

"No," she answered, "no, my friend. Your father and I have decided to accompany you for a day. This is not the hour of our separation, but it is the hour of our departure."

Carlos sighed, and got ready to leave without uttering a word. But he gazed at his wife often, and some tears at times rose to his tired eyes.

Luisa helped him with his preparations, as silent as and no less moved than he, and when the hour for the departure struck, don Francisco came to announce it.

Elvira watched them leave without being seen by Carlos. A long and sad look was the only farewell exchanged between the friend and the rival of Catalina.

33

Soon the news of the death of the Countess of S. spread through Madrid. Few suspected that she had deliberately asphyxiated herself. Her death was generally believed to have been caused by a fatal error, and the departure of Carlos de Silva was considered to be the natural result of his grief upon losing his lover.

Nothing disarms hatred like death. The day on which we owe others nothing is the day of fellow feeling. The sudden death of Catalina won her back all of her lost prestige. Her faults were forgotten, and her good qualities remembered. Her very weaknesses were poeticized and served to arouse greater compassion. She was no longer beautiful, distinguished, celebrated. She was no longer anything, and past merit is always granted the recognition that present merit is denied.

Men have this advantage over the other beasts. We never feed on dead bodies; we need living, pulsating victims to bleed beneath our nails, to groan between our teeth.

The funeral of the Countess, arranged by Elvira, was magnificent.

For a week or ten days all the talk was of the deceased, but when public interest was stirred by some other news, no one thought any more about the Countess or about Carlos.

Three months after the latter's departure, Elvira received the first and only letter she was to have from Luisa. The letter informed her that Carlos had been seriously ill, but the care of his wife and his father, as well as his youth, had saved him. That he did not seem to suspect that the Countess had taken her own life, or at least he did not say so. That his sadness was profound, but serene, and that although he was entirely at the disposal of his wife and his father, he seemed determined never to return to Spain.

This letter was written in London on March 20, 1820.

In 1826, on a rather cold afternoon of the same month of March, a handsome but rather worn-looking man was reading one by one the inscriptions on the tombstones that were legible in one of the oldest cemeteries in Madrid, and he did not stop until he found this epitaph, the letters of which had not yet suffered the ravages of time:

"Here lies the Countess of S. She died on December 18, 1819, at the age of 25 years, 9 months, and 11 days."

The man who was reading the epitaphs stood a few minutes before this one, deep in thought, and some tears flowed from his eyes, fixed on the marble gravestone.

Then he slowly left the cemetery and walked to one of the most well-known inns of Madrid at the time. Several notable people were waiting for him there; they had come to congratulate him and send him off at the same time. They wanted to congratulate him on having just obtained a brilliant appointment, and to send him off because the new appointment obliged him to leave Madrid the following day.

Two of those notables, leaving together after the visit, were speaking in rather loud voices.

"This diplomat of yesteryear is not making a bad career," said one. "What the devil favor does he enjoy at court, when he has almost never been there?"

"Quiet!" replied the other. "It's a scandal, but scandals of this kind are no longer labeled as such at a time when they have become so common and so frequent. Foreigners are right when they call Spain a second Turkey. It is impossible that the number of malcontents not quickly rise. While thousands of worthy Spaniards beg for their bread in foreign lands, trade stagnates, industry dies out, and the impoverished treasury is close to ruin, how can we impassively watch day after day these corrupt favors for those who improvise appointments, invent commissions, lavish honors on themselves? The lifeblood of the people destined to fatten up the chosen few!"

"But do you think it is only by favoritism that Carlos de Silva has risen?"

"If you are not aware of his merits . . ."

"He has one unquestionable merit."

"Which is?"

"His money. Silva is very rich."

"And he has a very pretty wife—and our Catholic monarch appreciates so much the husbands of beauties!"

"Quiet, you viper! The wife of Carlos de Silva is a model of virtue."

"That may be, but she is staying on in Madrid and her husband is leaving."

"She is staying in Madrid to care for her elderly father-in-law who is blind and sick, but she is a model wife who adores her husband."

"Yes, but the husband does not adore her. I have it on good authority."

"Nonetheless, Silva values his wife highly and is one of the most attentive, genteel husbands I have ever known."

"Yes, but they say that his only passion is ambition, and no matter how sweet and obliging he is to the lovely Luisa, I have been assured that in private he is a very sad, incommunicative companion. They say that he was devastated by the loss of a mistress, and he became ambitious as a distraction. His wife could find some distraction too, because after all, life has to have some interest, some object."

"Where are you headed?"

"I'm going to the Príncipe Theater."

"I to the home of the Secretary of the Treasury, where I have a meeting tonight."

The two gentlemen parted, after bowing deeply to a woman who passed by with two pretty girls. It was Elvira de Sotomayor with her daughters. The older one, who had just turned thirteen, was an angelic blonde. The younger, who was ten, was a brunette with fiery eyes named Catalina.

They were going to visit the Silva family, and an hour later they were returning home by the same street. Elvira looked so deeply sad that the older girl timidly asked her the reason.

"What is wrong, Mama? Why did you cry so much with that woman we visited?"

"Because that woman," said Elvira with a sigh, "is very good and very unhappy. When you are a few years older, girls, I will tell you a very sad tale: the story of two women, both very generous, very beautiful, and very unfortunate. That story will be a good lesson for you."

And the girls fell silent, and Elvira grew quiet too.

At this point our reliable news draws to a close. Whatever else we might add would be based on pure conjecture.

We do not know if Elvira did in fact relate to her daughters, as she had said she would, the story of the two women. And if she did, what impression did it leave on their young hearts? What truth did it reveal to them? What useful lesson might they have learned from this story?

Perhaps none; perhaps she told them nothing, revealed nothing, except that woman's lot is in any case unhappy. That the indissolubility of the very bond by which our laws claim to assure her future, often turns into a chain that is all the more unbearable for being unbreakable. Passionate and weak beings, now wrongdoers, now wronged, it is they who end up broken, and they who, whether through their own mistakes or those they are the victims of, always present to a cold, indifferent world the spectacle of those silent sorrows, those profound misfortunes that could serve as atonement for a thousand crimes.

The guilty woman finds wherever she turns harsh judges, ruthless executioners. The virtuous woman goes unnoticed, and at times—alas!—slandered. And the guilty and the virtuous are both equally unhappy, and perhaps also equally fine and generous!

Afterword

The nineteenth-century Cuban author Gertrudis Gómez de Avellaneda y Arteaga (1814–1873), or "la peregrina" (the pilgrim or wanderer), as she called herself, was indeed a traveler, growing up on the Caribbean island and spending most of her adult life in Spain. The oldest child and daughter of a Spanish nobleman, a naval officer who was posted in Cuba, and a beautiful and affluent Creole woman from a prominent Cuban family, Gertrudis was a child of privilege, leading a comfortable life in the central provincial capital of Puerto Príncipe (now Camagüey) surrounded by relatives, servants, and slaves. From an early age she showed a love and a gift for reading and writing, learning fluent French and immersing herself in the great works of French and English Romanticism that were the hits of the day. When at the age of twenty-two her Spanish stepfather took the family back to Spain, Gómez de Avellaneda embarked on a highly successful literary career, first in Seville and then in Madrid, establishing herself as a poet, novelist, and dramatist who recited her own poetry in literary salons and at the royal court in Madrid, and whose plays were applauded in the major cities of Spain. A prolific writer who was celebrated both in Spain and in Cuba during her lifetime, she nonetheless underwent bitter struggles and anguish in both her personal and her professional life, as an educated woman with highly advanced ideas and forms of behavior who found herself caught within the confines of a traditional, Catholic, strongly chauvinistic society. The men she knew, and the male establishment in general, while charmed by her beauty and grace, her poetic skills, and her scintillating personality, felt threatened by her remarkable intellect and creative gifts, allied with her outspoken feminism and liberal social ideas. Her plays took the Spanish public by storm and won high critical acclaim during her lifetime, but were also denigrated for their strong, self-determining female characters and their weak, vacillating male counterparts.[1] Despite the author's more conservative stance late in life, with her bold artistic vision, her openly feminist journalism, and her transgressive lifestyle (she had lovers and a child out of wedlock), she always remained a controversial figure.

In the years following her death, a paradoxical situation arose in regard to Gómez de Avellaneda's literary legacy and status. It seems that her name and her work were well known to her Cuban and Spanish compatriots, indeed she was viewed as a canonical author, and a few books and articles appeared validating her importance. At the same time, there was a concerted effort on the part of some members of the male critical establishment to minimize the significance of her work, through strategies like devoting only brief, scant references to her in literary anthologies as a "minor" playwright or poet, and systematically removing her name from such collections to replace it with those of other female authors, thereby seeking to exclude her from the canon of Hispanic Romanticism, a practice that has continued to this day.[2] It was not until the second half of the twentieth century, with the rise of transatlantic feminism, that her name began to resurface as a major, long-neglected figure of nineteenth-century Cuban and Spanish letters. In the new millennium, as part of the campaign to resurrect and revindicate important forgotten writers and artists of the past, interest in this fascinating woman has surged, leading to a tidal wave of articles, books, and symposia exploring various aspects of her life and work. She is now considered to be not only a leading figure of Spanish American Romanticism,[3] but according to María C. Albin, Megan Corbin, and Raúl Marrero-Fente, to this day one of the greatest female writers of Hispanic literature, and among the most important authors of the Spanish language.[4]

Gómez de Avellaneda's life and works grew out of the European Romantic tradition. Romanticism arose in the late eighteenth and nineteenth centuries as transformative literary, artistic, and social movements. With the momentous political and economic upheavals of the late eighteenth century, the advent of the Industrial Revolution and a rapidly growing middle class, the blind acceptance of old forms of authority was gradually giving way to a new emphasis on the individual, his desires, hopes, and dreams. There was both a call on the part of liberals for social and political reform, and a new valorization of the inner life. As an outgrowth of and a reaction to the eighteenth-century French Enlightenment, or Age of Reason, in the words of Elena Grau-Llevería and Roger Picard, "For the Romantic subject, feelings are the true bearers of Truth, not reason, because 'the passions carry within them a higher virtue based on a psychological truth, which guides our actions to the best outcome.'"[5] The Romantic is an ardent, highly sensitive individual who finds himself at odds with the world in which he lives. He envisions a pure realm of beauty and goodness that has no correspondence with a crass material outer world. In literary works like Rousseau's *Emile* and *La nouvelle Héloise*, Chateaubriand's *Atala* and *René*, and Bernardin de St. Pierre's *Paul et Virginie*, writers set up a contrast between the artificial and pernicious norms of a corrupt social world and the simple goodness of those who live in the heart of nature. Man in his natural state is good; it is civilization that has broken the bond between humanity and his surroundings, thereby destroying the harmony between man and the natural world. Emblematic of this disjunction is the opposition between "natural virtue" and "social virtue": the first is authentic virtue, which arises from the laws of nature that govern the world and human life; the second is a mere appearance of virtue, the hypocritical rules and conventions established by social man in his quest for glory, power, and control.[6] Those who follow the dictates of these destructive rules and norms are inevitably alienated from their core ethical and spiritual values, and thereby cut off from their fundamental humanity.

A common denominator of the European Romantic experience was that the world was viewed through the lens of a male subject; it reflected the masculine experience of life. For the male Romantic, woman exists as the object of man's desire; indeed she is often represented as the nucleus or emblem of an unsatisfactory object world. By the Romantic playbook, women had no place as desiring subjects. The nineteenth-century patriarchy did not accept the idea that women too had inner lives and dreams; it tended to view women from the outside in terms of simplistic dichotomies—good or evil, angel or monster, the Virgin Mary or the temptress Eve—stereotypes that could not capture the nature of women's experience. According to nineteenth-century gender ideology, man's place was in the outer public world, while woman was assigned to the inner domestic sphere as nurturing wife and mother, the "angel of the hearth." As Susan Kirkpatrick explains in her illuminating study of the Spanish female Romantics, the idea of defining men and women as essentially different in one sense gave women a kind of empowerment, because it granted them their own area of expertise, their special gifts in the realm of feelings and personal relationships. Moreover, the Romantic movement valorized the individual's inner life, the life of the emotions, which was considered to be woman's strong point. But in so doing it also greatly limited women's range of self-expression: women were allowed to know "tenderness" but not "passion"; they were denied the experience of erotic desire and the entire spectrum of possibilities for self-development offered by the public world outside the home.[7]

Gómez de Avellaneda was endowed with a strong personality and a romantic temperament, and from an early age she struggled against the deadening strictures constraining female behavior and self-expression. We are fortunate enough to have an intimate account of the author's early life in the short epistolary autobiography she wrote at the age of twenty-five to the law student Ignacio Cepeda during her sojourn in Seville, soon after emigrating to Spain.[8] As the daughter of an affluent Spanish-Creole family living in the Cuban provinces, in her childhood and adolescence Gertrudis enjoyed a kind of freedom that would have been virtually unthinkable in the more rigid and hierarchical ambience of peninsular Spanish society. She was allowed to fully indulge her love of reading and writing as she was growing up. However, she soon found that she was not exempt from the prejudices that limited and impeded female experience in the Hispanic world. After her beloved father died when she was only nine, her mother quickly remarried, giving her and her brother a stepfather whom the girl resented as a hasty replacement for her father. At the age of thirteen she was betrothed to a young man she hardly knew, who was considered to be the most eligible bachelor in her native region of Puerto Príncipe. Her grandfather, who favored her mother and her and was set on the match, had offered the young man a large portion of his estate if he married Gertrudis; that was the motivation for his proposal. As an innocent young girl and with the prospect of marriage still years off, she was flattered by the idea of marrying the wealthiest man in the region, and fantasized that he was the man of her dreams. But when she got to know him better at a later age she realized her mistake, seeing that her fiancé was quite ordinary and in every way unsuited to her in temperament and approach to life. When her mother and stepfather decided in turn to hasten the marriage, Gertrudis finally realized that she could not go through with it, and took refuge in her grandfather's home. The grandfather was sympathetic to the girl, but breaking off the marriage caused an uproar among her extended family, and when the grandfather later had a falling-out with her stepfather, Gertrudis was blamed for the rupture. The relatives joined forces to turn her grandfather against her, and just before his death he drew up a new will denying her the promised portion of his estate.[9]

Gertrudis's personal story, along with the plight of several of her closest female relatives, conspired to make her into a fierce opponent of arranged marriages and of marriage in general, with its harsh patriarchal laws designed for the subjugation and control of women. Her parents' arranged marriage had not been a happy one (perhaps partly due to the age difference between them, her father having been much older than her mother). Moreover, her favorite cousin quickly found disappointment in marriage; her husband, whom she had married for love, turned into a tyrant soon after taking the nuptial vows. From an early age Gertrudis had resolved to be a writer, but she soon learned that in the Spanish-speaking world such aspirations were incompatible with the role of wife and mother; indeed, some of the men who courted her expressed a strong disapproval of her literary vocation. She rejected a number of men who asked for her hand in marriage, preferring her freedom and independence to a stunted, confined existence.[10] And yet, as a highly feminine and romantic woman, she felt a strong need for love, the urgent desire to find the dreamed-of union of hearts and souls with a man who was her equal. While she sometimes made defiant statements against marriage, she at one point confessed in a letter to Cepeda, the man she loved for many years who proved wholly unworthy of her devotion, that while she had not and would not marry, she believed that she "would not tremble" to bind herself to another for life if she found a man who inspired in her an estimation such that she believed that her love would last.[11] Indeed, in an earlier letter to Cepeda she went further, voicing her profound desire for a fulfilling romantic relationship: "I was born to have my world in a man who loved me. . . . I have not achieved this, and I remain a wanderer on earth, alone in the midst of creation."[12] As a woman artist she felt the need for a full life on her own terms, yet found to her dismay that her feminine emotional needs could not be reconciled with her "masculine" strength of will and creative powers in a strongly misogynous society.

In many ways Gómez de Avellaneda lived out the life of a female Romantic artist. She shattered social barriers by leading a glamorous, unconventional life and gaining fame and income as a successful author in all the major literary genres: poetry, novels, legends, plays (both tragic and comic), and essays. Her literary works became the chosen vehicle to fight tirelessly against the injustices and backwardness of the societies in which she lived; indeed soon after her arrival in Spain she published *Sab* (1841), the first antislavery/feminist novel in the New World, which predated by eleven years Harriet Beecher Stowe's *Uncle Tom's Cabin* and was in some ways more radical than the later work.[13] Endowed with an exalted romantic temperament and plagued with misfortune, she led a stormy personal life filled with unsatisfactory and fractured relationships.[14] Her charm and appeal in Spain were enhanced by her exotic background as a Cuban Creole, but on a deeper level, as a woman and a colonial living in the imperial capital, she did not feel fully accepted in either the mother country or the island paradise of her youth. Indeed, in an 1839 letter to Cepeda she wrote, "Judged by society, which does not understand me, and tired of a way of life which perhaps makes me look ridiculous; superior and inferior to my sex, I am an outsider in society and isolated in nature. I feel the need to die. And yet I live, and probably appear fortunate in the eyes of the multitude."[15]

Gómez de Avellaneda was an outspoken feminist at a time when the seeds of early feminism were being sown in Europe and the United States, and when it was virtually nonexistent in the Spanish-speaking lands. In this regard she was inspired above all by the literary works of two Frenchwomen, Germaine de Staël and George Sand, whose novels provided a lens through which to view European women's current situation and concerns. Mme de Staël's novel *Corinne ou l'Italie* offered her the model of a brilliant woman artist who could not reconcile her artistic career with a fulfilling love relationship with a man, leading to a tragic end. Sand's early novels *Indiana* and *Valentine* showed how women were victimized by the unfair patriarchal laws governing marriage and family in the Western world, whereby women had no autonomous power, remaining ever subject to the full control of father, male relative, or husband. These works served as a model for the narrative of her own early life story or "autobiography," written in epistolary form to Ignacio Cepeda, and for her first two novels written soon after, *Sab* and *Two Women* (*Dos mujeres*), which are considered to be her most radical literary works.[16] The autobiographical account she wrote Cepeda had as its aim to awaken the interest, understanding, and love of a man who had become the object of her desire; she mistakenly thought that in Cepeda she had found a kindred soul who would admire her creative gifts and empathize with her struggles as a woman. *Sab*, a Romantic novel that recounts the love of a mulatto slave for the white daughter of his master, attacks various forms of social injustice and oppression that were prevalent in nineteenth-century Cuban society. Despite being barred from sale by the royal censors in Cuba, her antislavery novel was published in 1841 in Madrid and later in serial form in the Cuban and United States press; it circulated widely on the island, exerting an important influence on public opinion until the eventual abolition of slavery in Cuba in 1886.[17] Moreover, by openly comparing the situation of women to that of slaves, the work broadened the scope of criticism to include women as another marginalized and oppressed social group. *Two Women*, written a year later and set in contemporary Spain, was the first full-fledged feminist novel to appear in the Hispanic world, promoting ideas that are still topics of debate in the Spanish-speaking world today, nearly two centuries later. Gómez de Avellaneda's first two novels were so controversial that they were banned in Cuba,[18] and near the end of her life the author decided not to include them in the Spanish edition of her complete works. They first appeared in a collection of her complete works in the 1914 Cuban edition which marked the centennial of the author's birth.[19] The first English-language edition of *Sab*, translated by Nina M. Scott, came out in 1993 from the University of Texas Press.[20]

As Susan Kirkpatrick declares, Gómez de Avellaneda both embodied the female Romantic in her own life, and created the female Romantic subject in the Hispanic world of letters.[21] In her autobiographical account, poetry, and prose, we find the notion of "superior souls," individuals with exceptional imaginative gifts, a depth of feeling and understanding that are beyond the capacity of the common order of humanity. These are highly sensitive individuals who experience life more intensely than the average person, who know the heights and depths of joy and sorrow, suffering both on their own account and for the plight of all who are victimized by a hard, cruel world. For such individuals, love, the mutual understanding and union of two like minds and souls, is the supreme experience of life. But in contrast to the works of the male Romantics, for Gómez de Avellaneda there is a crucial difference when the world is viewed from a female perspective: here *woman* is the subject of experience, while *man* is the ever unsatisfactory object of female desire. In her autobiographical account to Cepeda, Gertrudis exclaims,

> Cepeda! . . . Where is the man who can fulfill the desires of this sensitive nature which is as fiery as it is delicate? For nine years I have searched in vain! . . . I have found men! Men who are all alike, to none of whom I could submit with respect and declare ardently: You are my God on this earth, and the absolute master of this passionate soul. For this reason my affections have been irresolute and short lived. I searched for a goodness I was unable to find and which perhaps does not even exist on earth. (*Sab and Autobiography*, 6)

Likewise Carlota, the heroine of her first novel, *Sab*, has a prototypical Romantic sensibility and is destined to suffer disillusionment in her love relations with man, as the narrator observes,

> Carlota loved Enrique, or perhaps we should say that she loved in Enrique the ideal object of her imagination . . .
> . . . she suddenly felt in the most hidden corner of her heart some terrible instinctive revelation of a truth which heretofore she had not clearly understood: that there are loftier souls on the earth who are endowed with feelings unrecognizable to more common ones, souls rich in sentiment, rich in emotions for which are reserved terrible passions, terrible virtues, immense sorrows . . . and that Enrique's soul was not one of these. (*Sab and Autobiography*, 40, 48)

When Carlota later confronts the naked truth about her husband's character and loses all hope of happiness, the sole consolation she can find is in her bonding with another unfortunate being, her indigent cousin Teresa, and in the knowledge she receives through

Teresa of the now deceased Sab's secret love for her—in the shared suffering and compassion of the Creole girl, the illegitimate cousin, and the mulatto slave. For this author, nobility of soul transcends race, gender, and class; despite their disparity in social status, these three superior souls are spiritually united in a bond of empathy and understanding that serves to lighten their load. In Sab's final letter to Teresa, written just before his death, he equates the lot of woman to that of the slave, going even further to underscore the powerlessness of the female condition:

> Oh, women! Poor, blind victims! Like slaves, they patiently drag their chains and bow their heads under the yoke of human laws. With no other guide than an untutored and trusting heart, they choose a master for life. The slave can at least change masters, can even hope to buy his freedom some day if he can save enough money, but a woman, when she lifts her careworn hands and mistreated brow to beg for release, hears the monstrous, deathly voice which cries out to her: "In the grave." (*Sab and Autobiography*, 144–145)

With these words Sab becomes the champion of women in their servitude, and the mouthpiece for the author in her denunciation of iniquity in all its forms, her call for a new era of freedom and social justice.

Where Gómez de Avellaneda's first novel *Sab* portrays women's suffering and unhappiness in the framework of a broader range of social issues, it is in her second novel, *Two Women*, that woman takes center stage as the object of her interest and concern. In contrast to her earlier book, the story takes place in Spain, and the characters are all from a privileged upper-class milieu. The plot line of the novel is simple: it depicts a romantic triangle in which two very different women vie for the love of one man. At the outset, the narrative follows the typical paradigm of sentimental novels of the period. Carlos and Luisa, two cousins from a Sevillian aristocratic family, are betrothed by their parents during their childhood. Owing to the early death of Carlos's mother, the two grew up together under the maternal care of doña Leonor, Carlos's aunt and Luisa's mother. They are united by a strong childhood affection and by the common spiritual values instilled in them from birth. But the boy and girl are soon subject to the disparate gender norms of patriarchal Spain. Carlos's father, don Francisco, sends his son to France to receive a worthy education, while Luisa remains at home and learns from her mother the basic domestic skills of reading and writing, religion, and homemaking. The omniscient female narrator subtly mocks the paltry education doña Leonor finds satisfactory for her daughter:

> . . . her mother had taken the greatest pains with her upbringing. She was not of a mind to adorn her with distinguished talents, and Luisa's upbringing was more religious than brilliant. . . . She did not have music or dancing lessons, or training in any other kind of skill; but in exchange she knew all the secrets of housekeeping, and excelled in embroidery and needlework; she knew basic arithmetic and geography; she could recite biblical history by heart and was somewhat proficient in the profane; with which, in the opinion of her mother, nothing was lacking for her to be called an educated woman.

When Carlos returns from an eight-year sojourn in France, Luisa has developed into a beautiful, pure young woman, and the two fall in love with the joy and innocence of first love. Under the mother's influence they are quickly married, before either has had any real experience of life. At this juncture the narrator interjects her own sober commentary on the situation; while praising the idyllic joys of pure young love, she voices her forebodings about the duration of a love grounded in the ignorance and inexperience of early youth, and laments the inconstancy of human feelings over life's course:

> If there exists happiness for mankind, if it is attainable on earth, it is only the union of love and virtue that can provide it. Love sanctified by religion, love tempered by security and habit, love

that takes the form of duty, duty embellished by love . . . how sublime, what blissful harmony! Why does fickle nature wrest from man this state of divine bliss? Why can we not solidify the concordance between feeling and duty? Oh imperfection and inconsistency of human nature, that eternal love, the soul's desire, cannot be realized by the heart!

But Carlos and Luisa are so happy! Away, cold thoughts, away sad lights of truth, for I want to relish the charming spectacle of a happy and chaste love.

After a year of serene conjugal happiness, Carlos is sent to Madrid to straighten out the estate of a deceased relative of whom they are the sole heirs. While there he meets another relative, a young widowed countess named Catalina of S., whose nature and temperament are in sharp contrast to those of his wife. Catalina is a woman of charm, superior intellect, and artistic gifts who is at the center of the salon life of Madrid. After the painful experience of an early arranged marriage, she has become a woman of the world who lives life on her own terms. Yet bored with the hypocrisy and superficiality of high society and a Romantic at heart, she yearns for the fulfillment of a love she has never known, for the union of two like minds and souls. She finds in Carlos the rare individual who can understand and love her, and despite much inner turmoil and anguish at the prospect of disrupting an honorable marriage, she promotes their relationship, unwilling to sacrifice their mutual love on the altar of social convention.

There is little external action in *Two Women*; the narrative consists of an introspective exploration of the psyches of the three protagonists. The book is Romantic in the characters' ardent sensibilities, its elegant language, and the subtle analysis of human behavior, thoughts, and feelings, while it is Realist in the narrative description of people and events, using the vehicle of an omniscient female narrator who relates the tale and often intervenes to comment on the action. It is through the intricate portrayal of Catalina's consciousness, as well as the thoughtful depiction of Carlos and Luisa in their reaction to the course of events, that

Gómez de Avellaneda subverts the conventional paradigm of sentimental novels of the period. In the traditional pattern, the two female rivals represent opposites: good and evil, the angel of the hearth and the femme fatale. At the end of the tale, the husband returns to the stable happiness of wife and home, the evil temptress is duly punished, and the social order is restored. One could say that on the surface this is an outline of the plot of *Two Women*: in the final chapters Catalina dies, and Carlos returns to his wife and family. But the entire fabric of the story serves to debunk these simplistic stereotypes, and the myth of eternal marital bliss.[22] Throughout the story the three main characters are all deeply wretched, enduring endless inner conflict and torment, and the ending provides no satisfactory resolution, culminating only in physical and psychic annihilation. What's more, the dichotomy between the good woman and the bad is undone; the two so different women of the book's title both prove themselves to be of a kind, generous, and noble nature.

Catalina, the foremost protagonist of the book, is the fictional persona of the author herself. In recounting her life story to Carlos during a night when they are intimately thrown together by the sickbed of a close relative, Catalina becomes a mouthpiece for her creator, her words reflecting the bitterness of a woman of exceptional beauty, intellect, and talent who on a personal level found herself played with, rejected, and censured by the men around her for the very attributes that made her unique:

> Oh! How dangerous for a woman of a vivid imagination is this period of her life when she needs, seeks, and waits for a protective, loving being to whom to offer her soul, her future, her very existence! How she deludes herself! . . .
>
> . . . The lover in whom I thought I had spied my ideal mate abruptly turned into a vulgar, hateful, and petty being. . . .
>
> During those two years I went through a costly and sad apprenticeship. My affections were disappointments; my hopes madness; my very virtues disastrous to me. My experiences day by day, hour by hour showed me that whatever good, great, and

beautiful there was in my soul was an obstacle to my happiness: that my enthusiasm led me astray, my credulity made me the plaything of so-called clever people, . . . in short, Carlos, my very intelligence, that priceless gift that brings us close to the divine, was for common minds a dangerous quality that would sooner or later be my undoing.

Catalina embodies the tragic figure of a woman with an artistic sensibility who has no outlet for her creative potential. She is gifted in all of the arts: music, dance, painting, languages and literature, and Carlos is soon entranced by her exceptional knowledge and talents:

She chose an aria by Rossini, and her voice, so whole and melodious, was a little weak and insecure upon starting the song. But she soon overcame such an inexplicable emotion, and her wondrous talent and great gifts shone forth in their full splendor. At the delightful strains of the song, Carlos raised his eyes toward her and could no longer withdraw them. The Countess's face was divine as she sang; never did such expressive features accompany beautiful music. As Catalina sang, Carlos could not breathe, totally captivated by the power of the melody.

Carlos is further dazzled by the readings and conversation Catalina undertakes to entertain her friend Elvira during the latter's convalescence:

Carlos . . . admired ever more the Countess's great gifts, and her vast and yet modest learning. . . . He was . . . delighted to hear her recite the most beautiful lines of the great French and Spanish poets with exquisite sensitivity and understanding, and when he discussed with her the quality of various poets, he was always surprised at the speed of her analysis and the accuracy of her judgments. . . . She analyzed like a philosopher and painted verbally like a poet, her ideas had the vigor and independence of a man's, and she expressed them with all the charming fantasy, and even some of the pleasant versatility, of a woman.

Yet this remarkably gifted individual has no meaningful channel for self-expression, and squanders her hours in frivolous, superficial pastimes before an audience who cannot understand or appreciate her worth. The Countess has found no deep emotional fulfillment in either the outer world or the inner world of personal relationships. The entrance of Carlos on the scene is for her a unique event that changes her life forever. As a profound and complex woman with a highly romantic temperament, she feels that she deserves the love she has awakened in Carlos and the joy they could share together. But at the same time, her conscience arouses feelings of guilt and anguish for destroying the serene marriage of an innocent young couple.

As a true Romantic, throughout the text Gómez de Avellaneda gives voice to her belief that love is a force of nature, which cannot be subject to artificial laws and social conventions. She also feels that as all in nature flows and changes, so human feelings can change over time; humans should respect and accept the dictates of nature, supreme arbiter of life and death. In her view, arranged marriages and the indissolubility of the marriage vow violate natural law. As two kindred spirits, Catalina and Carlos come to believe that their love is more valid than the ties sanctioned by Spanish law and the Catholic Church. As Catalina declares to Carlos, "What is love? Isn't it the most involuntary and the most beautiful of the human emotions? They say adultery is a crime, but there is no adultery for the heart." Moreover, Catalina has become pregnant with Carlos's child; by the world view propounded in the book, the fruit of their union bestows on her a claim to his love and loyalty that supersedes all man-made ties, as the narrator affirms: "Catalina was no longer only the seductive lover, the sublime friend. Nature, dressing her with majesty, with an indisputable right, now tied her to Carlos with the sweetest and most sacred of bonds. This bond was stronger than all those created by men."

All three of the main characters change and grow over the course of the story, while enduring the painful straitjacket in which they are forced to live. The innocent young Carlos and Luisa learn about the nature of life and love in their social world, and struggle to adapt to a new reality. Among the three protagonists, it is Carlos who proves the most weak and passive; the women have a core of inner strength that the man lacks. Carlos, who is in essence a man of fine character who wishes to do the right thing, feels bound by ties of affection, respect, and loyalty to his pure and devoted wife, while he is driven by the deeper, fuller love he has found with the Countess, a union of two minds and souls. Torn apart by the situation he is in, he cannot choose between the women and what they represent, and time and again leaves it up to Catalina to decide their fate.

The angelic Luisa in her own way grows and develops through the tragic situation that has fallen to her lot. Initially a timid, sheltered young girl with no experience of life, she spends the months following her husband's departure suffering in silence, patiently awaiting his return. But this long period of dormancy leads to her emergence as an active subject: when she hears that Carlos is sick, she insists on going to Madrid with her father-in-law to find him, asserting her position as his wife. Upon gradually learning the truth about Carlos's affair, she is filled with sadness and despair, and finally reveals what she has discovered to her father-in-law in an attempt to save her marriage. Yet when this in turn brings the situation to a head and she thinks that she has put the couple at risk, she crushes her own jealousy and anger and goes with her cousin Elvira to rescue the wayward lovers, leading to the riveting final episodes in which the two women rise to the full height of their humanity.

The confrontation between the female rivals is the emotional high point of the book. Meeting as bitter adversaries, in their single interview each woman on some level comes to understand and connect with the other. When Luisa meets Catalina, she intuits that the Countess possesses the distinguished qualities she lacks, and which are necessary for Carlos's happiness. What's more, she suddenly perceives that Catalina is pregnant with Carlos's child, and in her mind the fruit of nature the two share endows her husband's lover with a legitimate claim to his loyalty and love. As the scene unfolds, Catalina in turn recognizes the beauty, purity, and supreme virtue of this young wife who is willing to relinquish all she holds dear for the sake of the man she loves. Catalina has also come to realize that she and Carlos will not be able to achieve real and lasting happiness together; they will live a life of exile, ostracized from respectable society, and their child will be an outcast, scorned and shunned by the world. She moreover fears that Carlos's guilt and regrets will eventually undermine his love for her, leaving her in a state of complete abandonment. She concludes that it is in Carlos's interest to restore him to the serene life of honorable home and family. Thus the two women finally transcend their basic instincts to bond and come together in an outpouring of empathy and compassion, weeping in each other's arms in an alliance borne of shared suffering. Luisa's supreme act of self-sacrifice in choosing to relinquish her husband in favor of her rival, leads in turn to Catalina's resolve to make the ultimate sacrifice for the welfare of her lover and his spouse, removing herself from the scene by taking her own life. Both women are prepared to carry out sublime acts of self-denial for the sake of others, acts that, in the author's view, women alone are capable of.

In her final meeting with Carlos, who is unaware of her intention, Catalina hints at their possible separation through death. She exhorts her lover to promise that in the event of her death, he will wholeheartedly return to his neglected duties as husband and family man, graciously accepting his allotted destiny in atonement for his earlier abandonment; she even demands from him an oath to that effect, to ensure her peaceful final rest. But the concluding pages of the book reveal a starkly different outcome. Carlos and Luisa are viewed at a distance, through the narrator's voice or the words of others, as though the two surviving characters have lost their own voices as desiring subjects. The narrator reports that following a stay of many years abroad, on a dreary March day a world-weary man goes to an old Madrid cemetery, where he seeks out and quietly sheds some tears at the grave of the Countess of S., lost in thought. We then hear through the social grapevine that Carlos and Luisa's marriage has not thrived, that Carlos is emotionally distant from his wife and the two remain without offspring, implying the end of physical intimacy between the pair.[23] Carlos spends long periods of time away from their home in Madrid, focusing his energies on his diplomatic career, while the ever devoted Luisa remains at home to care for her husband's ailing father. There is no "happily ever after" for their story.

In the Romantic world view, life cannot measure up to man's limitless hopes and dreams. This is due to society's ills, but for many Romantic artists it transcends the particulars of contemporary life to stem from the very nature of the human condition, the inexorable facts of life and death. Yet for Gómez de Avellaneda and other nineteenth-century female Romantics, women's unhappiness is due less to a metaphysical angst than to a concrete social injustice that targets women as its victim. Indeed, the oppressive nature of patriarchal laws and attitudes denies women a fulfillment that *is* attainable on earth, a full life in which they could realize their human potential and dreams. For this author, emotional fulfillment through love is the transcendent experience of life. Her text makes clear that the unhappiness of her three protagonists is primarily due to the laws and practices governing the institution of matrimony in the Hispanic lands. Indeed, in a more enlightened world one can imagine alternative scenarios for her novel: if Carlos and Luisa had not been bound to each other from early childhood, Carlos might well have gone to Madrid after his return from France and there met Catalina, the love of his life. Barring that circumstance, if divorce were an accepted practice in Spain, with great pain Carlos and Luisa could have terminated their marriage, giving the protagonists a second chance to find happiness. But beyond this, for our visionary author love alone is not the key to self-realization for persons of either sex. Each individual should have the chance to find an interesting, purposeful activity that gives her or his life meaning—and in the absence of a satisfying personal relationship, having other vital outlets for one's energies and drives is even more important. It is this which makes woman's fate all the more tragic, confined as she is to a constrained, limited existence, as Catalina explains in prophetic words to her lover:

> When one arrives at a state where the dreams of love and happiness have vanished, Carlos, man finds before him the path of ambition. But for woman, what recourse is left to her when she has given up on love, her only good, her unique destiny? She must fight hand to hand, weak and helpless, against the frozen phantoms of boredom and starvation. Oh! When we still find ourselves fertile in thought, thirsty in soul, and our heart does not give us what we need, ambition is very beautiful. Then one should be a warrior or a politician, one should create for oneself a campaign, a triumph, a ruin. The thrill of glory, the turmoil of danger, the zeal for and fear of success, all those vital emotions of pride, valor, hope and fear. . . . But poor woman, with only one destiny in the world! What can she do, what can she be when she cannot be the one thing that is allowed to her?

The novel concludes with a sad and pessimistic assessment of women's fate:

> . . . woman's lot is in any case unhappy . . . the indissolubility of the very bond by which our laws claim to assure her future, often turns into a chain that is all the more unbearable for being unbreakable. . . .
>
> The guilty woman finds wherever she turns harsh judges, ruthless executioners. The virtuous woman goes unnoticed, and at times—alas!—slandered. And the guilty and the virtuous are both equally unhappy, and perhaps also equally fine and generous!

Implicit in the author's bitter words is a call for radical social reform. She is advocating the end of arranged marriages in which women are no more than mercantile objects of exchange, and the right of individuals to choose their spouse in accordance with their own inclination and temperament. In conjunction with this, she implicitly argues for the institution of divorce in the Hispanic world as a means of rectifying errors of judgment or changes of heart, thereby giving individuals another chance to attain happiness. Finally, she strongly supports the full education of women, enabling them to realize their complete humanity. In a series of feminist essays she wrote as founding editor of a women's journal upon her return to Cuba late in life, she postulates not only women's equality with men, but women's superiority, grounded in their dominance in the affective realm, their ability to understand and connect with others on the personal level. She argues, based on Pascal, that great thoughts and deeds arise from the heart,[24] and demonstrates with historical evidence that women's preeminence in this domain has inspired them to carry out countless heroic acts in both the public and private spheres of life. In her essays and her short biographies of illustrious women that appeared in the same journal, she gives numerous examples of famous women throughout history who against all odds have distinguished themselves as wise rulers and warrior queens, saintly mothers and martyrs, and brilliant intellectuals and artists. She deliberately chooses celebrated women of widely diverse temperaments and deeds, in order to show women's limitless potential for achievement. Based on this historical evidence, she declares unequivocally that woman is a rational being with capabilities equal to those of man, and calls for women's full admittance into all spheres of activity in the outer world. She declares that the education of women will empower them to make informed choices in life and to develop their gifts and potential. What's more, she glowingly predicts that their contributions will redound not only to the benefit of women but to the progress of society as a whole.[25]

Despite the somber ending of *Two Women*, in the final pages one finds a faint glimmer of hope for the future. As Lucía Stecher Guzmán affirms in her excellent article on the book, hope is embodied in two images.[26] First is the highly moving image of

Luisa and Catalina's warm embrace, which evinces a new female solidarity grounded in mutual empathy, understanding, and love. The final image of the book moves from the present into the future, with a picture of two small girls of the next generation. Luisa's cousin Elvira has gone to visit her with her two young daughters who, akin to Luisa and Catalina, are an angelic blonde and a fiery brunette, the latter named Catalina in honor of Elvira's dearest friend. Elvira cries so much during the visit with Luisa that afterward her daughters ask her the reason for their sadness. Elvira tells them that when they are older she will relate to them the sad story of two women, "both very generous, very beautiful, and very unfortunate." In this way one imagines that their story may be transmitted orally from generation to generation, gradually giving rise to a collective female consciousness, which will in turn crystallize in ardent sisterhoods who will take up the struggle for social change. And indeed, in the tale we have just read the story of the two women is being passed on to readers through the written word, amid the darkness portending a new dawn of human joy and enlightenment.

Barbara F. Ichiishi

Notes

1. Librada Hernández, "El 'no' de las niñas: Subversive Female Roles in Three of La Avellaneda's 'Comedias,'" *Hispanic Journal* 12, no. 1 (1991): 27–45. Most contemporary critics simply ignored the feminist dimensions of her works.
2. María C. Albin, Megan Corbin, and Raúl Marrero-Fente, "Gertrudis the Great: First Abolitionist and Feminist in the Americas and Spain," in "Gender and the Politics of Literature: Gertrudis Gómez de Avellaneda," ed. María C. Albin, Megan Corbin, and Raúl Marrero-Fente, *Hispanic Issues On Line* 18 (2017): 9, 12.
3. Brígida M. Pastor, "The Bicentenary of Gertrudis Gómez de Avellaneda: A Life and a Literature of Her Own," *Romance Studies* 32, no. 4 (2014): 217.

4. Albin, Corbin, and Marrero-Fente, "Gertrudis the Great," 13.

5. Elena Grau-Llevería, "El romanticismo social en *Dos mujeres* de Gertrudis Gómez de Avellaneda," *Bulletin of Spanish Studies* 87, no. 1 (2010): 34, and Roger Picard, quoted in Grau-Llevería, "El romanticismo social," 34. Unless otherwise noted, all English translations are mine.

6. Alexander Selló Selimov, "La verdad vence apariencias: Hacia la ética de Gertrudis Gómez de Avellaneda a través de su prosa," *Hispanic Review* 67, no. 2 (1999): 215–241.

7. Susan Kirkpatrick, *Las Románticas: Women Writers and Subjectivity in Spain, 1835–1850* (Berkeley: University of California Press, 1989), 1–9, 23–35.

8. Gertrudis Gómez de Avellaneda, "Autobiografía y Cartas," in *Obras de la Avellaneda* 6: 125–153 (Havana: Imprenta de Aurelio Miranda, 1914).

9. Ibid., 127–140.

10. Ibid., 128, 140, 143–152.

11. Ibid., 207. Gertrudis did get married twice, first to Pedro Sabater in 1846 and then to Domingo Verdugo in 1855. Both men died soon after the marriage in the most unfortunate circumstances. She and Sabater knew he was gravely ill when they married; he died three months after the wedding. Verdugo was seriously wounded by an assailant in 1858 after defending his wife from slander; in 1863 he finally succumbed to his wounds.

12. Ibid., 199–200.

13. Gertrudis Gómez de Avellaneda, *Sab and Autobiography*, trans. Nina M. Scott (Austin: University of Texas Press, 1993), ix.

14. Besides her prolonged unrequited love for Ignacio Cepeda, she also had a turbulent affair with the poet Gabriel García Tassara, father of her daughter Brenhilde, who was born in 1845 and died seven months later. García Tassara abandoned Gertrudis before the child's birth.

15. Gómez de Avellaneda, "Autobiografía y Cartas," 159.

16. Gómez de Avellaneda, *Sab and Autobiography*, xv.

17. Albin, Corbin, and Marrero-Fente, "Gertrudis the Great," 45–49.

18. *Sab* (1841) and *Dos mujeres* (1842–1843) were published in Spain, but were banned by the royal censors from sale in Cuba. A royal decree in the Cuban National Archives states that *Sab* contains "doctrines

subversive to the system of slavery on this Island and contrary to moral and good habits," and that *Dos mujeres* is infected with "doctrines prejudicious to Our Holy Religion and attacking therein conjugal Society and canonizing adultery." Gómez de Avellaneda, *Sab and Autobiography*, xv.

19. Gertrudis Gómez de Avellaneda, *Obras de la Avellaneda*, Edición nacional del centenario, 6 vols. (Havana: Imprenta de Aurelio Miranda, 1914).
20. Gómez de Avellaneda, *Sab and Autobiography*.
21. Kirkpatrick, *Las Románticas*, 133–173.
22. Lucía Stecher Guzmán, "'Y vivieron infelices para siempre': Ilusiones románticas y desengaños realistas en *Dos mujeres* de Gertrudis Gómez de Avellaneda," *Revista de Estudios Hispánicos* 50, no. 1 (2016): 37–54.
23. In his prologue to the 2000 Cuban edition of *Dos mujeres*, Antón Arrufat offers a provocative analysis of the conclusion of the novel, in particular, of the motives behind Catalina's suicide and its consequences. Arrufat affirms that there were multiple and complex reasons why Catalina chose to take her own life. He foregrounds the issue of the love triangle among Carlos, Luisa, and Catalina. His thesis is that Catalina knows that the main obstacle to her own fulfilling future life with Carlos is his ongoing love for and loyalty to Luisa. This stems from the Romantic idea that the dreamed-of ideal love union cannot be realized on earth: Carlos loves the two women in different ways and cannot wholly detach himself from either. Catalina, who feels guilt and compassion toward her hapless rival, sacrifices herself by taking her own life in order to restore Carlos to Luisa and to a serene, respectable life. But on another level, as the consummate Romantic, Catalina cannot entirely give him up and thus puts her faith in an eternal union with her lover after death; she hints at her imminent death in her final meeting with Carlos, and speaks of their eternal union in heaven. Arrufat believes that the fact that Carlos realizes that his lover committed suicide for his sake binds him to Catalina emotionally forever, and drives a wedge between him and his wife. So in this sense, Catalina emerges victorious over her rival in the contest for Carlos's love.

I do not think that the theories of Catalina's "altruistic" motives and those of her "egoistic" motives in taking her own life are mutually exclusive. Catalina is a highly complex character who combines generous, altruistic instincts with the strong ego of one who knows her own worth, as one of the author's "superior souls." The Countess understands human nature well: she knows that in the tragic situation in which she and Luisa find themselves, neither can really win; in fact, the one who physically gains Carlos will lose him emotionally, due to his relentless, everlasting guilt and regrets, and the one who loses him will reign supreme in his heart. By the final episodes, she sincerely wants Carlos to give Luisa what she deserves as his loving, devoted wife, and she is willing to make the ultimate sacrifice in order to achieve this. But she also knows that she and Carlos are kindred souls who share a unique human bond, and she cannot give up the compensatory hope that she will live in his heart forever, and that they will be rewarded for their sacrifice after death through an eternal union in heaven. Carlos loves and respects Luisa for her innate goodness and virtue—but Catalina is also an innately good, generous individual who has suffered at the hands of society. It would seem that in the author's view, the three protagonists are not victims of human frailty or the human condition so much as victims of the unjust laws of men. Adriana Méndez Rodenas kindly brought to my attention the Arrufat prologue to the 2000 Cuban edition of the book. See Gertrudis Gómez de Avellaneda, *Dos mujeres*, ed. Antón Arrufat and Ana María Muñoz Bachs (Havana: Editorial Letras Cubanas, 2000), lix–lxviii.

24. Pascal argues in *Les pensées* that great thoughts arise from the heart, that is, from the realm of intuition, instinct, feeling, rather than from the rational mind. Gómez de Avellaneda extends this idea: in her view, great thoughts in turn inspire great deeds, so both originate from the affective realm of life.

25. Gertrudis Gómez de Avellaneda, "La mujer," in Gómez de Avellaneda, *Obras de la Avellaneda*, Edición nacional del centenario, 6: 83–101 (Havana: Imprenta de Aurelio Miranda, 1914). The essays and short biographical sketches on women first appeared in Cuba in *Album cubano de lo bueno y de lo bello: Revista quincenal de moral, literatura, bellas artes y modas* I (1860). Some of the articles came out earlier (in the 1840s and 1850s) in several women's journals in Spain.

26. Stecher Guzmán, "'Y vivieron infelices para siempre,'" 48–51.

Select Bibliography

Gómez de Avellaneda's Cited Works

Autobiografía y cartas. Prologue and eulogy by Lorenzo Cruz de Fuentes. 2nd ed. Madrid: Imprenta Helénica, 1914.

"Autobiografía y Cartas." In *Obras de la Avellaneda*. Edición nacional del centenario. Vol. 6, 125–246. Havana: Imprenta de Aurelio Miranda, 1914.

Diario íntimo. Edited by Lorenzo Cruz de Fuentes. Buenos Aires: Ediciones Universal, 1945.

Dos mugeres. Madrid: Gabinete Literario, 1842–1843.

Dos mujeres. Edited by Antón Arrufat and Ana María Muñoz Bachs. Havana: Editorial Letras Cubanas, 2000.

Dos mujeres. In *Obras de la Avellaneda*. Edición nacional del centenario. Vol. 5, 5–210. Havana: Imprenta de Aurelio Miranda, 1914.

"La mujer." In *Obras de la Avellaneda*. Edición nacional del centenario. Vol. 6, 83–101. Havana: Imprenta de Aurelio Miranda, 1914. First published in Cuba in *Album cubano de lo bueno y lo bello: Revista quincenal de moral, literatura, bellas artes y modas* 1, 1860.

"La mujer." In *Obras literarias*. Vol. 5, 283–306. Madrid: Rivadeneyra, 1871.

Obras de la Avellaneda. Edición nacional del centenario. 6 vols. Havana: Imprenta de Aurelio Miranda, 1914.

Obras literarias. 5 vols. Madrid: Rivadeneyra, 1869–1871.

Sab. Prologue and notes by Mary Cruz. Havana: Instituto Cubano del Libro, 1973.

Sab. Edited by José Servera. Madrid: Ediciones Cátedra, 1997.

Sab. Edited by Catherine Davies. Manchester, UK: Manchester University Press, 2001.

Sab. In *Obras de la Avellaneda*. Edición nacional del centenario. Vol. 4, 401–541. Havana: Imprenta de Aurelio Miranda, 1914.

English Translations of Gómez de Avellaneda's Works

PROSE/PLAYS

Baltasar: A Biblical Drama in Four Acts and in Verse. Translated by Carlos Branby. New York: American Book Company, 1908.

Belshazzar. Translated by William Freeman Burbank. London: B. F. Stevens & Brown, 1914.

Cuahtemoc: The Last Aztec Emperor, A Historical Novel. Translated by Wilson W. Blake. Mexico City: F. P. Hoeck, 1898.

Love Letters. Translated by Dorrey Malcolm. Havana: Tall. Gráf. de Juan Fernández Burgos, 1956.

Sab and Autobiography. Translated by Nina M. Scott. Austin: University of Texas Press, 1993.

"'Women' by Gertrudis Gómez de Avellaneda." Translated by Nina Scott and Doris Meyer. In *Rereading the Spanish American Essay: Translations of 19th and 20th Century Women's Essays*, edited by Doris Meyer. Austin: University of Texas Press, 1995.

POEMS

"A él" (To Him). Translated by Thomas Walsh. In *Hispanic Anthology: Poems Translated from the Spanish by English and North American Poets*, 434–436. New York: G. P. Putnam's Sons, 1920.

"A él" (fragmento) (To Him) (excerpt), 49–54; "A la luna" (To the Moon), 61–62; "A las estrellas" (To the Stars), 41–42; "A una mariposa" (To a Butterfly), 43–48; "A ***" (To ***), 65–68; "Al destino" (To Destiny), 63–64; "Al partir" (Leaving), 37–38; "El recuerdo importuno" (Unwelcome Remembrance), 59–60; "Imitación de Petrarca" (In Imitation of Petrarch), 39–40; "Mi mal" (My Torment), 55–56; "Romance" (Ballad), 71; "Significado de la palabra yo amé" (The Meaning of the Words I Loved), 69–70; "Soneto imitando una oda de Safo" (Sonnet in Imitation of an Ode by Sappho), 57–58. Translated by Anna-Marie Aldaz and W. R. Walker. In *An Anthology of Nineteenth-Century Women's Poetry from*

Spain: In English Translation, with Original Text. New York: Modern
Language Association of America, 2009.

"A la esperanza" (To Hope), 280–281; "A la juventud" (To Youth), 324–325;
"A una mariposa" (To a Butterfly), 394–395; "A Washington" (To Wash-
ington), 388–389; "Al sol" (To the Sun), 390–391; "El día final" (The
Final Day), 350–351. Translated by Ernest S. Green and Harriet von
Lowenfels. In *Mexican and South American Poems (Spanish and English)*.
San Diego: Dodge and Burbeck Booksellers and Stationers, 1892.

"A Washington" (To Washington) (1841). Translated by Agnes Blake Poor. In
Pan-American Poems: An Anthology, 50. Boston: The Gorham Press, 1918.

"A Washington" (To Washington) (1869). Translated by Edith L. Kelly. "La
Avellaneda's Sonnet to Washington." *The Americas* 4 (1948): 242.

"Al partir" (On Leaving Cuba). Translated by Alice Stone Blackwell. In *Some
Spanish American Poets*, 490. New York: D. Appleton & Company, 1929.

"Al partir" (On Leaving). Translated by Seymour Resnick. In *Spanish-
American Poetry (Dual Language)*, 12–13. Mineola, NY: Dover, 1996.

Secondary Sources

Albin, María C., Megan Corbin, and Raúl Marrero-Fente. "Gertrudis the
Great: First Abolitionist and Feminist in the Americas and Spain." In
"Gender and the Politics of Literature: Gertrudis Gómez de Avellaneda,"
edited by María C. Albin, Megan Corbin, and Raúl Marrero-Fente.
Hispanic Issues On Line 18 (2017): 1–66. https://conservancy.umn.edu
/handle/11299/192190.

Arrufat, Antón. Prologue to *Dos mujeres*, by Gertrudis Gómez de Avellaneda, v–lxviii. Edited by Antón Arrufat and Ana María Muñoz Bachs.
Havana: Editorial Letras Cubanas, 2000.

Ayala, María de los Angeles. "*Dos mujeres*, novela reivindicativa de Gertrudis Gómez de Avellaneda." *AIH*, Actas 12 (1995): 76–83.

Beyer, Sandra, and Frederick Kluck. "George Sand and Gertrudis Gómez
de Avellaneda." *Nineteenth-Century French Studies* 19, no. 2 (1991):
203–209.

Bravo-Villasante, Carmen. *Una vida romántica: La Avellaneda*. Madrid:
Cultura Hispánica, 1986.

Cotarelo y Mori, Emilio. *La Avellaneda y sus obras: Ensayo biográfico y crítico*. Madrid: Tipografía de Archivos, 1930.

Cruz, Mary. "Gertrudis Gómez de Avellaneda y su novela *Sab*," *Unión* 1 (1973).

Ezama Gil, Ángeles, ed. *Gertrudis Gómez de Avellaneda, Autobiografía y otras páginas*. Edición, estudio y notas de Ángeles Ezama Gil. Madrid: Real Academia Española, 2015.

Fernández-Marcané, Leonardo. "Gertrudis Gómez de Avellaneda y el romanticismo europeo." *Baquiana: Revista Literaria* 1 (1999–2000): 103–111.

Figarola-Caneda, Domingo. *Gertrudis Gómez de Avellaneda*. Notes by Emilia Boxhorn. Madrid: Industrial Gráfica, 1929.

Foerster, Maxime. "A Man Is Crying: The Progression of Heterosexual Trouble in Gómez de Avellaneda's *Dos Mugeres*." *Romance Studies* 33, no. 1 (2015): 68–79.

Gies, David Thatcher. *The Theatre in Nineteenth-Century Spain*. Cambridge: Cambridge University Press, 1994.

Gilbert, Sandra M., and Susan Gubar. *The Madwoman in the Attic: The Woman Writer and the Nineteenth-Century Literary Imagination*. New Haven: Yale University Press, 1979.

Gold, Janet N. "The Feminine Bond: Victimization and Beyond in the Novels of Gertrudis Gómez de Avellaneda." *Letras femeninas* 15, nos. 1–2 (1989): 83–90.

Grau-Llevería, Elena. "El romanticismo social en *Dos mujeres* de Gertrudis Gómez de Avellaneda." *Bulletin of Spanish Studies* 87, no. 1 (2010): 31–49.

Guerra, Lucía. "Estrategias femeninas en la elaboración del sujeto romántico en la obra de Gertrudis Gómez de Avellaneda." *Revista Iberoamericana* 51 (1985): 707–722.

Harter, Hugh A. *Gertrudis Gómez de Avellaneda*. Boston: Twayne, 1981.

Henríquez Ureña, Max. *Panorama histórico de la literatura cubana*. New York: Las Américas Publishing Co., 1963.

Hernández, Librada. "El 'no' de las niñas: Subversive Female Roles in Three of La Avellaneda's 'Comedias.'" *Hispanic Journal* 12, no. 1 (1991): 27–45.

———. "On the Double: *Tres amores* and the Postponement of Love in Avellaneda's Theater." *Letras femeninas*, Número Extraordinario Conmemorativo 1974–1994 (1994): 39–47.

Kelly, Edith L. "Avellaneda's *Sab* and the Political Situation in Cuba." *The Americas*, 1 (1945): 303–316.

Kirkpatrick, Susan. *Las Románticas: Women Writers and Subjectivity in Spain, 1835–1850*. Berkeley: University of California Press, 1989.

Méndez Rodenas, Adriana. "Gómez de Avellaneda y Arteaga." *Escritoras Latinoamericanas del Diecinueve, Colección Virtual*. ELADD, 2015. https://eladd.org/autoras-ilustres/gertrudis-gomez-de-avellaneda-y-arteaga/.

———. "Mujer, nación, y otredad en Gertrudis Gómez de Avellaneda." In *Cuba en su imagen: Historia e identidad en la literatura cubana*, 13–29. Madrid: Editorial Verbum, 2002.

———. "Picturing Cuba: Romantic Ecology in Gómez de Avellaneda's *Sab* (1841)." In "Gender and the Politics of Literature: Gertrudis Gómez de Avellaneda," edited by María C. Albin, Megan Corbin, and Raúl Marrero-Fente, 153–172, *Hispanic Issues On Line* 18 (2017). https://conservancy.umn.edu/handle/11299/192150.

Miller, Beth. "Gertrude the Great: Avellaneda, Nineteenth-Century Feminist." In *Women in Hispanic Literature: Icons and Fallen Idols*, edited by Beth Miller, 201–214. Berkeley: University of California Press, 1983.

Miller, Beth K. "Avellaneda, Nineteenth-Century Feminist." *Revista/Review Interamericana* 4, no. 2 (Summer 1974): 177–183.

Molloy, Sylvia. *At Face Value: Autobiographical Writing in Spanish America*. Cambridge: Cambridge University Press, 1991.

Orozco Vera, María Jesús. "Estética romántica y denuncia social en *Sab*, de Gertrudis Gómez de Avellaneda." In *Romanticismo europeo: historia, poética e influencias*, edited by Juan Antonio Pacheco and Carmelo Vera Saura, 87–96. Seville: Universidad de Sevilla, 1998.

Parrack, Jennifer Patterson. "Masquerade and Women's Writing in Spain: Gertrudis Gómez de Avellaneda's *Dos mujeres*." *Philological Review* 29, no. 1 (2003): 27–45.

Pastor, Brígida M., ed. "Beyond the Canon: A Life and a Literature of Her Own (Essays on the Bicentenary of the Birth of Gertrudis Gómez de Avellaneda, 1814–1873)." Special issue, *Romance Studies* 32, no. 4 (2014).

———. "Cuba's Covert Cultural Critic: The Feminist Writings of Gertrudis Gómez de Avellaneda." *Romance Quarterly* 42, no. 3 (1995): 178–189.

———. "'El ángel del hogar': Imaginario patriarcal y subjetividad femenina en *Dos mujeres* de Gertrudis Gómez de Avellaneda." *Revista de Estudios Hispánicos* 30, no. 2 (2003): 19–31.

———. *Fashioning Feminism in Cuba and Beyond: The Prose of Gertrudis Gómez de Avellaneda*. New York: Peter Lang, 2003.

———., ed. "Gender, Writing, Empowerment: Essays on the Bicentenary of the Birth of Gertrudis Gómez de Avellaneda, 1814–1873." Special issue, *Romance Studies* 33, no. 1 (2015).

———. "Gender, Writing, Empowerment: Essays on the Bicentenary of the Birth of Gertrudis Gómez de Avellaneda, 1814–1873," ed. Brígida M. Pastor, special issue, *Romance Studies* 33, no. 1 (2015).

Picón Garfield, Evelyn. *Poder y sexualidad: El discurso de Gertrudis Gómez de Avellaneda*. Amsterdam: Rodopi, 1993.

Rodríguez, Milena, ed. "Entre Cuba y España: Gertrudis Gómez de Avellaneda en su Bicentenario (1814–2014)." Special issue, *Arbor* 190, no. 770 (2014).

Romero, Cira, ed. *Lecturas sin fronteras (Ensayos sobre Gertrudis Gómez de Avellaneda), 1990–2012*. Havana: Ediciones Unión, 2014.

Romero Mendoza, Pedro. *Siete ensayos sobre el romanticismo español*. Vol. 1. Cáceres: Servicios Culturales de la Excma. Diputación de Cáceres, 1969.

Roselló Selimov, Alexander. "La verdad vence apariencias: Hacia la ética de Gertrudis Gómez de Avellaneda a través de su prosa." *Hispanic Review* 67, no. 2 (1999): 215–241.

———. "Sensibilidad y verosimilitud en la prosa romántica: Un acercamiento al arte narrativo de la Avellaneda." *Salina: Revista de Lletres* 11 (1997): 100–107.

Schlau, Stacey. "Stranger in a Strange Land: The Discourse of Alienation in Gómez de Avellaneda's Abolitionist Novel *Sab*." *Hispania* 69, no. 3 (1986): 495–503.

Schlünder, Susanne. "Autoproyección literaria y codificación romántica de los afectos: Gertrudis Gómez de Avellaneda." In *El andar tierras, deseos y memorias*, edited by Jenny Haase, Janett Reinstädler, and Susanne Schlünder, 455–467. Madrid and Frankfurt: Vervuert, 2008.

Scott, Nina M. "Shoring Up the 'Weaker Sex': Avellaneda and Nineteenth-Century Gender Ideology." In *Reinterpreting the Spanish*

American Essay: Women Writers of the 19th and 20th Centuries, edited by Doris Meyer, 57–67. Austin: University of Texas Press, 1995.

Selimov, Alexander. "The Making of *Leoncia:* Romanticism, Tragedy, and Feminism." In "Gender and the Politics of Literature: Gertrudis Gómez de Avellaneda," edited by María C. Albin, Megan Corbin, and Raúl Marrero-Fente, 249–263. *Hispanic Issues On Line*, 18 (2017). https://con servancy.umn.edu/handle/11299/192133.

Sommer, Doris. "Sab, c'est moi." In *Foundational Fictions: The National Romances of Latin America*, 114–137. Berkeley: University of California Press, 1991.

Stecher Guzmán, Lucía. "'Y vivieron infelices para siempre': Ilusiones románticas y desengaños realistas en *Dos mujeres* de Gertrudis Gómez de Avellaneda." *Revista de Estudios Hispánicos* 50, no. 1 (2016): 37–54.

Zorrilla, José. "Gertrudis Gómez de Avellaneda." In *Hojas traspapeladas de los Recuerdos del tiempo viejo* 6:130–147. Madrid: Eduardo Mengíbar, 1882.

GERTRUDIS GÓMEZ DE AVELLANEDA (1814–1873) was an acclaimed Romantic author who was born and raised in Cuba and spent most of her adult life in Spain. Although she was a highly successful playwright, novelist, and poet during her lifetime, some of her works were denigrated (and even banned in Cuba) for their outspoken feminism and liberal social ideas. A multifaceted, prolific artist, she wrote twenty plays (both tragedies and comedies), seven novels and novellas, nine stories and legends, one volume of poetry, four autobiographies and memoirs, and numerous essays and articles. Author of the first antislavery/feminist novel in the New World (*Sab*, 1841), she waged an ardent campaign to promote freedom and justice for the marginalized and oppressed in her works, striving above all for social and economic equality for women.

BARBARA F. ICHIISHI received a BA in French literature from Mount Holyoke College, an MA in comparative literature from the University of California, Berkeley, and a PhD in Spanish from the University of Iowa. She is the author of *The Apple of Earthly Love: Female Development in Esther Tusquets' Fiction*, and the translator of some of Tusquets's major works, including *Never to Return*, *Seven Views of the Same Landscape*, *Private Correspondence*, and *We Had Won the War*. She has written articles on Spanish and Latin American women's literature, and is cotranslator of Édouard Glissant's *Monsieur Toussaint*.

BRÍGIDA M. PASTOR is Honorary Research Fellow at Swansea University in the United Kingdom. She is the author or editor of several books, including *Gertrudis Gómez de Avellaneda's Speech: Female Identity and Otherness* (2002), *Fashioning Cuban Feminism and Beyond: The Prose of Gertrudis Gómez de Avellaneda* (2003), and *A Companion to Latin American Women Writers* (2012), and has written many book chapters and academic articles on Spanish and Latin American women's writing.